全方位
英文閱讀

劉遠城——— 著

應用外語 44

ENGLISH

五南圖書出版公司 印行

PREFACE
前 言

　　坊間一般英文閱讀學習的書大都是以英文範文為主體，加上對範文的中文翻譯、文章中字彙的中文字義以及文法或句型的解釋。近年來隨著新的英文閱讀學習趨勢以及強調英文閱讀測驗文章或段落的主題之重要性，有關確認英文閱讀文章主題的書籍也應運而生。現今此類的英文閱讀書籍成為英文閱讀學習的主流之一。

　　然而，依據筆者英文教學三十多年的經歷，英文閱讀學習常遇到的困難或障礙不僅是無法掌握文章主題，還有對文章中字彙與文法的不瞭解。事實上，英文文章的閱讀是包含英文字彙、文法、句型以及文章主題的瞭解，缺一不可。因此，英文閱讀應該是一種包括上述項目的概括性學習，也是一種全方位的英文閱讀學習。

　　針對上述所說的全方位英文閱讀學習，本書提供一種包括英文字彙、文法、句型以及文章主題的學習方法。此種方法是一種筆者稱之為點 (字彙)、線 (句法)、面 (文章段落和全文的主題) 的全方位英文閱讀學習方法。換言之，從字彙的明白開始，經過句法的分析，進而瞭解段落或全文的主題或主旨，建構起完整的全面英文閱讀學習。這是一種按部就班的學習方式，也是一種依循漸進的學習方法。

　　本書的目的就是幫助讀者培養一個全面的英文閱讀能力。

因此，本書的設計是從第一章的字彙解讀來突破英文閱讀障礙的第一關。本章教導六種推敲字義的閱讀技巧與字彙記憶的十種要訣，使讀者在平時閱讀或考試時，面對閱讀測驗中不懂的單字時，能藉著推敲字義的閱讀技巧來明白其不懂的字彙。另一方面，藉著字彙記憶的十種要訣，記住大量的單字涵義，增進英文閱讀的實力。本書的第二章則是從英文句子的結構來分析句子的涵義。有別於傳統的文法分析，本書著重在以句子的架構來分析各種詞類之間的相關性，亦即先以圖示列出句子的構成要素，接著再將這些要素 (如動詞、名詞、代名詞等) 逐一分析解說，使讀者能明白句子的完整涵義，而不僅是詞類個別的用法，造成見樹不見林的片段瞭解。這也是很多英文學習者的學習盲點，無法理解英文句子變化所帶來的差異，其原因是不瞭解各種詞類在句子中功用及它對其他詞類的影響。這種功用與影響會造成對文章涵義的理解程度。例如，主詞是句子的頭，由名詞或代名詞所構成，但是不定詞、動名詞、甚至介系詞片語皆可作主詞用，只要其出現在主格的位置上。這種歸納相同功能卻是不同詞類的解釋會是本書句法章節中的重點之一。

　　明白字彙的涵義以及理解句法的結構與詞類的功能之後，掌握文章段落的主題或全文的主旨將是英文閱讀學習最後的一步。從筆者的教學經驗中發現許多學生都明白全文中字彙的涵義，文法與句型也沒問題，卻是不懂全文的主旨為何，不知段落的重點所在。究其原因，他們在高中之前所學的英文閱讀大都是著重在字彙的涵義與句子文法的解釋，也就是語言教學法中比較傳統的「文法 - 翻譯教學法 (Grammar-Translation

Approach)」，個別字義的瞭解與句子文法的分析是此種教學法的主要目標，對英語初學者而言，這是基本的教學方法之一。但是對想要英文閱讀進階的學習者而言，明白文章的主旨或段落的主題則是必要的學習目標，也是學習英文閱讀最終的目的之一。換言之，明白字彙的涵義以及理解句法的結構與詞類的功能是英文閱讀學習的過程與憑藉，最後的目的是瞭解文章的主題。而掌握主題就需要有合乎邏輯的思考，明白文章脈絡的發展。本書針對如何確認主題、主題句的位置以及文章的結構與風格有清楚的講解。

為了使讀者不僅明白上述字彙，句法以及文章主題的學習方法，並且也能結合三種不同項目的學習方法於實際文章的分析上，本書第四章提供八篇範文的示範，將前三章所介紹的各種英文閱讀學習方法綜合運用於這八篇範文中，並且詳細解說每一種項目中的方法運用，使讀者能明白如何結合字彙，句法以及文章主題的學習方法每一篇文章中。

本書的特色可分為下列幾項：

一、每一章開頭皆有該章的特色介紹並且以圖表呈現，使讀者迅速掌握該章的內容重點。

二、各章節中皆以精選例題示範該章節中的要點，逐點逐題說明，並且每一例題皆有詳細解析與中文的題譯。

三、各章節中多以圖表說明其內容，使讀者一目瞭然，立即清楚該章節中的內容重點，避免冗長的解釋。

四、每一章節末了皆有該章節的重點整理，將該章節所有的內容重點以流程圖或表列說明，使讀者能複習該章的內容精華。

本書的目的是教你如何自我學習英文閱讀技巧，進而能獨立閱讀英文文章。透過非傳統的方式，以全面向的學習學會英文閱讀。

作者

劉遠城 謹識

CONTENTS
目　錄

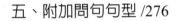

01

突破閱讀障礙的第一關

—— 字彙解讀

- ■ 第一節
  推敲字義的六種閱讀技巧
- ■ 第二節
  記憶字彙的十種要訣

閱讀導引

(一) 推敲字義的閱讀技巧：

閱讀技巧名稱 ▷ 閱讀技巧說明 ▷ 實例說明(各科考試題目) ▷

▷ 題目中譯 ▷ 題目中字彙解析 ▷ 重點整理 ▷ 習題&解答

(二) 記憶字彙的要訣：

記憶單字要訣解說 ➔ 圖表例舉說明 / 文字例舉說明 ➔ 實例練習 ➔ 解答&說明

本章特色

英文閱讀的基本障礙
→ 考試中的字彙涵義
→ 一般閱讀不懂的字彙

破解方法
→ 推敲字義的閱讀技巧（六大技巧）
　→ 推敲出考試中字彙的涵義
　→ 推敲出平時閱讀不懂字彙的涵義
→ 記憶字彙的要訣（十大要訣）
　→ 增加單字的正式＆另類記法

一石二鳥
→ 應付各種英文考試
→ 增進英文閱讀實力
→ 提升英文閱讀識字能力

一、同義字 / 片語推敲法

(一) 由單字的同位語來推敲：以位於單字後的其他單字、片語或子句形式出現的同位語來推敲單字的涵義

例 1

There is a superstition that if you break a mirror, you'll have bad luck for seven years.　　　　　　　　　　　　　　　　　(91 年度四技二專)

中譯　有一個迷信的說法說假如你打破一面鏡子，你就會有七年的厄運。

字彙解析

> That 子句是前面名詞的同位語，是解釋前面名詞的涵義。所以 that 子句的涵義就是解釋 a 之後的名詞。而 that 子句的意思是：「如果你打破鏡子，你就會有七年厄運。」這是一種迷信的說法，所以可以推敲其前的單字，superstition 也是與迷信涵義相似。由此推敲出 superstition 的字義爲迷信。

例 2

The famous wizard Harry Potter becomes a household figure all over the world.

中譯　著名的魔法師 (男巫) 哈利波特成了全世界家喻戶曉的人物。

Harry Potter(哈利波特) 在 wizard 後面，作 wizard 的同位語，所以 Harry Potter 指的就是 wizard。而 Harry Potter 是人人皆知的巫師。因此，可以推敲出 wizard 的涵義是指巫師。

例3

The summer in Taiwan is <u>humid</u>; the large quantity of water in the air makes it feel even hotter and more uncomfortable.　　(93 年度四技二專)

中譯 臺灣的夏天是潮濕的；空氣中大量的水分使得夏天令人覺得更熱與不舒服。

字彙解析

分號；是用來連接兩個句子，通常這兩個句子在涵義上是互相關聯的。所以分號之後的名詞片語 the large quantity of water in the air 是與前一句句尾的 humid 在涵義上是有關聯的。而「空氣中大量的水分」應就是指 humid 而臺灣的夏天 (The summer in Taiwan) 是 humid，依常識判斷，臺灣的夏天是如何被空氣中的水弄得人不舒服，應該就是意味著「潮濕」的天氣。Humid 正是此涵義。

例4

There was no <u>warning</u> that 2003 MN was coming.

中譯 沒有 2003 MN 小行星即將來臨的警告。

字彙解析

that 2003 MN was coming 這個名詞子句 (非形容詞子句) 在本句中作 warning 的同位語，亦即它是指其前 warning(警告) 的內容，否則就不

知 warning 所指為何。因此，warning 就是指 that 2003 MN was coming 這件事。其他類似的表達有：

The fact that he beat that policeman made him imprisoned for many years.

(他打那個警察的事實使他被監禁許多年。)

The scientist discovered the evidence that the disease was caused by the virus from mosquitoes.

(那位科學家發現那種疾病是由蚊子所有的病毒而引起的證明。)

(二) 由對單字的定義或解釋來推敲字義：出現在單字後的片語或子句，用來解釋單字的涵義

例 1

It's a robot bartender that can make drinks and tell jokes.

中譯 它是一種會製作飲料以及講笑話的酒保機器人。

字彙解析

bartender 的字義可以由其後的形容詞子句之涵義推敲出來，因為其後的形容詞子句是用來說明 bartender 為何。會製作飲料又會講笑話的這種人不會指一般飲料店的店員 (因為他們不需要講笑話給顧客聽) 所以只有酒吧中的酒保才會如此。

例 2

Asteroids are not stars; however, they are actually pieces of rock.

中譯 然而，小行星不是星星；他們實際上是岩石塊。

字彙解析

若 Be 動詞之後是名詞或名詞片語，他們就是與 Be 動詞之前的主詞涵義相似或一致。亦即

主詞 + be 動詞 + 名詞 / 名詞片語 (作主詞補語用)。

(涵義相同)

因此，本句的主詞 Asteroids 的意思就是 pieces of rock。其他相似的用
法還有如下列所示：

$$
主詞
\begin{cases}
\text{mean(意思是)} \\
\text{refer to(指)} \\
\text{indicate(顯示)} \\
\text{be called(稱作)}
\end{cases}
+ 名詞 / 名詞片語
$$

The name Koala means no drinks.

(無尾熊這個名字的意思是「不喝水」。)

The new rule only refers to the new employee of the company.

(這個新的規定只針對公司新進的員工。)

Fever and cough indicates illness.

(發燒與咳嗽顯示生病。)

Koalas are also called Australian bears.

(無尾熊也被稱為澳洲熊。)

(三) 由單字前後句子的同義字或片語來推敲字義：找出單字
　　前後句子或上下句子的相似字義的字或片語

例 1

Many Chinese people treat the rat as an auspicious symbol. They believe
the rat will bring good fortune.　　　　　　　　　　(104 年成大研究所)

中譯 許多中國人把老鼠視為吉祥的象徵。他們認為老鼠會帶來好運。

字彙解析

auspicious 的字義可由下一句中的 good fortune(好運) 來推敲。第一句中的 auspicious symbol 是指 rat(老鼠)，而第二句中指出 rat 會帶來 good fortune；所以 auspicious(形容詞) 應是與 good fortune 有關。因此，auspicious 的字義就是指與「好運」有關的「吉祥物」。

例2

There is real gratitude in the eyes of the lady whose life has been saved that night. You can find an unspoken "thank you" in her eyes.

中譯 在那晚那位性命被救的女士眼中有真誠的感謝。你可以在她眼中找到未說出口的「謝謝你」。

字彙解析

gratitude 的字義可以從下一句中的 "thank you" 而聯想出。因為兩個字或片語之後皆有 in ... eyes(在眼中)，所以 gratitude 就是指 thank you. unspoken(未說出口的) 來形容 thank you(感謝你) 更暗示是一種抽象的表達，如 gratitude(感謝) 的字義所表示。

(四) 由代名詞來推敲同義字的涵義

例句

The argument started between two women in front of the post office. Soon others joined in it and it became a real quarrel .

中譯 這場在郵局前面的爭論開始於兩個婦人之間。很快地，其他人也加入，演變成一場真正的爭吵。

要明白 quarrel 的涵義，就是要從句中的代名詞所連接的相關涵義來推敲。it 在句中是指 the argument(爭論)，而 it 至終變成了 quarrel。可見 quarrel 的涵義應是指 argument 的進一步發展。依常理而論，quarrel 應是指爭吵。

(五) 由連接詞 and 推敲同義字的涵義：and 連接兩個涵義相關的單字或片語

例句

Robots paint and assemble cars and put together electronic devices.

中譯 機器人油漆及組裝汽車並組裝電子裝置。

字彙解析

本句主詞是 Robots(機器人)，而主要動詞則分別由 and 所連接的三個涵義相同的動詞所組成：paint, assemble 以及 put together. paint 與 assemble 的受詞都是 car，而 paint 是「上漆」之意。所以 assemble 應是另一種不同的涵義，而 assemble 之後的動詞片語是 put together〔組合〕，所以 assemble 的涵義應與 put together 有關，因為組裝電子裝置和車子也是被組裝的涵義相似。所以 put together 就是 assemble 的同義字。

(六) 由連接詞或推敲同義字 / 反義字的涵義：or 連接兩個涵義相似或相反的單字或片語

例句

Some people believe that children may lie or fabricate stories about abuse. In fact, children do not invent stories about their own abuse.

有些人相信孩子可能說謊或捏造有關虐待的故事。事實
上，孩子不會虛構有關他們自己受虐的故事。

字彙解析

本劇中的 or 連接兩個字義相似的單字，因為後一句的涵義：事實上，
孩子不會虛構有關他們自己受虐的故事。後一句的涵義是與前一句的
涵義相反。所以前一句中的 lie 和 fabricate 是相似的涵義，都表示說謊
或虛構。而 fabricate(捏造) 正是類似的涵義。

二、反義字推敲法
(一) 由反義字或片語來推敲字義

例 1

Group registrations are not allowed. Each member must register for the
conference individually.

中譯 團體報名是不允許的，每個成員必須個別的報名進入會
場。

字彙解析

本句的前後兩句的涵義是相似的。但是因為前句中有 not，所以 group
registrations(團體報名) 的否定就是後面句子涵義。換言之，團體報名
是表示一種不被允許的方式，所以第二句就指出個人的報名才是可以
的。而 each other(每一個成員) 之涵義由句尾的 individually(個別地)
來加強語氣。因此，individually 的字亦可由 group(團體) 這個反義字
來推敲出。

The gamer wanted to live in the <u>virtual</u> world because his real life was much less interesting than his game life.

中譯 那位電玩者想要生活在虛擬的世界裡，因為他真實的生活比他的電玩生活無趣多了。

字彙解析

> virtual 的字義要從 because 子句中的 real(真實的) 推敲出來。因為後一句的涵義是真實生活比電玩生活無趣多了，所以前一句中的 wanted to live in virtual world 中的 virtual 就是「不真實」的涵義，他就是 real 的反義字。

(二) 由表示相反涵義的介系詞片語來推敲字義：instead of, unlike, in contrast to, despite, in spite of 等等

例1

Puppet theater uses puppets instead of real people to portray the characters in the play.

中譯 木偶劇院運用木偶取代真人來描寫劇中的人物。

字彙解析

> instead of(取代) 是用來表示與其相反或不同的涵義。因此，本句中的取代真人而用 puppets 來扮演戲中的角色。所以由此可知 puppets 是假的，使用 puppets 的戲院就是指木偶之類的劇院。

例2

John should <u>interact</u> more often with his friends and family after work, instead of staying in his room to play computer games.　　(104 年學測)

中譯 約翰應該在下班後更常和他的家人朋友互動，取代待在房間玩電腦遊戲。

字彙解析

instead of 表示「取代」之意。所以，依據第二句的涵義：取代待在他的房間玩電腦遊戲，前一句是與本句涵義相反。因此，interact ... with 應是指與人之間更多的來往的涵義。interact(互動) 就是這種類似的涵義。

例3

Despite his father's warning, he insists on taking the moonlighting as a mean for his business profits. (A) avocation (B) making illegal wines (C) smuggling (D) salvation (84 年中興研究所)

中譯 不顧他父親的警告，他堅持兼差作爲他事業獲利的慰藉。

字彙解析

由 Despite(不顧；不管) 所接的涵義，可見他做了他父親不該做的事。但是 (B) 與 (C) 揭示非法的事：製造私酒與走私，所以不能同時都是答案。(D)salvation(拯救) 的涵義則與前文不符，因爲他父親不會反對他拯救他的事業利潤。所以只剩 (A)avocation；而，moonlighting 由字面上分析應與晚上的活動有關 (月光)，而可能就是他晚上出去工作來賺取更多利潤。而 avocation 就是「兼差」之意。

例4

The two professions are not akin in spite of what people commonly think. (A) challenging (B) related (C) esteemed (82 年政大研究所)

中譯 儘管人們一般都這樣，但是這兩個職業是不相關的。

字彙解析

> in spite of(儘管) 所接的子句是表示與前半句相反的涵義，所以前半句中的 akin 不是正面，就是負面的涵義，但是一般而言 akin 的涵義是否定的機率比較低，否則就變成雙重否定的表達：not akin(不是不…)，所以應是正面或肯定的涵義。而 akin 的涵義又與 kin(親屬) 的字形接近，加上 a 在 kin 之前就成為形容詞 (如 a + live = alive, a + fire = afire) 所以表示這兩種職業是有關係的，只有 (B)related(相關的) 符合上下文義。

(三) 由表示相反涵義的連接詞來推敲涵義：but, while, although, even if

例 1

Types Os are curious and generous but stubborn.　　　　(105 年學測)

中譯 O 型血型的人士是好奇又慷慨的，但是卻固執己見。

字彙解析

> but 是連接兩個涵義相反的單字或片語。本句中的 curious(好奇的) 與 generous(慷慨的) 都是正面涵義的形容詞，所以 but 之後的 stubborn 就是表示負面意義的形容詞。雖然不能得知 stubborn 的確切意義，但是可以從常識判斷 O 型血型的人之負面個性是頑固且固執的，因此，stubborn 可能是此種涵義。

例 2

It is often said that an American starts a speech with a joke, while Japanese has an apology to make.　　　　(103 年輔大轉學考)

中譯 人們常常說美國人是以笑話爲開場白，然而日本人卻是以道歉爲開場白。

字彙解析

> while 有兩個意思：一是「當…時刻」，二是「然而」。在本句中 while 表示對比涵義的「然而」。前半句的涵義是美國人以笑話做開場白，所以後半句的涵義應是與前半句相反。說笑話是很輕鬆的，因此後半句中的 has an apology 中的 apology 應是嚴肅或正式的表示。所以 apology 的涵義應是與日本人的禮儀或習慣有關。

例 3

Although Mr. Chen is rich, he is a very <u>stingy</u> person and is never willing to spend any money helping those who are in need. (101 年學測)

中譯 雖然陳先生富有，但是他是個吝嗇的人，從不願意花任何錢去幫助那些需要幫助的人。

字彙解析

> stingy 的字義可由兩方面推敲出來，一是 although(雖然) 所連接的是兩個涵義成對比的句子，另一方面則可由 and 之後的解釋推敲出。因爲前半句說出陳先生是有錢人，後半句的涵義則與 rich 成對比。而與 rich 成對比的是不慷慨 (不可能是 poor，否則涵義前後矛盾)。and 之後的進一步解釋更確定 stingy 做「吝嗇的」解釋，因爲他不願意花錢幫助需要幫助的人。

例 4

Even if the police <u>postulate</u> that the suspect had a motive for the murder, that still doesn't mean that he did it. (83 年臺大研究所)

中譯 即使警方主張那個嫌疑犯有謀殺的動機，那仍然不能表示他做了那件事。

字彙解析

Even if(即使) 這個連接詞所連接的子句是表達相反或對比的涵義。後半句 that still doesn't mean that he did it 是表示否定那個嫌疑犯犯案的可能，所以前半句中警方應是認為或提出那個嫌疑犯有謀殺的動機。換言之，postulate 的涵義應是肯定且表達一種看法，這與 postulate「主張」的原意十分接近。

(四) 由表示相反或對照涵義的連接性副詞或副詞片語來推敲字義：however, nevertheless, in contrast

例句

In contrast to the fall of the stock market in Taiwan, the stock market in Hong Kong soared to another high peak.

中譯 與臺灣下跌的股市對照之下，香港的股市漲到另一高峰。

字彙解析

In contrast to 有兩種主要涵義：「對照之下；與…顯然有別」，所以其連接的是兩種對比的涵義。在本句中與臺灣股市的下滑成對比的是香港股市的上漲，而且 another high peak(另一高點) 也加強這種語意的解釋。因此，soar 的涵義可推敲為「上漲」，而其原意正是如此。

三、句子上下文意判斷法 (Guessing meaning from context)

(一) 利用表示因果關係的連接詞來推敲字義：because, as, so, since, therefore

例 1

The angry passenger argued <u>furiously</u> with the airline staff because their flight was cancelled without any reason. (104 年學測)

中譯 那位生氣的旅客憤怒地與航空公司的員工爭吵，因為他們的班機無故被取消。

字彙解析

> 本句的原因是：班機無故取消，所以結果自然就是乘客與航空公司的員工爭論，而 furiously 是副詞，用來形容 argued(爭論)，所以應是指「生氣」或「憤怒」等涵義。再加上 passenger 有 angry 來形容乘客，更確認 furiously 作為「憤怒」的解釋。

例 2

The traffic in the city was <u>light</u> today, so Jane got home earlier than usual. (89 年學測)

中譯 今天在城市的交通流量少，所以珍比平常更早回家。

字彙解析

> 這是一句表示因果關係的句子。前半句表示原因，後半句表示結果。所以 light 的字義可以由後半句的結果反推回去。因為「珍比平常更早回家」意味著她回家的路上的交通是順暢的，所以 light 的涵義應是與交通順暢有關。換言之，交通順暢與交通流量少在涵義很接近。

例3

She spent the summer brushing up on her Taiwanese history as she was to teach that in the fall.　(A) reviewing　(B) reading (C) taking　(D) writing　　　　　　　　　(82 年臺大研究所)

中譯　她花了整個暑假溫習她的臺灣歷史，因為她要在秋季教授那個課程。

字彙解析

後半句表示她要在接下來的秋季教授歷史課，所以前半句應是與課程有關。而，spent summer 在 brushing up on ... history 前，可見是花時間來預備歷史課程，因為 spend + 時間 + Ving(行動) 是「花時間在…上面」。

例4

Since I do not fully understand your proposal, I am not in a position to make any comment on it.　　　　　　　　　(102 年學測)

中譯　因為我沒有完全明白你的提議，我不便做任何對它的結論。

字彙解析

since(因為；既然) 表示原因，不瞭解那人的提案，所以結果就不予置評，可見 comment 就是表示「評論或意見」之意。

例5

Steve has several meetings to attend every day; therefore, he has to work on a very strict schedule.　(A) dense　(B) various　(C) tight (D) current　　　　　　　　　　　　　(99 年學測)

中譯 Steve 每天都要參加好幾個會議；因此，他必須依據緊湊的行程表而工作。

字彙解析

Therefore(因此) 連接表示結果的句子，所以前半句是原因。Steve 每天都有幾個會議要參加，所以他的工作必定很忙。可見他的行程 (schedule) 是很緊湊的，strict 的涵義就可推敲出來，就是 tight(緊湊的) 的同義字。

(二) 利用表示時間關聯的連接詞來推敲字義：when, before, after, until

例 1

When people feel uncomfortable or nervous, they may fold their arms across their chests as if to protect themselves. (98 年學測)

中譯 當人們覺得不舒服或緊張時，他們可能會兩臂交叉在他們的胸前好像要保護自己。

字彙解析

When(當…之時) 就呈現一種同時發生的行動或情況，而且是互相關聯的。When 的子句所表示的是一種不安的情況，所以同時就有對應的動作。To protect themselves(保護他們自己) 就與 fold their arms across their chests(手臂交叉胸前)，across(交錯)，可見 fold 就是表「交叉」的動作。

例 2

Before John got on the stage to give the speech, he took a deep breath to calm him down. (103 年學測)

中譯 在約翰上臺發表演講之前，他深呼吸使自己冷靜下來。

字彙解析

> Before(在…之前) 說出約翰上臺之前的情形，因爲是演講之前，所以自然會緊張，Before 將兩個相關的前後動作在此串聯，因此他要深呼吸 (deep 更加強此種涵義)，而 calm down(使…冷靜下來) 也加強此種解釋。

例3

After working in front of my computer for the entire day, my neck and shoulders got so stiff that I couldn't even turn my head. (102 年學測)

中譯 在我的電腦前工作一整天之後，我的頸脖與肩膀非常僵硬以致無法轉頭。

字彙解析

> After(在…之後) 表示先前的動作或情況造成後來的結果。既是一整天在電腦前工作，頸肩自然就會造成僵硬的結果，而 not even turn my head(甚至不能轉頭) 更意味著 stiff 是指肩頸僵硬。

(三) 利用表示比較關係的連接詞來推敲字義：than

例句

It has been estimated that The Linden Trust Fund's investment netted more than $80 million annually. (103 年輔大轉學考)

中譯 據估計琳達信託基金的投資每年獲得的淨利超過八千萬美元。

than(比…更…) 是連接兩個同性質的事物或人。than 之後連接錢 ($80 million)，所以前面的投資 (investment) 所接的動詞也與錢有關。more than(超過) 是正面的涵義，所以 (netted) 應與「賺錢」有關，推敲 netted 字義已接近原意了。

(四) 利用表示目的或結果的連接詞來推敲字義：so that, so ... that

例 1

A police officer takes money from a driver so that he does not give the driver a ticket for speeding. This is called bribery.

(103 年私醫轉學聯招)

中譯 那位警官收取駕駛的錢爲的是不給他開超速的罰單。這就稱爲賄賂。

字彙解析

so that(爲了…) 表示目的之連接詞，從前後又可看出警察收取賄賂，所以後面的代名詞 this 就是指這一件事，is called(被稱爲) 更直接說明此行爲的名稱。

例 2

It rained so hard yesterday that the baseball game had to be postponed until next Saturday.　　　　　　　　　　　　　　　　　(102 年學測)

中譯 天雨下得太大以至於棒球賽被迫延期至下週六。

字彙解析

so ... that 子句 (太…以至於) 是表示結果的連接詞句型。原因下大雨，

所以球賽必定是延期 (until next Saturday)，有預告的未來時間，可見 postpone 是「延期」之意。

(五) 利用表示條件的連接句來推敲字義：if, unless

例 1

If you want to know what your dreams mean, now there are websites you can visit to help you interpret them.　　　　　　　　(101 年學測)

中譯 如果你想要知道你夢的意義，現在這裏有你可以瀏覽的網站來幫助你解釋它們。

字彙解析

由 if 所引導的條件子句，通常都是表示某種條件下的因果關係。亦即「若…，則…。」所以本句中的假設狀況是若你想要知道你夢的涵義，你就可以去尋訪找出對夢的解釋的網站。可見 interpret 和 "what ... mean" 有相關的涵義。換言之，interpret 就是找出 what dreams mean。

例 2

If we walk at this slow pace, we'll never get to our destination.

　　　　　　　　　　　　　　　　　　　　(87 年學測)

中譯 如果我們以如此慢的步伐走路，我們將不會到達我們目的地。

字彙解析

如同上一題，若…我會…。走路很慢 (walk ... slow)，就無法到達目的地。at(以…的…) 所以 pace 應是指步伐，walk(走路) 也加強此種涵義的解釋。

The buildings couldn't be <u>built up</u> unless the workers worked day and night.

中譯 除非工人日夜趕工，否則這棟建築無法落成。

字彙解析

> Unless(除非)是表示一種否定的假設情況：它表示「若不…我無法…。」的假設狀況。因此，前半句中的否定涵義表示 built up 是正面的涵義；否則就無法構成否定涵義的情形。

(六) 利用表示舉例或衍生解釋的片語來推敲字義：such as, like, for example, that is

例1

Studies show that asking children to do house <u>chores</u>, such as taking out the trash or doing the dishes, helps them grow into responsible adults.

(99 年學測)

中譯 研究顯示要求孩子做家事，就像倒垃圾或洗盤子，有助於使他們成長為負責任的大人。

字彙解析

> chores 的字義可以從其後的舉例 (such as taking out ... dishes) 看出 chores 是家事。因為 chores 的涵義必須是概括性的涵義，才能包括各種的家事，像是倒垃圾與洗盤子等家事。

例2

Islamic terrorists attacked the innocent people in <u>European</u> countries, such as the people in France, the UK, and Germany.

中譯 伊斯蘭的恐怖份子攻擊在歐洲國家的無辜人們，像在法國、英國以及德國的人們。

字彙解析

European countries 的涵義可從 such as 所舉的國家 (法國、英國與德國) 而反推出 European 是指歐洲的國家，因為法、英、德都是位於歐洲的國家。

例 3

Tokyo is a metropolis, like New York, where more than ten million people live.

中譯 東京是像紐約那樣的大都會，有超過千萬的人住在那裏。

字彙解析

like(像) 也是舉例的一種方式。New York 和 Tokyo 都是 metropolis，而且在這些 metropolis 都住有千萬以上的人。可見 metropolis 不是一般的城市，而是指大城市。metro 這個字首也有「大」的涵義。

例 4

Those adolescents that engage in risk-taking behaviors which have health compromising effects; for example, heavy alcohol or substance abuse, unprotected sexual-behavior, are likely to have a lower self-esteem.

中譯 那些從事危險行為的青少年，其行為有危及健康的效果。例如，酗酒或惡癮，未受保護的性行為，他們都可能有較低的自尊心。

For example(例如) 所舉的幾個例子都用來呈現甚麼是 health compromising effects，可見 compromising 所描寫的效果是負面的，因為都是指酗酒，惡癮及不安全性行為。因此，compromising 的涵義與對健康有害有關。這種推敲字義與 compromising 原意已十分接近。

例5

Many <u>weddings</u> are double-ceremonies, that is, both the bride and groom exchange rings.

中譯 許多婚禮是雙重的儀式，亦即新娘與新郎雙方要交換戒指。

字彙解析

that is(亦即) 連接前後兩句涵義相似的句子，所以 that is 之後提到新娘與新郎，可見前面的 weddings 就是婚禮了。

(七) 利用標點符號來推敲字義：由與單字相關的標點符號來
    判斷單字的涵義
1. 由冒號 (：) 的功用來推敲字義：冒號 (：) 是連接兩個涵義
    相同的字詞或片語

例1

Jack is a <u>courteous</u> person: he is polite, kind, and always shows respect for others.　　　　　　　　　　　　　　　　　　　　　　　(89 年學測)

中譯 傑克是個有禮貌的人：他是有禮貌，親切而且總是顯示出對別人的尊重。

冒號 (：) 是用來連接兩個意思相關的字或句子。通常冒號前是概要的表達，冒號後則是進一步相關的說明或解釋。所以 courteous 的字亦可從 polite, kind 以及 show respect for others 看出來。事實上，courteous 就是 polite 的同義字。

例 2

The old lady enjoyed numerous leisure activities: fishing, playing tennis, rowing and chatting.

中譯　那位老婦人喜歡許多的休閒活動：釣魚、打網球、划船及聊天。

字彙解析

Leisure 是用來形容 activities(活動)，冒號後的活動的共同性就是休閒的性質，所以 leisure 正是此意。

2. 由破折號 (-) 的功用來推敲字義：破折號連接兩個涵義相似的字或片語

例句

The act of shopping-of leaving the house and going to a store-is a check against the inertia of consumption. (104 年臺大轉學考)

中譯　購物的行動──離開屋子而去商店──是一種對消費慣性的檢視。

字彙解析

破折號 (-) 是用來連接兩個意思相同的字或片語，所以本句中的 shopping 的涵義就是 of leaving the house and going to a store。

3. 由括弧 ( ) 來推敲其前的單字：括弧內的單字或片語是用來說明括弧前的單字或片語的涵義

Research on the possibility of cell phone addiction is an emerging field, and a lot of it centers on the habits of the youngest millennials (now teens and young adults), a generation that can't remember what it was like to not have a cell phone.　　　　　　　　　　　　　(104 年成大轉學考)

中譯　對手機成癮的可能性之研究是一種新興的領域，它大多集中在最年輕的千禧時代 (現在的青少年和青年人)，一個無法回想沒有手機將會如何的時代。

字彙解析

置於單字或片語後的括弧是用來說明括弧前單字或片語的涵義。通常括號內的文字解說清楚易懂。所以本句中的 youngest millennials 之涵義就是現今的青少年和青年 (now teens and young adults)。

4. 由分號 (;) 來推敲前後兩句中單字的涵義：分號 (;) 是用來連接語意相關的句子

Playing crystal balls or drums are healing; or even that music can cure cancer.　　　　　　　　　　　　　　　(103 年臺師大轉學考)

中譯　玩水晶球或打鼓是有治療效果的；或者甚至有哪種能治療癌症的音樂。

字彙解析

分號 (;) 的功能相當於 and，連接兩個語意相關的句子。所以前半句說某些活動可以對人如何，後半句也是相似的意思。因此，cure(治

療) 就是與 healing 同意。由 cure(常見的字彙) 反推回去就知 healing
之意。

四、依據同一段落中的前後句子語意關係來推敲字義
(一) 以邏輯方式來尋求字義：依據同一段前後或上下句子之
間的關聯來推敲字義

例 1

Learning style means a person's natural habitual and preferred ways of
learning. Research about learning styles has identified gender differences.
For example, one study found various differences between boys and girls in
sensory learning styles.

中譯 學習方式意味著一個人天然習慣且偏好的學習方法。有關
學習方式的研究已確認了性別上的差異。例如：有一個研
究發現在知覺學習方式上男孩和女孩之間不同的差異。

字彙解析

Gender 的字義可由 for example 後的例子推敲出來，因為 various differences
between boys and girls(男孩和女孩之間的不同的差異) 是一個對 gender
differences 的例證，所以 gender 應是指性別的涵義。

例 2

In February of 2003, Hessam Ghane, an unemployed chemist, sat alone
in his apartment in Independence, Missouri, grappling with the familiar
clutch of depression. He called a crisis hotline and told the counselor who
answered that he was considering suicide. After he hung up, two police
officers arrived at his door. Ghane asked to be taken to a hospital with a
psychiatric unit.

中譯 在 2003 年 2 月海珊・蓋思，一位失業的藥劑師，在密蘇里的獨立鎮獨自坐在他的公寓中，與大眾所知的沮喪魔掌對抗。他打電話給危機處理熱線，告訴電話的諮詢師他正想自殺。在他掛上電話之後，兩位警官來到他的門口。蓋思要求被帶到有精神科的醫院去。

字彙解析

本段文章中有幾個表達負面情況的用詞，如 unemployed(失業的)，depression(沮喪) 以及 suicide(自殺) 都在描寫文中主角蓋思的心理狀況，所以他後來被帶到醫院的 psychiatric unit 去，unit 是單位，指醫院的某一部門，從上下文的涵義來看，這個單位應是與他的精神狀況有關，所以 psychiatric 就是這方面的意義。

例 3

In addition to taking steps to deliver more personalized messages, advertisers are using billboards to offer more useful information. Digital billboards can connect to the Internet to display information such as the time, weather, and news headlines.　　　　　　　　　　　　(103 年私醫轉學聯招)

中譯 除了採取步驟去傳達更個人化的訊息，廣告商正運用數位看板提供更有用的資訊。數位看板可以連接至網路來呈現像時間、天氣以及新聞標題這樣的資訊。

字彙解析

billboard 的涵義可從其後的不定詞片語 (to offer more useful information) 來推敲 billboard 的涵義。因為這個不定詞片語是用來形容 billboard，表示 billboard 是用來提供有效、有用的資訊。而主詞 advertisers(廣告商) 則是說明他們使用 billboard 這樣的媒介。可見 billboard 應該是在

街上看到的廣告看板。接下來的一句更印證此種解釋。因為 billboard 可以連接網路來呈現項時間、天氣和新聞標題這樣的資訊。從上下文的句子就可推敲出 billboard 的涵義。

(二) 尋找段落中的同義字來推敲字義

例 1

Obesity is a significant health problem that elevates one's mortality risk. Overweight people are more vulnerable than others to heart diseases, diabetes, hypertension, respiratory problems, gallbladder diseases, stroke, arthritis, muscle and joint pain, and back problems.

(102 年私醫轉學聯招)

中譯 肥胖是一個明顯提高個人致死風險的健康問題。體重過重的人相較於他人在心臟病、糖尿病、高血壓、呼吸問題、膽囊疾病、中風、關節炎、肌肉及關節疼痛以及背部問題的方面更脆弱。

字彙解析

Obesity 的字義可從下一句中的 overweight(過重的) 形容詞來聯想，因為 overweight 的人有許多的疾病，所以就像 obesity 是一個明顯的健康問題一樣。從上下文涵義可看出 obesity 與 overweight 是指同一件事。

例 2

The hunter climbed up to the top of the mountain which is the highest mountain of the area. After half of a day, the other hunters also reached the summit of the mountain.

中譯 那位獵人爬上這個區裏最高山的山頂。半天過後，其他的獵人也到達山頂。

字彙解析

第一句中有山頂 the top of the mountain，接下來 other(其他的) 加上 also(也) 強調做成同樣的事，所以 summit 應該就是指第一句中的 top。

(三) 以表示各種語氣的連接詞 / 介系詞片語來推敲字義

例 1

Before her death, when she lay bedridden and mute for two years, he maintained a spreadsheet listing the books he read to her: Lewis Carroll, Jane Austin, Shakespeare's sonnets.   (104 年政大轉學)

中譯 在她去世以前，當她臥床不起並且無法言語時，他維持在一份電子資料工作表列出他讀給她的書籍：露易絲‧卡羅、珍‧奧斯丁、莎士比亞的十四行詩。

字彙解析

Bedridden 的涵義可從 Before her death 推敲出。因為 lay ... for two years(躺在…兩年之久)，可見 bedridden 一定是指生病臥床，因為生病臥床才會導致死亡，所以 bedridden 與病床有關。事實上，bedridden 是由 bed(床)+ridden(受折磨) 兩字合成的詞，表示在床上生病的狀況。

例 2

Roberts hypothesized that the gender difference could mean that women use their phone to foster social relationship while men are more interested in entertainment and usefulness.

中譯 羅伯假設性別的差異可能意味女性使用她們的電話來培養社交關係，然而男性使用電話卻對娛樂和效用更有興趣。

字彙解析

Gender 的涵義可由 "while"(然而) 連接兩個涵義相反的子句所推敲出來。在 gender difference(差異) 後的解釋 (mean) 說到男、女性的使用手機之差異，所以 gender 應是與「性別」的涵義有關。

五、跨段落的字義搜尋：依據不同段落中的上下文意來推敲字義

例 1

It was my first day in this beautiful city. As I was walking to the beach, a stranger came up to me and tried to shake my hand. "Don't you remember me, my friend?" he said. But I couldn't <u>recognize</u> his face at all. I didn't know a soul in the city. I had just arrived by plane and still had jet lag.

中譯 那是我第一天在這座美麗的城市。當我走向海灘，一位陌生人向我走來，試著和我握手。他說：「我的朋友，你不記得我了嗎？」但是我完全認不出他的臉。在這城裡我誰都不認識，我才剛搭飛機抵達這裡而且仍有時差。

字彙解析

recognize 的字義可由兩個線索看出：(1)recognize 的下一句是我在城市裡誰都不認識，這是對前一句 I couldn't recognize his face 進一步的強調，可見 recognize 是指認識的涵義。另一處線索是他稱那人為陌生人，所以他不認識他。綜合以上兩點線索 recognize 的意思就很明顯。

The kilt can be worn with accessories. On the front apron, there is often a kilt pin, topped with a small decorative family symbol. A small knife can be worn with the kilt too. It typically comes in a very wide variety, from fairly plain to quite elaborate silver-and jewel-ornamented designs. The kilt can also be worn with a sporran, which is the Gaelic word for pouch or purse.

中譯 蘇格蘭短裙可以搭配配件而穿。在前面的圍裙常有大頭針，針頭上有小的家族象徵的飾品。小刀也可與蘇格蘭短裙搭配。小刀以十分廣泛多樣的方式出現，從十分平常的到非常精緻的銀子和珠寶裝飾的設計。蘇格蘭短裙也可以搭配毛皮袋，愛爾蘭語稱它為「袋子」或「錢包」。

字彙解析

accessories 的涵義可從接下來的舉例推敲出。因為下面說道 kilt 可以有很多配件一起穿戴，例如：a pin, a small knife, a sporran 等等。第一句是主題句，說出 kilt 可搭配其他東西，可見 accessories 就是包括這些東西的統稱。因此，accessories 的涵義應是概括性的，而非特定的涵義。這些 pin, knife, sporran 都是 accessories, 可見 accessories 應是指附屬的小東西。

六、由字彙結構來推敲字義
(一) 由單字的字首、字根和字尾來推敲字義

例 1

The audience were very interested in Charles Brown's monologue.

(82 年政大轉學)

中譯 觀眾對查理‧布朗的獨白劇很有興趣。

mono(單一的)+ logue(語言) → 獨自講說的語言。場景是有觀眾，可見 monologue 應是個人演出的獨白劇 (尤其是指出其名字)。

例 2

This is a retrograde development. (82 年政大轉學)

中譯　這是一種倒退的發展。

字彙解析

Retro(字首)：倒退的。grade(層級)，所以 retrograde 就是指倒退的情形。

例 3

She gave birth to a malformed baby. (82 年政大轉學)

中譯　她生了一個畸形的小孩。

字彙解析

Mal(字首) 意指「不良；壞的」form：形體，合起來就作「不良外型的」解釋。類似的字還有 malfunction：故障。

例 4

However, because it's hard to get them to sit still and "perform on command," some professional photographers refuse to photograph pets.

(101 年學測)

中譯　然而，因為要使寵物坐著不動以及依指令表演是困難的，有些專業攝影師拒絕為牠們拍照。

photo：相片。grapher：畫圖者。photo + grapher：攝影師，字尾 er 表示「…的人」。photography：攝影。

例 5

Besides these safety issues, bottled water has other disadvantages.

(99 年學測)

中譯 　除了這些安全問題之外，瓶裝水還有其他的缺點。

字彙解析

dis：不；非。advantage：好處；優點。dis + advantage：缺點。besides：除了…之外。

例 6

Since the information on storage and shipment is not always readily available to consumers, bottled water may not be a better alternative to tap water.

(99 年學測)

中譯 　因為在儲存與運送上的資訊對消費者不一定容易獲得，所以瓶裝水可能不是對自來水更好的取代品。

字彙解析

ship(船)+ ment(表示抽象涵義的字尾)：船運。其他相同字尾的字彙還有：entertainment, amusement。

例 7

In 1941, Hitler launched a gigantic attack on the Soviet Union.

中譯 在 1941 年希特勒發動對蘇聯的強大攻擊。

字彙解析

> Gigantic：巨大的。-ic 是表示形容詞的字尾。

例 8

Please feel free to interrupt me if you don't understand what I say.

(102 年東吳轉學)

中譯 如果你不明白我所說的，請勿在意打斷我的話。

字彙解析

> inter(字首)：插入。-rupt(字根)：打斷，所以，interrupt 就是「打斷」
> 之意。

(二) 由單字的複合字形來推敲字義：由兩個具有涵義的字結
合而成的字彙

例 1

This centuries-old Chinese mind-body exercise is now gaining popularity
in the United States. (104 年學測)

中譯 這個流傳幾個世紀之久的中式身心運動現今已在美國蔚為
流行。

字彙解析

> Centuries-old：幾世紀之久。mind-body：身心，這些用連字 (-) 符號構
> 成的字與原字涵義相似。

例 2

You've most likely heard the news by now: A car-commuting, desk-bound, TV-watching lifestyle can be harmful to our health.　　　　　(104 年學測)

中譯　到現在為止你們已經大都可能聽到此一消息：一種開車通勤，待在辦公桌看電視的生活方式有害我們的健康。

字彙解析

> 本句中連續三個複合形容詞，都可從其字面的涵義解釋。只不過兩個是名詞＋現在分詞 (car commuting & TV-watching)，一個是名詞＋過去分詞 (desk-bound) 表示被動的涵義。

例 3

Hard-working managers often prefer to do an MBA via distance learning.
　　　　　(102 年淡江轉學考)

中譯　殷勤的經理經常偏好經由遠距教學來修 MBA 的課程。

字彙解析

> Hard-working 是形容詞＋現在分詞的複合形容詞，表示主動的涵義，用來形容動作者的情形。

例 4

Irahim Hamadto is armless, but he became the Egyptian para-table tennis champion by holding the bat in his mouth and flicking the ball with his right foot.　　　　　(103 年臺師大轉學考)

中譯　伊巴謙·哈瑪度沒有手臂，但是他藉由用嘴咬住球拍並且用他的右腳打球成為埃及殘障桌球賽的冠軍。

para：不正常的；table tennis：桌球。Para 是字首，有「平行的；錯誤的；保護的」等涵義。

例 5

Soybean-based biodiesel has remained costly and is controversial in food security circles. (104 年學測)

中譯 由黃豆為基礎的生殖柴油仍然昂貴並且在糧食來源穩定循環上仍有爭議。

soybean：黃豆；based：以…為根基，所以 soybean-based 是名詞＋過去分詞的複合形容詞，用來形容 biodiesel。

例 6

Your liver is fully awake by midday, ready to help with the digestion of food. (103 年臺灣聯合大學轉學考)

中譯 你的肝在正午之前是充分復甦的，準備來幫助食物的消化。

mid：在…中間；day：白日，所以 midday 就是白天的中午。類似的還有：midway 中途。Midnight：午夜。Mid 是字根，day 是單字。

例 7

The boy once studied in an old-fashioned school near London.

中譯 那個男孩曾經在靠近倫敦的一所傳統學校就讀。

字彙解析

old-fashioned 是形容詞，而 fashioned 是擬分詞 (不是由動詞轉成的過去分詞)，而是名詞 +ed 所構成的類似分詞的形容詞 old：舊式的 fashion：風格。

◎重點整理◎

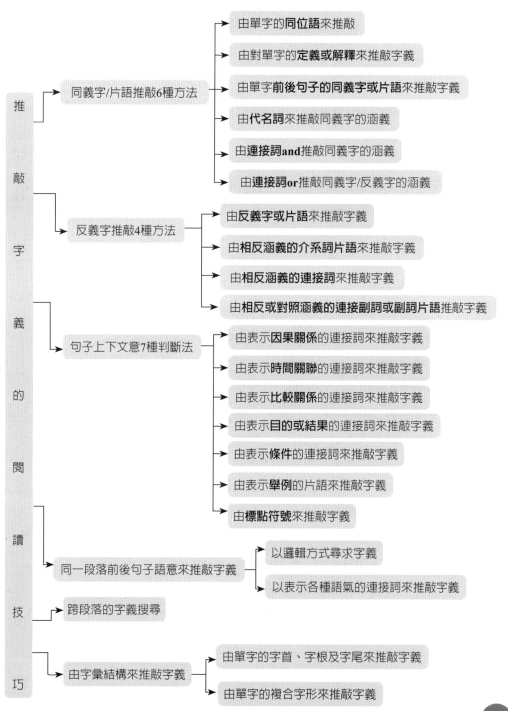

推敲字義的閱讀技巧

- 同義字/片語推敲6種方法
  - 由單字的**同位語**來推敲
  - 由對單字的**定義或解釋**來推敲字義
  - 由單字**前後句子的同義字或片語**來推敲字義
  - 由**代名詞**來推敲同義字的涵義
  - 由**連接詞and**推敲同義字的涵義
  - 由**連接詞or**推敲同義字/反義字的涵義

- 反義字推敲4種方法
  - 由**反義字或片語**來推敲字義
  - 由**相反涵義的介系詞片語**來推敲字義
  - 由**相反涵義的連接詞**來推敲字義
  - 由**相反或對照涵義的連接副詞或副詞片語**推敲字義

- 句子上下文意7種判斷法
  - 由表示**因果關係**的連接詞來推敲字義
  - 由表示**時間關聯**的連接詞來推敲字義
  - 由表示**比較關係**的連接詞來推敲字義
  - 由表示**目的或結果**的連接詞來推敲字義
  - 由表示**條件**的連接詞來推敲字義
  - 由表示**舉例**的片語來推敲字義
  - 由**標點符號**來推敲字義

- 同一段落前後句子語意來推敲字義
  - 以邏輯方式尋求字義
  - 以表示各種語氣的連接詞來推敲字義

- 跨段落的字義搜尋

- 由字彙結構來推敲字義
  - 由單字的字首、字根及字尾來推敲字義
  - 由單字的複合字形來推敲字義

Exercise

1. People used to wash clothes at the riverside, but now we do the _____ with the washing machine at home.

   (A) baking   (B) laundry   (C) figure   (D) function

2. Although Tom had been at the scene, he was _____ to act as a witness.

   (A) reasonable   (B) reluctant   (C) fatigue   (D) equal

3. He made his instruction explicit and direct that everyone could follow easily.

   (A) executirely   (B) exclusirely   (C) unspoken   (D) clear

4. The chairperson of the meeting asked everyone to speak up instead of _____ their questions among themselves.

   (A) reciting   (B) giggling   (C) murmuring   (D) whistling

5. I could not _____ the sweet smell from the bakery, so I walked in and bought a fresh loaf of bread.

   (A) insist   (B) resist   (C) obtain   (D) contain

6. The restaurant has a _____ charge of NT$250 per person. So the four of us need to pay at least NT$1,000 to eat there.

   (A) definite   (B) minimum   (C) flexible   (D) numerous

7. The story about Hou-I shooting down nine suns is a well-known Chinese _____ , but it may not be a true historical event.

   (A) figure   (B) legend   (C) miracle   (D) rumor

8. If you fly from Taipei to Tokyo, you'll be taking an international, rather than a _____ flight.

   (A) liberal   (B) domestic   (C) connected   (D) universal

9. Since organic food came into _____ decades ago, farmers became

more cautious about the use of pesticide.

(A) vogue　(B) contact　(C) voyage　(D) fan

10. Ms. Wilson opened the door for her daughter, although normally she would have done this for herself.

(A) volunteerly　(B) ordinarily　(C) abnormally　(D) surprisingly

11. Although salmon may travel hundreds of miles from where they were spawned, they will ultimately return there to lay eggs.

(A) probably　(B) reluctantly　(C) apparently　(D) eventually

12. If he keeps on harassing them, they will call the police.

(A) amusing　(B) bothering　(C) ignoring　(D) hurrying

13. Martin Luther King said,” The oppressed must never allow the conscience of the oppressed to slumber. To accept injustice or _____ passively is to say to the oppressor that his actions are morally right.

(A) presents　(B) recession　(C) inflation　(D) segregation

14. Most composers had not been idolized before they passed away.

(A) misguided　(B) dissatisfied　(C) reviewed　(D) worshipped

15. The United States Constitution mandates two houses of congress so that the large states will not be disproportionately represented.

(A) unequally　(B) illegally　(C) mistakenly　(D) suitably

16. Dancers exercise regularly, so they have supple bodies.

(A) aching　(B) limber　(C) thin　(D) coarse

17. Miss Jones was jubilant when she received her acceptance from the college.

(A) suspicious　(B) very happy　(C) surprised　(D) thankful

18. John was so engrossed in his novel that he forgot his appointment with his doctor.

(A) obliged　(B) absorbed　(C) excelled　(D) enlivened

19. Nothing could efface their memory of his cruelty although many years had elapsed.

(A) edify   (B) substantiate   (C) erase   (D) keep

20. Typhoon Maggie brought to I-Lan county a huge amount of rainfall, much greater than the _____ rainfall of the season in the area.

(A) average   (B) considerate   (C) promising   (D) enjoyable

21. The young couple decided to _____ their wedding until all the details were well taken care of.

(A) announce   (B) maintain   (C) postpone   (D) simplify

22. The patient's health did not _____ to the treatment; therefore, his doctor has to prescribe an alternative medication.

(A) reply   (B) improve   (C) activate   (D) respond

23. When people gamble more money than they can afford to lose, they can be in a _____.

(A) predicament   (B) prediction   (C) preservation   (D) procrastination

24. Music has healing properties -- whether it's quiet jazz or cacophonous rock anthems.

(A) estates   (B) effects   (C) proprietorship   (D) possessor ship

25. Mr. Lin is a very _____ writer; he publishes at least five novels every year.

(A) moderate   (B) temporary   (C) productive   (D) reluctant

26. Terrence Power, for example, complained that after his wife learned she had Wegener's disease, an _____ disorder of the immune system, they find it difficult to refuse to tests recommended by her physician.

(A) astonishing   (B) ordinary   (C) specific   (D) uncommon

27. Children normally have a _____ of new foods.

(A) confidence   (B) faith   (C) specific   (D) distrust

28. When I tried to lead her indoors she became frightened and refused to move. It took me some time to _____ her that her fear was ground less and that all was well.

    (A) persuade   (B) undermine   (C) cooperate   (D) disagree

Answers

1.	(B)	15.	(A)
2.	(B)	16.	(C)
3.	(D)	17.	(B)
4.	(C)	18.	(B)
5.	(B)	19.	(C)
6.	(B)	20.	(A)
7.	(B)	21.	(C)
8.	(B)	22.	(D)
9.	(A)	23.	(A)
10.	(B)	24.	(B)
11.	(D)	25.	(C)
12.	(B)	26.	(D)
13.	(D)	27.	(D)
14.	(D)	28.	(A)

一、字首、字根與字尾記憶法 (prefix, root, suffix)

英文屬於拉丁語系的一個分支語系，所以許多英文字彙的構成是由拉丁文衍生出。不僅如此，英文也受到法文、德文與西班牙文等語文的影響，所以英文有許多是由外來語所構成或衍生的字彙，這也就構成英文單字的慣用字首、字根、字尾，其中以字根最為重要。譬如西班牙中的 aqua(水) 是與英文中的 aqua(水) 視同字同義。因此，由 aqua 所衍生的英文單字就有不少、例如：aquaculture(養殖漁業)，aquarium(水族館)，aquarius(水瓶座)，aquashow(水上技藝表演) 等等。

由上述例子可知英文的字首、字根與字尾就如同中文的部首功用一般 (中文的部首「木」可以構成向「根」、「樹」等這些與「木」涵義相關的衍生字)。唯一不同的是中文的一些部首本身就具有獨立涵義的字彙，但在英文字首、字根、字尾中絕大部分是無法獨自成字。因此，英文中的字首、字根、字尾就須與單字結合，形成另一種涵義的字，正因為如此，他們就可產生出許多以其字首、字根與字尾為首與為尾的單字。請看下列範例說明：

※　dress(穿衣)+ un(不；非)= undress(脫衣)

　　lock(鎖住)+ un(不；非)= unlock(開鎖)

※　neighbor(鄰居)+ hood(狀態)= neighborhood(鄰近地區)

　　child(孩子)+ hood(時期)= childhood(孩童時期)

※　attend(參加)+ ant(人)= attendant(參加者，隨侍人員)

　　protest(抗議)+ ant(人)= protestant(異議者)

由上述例子可知英文的字首、字根與字尾就可知道許多單字的衍生涵義，對字彙的增進有很大的幫助。不過在英文字首、字根與字尾中，只有字尾有時並無特定的涵義，只是用來表示該單字的詞性，例如：active, act 是動詞，加 ive 就形成形容詞 (active 是主動的)。雖然如此，但是這些表示不同詞性的字尾還是有助於瞭解單字在文章中的相關涵義，因為大部分具有這類字尾的單字，涵義仍是相同的。此外，對句中的文法也有幫助。因為坊間有不少有關字首、字根與字尾的書，內容多且繁雜，不易記住。有些甚至冷僻的單字，沒有必要記住。因此，在此經過參考市面上的書籍，引出由 A 到 Z 常用 (考) 的字首、字根與字尾，且多以圖表方式陳列，使讀者一目瞭然。

重點 1、一般常見的字首、字根與字尾		
字首群	字義	舉例
A		
ab, abs	脫離；相反；不	abnormal(反常的)、absorb(吸去)
acro	高的；極度	acrobatics(特技)、acrophobia(懼高症)
aero, air	空氣；空中；氣體	aerologist(高空氣象學家)、airproof(不透氣的)
aeri, acr		airplane(飛機)、airlines(航空公司)
agri	田野	agriculture(農業)
alt	高的	althorn(高音喇叭)、altitude(海拔)
ambi, amphi	兩側；兩者；環繞	ambiguous(模稜兩可)、amphibian(水陸兩棲的)
an	無；非；不	anarchy(無秩序的)、anesthetic(無趣的；麻醉的)

ante	前；先；原來	anterior(在前的)、antetype(原型)
anti	相反；反對；防止	antibody(抗體)、antipathy(厭惡)
aqua	水；關於水的	aquarium(水族館)、aquaplane(滑水板)
aster, astro	星球；星	astronaut(太空人)、asterisk(星形符號)、astrology(占星學)
audi, audio	聽	audience(觀眾)、audiphones(助聽器)
auto	自動；自己	automobile(汽車)、autobiography(自傳)
avi	鳥類的；航空	aviarist(鳥類飼養家)、aviator(航空員)
B		
back	背後	backache(背痛)、backup(支援者、代理人)
bacter	細菌	bactericide(殺菌劑)、bacterin(疫苗)
be	使…變作	belittle(使縮小；貶低)、becloud(蒙蔽)
bene, beni	善的；好的	benefit(好處)、benefactor(恩人)
bi	雙；二；複	bilingual(雙語言的)、binate(雙生的)
bio	生命；生物	biology(生物學)、biolysis(生物分解)
C		
carn	肉	carnal(肉體的)、carnivorous(食肉的)
cent	一百爲單位	century(一世紀)、centuple(一百位)

chron	慢性的；長期的	chronicle(年代史)、chronic(慢性的)
circ, circum	周圍；環繞；圍起	circle(圓圈)、circumstance(環境)、circulate(使循環)
co, col	共同；和；一起	coexist(共存)、collaborate(合作)
com, con, cor	共同；互相；更～	compete(競爭)、combine(聯合)、concentrate(集中)、community(社區)、communication(溝通聯繫)
contra, contro, counter	相反；反對；相對	contradiction(矛盾)、counteract(抵制)
cosmo	宇宙；太空；秩序	cosmos(宇宙)、cosmonaut(太空人)(特指蘇聯的)
craft	技術；技巧	craftsman(技藝家；技工)、craftwork(工藝品)
cur	跑走	currency(流通)、current(水流；電流)
cycle	循環	cyclist(騎腳踏車的人)、cycle-track(腳踏車道)
D		
de	減少；取消；非	debase(貶低)、descent(下降)、destructive(毀滅的)
dia	相對；貫通	dialogue(對話)、diameter(直徑)
dic, dict	說	diction(用語)、dictionary(字典)
dif	分開；否定；不	differ(不同)、diffuse(散開)
dis	不無；相反；分離；取消；除去	disagree(不同意)、discount(折扣)、discover(發現)
down	降落；降低	downdraft(下降氣流)、downhill(下坡路)

dys	惡化；不良；困難	dyspeptic(消化不良的)、 dysphonia(發聲障礙)
E		
ef	趕出；外面	effable(可說明的)、efface(抹掉)
electro	電	electrician(電工)、electronics(電子學)
en, em	使～；在～之中	encouraging(激勵人的)、enlarge(擴大)、endanger(危害)、endearing(可愛的；惹人愛的)
equ	相同	equal(相等)、equate(使～相等)
eu	良好；善	eugenic(優生的)、eulogist(頌揚者)
ex, exo	來自；出自；完全；伸開	expose(暴露)、extend(延伸)、export(出口)
extra	以外；超越；在～之外	extraordinary(奇特的)、extravagant(浪費的)
F		
fam	名聲	famed(聞名的)、famous(有名的)
flu, flux	流暢	fluency(流暢)、fluxion(流動)
for	禁止	forbid(禁止)、forbear(避免)
fore	在～之前；預先；先	foresee(預見)、foretell(預言)
G		
geo	地球；土地	geognosy(地球構造學)、geography(地理)
H		
hem, hemi	半	hemicycle(半圓形)、hemisphere(半球)

herte, hereto	其他的；相異的	heterodox(異端的)、heterosexual(異性的)
homo, homeo	相同；相似	homosexual(同性戀的)、homotype(同型)
hyper	上方；超過；太甚	hypermarket(大規模超市)、hypersensitive(太過敏感的)
hypo	低；少；在～下	hypodermic(皮下的)、hypostasis(血液沉積症)
I		
im, in	不無；非；向內入；使得	income(收入)、infuriate(使～憤怒)、inappropriate(不合適的)
il	不；無；非或加強之意	illogical(不合邏輯的)、illegal(非法的)
inter	在～之內；互相	interact(互相作用)、intercity(城市間)
intra, intro	在內；內部；向內；入內	intraparty(政黨內的)、intramural(學校內的)
ir	不；無；內向；入	irregular(不規則的)、irrational(非理性的)、irresponsible(不負責任的)
M		
macro	大；宏；長	macrocosm(大世界)、macromarket(量販店)
magn, magni	大	magnate(達官貴人)、magnify(放大)
mal, male	惡；壞；並；不良	malediction(誹謗)、malefic(有害的)
micro, micr	微；極少；使擴大	microwave(微波)、microphone(麥克風)

mini	小	minibus(小型公車)、miniskirt(迷你裙)
mis	誤;錯;惡;小	mischief(災禍;災害)、misfortune(不幸)
mon, mono	單一的	monoatomic(單原子的)、monarch(獨裁者)
multi	許多的;多面的	multiform(多樣的)、multinational(多國的)
N		
nav	船	navy(海軍)、navigation(航海)
neo	新	neoclassic(新古典主義的)、neo-facism(新法西斯主義)
neut	中性;中立	neuter(中性的)、neutron(中子)
noct (i)	夜間	nocturnal(夜間的)、nocturne(夜曲)
nom	有關姓名	nominal(名義上的)、nominate(提名)
non	沒有	non-delivery(沒有送達)、nonhuman(非人類的)
not	使知道	notable(值得注目的)、notary(公證人)
nov	新的	novice(新生)
num	號碼	number(數字)、numbery(有基本的計算能力)
O		
oct	「八」的意思	octavo(八開紙)、octet(八重奏)、octopus(八爪魚)
oper	工作	operation(手術;行動)、operator(技工)

opp	對抗；反對	oppress(壓迫)、opponent(對手)、opposite(相反的)
omni	全；總；公；皆	omnibus(公共汽車)、omniscient(無所不知的)
out	勝過；過度；外；出；除去	outdoor(戶外的)、outlive(活得比～久)、outweigh(勝過)
over	太甚；在上；在外；顛倒	overseas(海外的)、overturn(傾倒)
P		
pan	全；海；總；泛	panorama(全景)、panacea(萬靈丹)
pass	經過	passport(護照)、passenger(乘客)
pater, patri	「父」之意	paternal(父親的)、patricide(弒父)
ped	「足」之意	pedal(踏板)、padestrian(行人)
per	穿過；通；透；全；遍；完全的	perceive(理解)、pervade(遍布)
pharmac	藥	pharmacy(藥學；藥房)、pharmacist(藥劑師)
phil	愛	philanthropy(博愛)、philosophy(哲學；原意為「愛智」)
photo	「光；照相」之意	photocopy(影印)、photograph(照片)
plen, plet, pl	充滿	plentiful(很多的)、complete(完全的)
popu, pub	人民	population(人口)、public(一般人民的；共同的)
poly	多	poly-crystal(多晶體)、poly-archy(多頭政治)

post	郵政；在～之後	postoffice(郵局)、postwar(戰後的)
pre	在～以前；預先	preface(前言)、prehistoric(史前的)、predict(預言)
prim	首要；第一	primary(首要的)、primer(預言；初學者)
pro	在前；代替；擁護；意見	progress(向前進；進步)、proceed(前進)
pseudo	假	pseudonym(筆名)、pseudograph(偽造文書)
psycho	心靈	psychology(心理學)、psychotherapy(心理療法)
Q		
quadri, quart	「四」的意思	quartet(四重奏曲)、quarter(四分之一)
quest, quer	問	question(疑問)、query(問題)
R		
radic	根本	radical(根本的)、radicate(生根)
radi, radio	光線	radiant(發光的)、radiocast(用無線電廣播)
re	回；向後；在；重新；相反；反對	remove(移除)、reread(重讀)、renew(更新)
retro	向後；回；反	retroact(違反)、retrogress(退化)
S		
sacer, sacr	神聖的	sacred(神聖的)、sacerdotal(聖職者的)
se	分開；離開	separate(分開)、segmental(部分的)

self	自己；自動的	self-help(自助)、self-abasement(自卑)
semi	一半	semicircle(半圓的)、semimonthly(每半個月一次的)
sens, sent	感覺的	sensation(感覺)、sentimental(感傷的)
sim	相像	similar(相似的)、simple(簡單的)
soci	相聚	social(社會性的)、socialist(社會主義者)
solut, solv	散開；解開	solution(解答)、solvent(溶劑)
stereo	固；硬；立體	stereograph(立體畫)、stereophonic(立體音響)
sub, suf, sup	下；稍；略為；副；分反	subacid(微酸的)、subarid(半乾燥地帶)、submarine(潛水艇)
super, supra	超級；超越；在～之上	supermarket(超級市場)、superpower(超級大國)、superficial(表面的)
sur	超過；外；上	surpass(超越)、surtax(附加稅)
sym, syn	共同；相同	synthesis(綜合)、symptom(表徵)
T		
tang, ting	觸；碰	tangent(接觸)、tingle(刺痛)
techn	技藝	technical(技術的)、technician(技術員)
tele	遙遠的；電信；電視	telegram(電報)、telephone(電話)、telescope(望遠鏡)
terr	土地	terrier(地籍冊)、terra(土地)、territory(領土)
the	關於神的	theism(一神論；有神論)、theology(神學)

trans	橫越；超過；貫穿；移轉	transmit(傳送)、transport(運輸)、transform(變形)
tri	三；三重	tripod(三腳架)、triangle(三角形)
twi	二；二重	twice(兩次)、twins(雙胞胎)
U		
ultra	極端；超越；以外	ultraist(極端主義者)、ultrasonic(超音波的)
un	不；非；相反；無；由～中弄出	unlock(開鎖)、unreal(不真實的)、unexpectedly(無法預期的)
under	下；內；少；不；足；次	underworld(下層社會)、underwear(內衣)
up	向上；在上	upland(高地)、uphill(上坡的)
V		
vice	副(都以〔-〕連接)	vice-president(副總統)、vice-consul(副領事)
vid, vis	看；視	video(影像的)、vision(視野)
vig, vit, viv	生命	vigor(體力)、vital(生命的)
W		
with	離開；向後；相反	withhold(制止)、withstand(抵擋)、withdraw(後退)

重點2、涵義籠統的字尾

A		
able, ably	可～的；有～性質的	readable(值得讀的)、changeably(易變的)
ability	可～性；易～性；可～	lovability(可愛)、knowledgeability(博識的)
acle(n)	構成實物或抽象名詞	spectacle(景物)、miracle(奇蹟)

age	屬於～的；具有～性質的；像～的	damage(損害)、percentage(百分比)、bandage(繃帶)
al(adj.), ally(adv.), al(n)	集合名詞；表示地點、費用、狀態、身分、事物	digital(數位的)、traditionally(傳統的)、hospital(醫院)
ance, ancy	表示狀態、情況、性質	allowance(津貼)、constancy(堅貞)
ant	做；造成；有～性質的人	merchant(商人)、servant(僕人)
ary	做；造成；有～性質的	library(圖書館)、reactionary(反映的)
ate	有～性質的；關於的；表示場所、物體、人	fortunate(幸運的)、private(私人的)
D		
dom	領域；身分；狀態	wisdom(智慧)、kingdom(國度)
E		
en	使變成～；由製成～；含有～的	deepen(使加深)、golden(金製的)
ence, ency, ent	表示性質；狀態；行為；關於～的	dependence(依賴)、tendency(趨勢)、confident(自信的)
F		
ful, fully	有～的；～的	peaceful(和平的)、fearfully(可怕地)
fy, fication	使～成為；～化	purify(使淨化)、solidification(團結)

H		
hood	時期；狀態；身分	neighborhood(鄰近地區)、parenthood(父母身分)、adulthood(成年時期)

I		
ible	可～的；易～的；能～的	terrible(可怕的)、corruptible(易腐敗的)
ic	～的；～的人	historic(歷史的)、romantic(浪漫的)
ish	如～的；性質的；略有；做～	foolish(愚蠢的)、finish(結束)
ion	行為；情況；狀態	action(行動)、discussion(討論)
istic	的	linguistic(語言的)、theistic(一神論者)

重點 3、有特定涵義的字尾

ain, aire, an, ant, ard, ar, ate	左側字尾都表示某種人或某種事業人士	captain(船長)、millionaire(百萬富翁)、American(美國人)、attendant(出席者)、coward(懦弱者)、candidate(候選人)
cracy, crat	統治的人	autocrat(獨裁者)、bureaucrat(官吏)
ee, en, er, eer	～的人	absentee(缺席者)、trainee(受訓者)、citizen(公民)、teacher(老師)、engineer(工程師)
ese	種族或國籍	Chinese(中國人)、Japanese(日本人)
esque	格式；形式	gardenesque(花園般式的)、picturesque(如畫的)
ess	女性或雌性動物	tigress(母老虎)、princess(公主)

ette	表示小的	novelette(短、中篇小說)、roomette(小房間)
form	有～形狀的；像～形狀的	uniform(制服)、transform(變形)
ics	學問；科目	statistics(統計學)、politics(政治學)、mathematics(數學)
ior	比較	superior(較好的)、prior(較早的)、inferior(較差的)
ism	學說；理論	capitalism(資本主義)、Marxism(馬克思主義)
ist, ive	某種信仰的人；某種職業的人	socialist(社會主義者)、tourist(觀光客)、detective(偵探)
less	無～的；不～的	careless(不小心的)、hopeless(無望的)
let	表示「小」	starlet(小明星)、booklet(小冊子)
like	如～的；有～的	childlike(孩童般的)、dreamlike(如夢般的)
logy	～學；～學說	zoology(動物學)、biology(生物學)
meter	措施；度量	diameter(直徑)、kilometer(公尺)
nomy	科學	astronomy(天文學)、agronomy(農耕學)
nym	名字	anonym(匿名)、pseudonym(筆名)
or	～的人	creator(創造者)、debtor(負債人)
proof	防～的；不透～的	airproof(不透氣的)、waterproof(防水的)
scape	景色；圖畫	seascape(海景)、nightscape(夜景)、landscape(風景)

um	場所；實物	aquarium(水族館)、stadium(體育館)
verse	轉向	reverse(逆轉)、diverse(互異的)
ward	向～的；朝～的	upward(向上的)、northward(朝北的)、outward(向外的)、forward(向前的)
ive	使～	selective(選擇性的)、creative(創意的)
ization, ize	有～的性質；有～作用的；屬於～的；有～傾向的	civilization(文明)、centralize(使集中)、criticize(批評)
ly	每～地；狀態；程度「地」，如～的；有特徵；屬於的	badly(惡劣地)、lovely(可愛的)、godly(神的)
ment	行為；過程或結果；組織	government(政府)、entertainment(娛樂)
ness	抽象名詞；表示性質、狀態	unwillingness(不情願的)、darkness(黑暗)
ous	～的；如～的；屬於～的；多～的	famous(有名的)、vigorous(充滿活力的)
ship	情況；性質；關係；身分；職位；技藝	citizenship(公民身分)、friendship(友誼)
some	充滿～的；易於～的；產生～的；有～傾向的	troublesome(麻煩的)、lonesome(孤獨的)
th	抽象名詞：表示其行為、性質、狀態	depth(深度)、truth(真理)

tion	形成、結果、行為、狀態	immunization(免疫法)、abortion(墮胎)
ty	抽象名詞：表示其行為、性質、狀態	safety(安全)、royalty(王位)
ure	行為、行為的過程或結果狀態、物體	culture(文化)、mixture(混合)
y	多～的；有～的；如～的；屬於～的；表性質、狀態、情況、行為、形成抽象名詞	sunny(陽光充足的)、discovery(發現)、inquiry(詢問)

Exercise

1. The doors of these department stores slide open _____ when you approach them. You don't have to open them yourself.

    (A) necessary   (B) diligently   (C) automatically   (D) intentionally

2. To _____ our industrial base, we must find overseas markets for our products.

    (A) expose   (B) expand   (C) export   (D) expound

3. The defendant pleaded guilty after he was _____ with incontrovertible evidence of guilt.

    (A) confronted   (B) confined   (C) construct   (D) constructed

4. Dr. James Lin _____ his entire career to the research of food safety.

    (A) explored   (B) devoted   (C) imposed   (D) resisted

5. It rained so hard yesterday that the baseball game had to be _____ until next Saturday.

    (A) surrendered   (B) postponed   (C) abandoned   (D) opposed

6. Please _____ yourself from smoking and spitting in public places, since the law forbids them.

   (A) restrain (B) hinder (C) restrict (D) refrain

7. The _____ capacity of this elevator is 400 kilograms. For safety reasons, it shouldn't be overloaded.

   (A) delicate (B) automatic (C) essential (D) maximum

8. I couldn't _____ the sweet smell from the bakery, so I walked in and bought a fresh loaf of bread.

   (A) insist (B) resist (C) obtain (D) contain

9. Peter has a _____ mind; he remembers almost everything he sees or hears.

   (A) retentive (B) reflexive (C) responsive (D) reproductive

10. The science teacher always _____ the use of the laboratory equipment before she lets her students use it on their own.

    (A) tolerates (B) associates (C) demonstrates (D) exaggerates

11. The police chief _____ an emergency statute as a reason for his decision to present any protesters from moving into the government office building.

    (A) incited (B) induced (C) invoked (D) instilled

12. Your membership card is due to _____ the impact of inflation.

    (A) exempt (B) extend (C) expel (D) expire

13. Are you free this weekend? There is an _____ of paintings of Monet at Taipei Fine Arts Museum.

    (A) impression (B) exception (C) exhibition (D) inflation

14. A 27-year-old Alaskan girl went on a trip to the frozen North in which she _____ the blizzards, the mountains, and the temperatures that dropped to sixty degrees below zero Celsius.

    (A) battled (B) suspended (C) compromised (D) disturbed

15. Ms. Lee typically read an interesting story to the children, asking them questions about the story as they _____ through it.

(A) proceeded (B) procured (C) proclaimed (D) procrastinated

16. Life can be _____ to a candle and journey.

(A) disappointed (B) attracted (C) compared (D) impressed

17. The government is searching for oil industry _____ to tackle the undersea oil disaster.

(A) conclusion (B) consumption (C) consultants (D) construction

18. Stranded in a strange city without money, he was in a _____.

(A) presentiment (B) predicament (C) precedent (D) presumption

19. Though Kevin failed in last year's singing contest, he did not feel _____. This year he practiced day and night and finally won the first place in the competition.

(A) relieved (B) suspected (C) discounted (D) frustrated

20. As more people rely on the Internet for information, it has _____ newspaper as the most important source of news.

(A) distributed (B) subtracted (C) replaced (D) transferred

Answers

1. (C) automatically 自動地
2. (B) expand 擴展
3. (A) confronted 面對
4. (B) devoted 獻身於
5. (B) postponed 延期
6. (D) refrain 忍住；節制
7. (D) maximum 最大的
8. (B) resist 抵抗
9. (A) retentive 記性好的
10. (C) demonstrates 示範
11. (C) invoked 借助
12. (A) exempt 免除
13. (C) exhibition 展覽
14. (A) battled 迎戰
15. (A) proceeded 繼續
16. (C) compared 比較

17. (C) consultants 顧問

18. (B) predicament 困境

19. (D) frustrated 挫折

20. (C) replaced 取代

二、英文語音拼字法：由單字的發音來記憶單字的字母

	英文語音拼字法	傳統死記法
優點	利用聲音比文字好記的特性牢記單字，並且有助口說英文。	不需會唸音標，可以短時間內背較多單字。
缺點	要記住母音所對應的單字字母，變化較大。	背過後很快就會忘掉，只懂字涵義，不會發音。

語音拼字法的說明與用法 (以 K.K 音標為主)

　　語音拼字法其實是許多以英文字母做母語人士的拼音法。它是一種「看字發音」的拼音法。簡單來說就是依據英文字母來發出單字的聲音。例如：pen 中的 p 字母與 n 字母就念作〔p〕與〔n〕，其字形與所對應的音標在外型上一致。所以就可以運用此原理來讀出大部分字的拼音。依據歌詞要比文字好記的優點 (即唱的內容要比讀的內容好記)，將「看字發音」的方法反推回來，變成「記音拼字」，亦即若記得〔dɛsk〕的音標，就可將音標轉換成字母 "desk"，因為子音〔d〕、〔s〕、〔k〕與字母 d、s、k 相同，剩下的只要記住母音〔ɛ〕是字母 e 的對應，即可拼出 desk 這個單字。這種記住拼音的方法可以使你的字彙量增加許多，此外，對於較長的單字也能藉著拼音來拼出完整的單字，以下舉例說明：

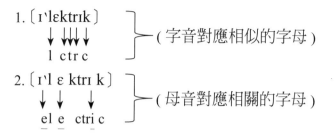

1. 〔ɪˈlɛktrɪk〕
   ↓ ↓↓↓ ↓   （字音對應相似的字母）
   l ctr c

2. 〔ɪˈl ɛ ktrɪ k〕
   ↓ ↓ ↓   （母音對應相關的字母）
   el e ctri c

　　以上這樣較長的字彙可以用「記音拼字」而拼出，就不會像死背字母來拼字辛苦並且容易拼錯，短的字更是容易用此方法記住，如：〔bʌs〕→ bus

　　因為英文的母音不是有相似的對應，而是有兩個以上的字母之對應，所以需要先記住母音所可能對應的字母，還好母音對應字母也是有一些規則可以遵循而拼出相對應的字母。接下來會以圖表顯示子音與母音個別所對應的字母。

(一) 子音部分：有下列兩種方式

1. 子音與對應字母相同者			2. 子音與對應字母不同者		
音標	對應字母	舉例	音標	對應字母	舉例
[b]	b	[bar] → bar	[dʒ]	j ge	[dʒɑb] → job [kedʒ] → cage
[p]	p	[pʊt] → put	[tʃ]	ch	[tʃɜtʃ] → church
[t]	t	[taɪm] → time	[ʒ]	su ge	[lɛʒɚ] → leisure [gəˈrɑʒ] → garage
[d]	d	[dæns] → dance	[ʃ]	sh	[ʃɜt] → shirt
[f]	f	[faɪv] → five	[θ]	th	[θɪk] → thick
[v]	v	[vɔɪs] → voice	[ð]	th	[ðɛr] → here
[s]	s	[smart] → smart	[ŋ]	ng	[stɪŋ] → sting
[z]	z	[zu] → zoo	[kw]	q	[kwin] → queen

1. 子音與對應字母相同者			2. 子音與對應字母不同者		
音標	對應字母	舉例	音標	對應字母	舉例
[h]	h	[hæt] → hat	[j]	y	[jɪr] → year
[k]	k	[kɪk] → kick	[hw]	wh	[hwaɪl] → while
	c	[kek] → cake			
	ch	[kraɪst] → Christ			
[g]	g	[gɑd] → God			
[m]	m	[mek] → make			
[n]	n	[nem] → name			
[l]	l	[ledɪ] → lady			
[r]	r	[rɛst] → rest			
[w]	w	[we] → way			

3. 特殊字母與子音的對應			4. 不發音的字母	
音標	對應字母	舉例	字母	舉例
[f]	ph	['maɪkrə,fon] → microphone	bt	[daʊt] → doubt
[g]/[f]	gh	[gost] → ghost [tʌf] → tough	gh	[haɪt] → height
[l]	ll	[tɔl] → tall	kn	[nɑk] → knock
[s]	ss	[tɔs] → toss	wr	[raɪt] → wright
[ʃən]	tion	[ræʃən] → ration	ps	[saɪ'kɑlədʒɪ] → psychology
[ʒən]	sion	[ə'keʒən] → occasion	mn	[hɪm] → hymn
			mb	[bɑm] → bomb
			que	[æn'tɪk] → antique

3. 特殊字母與子音的對應			4. 不發音的字母	
音標	對應字母	舉例	字母	舉例
			s<u>t</u>en	[lɪsn] → lis<u>t</u>en
			s<u>t</u>le	[bʌsl] → bus<u>t</u>le
			<u>l</u>alf ⎫ a<u>l</u>m ⎬ 中的 l a<u>l</u>n ⎭	[hɑf] → ha<u>l</u>f [kɑm] → ca<u>l</u>m [wɔr] → war<u>l</u>m
			<u>i</u>r	[aɪən] → <u>i</u>ron

(二) 母音部分：一母音對應兩個以上的字母，以下分為四種
不同母音與字母的對應

1. 子音與對應字母相同者			2. 子音與對應字母不同者		
音標	對應字母	舉例	音標	對應字母	舉例
[ɪ]	i e a y	[lɪŋk] → l<u>i</u>nk [ˈpɑrtɪ] → part<u>y</u> [ˈpæsɪdʒ] → pass<u>a</u>ge [taɪdɪ] → tid<u>y</u>	[aʊ]	ou ow	[laʊd] → l<u>ou</u>d [taʊɚ] → t<u>ow</u>er
[i]	ea ee ie e	[lif] → l<u>ea</u>f [fid] → f<u>ee</u>d [θɪf] → th<u>ie</u>f [hi] → h<u>e</u>	[ɔɪ]	oi oy	[sɔɪl] → s<u>oi</u>l [bɔɪ] → b<u>oy</u>
[e]	ai ay a	[ˈdelɪ] → d<u>ai</u>ly [he] → h<u>ay</u> [sem] → s<u>a</u>me	[aɪ]	i+ 字母 +e ie igh y	[laɪf] → l<u>i</u>fe [taɪ] → t<u>ie</u> [haɪ] → h<u>igh</u> [draɪ] → dr<u>y</u>

1. 子音與對應字母相同者			2. 子音與對應字母不同者		
音標	對應字母	舉例	音標	對應字母	舉例
[ε]	ea a e	[rɛd] → read (過去式) [fɛr] → fare [lɛmən] → lemon	[ʊr]	oor our ure	[pʊr] → poor [tʊr] → tour [lʊr] → lure
[æ]	a	[bæt] → bat [ˈæpl] → apple	[εr]	are air	[kεr] → care [ˈdεrɪ] → dairy
[ɔ]	o a ou au aw	[tɔl] → tall [lɔst] → lost [bɪˈkɔz] → because [lɔn] → lawn	[ɪks]	ex	[ɪksˈklud] → exclude
[o]	ow oa o	[ro] → row [lon] → loan [rop] → rope			
[ʊ]	ou oo u	[ʃʊd] → should [fʊt] → foot [bʊl] → bull			
[u]	ou oo u o	[sup] → soup [tul] → tool [lut] → lute [tum] → tomb			
[ə]	a o e	[əˈhɛd] → ahead [əˈkeʒən] → occasion [ˈʌvən] → oven			
[ɚ]	or er ure	[ˈtelɚ] → tailor [ˈdraɪvɚ] → driver [ˈkʌltʃɚ] → culture			

1. 子音與對應字母相同者			2. 子音與對應字母不同者		
音標	對應字母	舉例	音標	對應字母	舉例
[ɝ]	ir er ur ear	[ˋdɝtɪ] → dirty [hɝd] → herd [tɝn] → turn [lɝn] → learn			
[ɑ]	o a	[ˋbɑdɪ] → body [lɑrdʒ] → large			
[ʌ]	u o ou	[kʌt] → cut [lʌv] → love [əˋnʌf] → enough			

3. 不發母音的字母		4. 特殊字音的母音		
字母	舉例	音標	對應字母	舉例
ey	[he] → hey	[I]	o	[ˋwɪmin] → women
ei × ei ×	[ˋnebɚ] → neighbor [ˋliʒɚ] → leisure	[ʌ]	oo	[blʌd] → blood
母音＋ 字母 ＋e 或 e 為字尾	[tek] → take [luz] → lose	母音	ll lk	[bɔl] → ball [wɔk] → walk
		[ɔ]	com con	重音在第一音節 com → [a] [ˋkampətəns] → competence 重音在第二音節 com → [ə] [kəmˋpit] → compete

Exercise

請將下列音標轉為單字：

1. [əˋkædəmɪ] → _____ 中文：_____

2. [əˋdʌlt,hʊd] → _____ 中文：_____

3. [ˋætɪk] → _____ 中文：_____

4. [buθ] → _____ 中文：_____

5. [ˋbəʊndərɪ] → _____ 中文：_____

6. [brɪŋk] → _____ 中文：_____

7. [ˋkævətɪ] → _____ 中文：_____

8. [ˋkort,jɑrd] → _____ 中文：_____

9. [dɛstəˋneʃən] → _____ 中文：_____

10. [ɪnˋk,oʒɚ] → _____ 中文：_____

11. [əˋstet] → _____ 中文：_____

12. [frʌnˋtir] → _____ 中文：_____

13. [ˋhæbə,tæt] → _____ 中文：_____

14. [ˋlætə,tjud] → _____ 中文：_____

15. [laundʒ] → _____ 中文：_____

16. [ˋmænʃən] → _____ 中文：_____

17. [mɪdˋivl] → _____ 中文：_____

18. [ˋɔrtʃɚd] → _____ 中文：_____

19. [ˋaut,skɝts] → _____ 中文：_____

20. [ˋpravins] → _____ 中文：_____

21. [səˋbɝbən] → _____ 中文：_____

22. [ˋtrɛʒərɪ] → _____ 中文：_____

23. [ˋʌltəmɪt] → _____ 中文：_____

24. [ˋwɛr,haus] → _____ 中文：_____

25. [ˋwɪldɚ,nɪs] → _____ 中文：_____

1. academy 學院
2. adulthood 成人期
3. attic 閣樓
4. booth 亭子
5. boundary 邊境
9. brink 邊緣
7. cavity 蛀牙
8. courtyard 庭院
9. destination 目的地
10. enclosure 包圍
11. estate 房地產
12. frontier 邊界
13. habitate 棲息地
14. latitude 緯線
15. lounge 休息室
16. mansion 豪宅
17. medieval 中世紀的
18. orchard 果園
19. outskirts 市郊
20. province 省
21. surburban 市郊的
22. treasure 寶藏
23. ultimate 最終的
24. warehouse 倉庫
25. wildness 荒野

三、句子上下文聯想法

　　利用容易記住的上下文內容，像歷史事件、時事、新聞、日常生活中常經歷的事等等，加深對句中單字的印象，來記住該字彙。依據像朱立民與顏元叔等英語學者的觀點，由閱讀文章的上下文內容來記憶字彙事更有效率的方式。直接拿字典來背，讀了後面，就忘了前面，最後的效果可想而知，因此在此介紹的記憶方法是比較有效又能較久記住單字的方法。請看下列說明：

例 1

Adolf Hitler ordered to <u>massacre</u> six million Jews.

中譯 阿道夫‧希特勒下令大屠殺六百萬位猶太人。

說明 這句陳述表達一個人盡皆知的事實,所以由上下文可以看出 massacre 的涵義與殺死、屠殺有關。下次在別的文章中看到同樣的也就比較容易想起字義。

例 2

Michale Jackson's concert <u>attracted</u> thousands of audience.

中譯 麥克傑克森的演唱會吸引數以千計的聽眾參加。

說明 世界級歌手麥克傑克森無人不知,所以他的甚麼吸引了觀眾,很明顯的是演唱會。

例 3

Islamic <u>terrorists</u> attacked the World Trade Center in New York City on September 9th (911) and destroyed the whole building.

中譯 伊斯蘭的恐怖分子在 9 月 11 日攻擊紐約的世貿大樓並且摧毀整棟建築。

說明 這件舉世轟動與令人震驚的恐怖攻擊是無人不曉,所以發動者 terrorists 的涵義很明顯,由此可以記住它的涵義。

例 4

Westerners like to eat <u>dairy</u> food like milk and cheese.

中譯 西方人喜歡吃奶製品,像牛奶和起士。

說明 西方人一般的主食就是奶製品,再加上後面有舉出牛奶與起士的例子,所以上下文就可明顯看出 dairy 的涵義,這也是日常生活的常識。

※ 其常類似的具有清楚且令人印象深刻的句子還有表示一般常識的用詞，情境式的用語或日常主題等等，現舉例說明如下：

例 1

The man couldn't swim and was drowned dead in the river.

中譯 那人不會游泳而在河中溺水而死。

說明 前半句證明那人不會游泳，在河中的結果顯然是溺水，加上 dead 形容那人的情形，更可以確定他是溺水而死。

例 2

The hotel receptionist helped the customer to check in.

中譯 飯店的的接待員協助那位顧客辦理入住手續。

說明 這是一幅常見的情境，飯店的櫃臺人員 (也就是接待人員) 是為了服務客人入住飯店。因此，由本句的上下文所表達的情境會使 receptionist 的字義深刻的印在讀者的腦海中。

＊**注意事項**：坊間出版的英漢或英英字典所舉出的例句，常是上下文涵義的關聯性不多。因此，讀者可自行創意造句，一旦造出富有涵義的句子，這個單字就容易成為你 (妳) 的「終身伴侶」。

Exercise

一、請依下列句子的前後文意推敲單字的中文涵義：

1. She was scared by the ghost. scared: _____

2. The lemon juice was so tart that I don't like drink it because I don't like

sour drink. tart: _____

3. The man peeked a woman taking a bath through the window of the bathroom.

   peeked: _____

4. The Republic of China was established in 1911. establish: _____

5. The terrible drought in Africa made food decrease. drought: _____

6. The huge whale died at the beach and biologists made it into a specimen

   to let people see it.   specimen: _____

7. Taiwan is located between the Taiwan Strait and the Pacific Ocean. locate:

   _____

8. Satellites are used to collect data from the surface of the Earth when it

   rotates the Earth. satellite: _____; rotate: _____

9. Wang Jingwei was a traitor who worked for Japanese government when

   Japan occupied parts of China. traitor: _____

10. John married Jane and Jane became his spouse. spouse: _____

11. J.K Rowling is a well-known author in the world. author: _____

12. Koalas only live in Australia and look like teddy bears. koala: _____

13. Lots of refugees from the Middle East rushed to European countries.

   refugee: _____

14. If a huge asternoid from outer space hit the Earth, almost all living things

   will die out. asteroid: _____

15. The Titanic sunk in the Atlantic Ocean and thousands of people got

   drowned in the freezing water. sunk: _____

16. Walt Disney is the founder of Walt Disney World resorts around the world.

   founder: _____

17. If one eats too much food, he or she will become obese and look fat.

   obese: _____

18. Earthquakes sometimes not only destroy lots of buildings on the land but

also cause tsunamis from the sea. tsunami: _____

19. Avalanches usually happen on snowy mountains and cover large part of the mountain area. Sometimes, they also bury people alive. Avalanche _____

20. Lions and tigers are carnivorous animals that feed on herbivorous animal, such as sheep, cattle, and even rabbits. Carnivorous: _____; herbivorous: _____

Answers

1. scared：害怕的
2. tart：酸的
3. peek：偷窺
4. establish：建立
5. drought：旱災
6. specimen：標本
7. locate：座落於
8. satellite：衛星　rotate：環繞
9. traitor：叛徒
10. spouse：配偶
11. author：作者

12. koala：無尾熊
13. refugee：難民
14. asteroid：小行星
15. sunk：下沉
16. founder：創立者
17. obese：肥胖的
18. tsunami：海嘯
19. avalanche：雪崩
20. carnivorous：食肉的
    herbivorous：食草的

四、押韻聯想法

通常適用於單音節的短字，其字母大都相似。

例如：bake [bek] 烘焙，make [mek] 製作，take [tek] 拿取，cake [kek] 蛋糕，fake [fek] 假的，wake [wek] 醒來，lake [lek] 湖泊，rake [rek] 耙子，sake [sek] 緣故等字，這些字的拼字都是 ake 為主體，由此串聯出一連串的單字。但是這些個別的單字

不易記住，所以需要運用一句以上的句子來串連這些相似的字，現舉例說明如下：

例 1

那些廚師正在製作 (make) 麵包，他先取出 (take) 蛋及麵粉，再攪拌後，又放入烤箱烘焙 (bake) 成蛋糕 (cake)。

例 2

那位遊客向人買取一張打折的車票，等他上車驗票時，才發現是假的 (fake) 車票，為此緣故 (sake)，他只好下車在湖邊 (lake) 等待別人幫忙。

運用上述的同音標的字母來衍生出更多的單字，因而擴充字彙量。

Exercise

請用下列音標串聯相關的字：

1. [le]：＿＿＿＿＿ 、＿＿＿＿＿ 、＿＿＿＿＿ 、＿＿＿＿＿
   造句：＿＿＿＿＿＿＿＿＿＿＿＿＿＿＿＿＿＿＿＿＿

2. [ɛr]：＿＿＿＿＿ 、＿＿＿＿＿ 、＿＿＿＿＿ 、＿＿＿＿＿
   造句：＿＿＿＿＿＿＿＿＿＿＿＿＿＿＿＿＿＿＿＿＿

3. [ɑu]：＿＿＿＿＿ 、＿＿＿＿＿ 、＿＿＿＿＿
   造句：＿＿＿＿＿＿＿＿＿＿＿＿＿＿＿＿＿＿＿＿＿

4. [ri]：＿＿＿＿＿ 、＿＿＿＿＿ 、＿＿＿＿＿
   造句：＿＿＿＿＿＿＿＿＿＿＿＿＿＿＿＿＿＿＿＿＿

5. [mɪ]：＿＿＿＿＿ 、＿＿＿＿＿ 、＿＿＿＿＿
   造句：＿＿＿＿＿＿＿＿＿＿＿＿＿＿＿＿＿＿＿＿＿

6. [nɚ]：_____、_____、_____、_____

   造句：_____

7. [em]：_____、_____、_____、_____

   造句：_____

8. [ɛn]：_____、_____、_____、_____

   造句：_____

9. [ɑut]：_____、_____、_____、_____

   造句：_____

10. [ɔl]：_____、_____、_____、_____

    造句：_____

Answers

1. lake, lady, lace, lane

   造句：那位穿著蕾絲 (lace) 裙子的女生 (lady) 穿過巷子 (lane) 到達湖邊 (lake)。

2. hair, bear, mare, care

   造句：那農場主人關心 (care) 他的雌鳥 (mare) 有否被熊 (bear) 攻擊，因為他看到地上的毛髮 (hair)。

3. ground, tower, hour, loud

   造句：他在地面上 (ground) 往上看那高塔 (tower) 上的時鐘，時間 (hour) 是很晚了，他仍覺得鐘很吵 (loud)。

4. report, repeat, reply, regress

   造句：那位軍官重複 (repeat) 報告 (report) 上面需要支援卻得不到回覆 (reply) 只好撤退 (regress)。

5. mistake, mischief, middle, military

   造句：那架軍機穿越海峽中間 (middle)，犯了軍事上 (military) 的錯誤，造成危害 (mischief)。

6. corner, donor, banner, greenery

   造句：那面有捐贈者 (donor) 名字的旗幟被放在溫室的 (greenery) 角落中 (corner)。

7. lame, game, aim, came

   造句：那位跛腳 (lame) 的選手來 (came) 參加這場比賽 (game) 的目標 (aim) 是贏。

8. intend, end, blend, attend

   造句：那位歌手打算 (intend) 參加 (attend) 這次比賽，作為他生涯的結束 (end)，他混合 (blend) 了兩種樂器來演唱。

9. outstanding, doubt, rout, stout

   造句：這位傑出的領袖面對烏合之眾 (rout) 仍然勇敢的 (stout) 面對他們，使他們不懷疑 (doubt) 他的帶領。

10. mall, almost, alter, altogether

    造句：那個商場 (mall) 改變 (alter) 銷售，吸引幾乎 (almost) 附近所有的人一同 (altogether) 前來。

五、單字字形衍生聯想法

與押韻聯想法有些類似，但不同之處乃在於此法是以單字字形為基礎，進而多面向衍生出更多的單字。請看下列步驟：

步驟 1：在常見的簡短單字之前後加上其他的字母而衍生出其他涵義的單字，可分為下列兩類：

(1) 單句衍生法：往前或往後添加字母

例 1

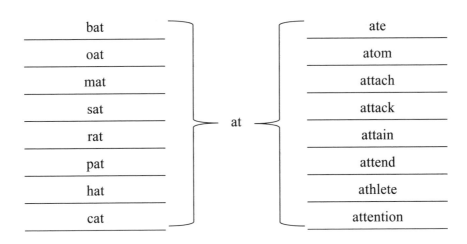

bat		ate
oat		atom
mat		attach
sat		attack
rat	at	attain
pat		attend
hat		athlete
cat		attention

例 2

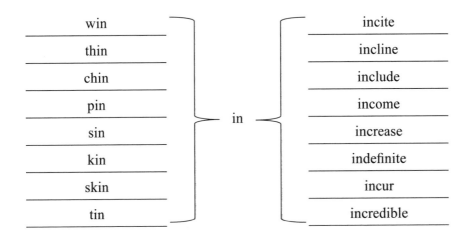

win		incite
thin		incline
chin		include
pin		income
sin	in	increase
kin		indefinite
skin		incur
tin		incredible

步驟 2：字義的串聯 & 聯想：由簡短單字衍生的單字必須經過連結成一句有涵義的句子，才容易記住其中單字的涵義。

at → bat(蝙蝠)、oat(燕麥)、mat(墊子)、sat(坐在)、rat(老鼠)、pat(輕拍)

　　將上述的句子串聯成一句有涵義的句子：一隻蝙蝠 (bat) 飛過一隻坐在 (sat) 墊子 (mat) 上正在吃燕麥 (oat) 的老鼠 (rat) 並且輕拍他 (pat)。

(2) 雙向衍生法：同時往前與往後添加字母

例 1

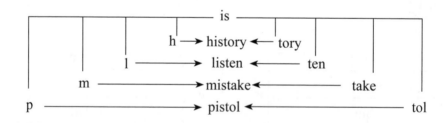

例 2

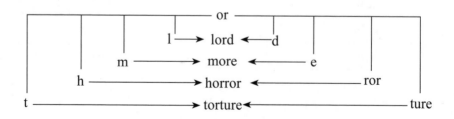

步驟 3：同樣將這些單字串聯成一句有意義的句子，以使記住
　　　　這些單字的涵義。

例 1

　　is 所衍生出來的單字有 history(歷史)、listen(聆聽)、mistake(錯誤)
及 pistol(手槍)。現在將這些單字串聯成以下的句子：

　　＊我們應當仔細聆聽 (listen) 手槍 (pistol) 在歷史 (history) 上所造成
　　的可怕事件。

例 2

　　or 所衍生出來的單字有 lord(主人)、more(更多的)、horror(恐懼)
以及 torture(折磨)。現在將這些單字串聯成以下的句子：

　　＊那位主人 (lord) 對待他的僕人更多的 (more) 折磨 (torture)，使她
　　非常恐懼 (horror)。

Exercise

一、請依下列所提供的字元以單向方式衍生字彙

1.

on

串聯句子：_____

2.

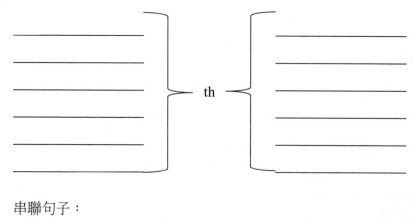

串聯句子：_____

二、請依下列所提供的字元以向前或向後雙向方式衍生
　　字彙

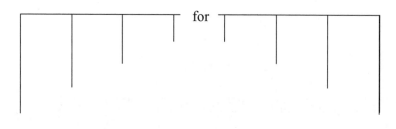

串聯句子：_____

一、

1.

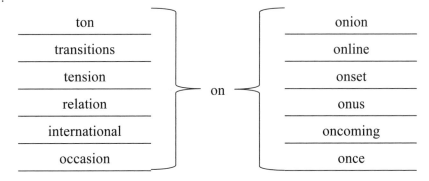

ton		onion
transitions		online
tension	on	onset
relation		onus
international		oncoming
occasion		once

串聯句子：他在線上 (online) 買了洋蔥 (onion)，卻遭到駭客攻擊 (onset)，他對要來的 (oncoming) 攻擊認為網路公司要負責任 (onus)。

2.

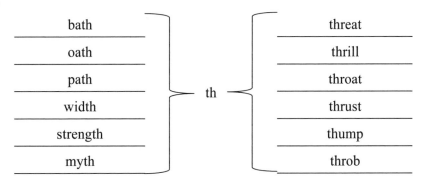

bath		threat
oath		thrill
path	th	throat
width		thrust
strength		thump
myth		throb

串聯句子：他感受到威脅 (threat)，因此衝入 (thrust) 安全之處，但仍被人重擊 (thump)，他嚇得心悸 (throb)。

二、

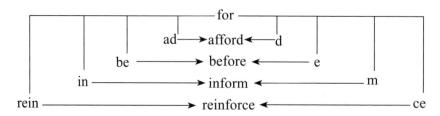

串聯句子：在為公司買東西前 (before)，要考量自己付得起錢 (afford)，並且通知 (inform) 老闆，強調 (reinforce) 那個東西是必要的。

註：以上為參考答案，你 / 妳也可以有自己的聯想字與字串。

六、中文諧音聯想法

　　即是從中文的語音中找出與英文單字發音相同的語音，而後刻意將此諧音與英文單字的涵義相連來記住其涵義。請看下列舉例說明：

例 1

penetrate [ˈpɛnətret] 穿過，與其類似的中文諧音為「攀了撬的」。
由此諧音可模擬出含有 penetrate 的字音與字義之句子：
「礦工攀了山岩，穿過撬開的隧道才到達礦坑。」
本句同時包含 penetrate 的字音 (攀了撬的) 與字義 (穿過)。利用中英文字的諧音可以一舉兩得同時記下字音與字義，比較不易忘記。這是幫助考生應考前的快速記字訣竅，是另類記憶單字方法，不過平常還是以一般記單字的標準發音與拼法記住。

例 2

fraud [frɔd] 欺詐

中文諧音 福落得

諧音句 那個騙子想從欺詐別人得到個人福利，卻落得入監下場。

例 3

lethal [ˈliθəl] 致命的

中文諧音 利得

諧音句 這把刀鋒利得可以致命。

例 4

chord [kɔrd] 弦

中文諧音 扣的

諧音句 他扣的弦律令人沉醉。

Exercise

1. cater [ˈketə] 外燴

   中文諧音：_____

   諧音句：_____

2. bonus [ˈbonəs] 獎金；紅利

   中文諧音：_____

   諧音句：_____

3. bid [bɪd] 出價

   中文諧音：_____

   諧音句：_____

4. wreath [riθ] 花圈

   中文諧音：＿＿＿＿＿＿＿＿＿＿＿＿＿＿＿＿＿＿＿＿＿＿

   諧音句：＿＿＿＿＿＿＿＿＿＿＿＿＿＿＿＿＿＿＿＿＿＿＿

5. veil [vel] 面紗

   中文諧音：＿＿＿＿＿＿＿＿＿＿＿＿＿＿＿＿＿＿＿＿＿＿

   諧音句：＿＿＿＿＿＿＿＿＿＿＿＿＿＿＿＿＿＿＿＿＿＿＿

6. torch [tɔrtʃ] 火把

   中文諧音：＿＿＿＿＿＿＿＿＿＿＿＿＿＿＿＿＿＿＿＿＿＿

   諧音句：＿＿＿＿＿＿＿＿＿＿＿＿＿＿＿＿＿＿＿＿＿＿＿

7. deem [dim] 認為

   中文諧音：＿＿＿＿＿＿＿＿＿＿＿＿＿＿＿＿＿＿＿＿＿＿

   諧音句：＿＿＿＿＿＿＿＿＿＿＿＿＿＿＿＿＿＿＿＿＿＿＿

8. caution ['kɔʃən] 小心

   中文諧音：＿＿＿＿＿＿＿＿＿＿＿＿＿＿＿＿＿＿＿＿＿＿

   諧音句：＿＿＿＿＿＿＿＿＿＿＿＿＿＿＿＿＿＿＿＿＿＿＿

9. strand [strænd] 一條；一線

   中文諧音：＿＿＿＿＿＿＿＿＿＿＿＿＿＿＿＿＿＿＿＿＿＿

   諧音句：＿＿＿＿＿＿＿＿＿＿＿＿＿＿＿＿＿＿＿＿＿＿＿

10. chunk [tʃʌŋk] 大塊

   中文諧音：＿＿＿＿＿＿＿＿＿＿＿＿＿＿＿＿＿＿＿＿＿＿

   諧音句：＿＿＿＿＿＿＿＿＿＿＿＿＿＿＿＿＿＿＿＿＿＿＿

Answers

1. cater ['ketɚ] 外燴

   中文諧音：開的

   諧音句：那主人開的外燴十分成功，賓主盡歡。

2. bonus ['bonəs] 獎金；紅利

中文諧音：蹦樂死

諧音句：那人贏得大筆獎金，又蹦又跳，快樂死了。

3. bid [bɪd] 出價

中文諧音：逼得

諧音句：那買主被逼得出價買下那件骨董。

4. wreath [riθ] 花圈

中文諧音：蕾絲

諧音句：女裝上的蕾絲像花圈一樣。

5. veil [vel] 面紗

中文諧音：飛蛾

諧音句：他帶著面紗看不清楚前面的飛蛾。

6. torch [tɔrtʃ] 火把

中文諧音：偷取

諧音句：他偷取奧運的聖火火把。

7. deem [dim] 認為

中文諧音：地目

諧音句：那地主認為他的地目不清楚。

8. caution ['kɔʃən] 小心

中文諧音：夠鮮

諧音句：在外用餐要小心食物夠不夠鮮。

9. strand [strænd] 一條；一線

中文諧音：絲傳得

諧音句：他能將一絲棉條穿得過針眼。

10. chunk [tʃʌŋk] 大塊

中文諧音：強嗑

諧音句：那位毒販逼迫吸毒者強嗑一大塊毒品。

註：以上爲參考答案，你／妳也可以有自己的中文諧音與諧音
　　句。

七、折字法

1. 將一個長的單字拆成兩個 (或兩個以上) 的有涵義的單
字，此法特別用於長的單字。請看下列說明：

oatmeal(燕麥粥) → oat(燕麥)+ meal(餐點)

wardrobe(衣櫥) → ward(寢室)+ robe(衣服；長袍)

breakthrough(突破) → break(破)+ through(穿越)

capability(能力) → cap(帽子)+ ability(能力)

outgoing(外向的) → out(外在的)+ going(行動)

shortcoming(缺點) → short(短缺的)+ coming(來到)

safeguard(防衛) → safe(安全的)+ guard(保護)

surpass(超越) → sur(超級的)+ pass(越過)

undertake(擔任) → under(在～下)+ take(接受)

upgrade(升級) → up(上升)+ grade(等級)

underestimate(低估) → under(在～下)+ estimate(評估)

viewpoint(觀點) → view(看法)+ point(點)

以上的單字大都是像中文的詞 (像茶 + 杯 = 茶杯)，由
兩個單字的涵義結合而成立另一個包含兩個單字原意的
新字彙。

2. 另有一類的單字，可以拆開成有字義的單字，但是卻與
原字涵義完全不同，請看下列例子說明：

blacksmith(鐵匠) → black(黑色的)+ smith(鐵匠)

contractor(立約人) → con(反對)+ tractor(牽引機)

hostage(人質) → host(主人)+ age(年級)

peasant(農夫) → peas(豌豆)+ ant(螞蟻)

patriot(愛國者) → pat(輕拍)+ riot(暴動)

※ sovereign(最高統治者) → so(如此)+ very(非常的)+ reign(統治)

tenant(房客) → ten(十隻)+ ant(螞蟻)

therapist(治療師) → the(這、那)+ rapist(強姦者)

beseige(圍攻) → be(被)+ siege(包圍)

boycott(抵制) → boy(男孩)+ cott(欄舍)

calligraph(書法) → call(稱作)+ I(我的)+ graph(圖表)

kidnap(綁架) → kid(小孩)+ nap(小睡)

metaphor(隱喻) → met(遇到)+ aphor(格言)

※ purchase(購買) → purr(發出愉快的低哼聲)+ chase(追趕)

tresspass(侵入) → tress(髮束)+ pass(越過)

molecule(分子) → mole(間諜)+ cule(小的)

※ barometer(氣壓計) → bar(木條)+ of(的)+ meter(計量計)

carton(紙板盒) → car(汽車)+ ton(噸)

charcoal(木炭) → char(燒黑的)+ coal(煤炭)

compass(羅盤) → com(共同的)+ pass(通過)

compound(混合物) → com(共同的)+ pound(搗碎)

antarctic(南極) → ant(螞蟻)+ arctic(北極)

carnation(康乃馨) → car(汽車)+ nation(國家)

chestnut(栗子) → chest(胸部)+ nut(堅果)

peacock(孔雀) → pea(豌豆)+ cock(公雞)

※ swamp(沼澤) → swam(游泳)+ pool(池塘)

tornado(龍捲風) → torn(撕裂)+ ado(麻煩而忙亂)

※ walnut(胡桃) → wall(牆)+ nut(堅果)

※ robust(強健的) → rob(搶劫)+ bust(雕像)

astray(迷途地) → as(像)+ tray(小碟子)

上述所拆開的字雖然與原字的字義無關,但是仍可以運用聯想力,記住原字的涵義,同時又能增加拆字後的單字量。例如:walnut(胡桃) → wall(牆)+ nut(堅果) 就可聯想成像牆一樣硬的堅果。上述的單字打 ※ 的部分有稍作變化,以便拆開記憶。

Exercise

請將中文涵義填入下列空格:

1. barber(理髮師)+ shop(商店)= _____

2. along(沿著的)+ side(一邊)= _____

3. before(在～之前)+ hand(管理)= _____

4. con(同)+ temporary(當代)= _____

5. court(空地)+ yard(庭院)= _____

6. day(白天)+ break(開啓)= _____

7. check(檢查)+ out(外出)= _____

8. door(門)+ way(路徑)= _____

9. door(門)+ step(階梯)= _____

10. down(下)+ ward(方向)= _____

11. drive(開車)+ way(道)= _____

12. forth(向前的)+ coming(來)= _____

13. here(此處)+ after(之後)= _____

14. in(在～之內)+ land(土地)= _____

15. inter(互相的)+ section(區域)= _____

16. life(一生的)+ long(之久)= _____

17. long(長的)+ itude(度)= _____

18. main(主要的)+ land(陸地)= _____

19. suit(衣服)+ case(箱子)= _____

20. no(沒有)+ where(到處)= _____

21. out(外面的)+ skirts(邊緣)= _____

22. over(在～之上)+ head(頭)= _____

23. sub(下)+ urban(都市的)= _____

24. ware(物品)+ house(房子)= _____

25. where(地點)+ abouts(附近)= _____

Answers

1. barbershop = 理髮店
2. alongside = 並排地
3. beforehand = 事前
4. contemporary = 當代的
5. courtyard = 庭院
6. daybreak = 破曉；黎明
7. checkout = 結帳櫃檯
8. doorway = 門階
9. doorstep = 門口
10. downward = 向下地
11. driveway = 私人車道
12. forthcoming = 即將到來的
13. hereafter = 從今以後

14. inland = 內陸
15. intersection = 十字路口
16. lifelong = 終生的
17. longitude = 經度
18. mainland = 大陸
19. suitcase = 行李箱
20. nowhere = 無處
21. outskirts = 市郊
22. overhead = 在頭上
23. suburban = 郊區的
24. warehouse = 倉庫
25. whereabouts = 行蹤

八、同義字 & 反義字串聯法

(一) 同義字串聯法：利用幾何圖形將一單字的同義字同時呈現。請看下列說明：

1.

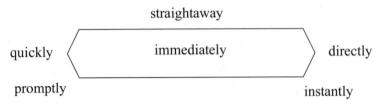

→ 這些都是表示「立即、即刻、直接」等涵義的字

2.

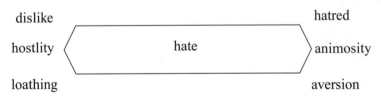

→ 這些都是表示「怨恨、仇恨、恨惡」等涵義的字

3.

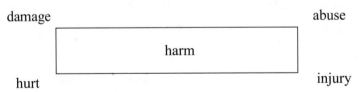

→ 這些都是表示「傷害、損害、受害」等涵義的字

4.

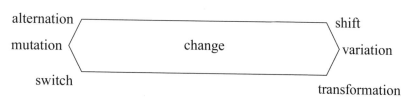

→ 這些都是表示「偉大、極好、極佳」等涵義的字

5.

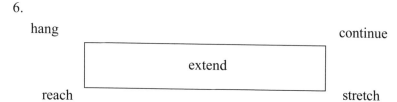

→ 這些都是表示「改變、變化、轉變」等涵義的字

6.

hang		continue
	extend	
reach		stretch

→ 這些都是表示「延伸、伸展、延續、延展」等涵義的字

備註：坊間有許多此類的同意字字典，可以買來當作工具書，
    增加你的字彙量及識字能力。

(二) 反義字對比法：以 ⇆ 符號顯示兩個 (或以上) 相反涵義
    的字

1. abrupt(突兀的) ⇆ polite(禮貌的)/prudent(謹慎的)

2. absent(缺席的) ⇆ present(出席)

3. abundance(豐富的) ⇆ shortage(缺乏)/lack(缺少)

4. accept(接受) ⇆ refuse(拒絕)/reject

5. accidental(意外的) ⇆ deliberate(故意的)

6. admire(讚美) ⇆ scorn(嘲諷)

7. agile(靈巧的) ⇆ clumsy(笨拙的)

8. allow(允許) ⇆ forbid(禁止)

9. approve(贊成) ⇆ veto(否決)

10. approximate(大約的) ⇆ exact(精華的)

11. ban(禁止) ⇆ permit(允許)/allow(許可)

12. barren(貧瘠的) ⇆ fertile(豐富的)

13. belittle(輕視) ⇆ praise(讚美)

14. better(較好的) ⇆ inferior(較差的)

15. bless(祝福) ⇆ curse(詛咒)

16. blunt(鈍的) ⇆ sharp(尖銳的)

17. boastful(自誇的) ⇆ modest(謙遜的)

18. brave(勇敢的) ⇆ cowardly(膽小的)

19. bright(明亮的) ⇆ dim(灰暗的)

20. full(充滿) ⇆ empty(空的)

文章中也會出現相同的用詞來做比較、對比等等的描述，所以記住這些反義字有助於提升閱讀的能力。

Exercise

一、請從下列句中選出與畫線單字相同的同義字：

1. The mean woman was resentful of other's success.

   (A) sweet　(B) envious　(C) bitter　(D) admiral

2. The policeman <u>bewared</u> of the drunk driver and stopped him from starting a probable car accident.

(A) wary   (B) bias   (C) ignorant   (D) focused

3. Africa once became one of the principal <u>colony</u> of Western countries.

(A) community   (B) section   (C) location   (D) settlement

4. Nowadays, there are many <u>conceited</u> young people who are arrogant and egocentric.

(A) excellent   (B) humble   (C) self-important   (D) complicated

5. The bad boy was <u>condemned</u> for his rude behavior.

(A) denounced   (B) admired   (C) neglected   (D) concentrated

6. The killer has <u>confessed</u> that he murdered the rich merchant.

(A) denied   (B) admitted   (C) pretended   (D) distrusted

7. The international <u>convention</u> was held in Geneva to discuss the problem of global warming.

(A) argument   (B) debate   (C) conjunction   (D) conference

8. The climate of the present world is changing <u>drastically</u>.

(A) radically   (B) mildly   (C) calmly   (D) tranquilly

9. Many Europeans are <u>fanatics</u> who love football crazily.

(A) players   (B) athletics   (C) members   (D) extremists

10. The horror movie <u>horrified</u> all the audience in the cinema.

(A) excited   (B) entertained   (C) marvelled   (D) appalled

11. The weather in Taiwan during summer is extremely <u>humid</u>.

(A) hot   (B) clammy   (C) warm   (D) changable

12. After the negotiation between the two countries, the threat of war has <u>diminished</u>.

(A) enhanced   (B) lengthed   (C) minimized   (D) manoeuvred

13. The poet pondered how to write a lyric about the city.

(A) contemplated　(B) depicted　(C) narrated　(D) outlined

14. The criminal expressed his regret of killing the innocent victim.

(A) repentance　(B) patience　(C) sacrifice　(D) restrain

15. The girl is lazy and her room looks untidy.

(A) ordered　(B) chaotic　(C) sequence　(D) variety

二、請從句中選出與畫線單字相反的反義字：

1. Most movie stars actually want to live an ordinary life.

(A) usual　(B) normal　(C) special　(D) conventional

2. The handicapped man, despite losing both hands, still live an optimistic life.

(A) pessimistic　(B) positive　(C) peculiar　(D) dreamlike

3. Her parents opposed her marrying that rascal.

(A) resisted　(B) objected　(C) surpported　(D) disagreed

4. The leather of the shoes is genuine, which is made from sheepskin.

(A) frank　(B) candid　(C) affected　(D) false

5. She suffered greatly from her husband's suicide and her grief made her frustrated.

(A) sorrow　(B) rejoice　(C) melancholy　(D) despair

6. The death of his father made her mad.

(A) sane　(B) barmy　(C) batty　(D) deranged

7. The affluent man lives a luxurious life that makes him jealous by lots of people.

(A) opulent　(B) sumptuous　(C) plain　(D) lavish

8. The weather was so hot that he loosened his tie.

(A) prefered　(B) tightened　(C) lessened　(D) mixed

9. The woman scattered the seeds over the farmland.

    (A) gathered   (B) sprinkled   (C) declared   (D) harvested

10. A sensible person will usually make a right decision while facing a choice.

    (A) sound   (B) severe   (C) sensitive   (D) foolish

Answers

一、

1. (C) bitter 怨恨的，sweet：甜美的 envious：羨慕的 admiral：海軍上將

2. (A) wary 留意，bias：偏見 ignorant：無知的 focused：專注

3. (D) settlement 定居地，community：社區 section：區域 location：位置

4. (C) self-important 自負的，excellent：卓越的 humble：謙卑 complicated：複雜的

5. (A) denounced 指責，admired：稱讚 neglected：忽視 concentrated：專注

6. (B) admitted 承認，Denied：拒絕 pretended：假裝 distrusted：不信任

7. (D) conference 會議，argument：爭論 debate：辯論 conjunction：連接

8. (A) radically 劇烈地，mildly：溫和地 calmly：安穩地 tranquilly：平靜地

9. (D) extremists 狂熱分子，players：選手 athletics：業餘選手 members：會員

10. (D) appalled 驚嚇，excited：興奮 entertained：娛樂 marveled：驚訝的

11. (B) clammy 黏濕的，hot：熱的 warm：溫暖的 changeable：多變的

12. (C) minimized 使縮小，enhanced：提升 lengthed：延長 manoeuvred：演習

13. (A) contemplated 沉思，depicted：描繪 narrated：敘述 outlined：略述

14. (D) repentance 悔改，patience：耐心 sacrifice：奉獻 restrain：限制

15. (B) chaotic 混亂的，ordered：有秩序的 sequence：連續 variety：變化

二、

1. (C) special 特別的，usual：通常的 normal：正常的 conventional：傳統的

2. (A) pessimistic 悲觀的，positive：肯定的 peculiar：特別的 dreamlike：夢幻的

3. (C) supported 支持，resisted：拒絕 objected：反對 disagreed：不同意

4. (D) false 假的，frank：坦白的 candid：率直的 affected：受影響的

5. (B) rejoice 欣喜的，sorrow：哀傷 melancholy：悲傷 despair：絕望

6. (A) sane 明智的，barmy：輕狂的 batty：瘋狂的 deranged：發狂的

7. (C) plain 純樸的，opulent：豐富的 sumptuous：豪華的 lavish：奢侈的

8. (B) tightened 弄緊，preferred：偏好 lessened：減少 mixed：混合

9. (A) gathered 聚集，sprinkled：播撒 declared：宣告 harvested：收穫

10. (D) foolish 愚蠢的，sound：健全的 severe：嚴重的 sensitive：敏銳的

九、相似字形單字辨識法

　　在英文閱讀中有時會遇到字形相似但涵義卻不同的字彙，造成讀者對文意領會的錯誤。因此，本辦法就是找出兩者之間字形差異的那個字母利用此字母發音的中文擬聲來串連兩字的涵義，如此即可同時記住兩字的字義，又可避免字義的混淆，請看下列舉例說明：

例1

expend(花費)/expand(擴張)

辨識差異之方法：兩字形只差在字母 e 與 a 的不同，所以利用字母 e 中的中文擬聲音「一」來形成下列這樣相關涵義的句子：

擴張店面花費一筆不少的錢。(expend 是 'e'，與中文「一」諧音)

例2

exit(出口)/exist(存在)

辨識差異之方法：逃離火場的人發現存在的出口已被封死。

(「死」是 s 的諧音) 所以 exist 與 exit 的字母差異在 's' 藉此就避免混淆兩字的涵義。

　　接下來列出常見的相似字形字彙表與相關的辨識法：

字組	字義	字形 & 字義辨識與速配法	關鍵字母音
accent ascent	重音 上升	這字的重音很重， 使得整個字音很難上升。	s
accept except	接受 除～之外	除了他自己以外， 一人的見解很難爲眾人接受。	e

字組	字義	字形 & 字義辨識與速配法	關鍵字母音
altar alter	講臺 改變	通常一上講臺，就變得緊張	e
adapt adopt	適應 採納	採納醫生的建議後， 那位產婦就比較適應飲食，不嘔吐了	o
bare bear	裸露的 出生	人一出生，就是裸露的	e
boarder border	住宿者 邊緣	這些住宿者的住屋邊緣住著一位老阿伯。	〔a〕取其字標
bit bite	一點 咬	她食慾一直不振，每餐只咬一點點的肉吃	e
coarse course	粗糙的 課程	這個課程是粗糙的，只有閒聊。	u
conscious conscience	有意識的 良心	他意識到他是有良心的，因為她一心要報恩。	en
confidant confident	密友 自信的	密友就是那種我們相信的人。	e
confirm conform	確認 使符合	那考生一直想確認他是否 符合應考資格。	e
corps corpse	特種部隊 屍體	特種部隊一下擊斃恐怖分子， 他們的屍體散布各處。	e
desert dessert	沙漠 甜點	在沙漠中，水對即將渴死的人來說，猶如甜點對飢餓的孩童一般。	s
effect affect	效果 影響	效果一但受到影響，就會有不同的結果。	e
flash flush	閃光 臉紅	攝影機的閃光使那害羞的女孩有點臉紅。	u

字組	字義	字形 & 字義辨識與速配法	關鍵字母音
great greet	偉大的 歡迎	偉大的人一直受人歡迎。	e
horse hose	馬 褲襪	啊！這真是怪事，馬居然被褲襪纏住。	r
invisible invincible	看不見的 無敵的	使萬物緊附於地表看不見的 地心引力是無敵的	s
kin king	親戚 國王	那位國王急於用自己的親戚。	g
tune turn	曲調 轉變	歌手的曲調一下變得很低沉。	e
patent pattern	專利品 型式	這種型式的專利品在代替舊產品。	t
peel peer	剝皮 同儕	他的蘋果削皮技術是同儕中有名的喔！	l
principal principle	主要的 原則	他主要的原則是一心一意的做一件事。	e
seem seam	似乎 接縫	他的衣服似乎有接縫，可能縫過。	e
vary very	轉變 非常	人在青少年時期一下轉變得很快。	e

Exercise

1. back：_____，beck：_____

2. beech：_____，beach：_____

3. beer：_____，bear：_____

4. bag：_____，beg：_____

5. bill：_____，bell：_____

6. bind：_____，band：_____

7. cold：_____，colt：_____

8. command：_____，commend：_____

9. duck：_____，deck：_____

10. grand：_____，grind：_____

11. great：_____，greet：_____

12. grab：_____，grip：_____

13. heard：_____，heart：_____

14. lag：_____，leg：_____

15. roam：_____，room：_____

Answers

1. back：後面，beck：點頭

2. beech：櫸，beach：海灘

3. beer：啤酒，bear：熊

4. bag：包包，beg：乞求

5. bill：鳥喙，bell：鈴鐺

6. bind：綁，bend：彎曲

7. cold：冷的，colt：小馬

8. command：命令，commend：表彰

9. duck：鴨子，deck：甲板

10. grand：盛大，grind：研磨

11. great：偉大的，greet：歡迎

12. grab：抓，grip：握

13. heard：聽見 (過去式)，heart：心

14. lag：落後，leg：腿

15. roam：漫遊，room：房間

十、英語圖像速記法

利用圖像與相關的聲音來記住字彙，請看下列說明：

anchor['æŋkɚ] 錨 (擬聲音：安可)

他將錨放在安全可以放的地方。

glance [glæns] 看著；盯著 (擬聲音：隔欄死)

他隔著欄杆死 盯著她看

damage ['dæmɪdʒ] 損壞 (擬聲音：當不急)

他把窗子損壞 當作不急的事。

◎重點整理◎

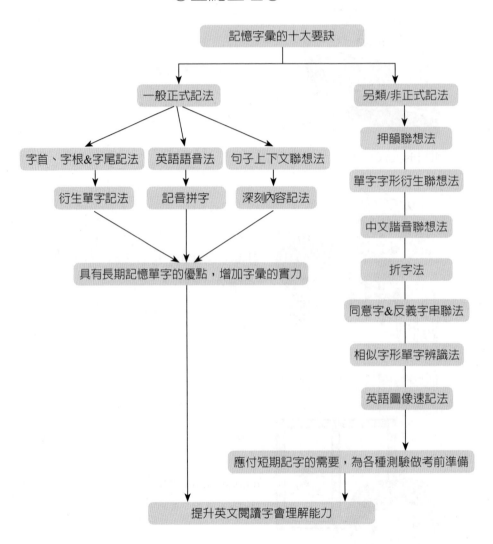

記憶字彙的十大要訣

一般正式記法

另類/非正式記法

字首、字根&字尾記法　　英語語音法　　句子上下文聯想法

押韻聯想法

單字字形衍生聯想法

中文諧音聯想法

折字法

同意字&反義字串聯法

相似字形單字辨識法

英語圖像速記法

衍生單字記法　　記音拼字　　深刻內容記法

具有長期記憶單字的優點，增加字彙的實力

應付短期記字的需要，為各種測驗做考前準備

提升英文閱讀字會理解能力

CHAPTER

02 突破閱讀障礙的第二關

—— 掌握句子結構 & 涵義

- 第一節
  句子基本結構 & 涵義
- 第二節
  特殊句型結構 & 涵義
- 第三節
  慣用句型結構 & 涵義

閱讀導引

(一) 句子基本結構 & 涵義：

> 句子主要要素的構成 ▸ 各主要要素的說明 ▸ 實例講解
>
> ▸ 各主要要素的重點整理(以圖表呈現) ▸ 句子的次要要素構成
>
> ▸ 各次要要素說明 ▸ 實例講解 ▸ 次要要素的重點整理

(二) 特殊句型結構 & 涵義：

> 各種特殊句型的結構分析 ▸ 以圖表呈現
>
> ▸ 實例講解(包含各類考試句子) ▸ 重點整理

(三) 慣用句型結構＆涵義：

各種詞類的慣用句型　　以句型公式呈現

實例講解(包含各類考試句子)　　重點整理(以總表呈現)

本章特色

英文閱讀的句子障礙　→　不明白句子涵義

不明白句子結構(文法)

破解方法　→　清楚句中詞類的彼此關聯　→　領悟這些關聯所表示的涵義

（八大詞類在句中的角色）

清楚各種句型的結構　→　領悟不同句型的不同解釋

（特殊 & 慣用句型的特別結構）

一體兩面的句子分析　→　基本句子結構的分析

特殊&慣用句型的分析　→　句子涵義的領會

解讀英文句子的五大迷思：

一、句子文法解析缺少重點，以致無法找出句子涵義的重心所在。

二、句子解析重在句中詞類的個別分析，缺少詞類之間的關聯性。

三、句子解析缺少歸納與整合，以致強調句中詞類的單一性解析。

四、句子解析缺少對中、英文之間句型與語法的差異之比較，以致閱讀英文句子時，常會誤解英文的原意，造成對句子涵義的誤解。

五、對慣用句型的字面解釋造成對句子涵義的誤解。

　　本章針對上述五大解讀英文句子的迷思提出辨別與破解之道並且提出各種詞類在句中的用法與彼此的關聯。現以下列圖表概括說明：

一、

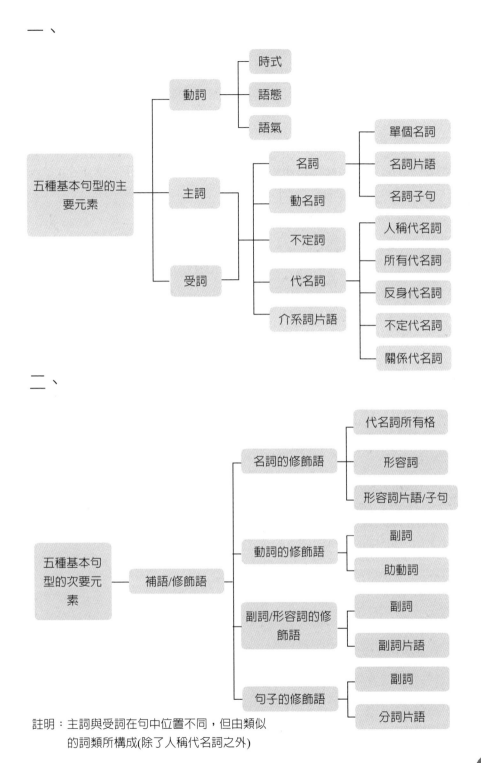

二、

註明：主詞與受詞在句中位置不同，但由類似
　　　的詞類所構成(除了人稱代名詞之外)

句型的主要要素 + 句型的次要要素 = 各種基本句子的組成
瞭解這些句子構成要素和要素之間的關聯 = 明白這些句子的涵義

現舉例說明如下：

範例：The man loves movies.(本句皆為主要元素)
　　　主詞　動詞　受詞

⇨ The young man loves romantic movies.
　　形容詞　　　　　形容詞
　　　　　　　　　　　(本句加上形容詞為修飾語)

⇨ The young man loves romantic movies very much.(本句加
上副詞為修飾語)　　　　　　　　副詞

⇨ The young man and his friends love romantic movies very
much.　　　　　代名詞所有格
　　　　　　　　(本句加上代名詞所有格為修飾語)

⇨ The young man and his friends who live together love romantic
movies very much.　　　　　形容詞子句
　　　　　　　　(本句加上形容詞子句為修飾語)

所以句子最主要的構成元素是動詞。其次是主詞，主詞與動詞是英文五種基本句型的必要詞類。請看下列五種基本句型中的主詞與動詞的組成：

一、五種基本句型的主要元素

順序	句型結構	例句說明
1	主詞＋完全不及物動詞	Money talks. （有錢好說話） 主詞 完全不及物動詞
2	主詞＋不完全不及物動詞	Old people often feel 主詞 不完全不及物動詞 lonely. (老人經常覺得寂寞。) 主詞補語
3	主詞＋完全及物動詞＋受詞	The early bird catches the worm. 主詞 及物動詞 受詞 (早起的鳥兒有蟲吃。)
4	主詞＋不完全及物動詞＋受詞＋受詞補語	All work and no play makes 主詞 不完全及物動詞 Jack a dull boy. 受詞 受詞補語 (只工作不消遣，使人遲鈍。)

5	主詞＋授予動詞(註2)
	＋{ 間接受詞＋直接受詞
	直接受詞＋介系詞＋
	間接受詞
		An honest man always tells
		    主詞 授予動詞
		＋{ people truth.
		   間接受詞 直接受詞
		    truth to people.
		   直接受詞 介系詞 間接受詞
		(誠實人對人總是說實話。)

註1：不完全不及物動詞包括「連綴動詞」及「感官動詞」。

註2：授予動詞 (dative verb) 是及物動詞的一種，其後必須接兩種受詞：
　　　「直接受詞」(真正接受者) 與「間接受詞」(給予者的憑藉，人或
　　　物皆有可能。)

上述五種基本句型的差異之關鍵在於動詞。請看下列圖解上述句型的不同：

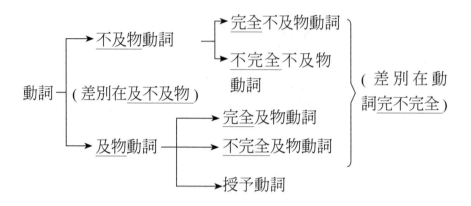

從以上圖表看出動詞的及物與不及物或完全與不完全是造成這五種句型的主要差異，因為這些差異直接影響動詞後所接（或不接）的受詞或補語，換言之，動詞的「及不及物」會造成它有無受詞，「完不完全」會影響動詞前的主詞或動詞後的受詞有無補語。

由此圖表可看出「動詞」會影響句子的「涵義」。因此，接下來會就動詞的三方面分別來說明它們對句子涵義的影響：
(一) 動詞的時式 (二) 動詞的語態 (三) 動詞的語氣

(一) 動詞的時式：十二種表示不同時間狀態的動詞時式

說到時式就是「時間 + 狀態」，因可歸納出下列三個時間，加上四種狀態，互相交叉的結果就產生十二種動詞的時式（或稱作「時態」），現以圖片說明如下：

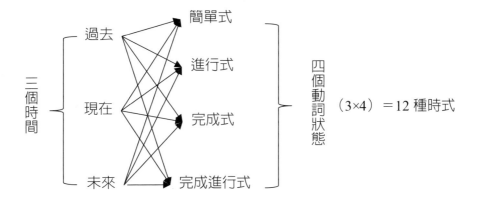

由上表可歸納出下列十二種動詞時式，每一種都表達不同的情境與涵義：

1. 過去簡單式 2. 過去進行式 3. 過去完成式 4. 過去完成進行式 5. 現在簡單式 6. 現在進行式 7. 現在完成式 8. 現在完成進行式 9. 未來簡單式 10. 未來來進行式 11. 未來完成式 12. 未來完成進行式

瞭解以上時式的形式與表達的狀態有助於瞭解句子的涵義，以下逐項說明其形式與表達的狀態：

1. 過去式相關時式：(1) 過去簡單式 (2) 過去進行式 (3) 過去完成式 (4) 過去完成進行式

時式	動詞形式	表達的狀態 / 情境	表達的方式
過去簡單式	動詞規則變化：V + ed 動詞不規則變化	1. 表示過去的歷史、軼聞、故事、紀錄等等。	與表示過去時間的副詞或副詞片語合用或副詞子句。
		2. 表示以往的例行事物或習慣。	與頻率副詞 / 表習慣的副詞片語合用。
		3. 表示特定意思的未來狀況	以慣用句型表達。
過去進行式	was } + Ving were	表示過去某時刻正在進行的動作	與表示過去特定時間的副詞 / 副詞片語合用。
		表示當兩個動作發生時，較早發生的動作進行時。	與表示過去時間的副詞子句 (主要子句 / 對等子句) 合用。
		表示過去同一時間都在進行的兩個行動。	與表示過去正在進行動作的副詞子句合用。
過去完成式	had + p.p.	表示某一動作或狀態在過去某時點開始並在過去某時點結束。	與表示過去某段持續時間的副詞片語 / 子句合用。
		表示比過去還早的過去。	與表示過去狀態的慣用句型合用。
		表示過去未曾實現的願望或計畫。	與表示期望、打算、計畫等動詞的過去完成式合用。
過去完成進行式	had been+Ving	強調在過去某一時段正在進行或持續的動作或狀態。	與表示持續或進行到過去某段時間的副詞片語或子句。

註解：Ving：現在分詞，p.p.：過去分詞

(1) 過去簡單式範例：Ved/ 不規則變化

例 1

World War II broke out in 1939.

中譯 二次大戰於一九三九年爆發。

文法解析

表示歷史事件的句子通常都有表示過去時間的副詞或副詞片語，在本句中有表示時間的副詞片語：in 1939，所以要用過去簡單式。

例 2

Jane often went for a walk in the morning, but she didn't do it anymore because of her illness.

中譯 珍以往經常在早晨散步，但是因為她的病，她不再如此做了。

文法解析

表示過去習慣的動作或例行的事，要用過去簡單式以及表示習慣的頻率副詞，如以下所顯示：

$$
主詞 + \begin{cases} always(總是；一直) \\ usually(通常) \\ often(經常)/frequently \end{cases} + 一般\ V
$$

$$
主詞 + \begin{cases} sometimes(有時) \\ occasionally(偶爾) \\ seldom(很少) \\ rarely(絕少)/scarcely/hardly \\ never(從未) \end{cases} + 一般\ V
$$

或

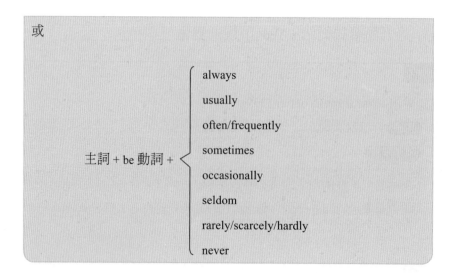

主詞 + be 動詞 +
- always
- usually
- often/frequently
- sometimes
- occasionally
- seldom
- rarely/scarcely/hardly
- never

例 3

The bartender told his customers in the pub that it is time that they went home.

中譯 那位酒保告訴在夜店的顧客該是他們回家的時候。

文法解析

It is time that + 主詞 + 過去式⋯。(該是⋯的時候。)

＊ 特定用法的句型，雖然是表示未來的狀況，卻要用過去簡單式。

(2) 過去進行式的範例

例 1

The Olympic athlete was running faster and faster then.

中譯 那時那位奧運選手正在愈跑愈快。

文法解析

本句句尾的 then(那時) 指出一個過去的特定時間正在進行的動作，所

以要用過去進行式來表達，表示過去某時刻正在發生的動作或事情。

例2

Abraham Lincoln was assassinated while he was watching a play in a theater.

中譯 亞伯拉罕‧林肯在戲院看戲時遇刺。

文法解析

本句由副詞子句與主要子句所構成。其中主要子句表示一個過去發生的事件，比主要子句 (Abraham Lincoln ... assassinated) 發生更早且正在進行的事情就要用過去進行式。

例3

While children were playing in the yard, their parents were preparing for the lunch for them.

中譯 當孩子們正在院子裡玩耍時，他們的父母正在為他們準備午餐。

文法解析

本句也是由表時間的副詞子句 (While... the yard) 與其後的主要子句所構成，這兩個子句都表示正在進行的事，所以都要用過去進行式。

(3) 過去完成式的範例

例1

The United Kingdom of Britain had lost many of her colonies from 1950's to 1970's.

中譯 大英國協從一九五零年代至一九七零年代已經失去她許多殖民地。

文法解析

1950's 到 1970's 的二十年間是一段過去的持續時間，所以描寫這段時間的動詞時式要用過去完成式。from 1950's to 1970's 就是表達過去完成式所需的時間狀態之副詞片語。

例 2

By the time the train arrived at the station, the author <u>had already finished</u> her draft of a chapter of a new novel.

中譯 在火車到達車站之前，那位作者已經完成她新的小說中的一章草稿。

文法解析

因為作者完成小說寫作的章節在先，所以同樣表示過去的時間但是較早發生的事情要用過去完成式，來表示比過去還早的過去。

例 3

The careless mother found that she <u>had left</u> her little daughter in her car when she went shopping.

中譯 那位粗心的媽媽發現當她去購物時，她把她小女兒留在她車上。

文法解析

本句中「小女兒留在車上」要比「發現」早，所以表示「過去中的過去」要用過去完成式。

The residents had scarcely been evacuated from the coast before the flood
covered the coast.

中譯 當居民一從海岸撤離，洪水就覆蓋海岸。

文法解析

有些特殊句型是用來表示過去所發生的前後連續的事情或是動作。本
句就是此種句型的表達：

$$主詞 + had + \begin{Bmatrix} scarcely \\ hardly \end{Bmatrix} + p.p.\cdots$$

$$\begin{Bmatrix} before \\ when \end{Bmatrix} + 主詞 + 過去式\cdots：一\cdots就\cdots$$

較先發生的就用過去完成式，較後發生的則用過去簡單式；因此，本
句中撤離較早，因此用 had scarcely been evacuated，洪水來襲較晚，所
以用過去簡單式：covered。

Her mother had intended to see her daughter's wedding, but she could not
live long enough to see it come true.

中譯 她母親原本預期看到她女兒的婚禮，但是她未能活到看到
此事成真。

文法解析

intend(企圖) 式表示意圖的動詞，若用過去完成式，則表示未達成的
計畫或計畫。其他這類的動詞還有：expect、hope、think、assume、
think、destine、plan、promise 等等動詞。

(4) 過去完成進行式的範例

Kevin <u>had been standing</u> on a ladder trying to reach for a book on the top
shelf when he lost his balance and fell to the ground.

中譯 當他失去他的平衡並且跌到地上,凱文當時正站在階梯
上,試著拿取在最上層書架的一本書。

文法解析

> When 子句表達一個發生在過去的動作,而其前的主要子句則表示時
> 正在進行得動作,這時就用過去完成進行式來表達此種正在發生的動
> 作:had been standing。

2. 現在式相關時式:(1) 現在簡單式 (2) 現在進行式 (3) 現在完
   成式 (4) 現在完成進行式

時式	動詞形式	表達的狀態 / 情境	表達的方式
現在簡單式	動詞　　　　　　　動詞 + s/es	表示現在存在的事實或不變的真理	不受句中其他時式的影響
		表示習慣或例行性的動作	表示習慣或頻率的副詞 / 副詞片語
		表示「條件」/「時間」的狀況	與表示條件或時間的子句合用
		取代未來簡單式,表示未來的狀態	大都是與來去或活動動詞合用

時式	動詞形式	表達的狀態 / 情境	表達的方式
現在進行式	is/am/are + Ving	表示現在正在進行中	與表示現在時刻的副詞 / 副詞片語合用
		表示連續性或反覆的動作	與表示持續性或習慣性副詞片語合用
		表示最近的未來狀況，取代未來簡單式	與表示未來時間的單字 / 片語 / 子句合用
現在完成式	has/have + p.p.	表示從過去某一時點一直延續到現在的狀態	與表示延續性的時間副詞 / 副詞片語 / 副詞子句合用
		表示經驗 / 經歷	與表示經歷 / 經驗的副詞 / 副詞片語合用
		表示從過去到現在剛完成的動作	與表示結果 / 完成的副詞 / 副詞片語合用
現在完成進行式	has/have been + Ving	表示由過去一直延續 / 進行至今仍在進行的動作 / 狀態	與表示持續時間的副詞 / 副詞片語 / 副詞子句合用

(1) 現在簡單式的範例：V/V+ s/es

例 1

In order to stay healthy and fit, John exercises regularly. (101 年學測)

中譯 爲了保持健美，約翰規律地運動。

文法解析

本句的涵義是說明一個因果關係的事實：爲了⋯而做。所以用現在簡單式來表達這種必然結果的事實。

Mei-ling has a very close relationship with her parents. She always consults them before she makes important decisions. (103 年學測)

中譯 美林與她父母有非常親密的關係。她在做決定前總是會先請教他們。

文法解析

從後一句中的 always(總是) 可以看出「美林」的習慣：做決定前先請教父母。因此，表示這種習慣就要用現在簡單式。always 是頻率副詞，所以本句要用現在簡單式。

例 3

If student enrollment continues to drop, some programs at the university may be eliminated to reduce operation costs. (103 年學測)

中譯 如果學生的註冊人數持續下降，大學中的某些計畫案可能被刪除來減少經營的費用。

文法解析

在表示條件狀況的 if 子句中，其動詞要用現在簡單式；即使這個狀況還未發生或將來可能發生。所以要用現在簡單式 continues 在本句中。主要句子則用表示未來狀況的 may be。

例 4

When you take photos, you can move around to shoot the target object from different angles. (98 年學測)

中譯 當你攝影時，你可以到處移動，從不同的角度來拍攝目標物。

文法解析

表示「當…，就…」的情況時，表示時間的 when 子句要用現在簡單式，所以本句中表示「當你…你就…。」的情況時，when 子句要用現在簡單式 take。

例 5

As soon as the couple <u>saves</u> enough money, they will buy a home.

中譯 這對夫婦一存夠錢，他們就會買房子。

文法解析

表示前後接續發生時的動作或事情，as soon as(一…就…) 中的動詞要用現簡單式表示未來會發生的事情。

例 6

The businessman <u>leaves</u> for Hong Kong tonight.

中譯 那位商人今晚前往香港。

文法解析

有些動詞可以用現在簡單式表示最近的未來之動作或事情，本句中的「今晚」tonight 就是表示最近未來的時間，加上動詞是表示未來去的動詞，所以可以用現在簡單式取代未來簡單式。像 go, come, arrive, reach 這類的未來動詞也可如此使用。

(2) 現在進行式：am/is/are + Ving

例 1

The government is doing its best to preserve the cultures of the tribal people for fear that they may soon die out. (99 年學測)

中譯 政府正在盡全力保存那個部落的文化，以免他們可能很快就消失。

文法解析

本句表是一件正在運行事情：保存部落文化，所以句中的動詞要用現在進行式：is doing。do its best：盡全力，是一慣用動詞片語。

例 2

The wife is always complaining her husband.

中譯 那位太太總是抱怨她的先生。

文法解析

表示連續且反覆的動作，用現在進行式來表達。本句中的太太抱怨是一直重複發生的事情，所以要用現在進行式來表達。

例 3

Henry is a little nervous because he is meeting his new boss tomorrow.

中譯 亨利有點緊張，因為他明天將要與他的新老闆見面。

文法解析

明天 (tomorrow) 是接近的時間，所以可以用現在進行式來取代未來簡單式，表示即將發生的事：會見他的新老闆 (is meeting his new boss)。

類似的狀況還有：The plane is taking off in five minutes.(飛機將在五分鐘
後起飛。)

(3) 現在完成式：has/have + p.p.

例 1

No one could beat Paul at running. He has won the running championship
continuously for three years.   (101 年學測)

中譯　在賽跑上無人能擊敗保羅。他已經連續三年贏得賽跑冠
　　　　軍。

文法解析

本句的涵義是保羅已經連續三年贏得冠軍，亦即他從三年前直到如今
都一直贏得冠軍。這種表示「從過去延續至今」的時間狀態，要用現
在完成式來表達。「for + 一段時間」表示「有…多久」是常與現在完
成式合用的介系詞片語 (在此作副詞片語用)。since+ 子句 / 名詞是另
一個常見的副詞表語，也與現在完成式合用。

例 2

Linda has gone to the United States many times.   (輔大轉學考)

中譯　琳達去過美國許多次了。

文法解析

表示一種經歷或經驗，要用現在完成式。通常會有表示經歷的副詞片
語 (many times) 與句子合用，以表達經歷的情形。此外，has been 的涵
義則是：曾經去過，與 has gone 涵義稍有不同。

例 3

The mechanic has just fixed his car when he arrives.

中譯 當他到達時，那位技師剛剛修好他的車。

文法解析

> 表示從過去到現在完成的動作，要用現在完成式。為了強調完成的結
> 果，通常都有表示「完成」涵義的副詞，像 already、just，等時間副詞。

例 4

Most major surveys in recent years has found that Americans are satisfied
with their family life. （中正大學轉學考）

中譯 近年來大部分主要的調查發現美國人對他們的家庭生活感
到滿意。

文法解析

> 表示最近時間的副詞片語常與現在完成式合用，例如，lately(近來)，
> recently(最近) 等等時間副詞，本句中有 recent(最近)，所以要用現在
> 完成式。

(4) 現在完成進行式：has/have been + Ving

例句

She has been waiting for her boyfriend for one hour.

中譯 她一直等她的男友有一小時之久。

文法解析

> 她等男友已經一小時了。這個等待的動作沒有中止，所以表示這種
> 從以前一直進行至今的動作或狀態，要用現在完成進行式：has been

waiting. 比較現在完成式與現在完成進行式的不同，請看下例說明：

He has repaired his car.(已完成)

He has been repairing his car.(尚在進行中)

3. 未來式相關時式：(1) 未來簡單式 (2) 未來進行式 (3) 未來完成式 (4) 未來完成進行式

時式	動詞形式	表達的狀態 / 情境	表達的方式
未來簡單式	will shall }+ 原形 V	表示未來計畫要實行或預期發生的事情	與表示未來時間的副詞 / 副詞片語 / 副詞子句合用或表示未來時間的名詞片語合用
		表示自然或物理現象的必然性	與表示時間或條件的副詞子句合用
		表示請求或邀約	通常以疑問句句型來表達
未來進行式	will shall }+ be + Ving	表示未來某時點 / 時段預定進行的動作或發生的事情。	與表示未來某時點 / 時段的副詞片語 / 子句合用
未來完成式	will shall }+ have + p.p.	表示預定在未來的特定時間之前要完成的事情或動作。	與表示未來某時點 (段) 為止的副詞片語 / 子句合用
		表示從現在或過去持續到未來某時段 (點) 為止的動作或狀態。	

時式	動詞形式	表達的狀態 / 情境	表達的方式
未來完成進行式	will shall + have + been + Ving	表示由現在 / 過去一直持續到未來某時點仍在進行的動作或狀態。	與表示未來某時點 (段) 為止的副詞片語 / 子句合用

(1) 未來簡單式的範例：will + 原形動詞

例 1

We hope that there <u>will be</u> no war in the world and that all people <u>will live</u> in peace and harmony with each other. (98 年學測)

中譯▶ 我們希望世界上將沒有戰爭並且所有人都將彼此生活在和平與和諧中。

文法解析▶

本句的涵義是表示一種對未來世界的期望，所以句中所有的動詞都用未來簡單式來表達：will be 與 will live。

例 2

The scientists <u>are going to</u> explore Mars by sending a spaceship to Mars.

中譯▶ 科學家們將透過向火星發射太空船來探索火星。

文法解析▶

be going to + 原形動詞也是表示未來行動或計畫的未來簡單式之另一種用法。它與 will + 原形動詞不同之處乃是 be going to 表示未來的計畫或打算，而非未來自然發生的事情，所以下列的情況不能用 be going to 而是要用 will + 原形動詞：

A huge typhoon <u>is going to</u> hit Taiwan tomorrow.(✗)

A huge typhoon will hit Taiwan tomorrow.(○)

例 3

The ship is about to leave the harbor.

中譯 這艘船即將離開港口。

文法解析

be about to + 動詞原形表示「即將…。」這是另一種表示未來即將發生的動作／事情的特殊發展表達方式。

例 4

Shall we have dinner together tonight？

中譯 我們今晚是否要共進晚餐？

文法解析

以 "Shall we ...？" 開頭的問句，表示一種邀約，而非詢問而已。事實上 Shall we = Let's 的涵義。

(2) 未來進行式：will/shall + be + Ving

例 1

President Obama will be having a meeting with the prime minister of Japan to discuss the situation of Asia tomorrow morning.

中譯 明天早上歐巴馬總統將與日本首相進行會談，討論亞洲的情勢。

文法分析

本句表示在明早 (未來預定的時間) 將要進行的事情，所以要用未來

進行式：will be having。而 tomorrow morning(明早) 就是表示未來時間的副詞片語。

例2

Sam will be sleeping at this time tomorrow.

中譯 山姆明天此時正在睡覺。

文法分析

at this time tomorrow(早天此時) 清楚指出未來的某時間點，所以本句要用未來進行式：will be sleeping。

(3) 未來完成式：will/shall + have + p.p.

例1

By the end of 2020, He will have worked in this company for twenty years.

中譯 在二零二零年底，他將在這個公司已經工作二十年之久。

文法解析

本句表示在未來的某一時間 (2020 年)，仍舊持續的狀態，所以用未來完成式：will have worked 來表達從而二十年前 (2000 年) 到如今 (2020 年) 持續的情況。

例2

The manager will have completed his project by next month.

中譯 那位經理預定在下個月之前完成他的計畫。

文法解析

表示未來在某一時段 (next month) 預定要完成的動作或事情，要用未來

完成式表達：will have completed。

(4) 未來完成進行式：will/shall + have been + Ving

例句

The forest fire in the north of California State will have been burning for nearly three weeks by the end of this month.

中譯 那場在加州北部的森林大火到本月底前已經延燒了三週。

文法解析

句中的森林大火是不斷地延燒，而且預定還會繼續延燒，所以句中的動詞要表達此種由過去到未來一直進行的狀態時，要用未來完成式進行：will have been burning。

◎重點整理◎

上述的十二種動詞時式形式可以整理如下表：

時式	動詞形式	時式	動詞形式
1. 過去進行式	1. 動詞規則變化：V+ed 2. 不規則變化	6. 現在進行式	is/am/are + Ving
2. 過去進行式	was/were + Ving	7. 現在完成式	has/have + p.p.
3. 過去完成式	had + p.p.	8. 現在完成進行式	has/have + been + Ving
4. 過去完成進行式	had + been + Ving	9. 未來簡單式	will/shall + 原形動詞
5. 現在簡單式	1. 動詞 2. 動詞 + s/es(第三人稱單數)	10. 未來進行式	will/shall + be + Ving

時式	動詞形式	時式	動詞形式
11.未來完成式	will/shall + have + p.p.	12.未來完成進行式	will/shall + have + been + Ving

備註：Ving：現在分詞，p.p.：過去分詞

　　將上述圖表的各種時式所表達的時間狀態整理分別整理如下：

一、過去式的各種時式

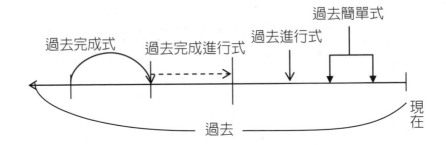

二、現在式的各種時式

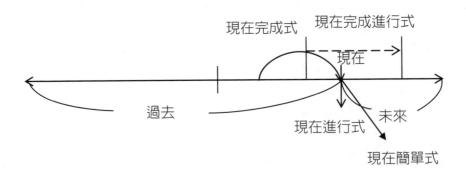

三、未來式的各種時式

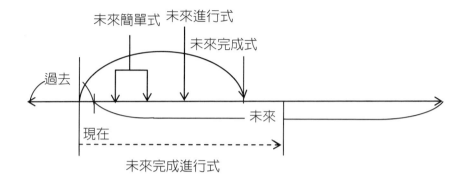

【圖表說明】

一、過去式的各種時式

　　1. 過去完成式：表示從過去的某一時點一直延續到過去另一時點的時段中所延續或存在的動作或狀態，亦即是表示「過去中的過去」。

　　2. 過去進行式：表示過去某一時點正在進行的動作或發生的事。

　　3. 過去完成進行式：表示過去某一段時間正在持續進行的動作或事情。

　　4. 過去簡單式：表示過去的事實或例行的事或動作。

二、現在式的各種時式

　　1. 現在完成式：表示從過去某一段時點 (段) 一直延續到現在的狀態或剛完成的動作。

　　2. 現在進行式：表示現在 (此刻) 正在進行的動作或發生的事情。

3. 現在完成進行式：表示從以往一直進行到現在的動作或還在發生的事情。

4. 現在簡單式：表示現在的事實或不變的事物或例行的事物與習慣。

三、未來式的各種式

1. 未來完成式：表示在未來某一時點預定要完成的動作或事物。

2. 未來進行式：表示在未來某一時點 (刻) 預定進行的動作或事情。

3. 未來完成進行式：表示現在 / 過去一直進行並且在未來某一時點預定要完成的動作或事情。

4. 未來簡單式：表示在未來計畫要做的事情或將會發生的事情。

Exercise

請選出最合適的答案選項

1. Jack is very proud of his fancy new motorcycle. He has _____ to all his friends about how cool it looks and how fast it runs.

   (A) boasted　(B) been boasted　(C) being boasted　(D) to be boasted

   (101 年學測改編題)

2. This course _____ students with a solid foundation for research. It is highly recommended for those who plan to go to graduate school.

   (A) provides　(B) provided　(C) will provide　(D) has provided

   (96 年學測改編題)

3. Ms. Lin business expanded very quickly. She _____ her first store two years ago; now she has fifty stores all over the country.

    (A) opened (B) had opened (C) has opened (D) would open

    (96 年學測改編題)

4. If the shrinking _____, India will disappear in 200 million years.

    (A) will continue (B) continues (C) continued (D) is continuing

    (96 年學測改編題)

5. The hip pop star must be so popular. Fans _____ in the queue for over 5 hours to buy her concert tickets.

    (A) had waited (B) waited (C) are waiting (D) have been waiting

    (104 年私醫聯招轉學考)

6. Japanese _____ one of the most popular courses at the university since the Asian studies program was established.

    (A) has become (B) became (C) become (D) is

    (104 年私醫聯招轉學考)

7. Mr. Brown _____ in this company for ten years after he graduated from a university.

    (A) has worked (B) worked (C) was working (D) will have worked

8. When the police found the injured person, he _____ for half an hour.

    (A) had bled (B) has bled (C) had been bleeding (D) was bleeding

9. The scientist estimated that the space shuttle _____ by July 23.

    (A) has been completed   (B) will have been completed

    (C) will be completed   (D) is completed

10. The old woman said that she _____ her key in her house.

    (A) left (B) has left (C) was leaving (D) had left

11. The soldier _____ his family again since he left home.

(A) has never seen   (B) had never seen

(C) never saw   (D) will have never seen

12. The new employee becomes nervous when he knows that he _____

his supervisor tomorrow.

(A) meets   (B) will have met   (C) will be meeting   (D) is meeting

13. When the terrible car accident happened, the driver of the car _____ .

(A) slept   (B) has slept   (C) was sleeping   (D) had slept

14. While it was raining heavily outside, Tom _____ an interesting movie.

(A) watched   (B) has watched   (C) was watching   (D) had watched

15. The young couple often _____ a walk in the morning.

(A) has taken   (B) take   (C) takes   (D) will take

16. By the time I arrived at the wedding reception, most of the guests _____

(A) pretending not have seen me   (B) had already left

(C) would have been   (D) are about to leave.

(102 年臺灣聯大轉學考)

17. When he _____ its throat, the little pig suddenly screamed, " Stop!"

(A) had cut   (B) has cut   (C) will cut   (D) was about to cut

18. By this time next year, we _____ here for five years.

(A) have lived   (B) will live   (C) will have lived   (D) will be lived

(97 年關務人員考試)

19. Susan _____ to lock the door before she went to bed.

(A) forgets   (B) had forgotten   (C) has forgotten   (D) forgot

(104 年地方特考)

20. I feel so tired this evening. I've been working hard _____ .

(A) all day   (B) every day   (C) each day   (D) day by day

(102 年地方特考)

1. (A)

2. (C) 由後半句 It is highly... 所以看出前面一句的涵義是指未來發生的事情。

3. (A) 有 ago(在…之前) 這個表示過去時間的片語，之句子要用過去簡單式。

4. (B) If 子句要用現在簡單式。

5. (D) for over five hours(有超過五小時之久)，表示一段延續至今的時間狀態，加上 wait(等待) 是表示持續的動作，所以要用現在完成進行式。

6. (A) 有 since 的子句，通常要用現在完成式。

7. (A) 有 for 的片語，通常要用現在完成式。

8. (C) bleed(流血) 是不會停止的動作，而 when 子句表示一件發生在過去的事情，所以其後的主要子句要用過去完成進行式。

9. (B) by(在…之前) 表示一個未來的時間，所以要用未來完成式，而 space shuttle 是事物，所以要用被動語態，因此本句要用未來完成被動語態。

10. (D) 遺留鑰匙的動作比說這個動作早，所以要用過去完成式。

11. (A)

12. (D) is meeting 是現在進行式，表示預定要發生的事。

13. (C) 兩件同時在過去發生的事，都要用過去進行式。

14. (C)

15. (C) often(經常) 形容動詞，表示這是一種習慣，所以要用現在簡單式。

16. (B) By the time ＋過去式動詞的子句 (在…之前) 與過去完成式合用，表示一前一後的時間先後順序。

17. (D) be about to ＋原形動詞：將要…。

18. (C) by this time next year(明年此時) 是表示未來某一時點，所以要用未來完成式。

19. (B) before(在…之前)，所以忘記鎖門要比去上床睡覺發生的早，因此要用過去完成式：had forgotten。

20. (A) all day(整天) 表示一段持續的時間，所以要用現在完成進行式：have been working。

(二) 動詞的語態

1. 四種基本被動語態句型

　　英文的被動語態的句型，都是由主動語態的句型轉變而來，亦即從四種基本句型轉變而來 (除了第一種基本的句型：主詞 + 完全不及物動詞)，因為轉變為被動語態的主動語態句型必須都要有受詞。請看下列比較說明：

　　Dog bark.(狗吠)(第一種基本句型)

　　本句動詞(bark)之後沒有受詞，所以無法轉變為被動語態。

　　The dog attack the cat.(那些狗攻擊那隻貓。)

　　本句動詞 attack 之後接受詞 the cat，所以可將它改為下列被動語態的句子：

　　The cat is attacked by the dog.(那隻貓被狗攻擊。)

⊙ 在中文句子中只要加上「被」字，就能將主語涵義的句子轉變為被動涵義的句子，但是英文中這樣的主動轉被動涵義的方式就複雜許多並且有一定的轉換模式。現在請看下列四種基本被動語態句型：

(1) 主詞 + 完全及物動詞 + 受詞 (五種基本句型中的第三種)

　　主詞 (I) + be + p.p. + 介系詞 + 受詞 (I)(被動語態)

例句

He loves sweet food.(主動語態)

Sweet food is loved by him.(被動語態)

中譯 他愛甜食 ⇨ 甜食是他所愛的。

文法解析

上句是主動語態的句子，轉變為被動語態時，句中的主要動詞就要轉變為 be + p.p.(過去分詞) 的形式。上下句子的主詞與受詞要互換位置，亦即上句中的受詞變為主詞 sweet food, by 本身的意思是「藉由」。而主詞則變為受詞 him，而且要以介系詞 by 來連接受詞 him。

(2) 主詞 + 不完全及物動詞 + 受詞 + 受詞補語 (五種基本句型中的第四種)

主詞 (I) + be + p.p. + 主詞補語 + 介系詞 + 受詞 (I)

例句

Most people think vegetables healthy.

Vegetables are thought healthy by most people.

中譯 大部分人認為蔬菜是健康的。

⇨ 蔬菜被大部分人認為是健康的。

文法解析

本句有受詞補語，所以在由主動語態轉變為被動語態的句子時，原主動語態中的受詞補語轉變為被動語態中的主詞補語 (緊接在過去分詞後)，來形容其前的新主詞 (其實，在原句中受詞補語本來就是修飾受詞。)

(3) 主詞 + 授予動詞 + { 間接受詞 + 直接受詞 (五種基本句型中的第五種)
直接受詞 + 介系詞 + 間接受詞

有兩種受詞的不同順序，所以有下列兩種被動語態的句型：

① 主詞 + 授予動詞 + 間接受詞 + 直接受詞

主詞 (I) + be + p.p. + 直接受詞 + by + 受詞 (I)

② 主詞 + 授予動詞 + 直接受詞 + 介系詞 + 間接受詞

主詞 (I) + be + p.p. + (介系詞) + 間接受詞 + by + 受詞 (I)

例 1

Jack gave me a big surprise on my birthday.　　　　(101 年初等考試)

I was given a big surprise by Jack on my birthday.

中譯　在我的生日傑克給我一個大的驚喜
　　　　⟹ 在我的生日我被給予一個大的驚喜。

文法解析

因為授予動詞有兩個受詞 (直接受詞 & 間接受詞)，所以其主動語態也可以轉換成兩種不同的被動語態。本句是以間接受詞 (動詞動作施予的憑藉者) 作被動語態句子的主詞。

例2

Jack gave me a big surprise on my birthday.

A big surprise was given (to) me by Jack on my birthday.

中譯 在我的生日傑克給我一個大的驚喜

⇨ 在我的生日一個大的驚喜給了我。

文法解析

> 本句是以直接受詞作被動語態句子的主詞,唯一的差異是它原先的主
> 動語態句中之介系詞在被動語態的句子中可有可無,所以用括號來表
> 示。

2. 被動語態的時式

如同主動語態的動詞時式,被動語態也有動詞時式,請看
下列圖表說明:

時式	動詞形式	例句
簡單式	am/are/is + p.p. was/were + p.p. will + be + p.p.	The song is liked by many people. The thief was caught by the police. Mars will be landed by man in 2001.
進行式	am/are/is + being + p.p. was/were + being + p.p.	The cat is being chased by dogs. When the rescue team found the man, he was being chased by a bear.
完成式	has/have + been + p.p. shall will + have + been + p.p.	The athletes have been trained for one year. The building will have been completed next month.

3. 特殊句型的被動語態

(1) 祈使句的被動語態：Let + 主詞 + be + p.p.

Let the thief be stopped stealing.

中譯 讓那個小偷停止偷竊。

文法解析

祈使句有兩種主動句型：(1) 原形動詞 (2)Let + 受詞 + 原形動詞 + 原形動詞的受詞，本句結尾於第二種變動語態句型：Let + 受詞 + be + p.p. + to + 原形動詞，所以 the thief 之後要用 be stopped。

(2) 具有感官 / 祈使句動詞句型的被動語態：主詞 + be + p.p. + to + 原形動詞

She was heard to sing a song.

中譯 她被人聽到在唱歌。

文法解析

這句中 heard 就是感官動詞，因為是被動語態，所以 heard 之後要接 to + 原形動詞。以下是本句的原主動語態句型轉變被動語態的句型的情形：

They heard her sing a song.

She was heard to sing a song (by them).

by them 表示一般的多數，所以可以省略。

4. 慣用句型的被動語態

(1) 主詞 + be + p.p. + by 之外的介系詞 + 受詞

例 1

The scientists are interested in the new virus.

中譯 那些科學家對新病毒有興趣。

文法解析

有些 be + p.p. 是被動語態的形式，卻表達主動的涵義，而且它們 p.p. 後面所接的介系詞是各有所不同，不是一般被動語態句子所接的介系詞 by。

主詞 +
$$
\begin{cases}
\text{absorbed, involved(專注於) + in} \\
\text{surprised, amazed, startled, shocked, astonished,} \\
\text{astounded(驚訝於～) + at} \\
\text{frightened, horrified, terrified(驚嚇於～) + at / by} \\
\text{distressed, annoyed, vexed(對～感到苦惱) + with + 受詞} \\
\text{be + pleased, delighted, amused(對～感到高興) + with} \\
\text{tired, wearied, exhausted, fatigued(因～而疲倦) + with} \\
\text{disappointed at(對～感到失望)，married to(嫁 / 娶)，engaged} \\
\text{to(與…訂婚)，satisfied with(滿意)，known to(為…所知道)}
\end{cases}
$$

例 2

Her mother is not satisfied with her grade.

中譯 她母親對她的成績不滿意。

文法解析

雖然本句動詞是被動語態的形式：is not satisfied with，但是卻沒有被動語態的涵義：對…不滿意。

(2) It is ＋p.p. ＋that 子句

例 1

It is said that there is water in Mars.

中譯　據說在火星有水存在。

文法解析

這是一種慣用的句型，以 It 爲虛主詞，眞正的主詞是後面的 that 子句，類似的句型還有：

It is/was ＋
$\begin{cases} \text{believed(據說)} \\ \text{reported(據報導)} \\ \text{expected(大家預期)} \\ \text{suggested(根據建議)} \\ \text{rumored(據傳言)} \\ \text{known(大家都知道)} \end{cases}$ ＋that 子句

上述的慣用被動句型常出現在新聞報導中的句中，表示一種普遍的看法。

例 2

It is reported that the ship eventually sank in the Pacific Ocean.

中譯　據報導那艘船最終沉沒於太平洋中。

文法解析

It is ＋p.p. 的動詞時式與 that 子句的時式常會不同，依據句子的上下文義而定。本句中船沉沒在先，報導在後，所以 It is 用現在簡單式，而 that 子句中的動詞用過去簡單式：sank。

(3) 主詞 +
$$\begin{cases} \text{need, want} \\ \text{require, deserve(值得)} \\ \text{merit(值得)} \end{cases}$$
+ Ving(動名詞)

例 1

The used car needs repairing.

中譯 那部舊車需要被修理。

文法解析

上述動詞常接不定詞做其受詞 (例：He needs to see a doctor.)。但是它們接動名詞時，是表示被動的涵義，所以本句也可相等於下列句型：

The used car needs repairing.

⟹ The used car needs to be repaired.

例 2

The villa deserves buying because of its splendid view.

中譯 因為它華麗的景觀，那棟別墅值得購買。

文法翻譯

deserve 一般是接不定詞做其受詞，但在本句中，它接動名詞時也是被動的涵義，它也可以等同 deserves to be bought。

(三) 動詞的語氣

動詞的語氣主要是指動詞的假設語氣，共計有五種基本的假設句型，分別以公式的方式說明如下：

1. 五種基本的假設語氣句型：

(1) 表示與過去事實相反的假設語氣句型

$$\text{If} + \text{主詞} + \text{had} + \text{p.p.}\cdots, \text{主詞} + \begin{Bmatrix} \text{would} \\ \text{should} \\ \text{could} \\ \text{might} \end{Bmatrix} + \text{have} + \text{p.p.}\cdots：$$

(那時) 若…，就…

例句

If Diana <u>had chosen</u> the correct box, she would have won the new car.

(103 年臺大轉學考)

中譯 如果黛安娜選對了箱子，她將贏得那部新車。

文法解析

> 從本句中的動詞時式就可看出它是表示與過去事實相反的假設：If 子句中用過去完成式 had chosen，主要子句中則用 would have won 這樣的動詞時式。這句的事實是：Diana didn't choose the correct box, so she didn't win the new car.(黛安娜沒有選對箱子，所以她沒有贏得新車。) 此種假設語氣的句子通常其動詞時式要比當時的事實所表達的時間早，所以 If 子句才用過去完成式，它比事實中的過去簡單式所表達的時間更早。

(2) 表示與現在事實相反的假設語氣句型

$$\text{If} + \text{主詞} + \text{過去簡單式動詞}\cdots, \text{主詞} + \begin{Bmatrix} \text{would} \\ \text{might} \\ \text{should} \\ \text{could} \end{Bmatrix} + \text{原形動詞}\cdots：$$

現在若…，就…

例 1

If he won a lottery of one million dollars, he would travel around the world.

中譯 若是他贏得百萬彩券，他將會環遊世界。

文法解析

> 本句表示一種與現在事實相反的假設情況，If 子句中要用過去簡單式，而主要子句則用 would + 原形動詞。本句的事實是：He does not win a lottery of one million dollars, so he will not travel around the world.(他沒有贏得百萬彩券，所以他不會去環遊世界。) 本句的假設語氣的動詞時式也是比表示事實的動詞時式要早：假設語氣的 If 子句中用過去簡單式，而表示事實的句子則用現在簡單式。

例 2

If he were a bird, he could fly to you.　　　　　　　　　(五專聯招)

中譯 如果他是隻鳥，他就能飛到你身邊。

文法解析

> 表示與現在事實相反的假設之 If 子句中要用過去簡單式。但是若是用 be 動詞時，則不論主詞是否為第三人稱單數 (he, she 或 it)，都要用 were 來表達。

(3) 表示未來發生可能性極小的假設語氣句型

$$\text{If} + 主詞 + \text{should} + 原形動詞\cdots,\ 主詞 + \begin{cases} \text{would} \\ \text{should} \\ \text{could} \\ \text{might} \end{cases} + 原形動詞\cdots:$$

萬一…，就…

例句

If the volcano near the city should erupt, it would be a huge natural disaster to the people living in the city.

中譯 萬一這座靠近城市的火山爆發，它對住在那城中的人而言就會是一場巨大的天然災難。

文法解析

> If 子句中用 should 作助動詞，表示一種可能性極小的情況，所以在意思上表示「萬一…，就…」的狀況。

(4) 表示未來絕不可能發生的假設性語氣句型

If + 主詞 + were to + 原形動詞…，主詞 + $\begin{Bmatrix} could \\ would \\ should \\ might \end{Bmatrix}$ + 原形動詞… :

如果…，才…

例句

If the sun were to rise in the west, she would marry the man.

中譯 如果太陽從西邊升起，她將會嫁給這位男士。

文法解析

> 從 If 子句中的 be 動詞 were 就知道這是與現在事實相反的事，亦即太陽不會從西邊升起，而 be + to + 原形動詞本來就是未來將發生的事，因此，結合兩者「were + to + 原形動詞」就表示這是一種未來不可能發生的事，所以本句是表示一種強烈否定的假設語氣。

(5) 綜合「與過去事實相反的假設句型」與「與現在事實相反
的假設句型」之假設句型

$$\text{If} + 主詞 + \text{had} + \text{p.p.}\cdots, 主詞 + \begin{cases} \text{would} \\ \text{should} \\ \text{could} \\ \text{might} \end{cases} + 原形動詞\cdots:$$

如果那時…，現在就…

例句

If I had stopped him from visiting the dangerous place then, he would not get hurt.

中譯 若是我那時阻止他們去那個危險的地方，他現在就不會受
傷了。

文法解析

> 表示過去的狀況影響到現在的情形的這種假設情況，是結合表示與過
> 去相反的假設句型和與現在事實相反的假設句型，因此採取一種，混
> 合兩種假設句型的方式來表達。

2. 基本假設句型的省略句型

在以上的五種基本句型中，有三種句型可轉變為簡化的句型
(1) 表示與過去相反的假設句型之省略句型

$$\text{Had} + 主詞 + \text{p.p.}\cdots, 主詞 + \begin{cases} \text{would} \\ \text{should} \\ \text{could} \\ \text{might} \end{cases} + \text{have} + \text{p.p.}\cdots:$$

如果 (那時)…，就…

Had I been sick, I would have missed the concert.　　　　（臺大轉學考）

中譯　若是當時我生病，我就會錯過那場音樂會。

文法解析

本句是由「與過去事實相反的假設句型」簡化而來：

If + 主詞 + had + p.p. ... ，主詞 + $\begin{cases} \text{would} \\ \text{should} \\ \text{could} \\ \text{might} \end{cases}$ + have + p.p. ...：

當時若…就…

⟹ ~~If~~ + 主詞 + had + p.p. ... ，主詞…。

⟹ Had + 主詞 + p.p. ... ，主詞…。

只有 If 子句簡化，主要句子不變。

(2) 表示與現在事實相反的假設句型之省略句型 (只有 be 動詞形式，不包括一般動詞)

Were + 主詞…，主詞 + $\begin{cases} \text{would} \\ \text{should} \\ \text{could} \\ \text{might} \end{cases}$ + 原形動詞…：

假如…，就…

例句

Were the rich man her father, she would live a luxurious life.

中譯　如果那個有錢人是她的父親，她就會過一種奢華的生活。

類似上一種「與過去事實相反的假設語氣」的省略句型，本句也是省略 If 和將動詞與主詞前後對調。

(3) 表示未來發生可能性極小的假設句型之省略句型

$$\text{Should} + 主詞 + 原形動詞\cdots\text{，}主詞 + \begin{cases} \text{would} \\ \text{should} \\ \text{could} \\ \text{might} \end{cases} + 原形動詞：$$

萬一…，就…

例句

Should World War III happen, there would be none surviving on the Earth.

中譯　萬一第三次世界大戰爆發，在地球上將無人生存。

文法解析

本句像上述兩種假設語氣的省略句型，也是省略 If 並將主詞與助動詞前後顛倒。由此可知，假設語氣的省略句型都是將 If 子句中的 If 省略並且將主詞與助動詞對調的模式。

3. 假設語氣的慣用句型

(1) 主詞 + wish (es) + that + 主詞 +
- 過去式 (表示與現在事實相反的假設)
- had + p.p.(表示與過去事實相反的假設)
- should/could/would/might + 原形動詞 (表示未來未能如願的事)

例 1

The teacher wishes that his students passed the entrance exam of that university.

中譯 那位老師希望他的學生通過那所大學的入學測驗。

文法解析

> wish 與 hope 的中文涵義是相同的,都表示「希望」。但是 wish 表示所希望的事並未成就,甚至是相反的結果,但是 hope 卻示可能會達成的希望。所以兩者在它們的隱涵義義是不同的,本句的 wish 是指現在發生的事與其期望之事相反,所以事實上他的學生沒有通過入學測驗:his students don't pass the entrance exam of that university。

例 2

The fireman wished that he had saved the old woman from her house afire.

中譯 那位消防隊員希望他能從那老夫人的房子中拯救她。

當 wished 是過去式時，其後的動詞要用過去完成式來表示一個「與過去事實相反的假設」，所以本句的意思是與字面的涵義相反，亦即那位消防隊員並沒有救出那位老婦人。

例 3

The singer's fans wish that they could see him at the airport.

中譯 那位歌星的歌迷希望他們能在機場見到他。

文法解析

wish 之後若用助動詞過去式 (could/should/would/might) 就表示一種與未來可能發生之事相反的情況。如本句中歌迷想在機場見他們的歌星偶像，卻未能如願。

(2) 主詞 + $\begin{cases} 1. 現在式動詞 \\ 2. 過去式動詞 \end{cases}$ + as if/though + 主詞 +

$$\begin{cases} 1. \begin{cases} were/ 過去式動詞 \\ had + p.p. \\ could/would/should/might + 原形動詞 \end{cases} \\ 2. had + p.p. \end{cases}$$

(…好像…。)

例 1

The child speaks as if he were an adult.

中譯 那個孩子說起話來好像他是大人。

as if 或 as though 是同樣的涵義之附屬連接詞，因爲其所引導的子句涵義所表示的不是眞的如此，所以 as if 子句中的動詞要用表示假設語氣的動詞，也就是比表示事實的動詞 (speaks) 更早的動詞：動詞過去式 were。

例2

The strong typhoon destroyed many wooden houses as if they had been bombed.

中譯 　那個強烈的颱風摧毀許多的木造房屋，好像它們是被轟炸過。

文法解析

像有 wish 的句子一樣，as if 子句前的動詞若是過去式，as if 子句中的動詞就要用比過去式更早的動詞時式：過去完成式 (had + p.p.)。

例3

These students look very confident as though they would pass the exam.

中譯 　這些學生看起來很有信心，好像他們會通過考試。

文法解析

as though 子句之前的動詞是現在簡單式動詞 look，所以學生看起來很有信心是現在發生的事，而通過考試則是未來才會發生的事，但是有時不一定是如此，所以就用 would + 原形動詞來表示。

(3) If only that + 主詞 + 假設語氣的動詞時式：但願⋯

例句

If only the rain would stop. （成大轉學考）

中譯 但願雨會停。

文法解析

> If only + that 子句的假設語氣句型，是表示與現在事實相反的假設，所以要用 would + 原形動詞，表示雨仍然在下，而希望它不要在下。

(4) But for + 名詞 / 名詞片語，主詞 + $\begin{cases} would \\ should \\ could \\ might \end{cases}$ + $\begin{cases} \text{have + p.p.(表示與過去事實的相反之假設)} \\ \text{原形動詞 (表示與現在事實相反之假設)} \end{cases}$:

若非⋯，就⋯

例 1

But for the doctor's help, the man in the train would have died.

中譯 若非那位醫生的幫忙，在火車上的那人早就死了。

文法解析

> But for 是接名詞或是名詞片語，本句是接 the doctor's help。但是從後面句子中的時式可以判斷這件事是發生在過去，並且表示與過去事與相反的假設，因此其時式是：would have + p.p.(died)。事實上，But for 就相當於 If + 主詞 + had + p.p. 的用法。

But for his adopted parent's assistance, the businessman would not be so successful.

中譯 若非他養父母的協助，那位商人不會如此成功。

文法解析

> 本句的助動式是 would + 原形動詞，所以表示與現在事實相反的假設情形，換言之，他現在是一個十分成功的商人。

◎重點整理◎

上述的動詞被動語態與假設語氣可以整理如下：

一、被動語態的句型
(一) 三種基本被動語態句型 & 被動語態的時式

種類	基本被動語態句型	時式	動詞形式
1	主詞 + be + p.p. + 介系詞 + 受詞	簡單式	am/are/is + p.p. was/were + p.p. will + be + p.p.
2	主詞 + be + p.p. + 主詞補語 + 介系詞 + 受詞	進行式	am/are/is + being + p.p. was/were + being + p.p.
3	主詞 1 + be + p.p. + 直接受詞 + by + 間接受詞 1 主詞 2 + be + p.p. + (介系詞) + 間接受詞 + by + 直接受詞 2	完成式	has/have + been + p.p. shall } + have + will been + p.p.

(二) 特殊句型的被動語態

    1. 祈使句的被動語態句型：Let + 主詞 + be + p.p.

    2. 具有感官、祈使動詞的句型之被動語態：主詞 + be + p.p.
      + to + 原形動詞

(三) 慣用句型的被動語態

    1. 主詞 + be + p.p. + by 之外的介系詞 + 受詞

    2. It is + p.p. + that 子句

    3. 主詞 + 特定動詞 (need/want/require/deserve/merit) +
      Ving(動名詞)

    4. (1) 主詞 + be + p.p. + by 之外的介系詞 + 受詞

      (2) It is + p.p. + that 子句

      (3) 主詞 + require, deserve(值得), merit, need, want + Ving(動名詞)

二、假設語氣的句型

(一) 五種基本的假設語氣句型

假設情況	動詞的假設句型
與過去事實相反的假設	If + 主詞 + had + p.p... ， 主詞 + { would / could / should / might } + have + p.p....
與現在事實相反的假設	If + 主詞 + 過去簡單式動詞…， 主詞 + { would / could / should / might } + 原形動詞…

假設情況	動詞的假設句型
未來發生可能性極小的假設	If + 主詞 + should + 原形動詞…， 主詞 + { would / could / should / might } + 原形動詞…
未來絕不可能發生的假設	If + 主詞 + were to + 原形動詞…， 主詞 + { would / could / should / might } + 原形動詞…
與過去事實相反的假設 ＋ 與現在事實相反的假設	If + 主詞 + had + p.p. …， 主詞 + { would / could / should / might } + 原形動詞…

(二) 三種基本假設句型的省略句型

與過去事實相反的假設	Had + 主詞 + p.p. ...，主詞 + { would / could / should / might } + have + p.p. …
與現在事實相反的假設	Were + 主詞…，主詞 + { would / could / should / might } + 原形動詞…

未來發生可能性極小的假設	Should + 主詞 + 原形動詞…, 主詞 + $\begin{cases} \text{would} \\ \text{could} \\ \text{should} \\ \text{might} \end{cases}$ + 原形動詞…

(三) 假設語氣的慣用句型

1. 主詞 + wish (es) + that + 主詞 +

   $\begin{cases} \text{過去式 (表示與現在事實相反的假設)} \\ \text{had + p.p.(表示與過去事實相反的假設)} \\ \text{should/could/would/might + 原形動詞 (表示未來未能如願之事)} \end{cases}$

2. 主詞 + $\begin{cases} \text{1. 現在式動詞} \\ \text{2. 過去式動詞} \end{cases}$ + as if/though + 主詞 +

   $\begin{cases} 1. \begin{cases} \text{were/ 過去式動詞} \\ \text{had + p.p.} \\ \text{could/would/should/might + 原形動詞} \end{cases} \\ 2. \text{had + p.p.} \end{cases}$

3. If only that + 主詞 + 假設性語氣的動詞時式…

4. But for + 名詞 / 名詞片語, 主詞 + $\begin{cases} \text{would} \\ \text{could} \\ \text{should} \\ \text{might} \end{cases}$ +

   $\begin{cases} \text{have + p.p.(表示與過去事實相反的假設)} \\ \text{原形動詞 (表示與現在事實相反的假設)} \end{cases}$

Exercise

一、選擇題：請從選項中選出最適合句子的答案選項

1. The painting _____ twice, most recently, in August 2004, with another Munch painting. (104 年政大碩士班)

   (A) has stolen (B) has been stolen (C) was stolen (D) had stolen

2. Passengers _____ to leave the priority seat for elderly people on public transportation.

   (A) suppose (B) are suppose (C) are supposed (D) has supposed

3. _____ your timely help, he could have failed.

   (A) But (B) Had it not been for (C) If it were not for (D) For

   (84 年二技入學測驗)

4. _____ some person overhearing what we talked about, or the news would not have been spread. (84 年二技入學測驗)

   (A) There could be   (B) It couldn't

   (C) It must be   (D) There must have been

5. If the old man hadn't ridden his grandson's tricycle down the hill, _____.

   (A) he couldn't have broken his leg

   (B) he will not break his leg (103 年臺大轉學考)

6. If Joseph had not gone to college, _____.

   (A) he would never have met his best friend, Marcel.

   (B) he would never meet his best friend, Marcel. (103 年臺大轉學考)

7. _____, she would have caught the train. (86 年二技入學測驗)

   (A) Had she hurried   (B) If she has hurried

   (C) If she hurried   (D) Had she had hurried

8. Benson told his wife, "If only I _____ that car!" as he saw it.

   (A) could buy (B) can buy (C) could have bought (D) would buy

9. _____ an enormous earthquake happen, along the sea, a tsunami might occur at the same time.

(A) Had　(B) Were　(C) Could　(D) Should

10. Though the police officer was not _____ the suspect's answer, he still released him.

(A) satisfied to　(B) satisfied with　(C) satisfy with　(D) satisfied in

二、文法挑錯題：請從下列句子中，挑出每句有文法錯誤的劃底線的部分

1. If a film exposes to light while it is being developed, the negatives will be
　　　　　　　(A)　　　　　　　　　　(B)　　　　　　　　　(C)
ruined
(D)

2. I thought Betty wanted to stay, but she was leaving right now
　　　　(A)　　　　　(B)　　　　(C)　　　(D)

3. The boy was given a present for his grandfather yesterday.
　　　　(A)　　　(B) (C)　　　　　(D)

4. It estimated that there are currently over 500,000 pieces of man-made
　　(A)　　　　　(B)　　　　　　　　　　　　　　(C)
trash orbiting the earth at speeds of up to 17,500 miles per hour.
　　　　　　　　　　(D)

5. Ground stations have built to monitor larger pieces of space trash to
　　　　　　(A)　　　　　　　(B)
prevent them from crashing into working satellites or space shuttles.
　　(C)　　　　　　(D)

6. The couple wished that their son was saved by the searching team after the
　　　　(A)　　　　　　　(B)　　　　　(C)
accident happened.
　　(D)

7. When the hunters saw the giant gray bear, they were so frightened as if
          (A)   (B)   (C)

    they saw a terrible monster.
          (D)

8. If the personal computer had not invented, will the information age have
        (A)   (B)

    arrived by other means?
          (C)   (D)

9. John was worried about the cost since last week when he heard prices
          (A)   (B)   (C)

    were rising.
        (D)

10. When he saw his cat in the street, it has chased by many dogs.
          (A)   (B)   (C)   (D)

Answers

一、

1. (B) 因為有表示「最近」時間的副詞 recently，所以要用現在完成
   式。而此動詞是事務 the painting，所以是用被動語態。綜合
   這兩種因素，所以要用現在完成式被動語態：has been stolen。

2. (C) be supposed to：應當，慣用表達。

3. (B) 與過去事實相反的假設語氣之省略句型：Had+ 主詞 +p.p...。
   因為本句後半句是表示與過事實時相反的假設句型：could
   have failed，所以前半句要用與過去事實相反的假設句型。

4. (D) 後半句是表示與過去事實相反的假設語氣句型：would not
   have been spread，所以前半句也應是表示與過去事實相反的
   假設句型，但是因為主詞 some person 在後，所以應用 There
   be 的句型。只有 (D) 切合文法型式。

5. (A) 從前半句可以判斷本句是表示「與過去事實相反的假設句

型」：would have broken

6. (A) 類似第 5 題的情況

7. (A) 本句是「與過去事實相反的假設語氣之省略句型」，因為後半句中的動詞是：would have+p.p，所以 Had 至於句首。主詞在後，型成倒裝句型。

8. (C) Only if+that 子句，若表示過去的願望，要用 could have+p.p 的動詞時式。

9. (D) 因為主詞 (an enormous earthquake) 之前還有助動詞，加上後半句是表示假設語氣的動詞，所以前面空格應是過去式的助動詞，根據前後文的涵義，是指「萬一」的情況下，所以要用助動詞 should.

10. (B) be satisfied with：滿足於…

二、

1. (A) exposes → is exposed

2. (D) was leaving → is leaving

3. (C) for → to

4. (A) It estimated → It is estimated

5. (A) have built → have been built

6. (B) was saved → had been saved

7. (D) saw → had seen

8. (B) will → would

9. (D) were rising → rising

10. (C) has chased → has been chased

(四) 主詞 (Subject)

    主詞的形式：1. 名詞 2. 名詞片語 3. 名詞子句 4. 代名詞

1. 名詞：(1) 單個名詞 (2) 複合名詞

(1) 單個名詞依其種類可分為下列各種名詞：

① 普通名詞

例 1

The lion is the king of beasts.

中譯 獅子為萬獸之王。

文法解析

> lion 是普通名詞，有單複數形式 (a lion/lions)。但是表示同種類的全體概念時，可用 the + 普通名詞來表示全體，所以本句中 The lion 不是特指那一隻獅子，而是代表所有的獅子。此外，用單數或複數也是如此。
>
> 請看下列說明：
>
>   The lion is the king of beasts.
>
> = Lions are the king of beasts.
>
> = A lion is the king of beasts.
>
> 一般而言，名詞的單、複數做主詞時在涵義上是相同的，並不需強

調它的單、複數之涵義；例如，A car is a modern invention 和 Cars are modern invention(汽車是現代的發明。) 是同樣的涵義。

例2

The rich often despise the poor.

中譯 富人經常瞧不起窮人。

文法解析

The + 形容詞 = 複數名詞。所以句中的 the rich = rich people, the poor = poor people。這是一種特殊的複數名詞之形式。

② 集合名詞

例1

When people feel uncomfortable or nervous, they may fold their arms across their chests as if to protect themselves. (98 年學測)

中譯 當人們覺得不舒服或緊張時，他們可能會兩臂交叉在胸前，好像要保護自己。

文法解析

集合名詞是「沒有複數形式 (字尾加 s/es) 卻有複數涵義的名詞。」因此，本句中的 people(人們) 是複數涵義的集合名詞 (沒有 s 的複數形式)。所以句中的動詞用複數動詞 feel。其他類似的集合名詞還有：family(家人)，furniture(傢俱)，cattle(牛)，clergy(神職人員)，audience(觀眾)，committee(委員)，faculty(全體教職員)，staff(員工)，mob(爆民) 等等。再看一例：My family are all well and they live in Taipei now.

例2

There are many different peoples in Singapore.

中譯 　在新加坡有許多不同的民族。

文法解析

> 有些集合名詞因爲涵義不同，而轉變成普通名詞，要以單數或複數的
> 形式來呈現。像本句中的 people 在本句中作「民族」解釋，所以它是
> 以普通名詞呈現，要以複數名詞 peoples 來表達。其他類似的集合名詞
> 還有：family(家庭，家族)，committee(委員會)。

③ 專有名詞

例1

Ta Chi Chuan is a type of ancient Chinese martial art.

中譯 　太極拳是一種古代的武術。

文法解析

> 專有名詞的字首要大寫，因爲「太極拳」是一種唯一而專有的用詞，
> 所以沒有複數的形式，也沒有單數 (a/an) 的形式，是不可數名詞，要
> 用單數動詞 is。

例2

President Obama was protested by many people outside the meeting.

中譯 　歐巴馬總統遭到會場外的人們抗議。

文法解析

> 稱謂或頭銜在英文中一定字首要大寫，所以本句中總統要用大寫
> President。它也是一種專有名詞的形式，因此要用單數動詞 was，其他
> 像 Mr., Mrs, Miss, Manger, Chairperson 等都是如此。

例 3

The Titanic sank in the North Atlantic Ocean in the early morning of 15
April, 1912.

中譯　鐵達尼號於一九一二年四月十五日清早沉沒於北大西洋
　　　中。

文法解析

鐵達尼號是一艘遊輪的名稱，所以是專有名詞，字首要大寫，並且
加上 the 於其前。其他像公司，公共建築物，學校，國名，街道名
稱，山川名稱，家族名稱等專有名詞，大部分都要加 the 於其前，並
且大寫。例如：The Tatung Company(大同公司)，The National Palace
Museum(故宮博物院)，The University of Oxford(牛津大學)，The Lincoln
Street(林肯街)，The Republic of China(中華民國)，The Alps(阿爾卑斯
山)，The Smiths(史密斯家庭) 等等。

例 4

The blind Chinese woman will become a Helen Keller of China.

中譯　那個眼盲的中國婦女將成為中國的海倫‧凱勒。

文法解析

a/an＋聞名的人、事、地或物可以表示「一個像…的人 / 事 / 地 / 物」，
例如：Shanghai is a New York of China.(上海是中國的紐約)，指兩者皆
是各自國家的臨海重要的大都會。

④ 物質名詞

例 1

All creatures need water to survive.

中譯 所有的生物都需要水才能生存。

文法解析

> 物質名詞也是不可數名詞，所以沒有單、複數的形式。其動詞也要用
> 單數動詞，例如：Too much salt is harmful to our health. 凡是不到的一個
> 個數算的名詞，大都是物質名詞，像 sugar, iron, gold, wheat, rice, coffee,
> tea, juice, oil, bread, meat 等等皆是。

例 2

The housewife bought two bottles of wine for her husband.

中譯 那位家庭主婦爲他先生買了兩瓶酒。

文法解析

> 物質名詞爲不可數名詞，亦即：數量 + 計量單位 + of + 物質名詞，這
> 種方式也可以在計量單位之後加 s/es 的複數形式來表達複數的涵義，
> 但是物質名詞本身仍不能以複數形式呈現，請看下列例子說明：

數量	計量單位	of	物質名詞	
two	cups	of	water	兩杯水
three	sheets	of	paper	三張紙
two	spoons	of	sugar	兩匙糖
four	bowls	of	rice	四碗米
five	slices	of	meat	五片肉
six	gallons	of	oil	六加侖油

例 3

The ship sailed across the waters of the Strait of Malacca.

中譯 那艘船航行過馬六甲海峽的水域。

文法解析

> 有些物質名詞以複數形式出現時，有不同的意涵。像本句中的 waters 就作「水域」解釋，而非「水」解釋。類似的字還有 woods(樹林)，glasses(眼鏡)。

⑤ 抽象名詞

例 1

The political pundit's advice exercises the opinion of the vast majority of the voters. (104 淡江碩士班入學考)

中譯 那位政治權威人士操弄他對大多數選民的建議。

文法解析

> 抽象名詞也是不可數名詞，所以其後的動詞是用單數動詞。advice(建議) 是抽象名詞，所以其後用單數動詞 exercises。其他表示抽象概念的皆是抽象名詞，像 strength(力量)，power(權力)，benefit(利益)，virtue(美德) 等等皆是。

例 2

Princess Diana was a beauty that attracted many people's attention in the ceremony.

中譯 在典禮中黛安娜是一位吸引許多人注意的美女。

有些抽象名詞做不同的解釋時，會轉變成可數名詞，有單、複數的形式。所以本句中的 a beauty(一位美女) 即是可數名詞，它與作「美麗」解釋的 beauty 在詞性上不同，因為 beauty(美麗) 是抽象名詞。類似的用法還有如下表所列：

抽象名詞	字義	普通名詞	字義
abstract	抽象	abstract (s)	摘要
accommodation	適應	accommodation (s)	住宿
room	空間	room (s)	房間
work	工作	work (s)	作品
wonder	驚奇	wonder (s)	奇觀
youth	年輕	youth (s)	青年
spectacle	光景	spectacles	眼鏡
beauty	美	beauties	美女
art	藝術	arts	技能
shock	打擊	shocks	震動
tone	風格	tones	音調
stress	壓力	stresses	重音

(2) 複合名詞

① 兩個字組合而成的複合名詞

例 1

Alice is Tom's girlfriend, who is a nurse in a hospital.

中譯 愛麗絲是湯姆的女朋友，她是一所醫院中的護士。

由兩個字組成的複合名詞，在英文單字中非常的多。涵義也是由這兩個字的字義結合而成，例如，bookshelf(書架)，roommate(室友)，housewife(家庭主婦)，bartender(酒保)，housekeeper(管家)，mankind(人類)，manmade(人工製品)，heartbeat(心跳)等等。

例 2

The boy's father was a rich man and sent him to a private school to study.

中譯 那男孩的父親是一位有錢人，並且送他去私校讀書。

文法解析

有些複合名詞是分開的兩個字，但是卻是綜合兩個字的字義之名詞，有點類似中文的字詞。例如，post office(郵局)，bus driver(公車司機)，seatbelt(安全帶)，alarm clock(鬧鐘)等等。

② 由連字符號 (–) 所連接而成的複合名詞

例 1

The missing he–goat was found in the desert.

中譯 那隻失蹤的公山羊在沙漠中被找到。

文法解析

這類的複合名詞之字義可從兩個組合的字之字義而得知。本句中的 he 是指男性的「他」，所以放在 goat(山羊)的名詞前，就形成「公山羊」的字義。其他類似的字還有：she–god(女神)，re–creation(改造物)。

His mother–in–law doesn't like him because she thinks him poor.

中譯　他的岳母不喜歡他，因為她認為他窮。

文法解析

有些英文複合名詞是三個字組合而成，如本句中的 mother–in–law，它的複數形式是在第一個字後加 s/es，所以 mothers–in–law 就是複數形式。其他類似的字還有：brothers–in–law(姊夫、妹夫)，lookers–on(參觀者)，editors–in–chief(總編輯)。

2.　名詞片語：(1) 不定詞片語 (2) 動名詞片語 (3) 介系詞片語

(1)　不定詞片語：to + 原形動詞

例 1

To master English needs a lot of practice and patience.

中譯　精通英文需要許多的練習與耐心。

文法解析

不定時片語可以作主詞用，所以本句中的 To master English 就是本句的主詞。而不定詞作主詞時，動詞一定要用單數動詞，因為不定詞片語被視為一件事情，不論其中的名詞是否為複數。例如，To collect stamps is an interesting hobby. 本句中的 stamps 雖然是複數但是仍然用單數動詞 is。

例 2

It is easy for us to tell our friends from our enemies. 　　(100 年學測)

中譯　對我們而言，要分辨敵友是容易的。

有種特殊句形式將作主詞的不定詞片語移到句尾，而又 It 代替它原來
的位置作虛主詞，以避免主詞過長的問題。其句型如下：

It is + 形容詞 + (for + 代名詞受詞 / 名詞) + to + V

(↑虛主詞)　　　　　　　　　　　　　　　(↑真正的主詞)

(2) 動名詞片語：Ving

例句

Pushing a wheelchair is not really as easy as it looks.

(104 年初等地方特考)

中譯　推輪椅不是真的像它看起來那麼簡單。

文法解析

動名詞片語可以置於句首作主詞用。本句中 Pushing a wheelchair 就是
名詞片語作主詞用。其後的動詞都是單數，因為動名詞片語被視為一
件事，所以不論動名詞後面接的是否為複數，仍要用單數動詞。例如
Saving people from fire is the task of firemen，people 是複數，但是動詞仍
然用單數 is。

(3) 介系詞片語：介系詞 + 名詞

例句

Over the border is Mexico.

中譯　越過邊境就是墨西哥。

文法解析

Over the border 在此是介系詞片語作主詞用，over 是介系詞加名詞 the
border，通常是用來加強語氣的用法。

3. 名詞子句：(1)That 子句作主詞 (2)Wh– 子句作主詞
(1) That 子句作主詞

例句

That the scientist won the Noble Prize was well–known to the world.

中譯 那位贏得諾貝爾獎的科學家是舉世聞名的。

文法解析

> That 子句若置於句首都是作名詞子句用，因為 That 子句是句中的主格。所以其後的動詞要用單數動詞：was。

(2) Wh– 子句作主詞

例 1

What also needs to be admitted is that the customer is a human being.

(89 年二技入學測驗)

中譯 還有必須承認的是顧客也是人。

文法解析

> Wh– 開頭的子句，若在句首，都作名詞子句用。所以本句中的 what... 也是名詞子句作句子的主格。is 之後 that 子句則是作主詞補語用，也是名詞子句。

例 2

Who saw the murderer is the key of this criminal case.

中譯 誰看到兇手是這件刑事案件的關鍵。

Wh– 的形式開頭的名詞子句在涵義上仍是具有原意，如本句中的 who 的涵義仍是誰，但已不是問句的口氣，而是表示一般的敘述，其他類似的還有：

$$
\left.\begin{array}{l}
\text{When} \\
\text{Where} \\
\text{Which} \\
\text{What} \\
\text{How}
\end{array}\right\} + 主詞 + 動詞 + 主要動詞（單數）
$$

4. 代名詞：(1) 人稱代名詞 (2) 指示代名詞 (3) 所有 (格) 代名詞 (4) 不定代名詞

(1) 人稱代名詞

例 1

Alice is hard to argue with because she is obstinate.

中譯 愛麗絲是很難理論的，因為她很固執。

文法解析

代名詞可以作主詞，在閱讀中代名詞代替先前提過人，所以本句中的 Mary，由 she 所取代。

下列是人稱代名詞的所有用法：

人稱	性	單複數	主格	受格	所有格		反身代名詞
					形容詞	代名詞	
第一人稱	通性	單數	I	me	my	mine	myself
		複數	we	us	our	ours	ourselves

人稱	性	單複數	主格	受格	所有格 形容詞	所有格 代名詞	反身代名詞
第二人稱	通性	單數	you	you	your	yours	yourself
		複數					yourselves
第三人稱	陰陽各表	單數	he	him	his	his	himself
		複數	she	her	her	hers	herself
		單數	it	it	its		itself
		複數	they	them	their	theirs	themselves

例2

It rained heavily when the typhoon came to Taiwan.

中譯 當那個颱風來到臺灣時，雨下得很大。

文法解析

it 原是取代事物的代名詞。但是在本句中，it 並非特指本句中的事物 (it ≠ typhoon)，在此情況下，it 通常是表示「天氣、季節、時間、距離」等事物。It 也不能作「它」解釋，而是要依據前、後文來解釋。例如，It is midnight now.(現在是午夜了。) 本句中的 It 就是指「時間」(It = the time)。再看一例，It is twenty miles from Taipei to Taoyuan.(臺北到桃園的距離是二十英哩。)It = the distance.(It 就是指距離)。

(2) 指示代名詞

① this, these, that & those 的用法

例1

The climate of Tokyo is cooler than that of Taipei in fall.

中譯 在秋天東京的氣候比臺北的氣候更涼爽。

that 是指示代名詞，在本句的比較句型中，一定要用 that 代替前面的 climate，以避免重複，而如果前面是複數的名詞，則要用 those 來取代，其句型式如下：

$$\text{The} + 名詞 + 介系詞 + \begin{cases} 單數名詞 \\ \\ 複數名詞 \end{cases} \text{than} + \begin{cases} \text{that} \\ \\ \text{those} \end{cases} 介系詞 + 名詞：$$

…比…更…

再看一例：The houses in London are more expensive than those in Taipei.

例2

Those who shy away from social contacts are seen to be stubborn and indecisive, to be mistrustful or prone to jealousy, or to overreact to certain situations with a sharp temper. （東吳轉學考）

中譯 凡是避開社會接觸的人被視為固執、優柔寡斷，猜疑人的或傾向嫉妒，或者以急躁的性情對某種情況過度反應。

文法解析

those who + 子句：凡是…的人，是一種慣用的表達，所以一定要用 those 來作先行詞，這類的用法常出現在格言或如俗諺中，例如，God helps those who help themselves.(天助自助者。)

He is allergic to weather change. <u>This</u> makes him sneeze easily.

中譯 他對天氣改變過敏。這使他的鼻子容易打噴嚏。

文法解析

This 不僅可以取代個別的單字，也可以表示其前提過的整個句子。所以在本題中的 This = He is allergic to weather change. That 也有類似的功用，指示用法稍有不同，請看下列說明：

<u>Tell</u> him to meet me, and <u>that</u> at once.(告訴他來見我，並且立刻如此。)

② such & so 的用法

例 1

Pizza is covered with all kinds of ingredients, <u>such as</u> oliver oil, herbs and meat.

中譯 披薩被各種食材覆蓋，像橄欖油、香草、和肉這類的食材。

文法解析

such as：像…這類的…。它是 such 作指示代名詞，代替其前的名詞，as 作「像… 」解釋，是介系詞，所以其後接名詞，所以 such as 就作「像…這類的… 」解釋。本句中的 such 取代 ingredients(食材)，所以後面的都是用在披薩中的食材。

例 2

A: Do you think the global warming is a serious problem?

B: Yes, I think <u>so</u>.

中譯 甲：你認爲全球暖化是一個嚴重的問題嗎？

乙：是的，我這樣認爲。

文法解析

> so 在本句中是取代 the global warming is a serious problem 這一句，它作代名詞。so 可以取代片語或句子。

(3) 所有 (格) 代名詞

例 1

Gary's house is very expensive. In contrast, mine is very cheap.

中譯 蓋瑞的房子非常貴。對照之下，我的房子就很便宜。

文法解析

> 因爲前、後兩句是比較同類的事物：house，所以後面一句的同類事物 house 就可以用所有格代名詞 mine 取代 my house，以避免重覆。mine 在此句中是位於主格，所以所有代名詞也可以作主詞用。

例 2

Mary's flowers are blooming, but yours are withering.

中譯 瑪麗的花正在盛開，但你的花正在枯萎。

文法解析

> 後一句的 yours = your flowers，所以 yours 可以取代複數也可以取代單數，像上一例句所顯示的。所有代名詞也有單複數之分，例如，mine = my + 名詞，只是後面所接的名詞單複數皆可。詳細的所有 (格) 代名詞請參閱前面所列的表格。

(4) 不定代名詞

① one, the other, another 的用法

例 1

One of the world's most powerful women is Oprah Winfrey.

中譯 世界最有權勢的女人之一是歐普拉・溫弗瑞。

文法解析

> one(某一者) 是不定代名詞，代替一個非特定的人或事物。例如，
> There are many books in the shelf and I choose one from them. 本句中的 one
> 是指 many books 中的任一本。此外，常用的 one 句型就是本例句所顯
> 示的：One of the + 複數名詞 + 單數動詞… : …中的之一。

例 2

The two children may look exactly the same to you, but the parent has no
trouble telling one from the other.   (103 年地方特考)

中譯 這兩個孩子對你而言可能看起來完全一樣，但是其父母在
辨識其中一人與另一人的差異上就毫無困難。

文法解析

> one ...; the other ...(一者…，剩下一者…。) 是一種慣用句型，是指兩者
> 中的一者與另一者。例如：The man has two dogs: One is black; the other is
> white.

例 3

Four prisoners escaped from the local jail. One of them was caught by the
police nearby; another was found in an abandoned house.

中譯 四個犯人從當地的監獄逃脫。他們其中一人在附近被警方逮捕；另有一人在一間荒棄的屋中被尋獲。

文法解析

another 是指非特定的另一者。所以本句中的 another 是代替 four prisoners(四個犯人) 中的任一者，another 與 the other 之差異在於 the other 只能用於兩者中的其中之一，而 another 則不受數目的限制，可以指三者 (含三者) 以上的任何一者。

② some... others... 的用法

例句

A storm struck the ship at sea. Some on the ship got drown; others were saved by another ship.

中譯 一個暴風襲擊那艘在海上的船。有些在船上的人溺死，有些人則被另一艘船救起。

文法解析

some 在本句中是代名詞，others 也是代名詞，但是兩者必須一前一後搭配，因為它們是慣用的句型。其涵義則作：有些…；有些…的解釋，不能依其存有涵義作：有些…其他…的解釋。

③ each, either, neither 的用法

例 1

Venomous snakes are always dangerous. Each of them may be injurious or even lethal to other creatures.

中譯 毒蛇總是危險的。牠們每一種對其他的生物可能都會造成傷害或致死。

文法解析

Each 在本句中作代名詞用，取代 every venomous snake(每一種毒蛇)。
Each 是因爲單數代名詞，所以其後的動詞要用單數動詞。其相關的句
型爲：

$$\text{Each of} + \begin{cases} 代名詞 \\ \\ \text{the} + 名詞 \end{cases} + 單數名詞\cdots : \cdots 之中的每一\cdots$$

例2

Waitress: Which do you prefer, tea or coffee？

Customer: Either will do.

中譯 　侍者：你比較喜歡何者，茶或咖啡？

　　　　顧客：任何一者皆可。

文法解析

either 在本句中作代名詞，作「任一者」解釋。Either 是取代兩者中的
任一者，所以其代替的對象都是兩個人或兩件事物中的任何一者。
因此，本句中 either 取代的問句中的茶或咖啡中的任一者。再看另外
一種相關的用法：

$$\text{Either of} + \begin{cases} \text{the} + 名詞 \\ \\ 代名詞 \end{cases} + 單數動詞\cdots :$$

$$\cdots(兩者) 之中的任一\cdots$$

例 3

The police found two suspects involved into the murder, but neither of them admitted murdering the woman.

中譯 警方發現涉及那件謀殺的兩位嫌犯，但是他們倆人都否認謀殺那女人。

文法解析

neither(兩者都不⋯) 是取代兩者的否定涵義之代名詞。所以本句中的 neither of them 應作「他們兩人都不⋯」之解釋。neither 的否定對象一定是兩者。本句中呈現 neither 的特殊句型：

$$\text{neither of} + \begin{cases} \text{the} + 名詞 \\ \\ 代名詞 \end{cases} + 複數動詞\cdots : 兩者都不\cdots$$

④ few, a few, both, many, several 的用法

$$\begin{rcases} \text{Few} \\ \text{A few} \\ \text{Both} \\ \text{Many} \\ \text{Several} \end{rcases} + \text{of} + \begin{cases} \text{the} + 複數名詞 \\ 代名詞受格 \end{cases} + 複數動詞\cdots : \begin{cases} 幾乎沒有\cdots \\ 一些\cdots \\ 兩者\cdots \\ 許多\cdots \\ 幾個\cdots \end{cases}$$

例 1

The earthquake was so intensive that few of the villagers survived.

中譯 那個地震是非常強烈，以至於那些村民幾乎沒人存活。

few 在本句中是代名詞，代替村民 (villagers)。它的涵義是「幾乎沒有；很少」所以本句是部分否定的表達。few 相關的句型是：few of the + 複數名詞 + 複數動詞。few 是只能取代可數名詞，不能取代不可數名詞。

例 2

Two persons were saved by the firemen from the big fire and both of them were hurt by the fire.

中譯 兩個人被那位消防員從大火中救出，並且他們兩人都被火燒傷。

文法解析

both 是指兩者，包括人或事物。所以本句中的 both of them 是指那兩個被消防員救出來的人。both 有時會和 and 合用，但那是 both 作形容詞用。both 的相關用法是：

$$\text{both of} + \begin{cases} \text{the + 名詞} \\ \\ \text{代名詞} \end{cases} + \text{複數動詞} \cdots : \text{兩者都} \cdots$$

例 3

Many of Taiwan's young people face unemployment.

中譯 臺灣的許多年輕人面臨失業。

Many 在本句是代名詞，代替 many young people。因爲 many 是用在可
數名詞，所以其後的名詞一定是複數名詞並且動詞也要用複數(face)。
其相關的句型是：

$$
\text{Many of} + \begin{cases} \text{the} + 名詞 \\ \\ 代名詞 \end{cases} + 複數名詞 + 複數動詞
$$

例 4

The police attacked the base of the terrorists, and <u>several</u> of them escaped
from the base.

中譯　警方攻擊恐怖份子的基地並且有幾個恐怖份子從基地逃
　　　　脫。

文法解析

several(幾個) 在本句中是不定代名詞，取代 terrorists。因爲 several 是
複數的代名詞，所以其後的名詞與動詞都是複數。其相關的句型如
下：

$$
\text{Several of} + \begin{cases} \text{the} + 複數名詞 \\ \\ 代名詞 \end{cases} + 複數動詞… : …之中的幾個…
$$

⑤ a little, little, much 的用法

$$
\left.\begin{array}{l}
\text{A little} \\
\text{Little} \\
\text{Much}
\end{array}\right\} \text{of} + \text{不可數名詞} + \text{單數動詞}
$$

例 1

A little of the toxic substance in the drinking water makes people sick.

中譯 飲用水中的毒性物質只要一點點就會使人生病。

文法解析

為了強調「一點點」的涵義，用 A little 作代名詞用，代替 toxic substance(毒性物質)。因為 A little 適用於不可數名詞，所以 A little 後面所接的名詞是不可數名詞 (substance)，動詞也要用單數 makes。

例 2

Little of the polluted water flowed to the river after the experts stopped the water flowing from the big container.

中譯 在專家阻止水從那個大容器流出後，幾乎沒有污染的水流入河中。

文法解析

Little 是作「幾乎沒有」解釋，並且用來取代不可數名詞，所以 Little of 後面是不可數名詞 water，而 Little 的相關句型是：

$$
\text{Little of} + \left\{\begin{array}{l}
\text{the} + \text{不可數名詞} \\
\\
\text{代名詞}
\end{array}\right\} + \text{單數動詞}
$$

Little of 與 A little of 最大不同在於 Little of 是部分否定的涵義。

例3

The gold in the bank was stolen and <u>much of it</u> was found in a deserted house.

中譯 在銀行裏的黃金被盜走，其中許多黃金在廢棄的屋中找到。

文法解析

much 在本句中作代名詞用，取代不可數名詞 gold(也就是 it 所代表的)，所以其後的動詞要用單數 was stolen。與 much 相關的句型如下：

much of $\begin{cases} \text{the} + 不可數名詞 \\ \\ 代名詞 \end{cases}$ + 單數動詞… : …許多…

⑥ all, most, some, any, half, the rest 的用法

$\left.\begin{array}{l} \text{All}(\ 所有\ ) \\ \text{Most}(\ 大多數\ ) \\ \text{Some}(\ 有些\ ) \\ \text{Any}(\ 有些\ ) \\ \text{Half}(\ 一半\ ) \\ \text{The rest}(\ 其餘\ ) \end{array}\right\}$ + of + the $\begin{cases} 複數名詞 + 複數動詞 \\ \\ \\ 不可數名詞 + 單數動詞 \end{cases}$

例 1

Seven people with their guide climbed Mt. Everest and all of them died from sudden avalanche from the mountain.

中譯 七個人與他們的嚮導攀登艾佛勒斯峰，他們所有人都在一個突如其來的山上雪崩中罹難。

文法解析

All 在本句中是取代其前半句中的七人 (seven people) 與他們的嚮導 (their guide)。所以句中的 them 是指這七人，而 all 則用來強調所有七人都罹難。All of 之後可以接可數名詞或不可數名詞，也可接相關的複數動詞或單數動詞，所以決定 all 可以接何種動詞在於 all 之後的名詞是可數或不可數名詞。

例 2

For most of us, the holidays are a great time to gather family.

中譯 對我們大多數人而言，假日是家人聚集的美好時光。

文法解析

most 在本句中是取代「我們」(us) 的代名詞，most 之後可數或不可數名詞，其後的動詞也依所接的名詞而可接單數動詞或複數動詞，其相關的句型如下：

$$
\text{Most of} + \begin{cases} \text{代名詞 / 可數名詞} \\ \\ \text{不可數名詞} \end{cases} + \begin{cases} \text{複數動詞} \\ \\ \text{單數動詞} \end{cases} \cdots :
$$

…的大多數…

例 3

In 1973, <u>some</u> of the countries that sold oil to the United States stopped selling it.

中譯 在一九七三年，某些賣石油給美國的國家停止銷售給它。

文法解析

some 在本句中是取代 some countries 的代名詞，some 之後可接可數或不可數名詞，而句中的主要動詞也是依據some 之後所接的名詞而定。因此，本句中的 some 之後應用複數動詞，但是因為是過去式所以沒有差別。但是 some of 這樣的用法只能用於肯定句中。

例 4

<u>Any</u> of the people who don't get permission are not allowed to enter this area.

中譯 任何未得到允許的人不得進入此一區域。

文法解析

Any 在本句中是取代 any people，它的用法與 some 類似，其後都可接可數或不可數名詞以及與名詞單複數一致的複數或單數動詞。但是 any 在涵義上與句型上與 some 有所不同，any 在本句中作「任何」解釋而且any 只能用在否定、疑問以及條件句中，但不能用於肯定句中。

例 5

During the civil war of Syria, almost <u>half</u> of her citizens fled from the country to other nations like Italy and Turkey.

中譯 在敘利亞內戰期間，幾乎她半數的國民都從該國逃離到其他像義大利和土耳其這些國家。

文法解析

half 在句中作代名詞,代替 half citizens,爲了強調,所以用 half of(…的一半) 來加強語氣。half of 之後可接可數或不可數名詞,以及與名詞單複數一致的複數或單數動詞。

例 6

The tsunami destroyed most of the houses of the island and <u>the rest of the houses of the island</u> were badly damaged.

中譯 那個海嘯摧毀了那座島上大部分的房屋,島上剩下的房子都嚴重的受損。

文法解析

rest 在本句中作「剩下;剩餘」解釋。其後可接可數或不可數名詞,rest of 的句型如下:

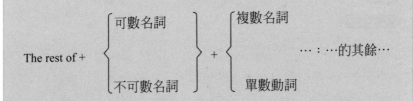

此句型與其他相似用法的句型之差異在於 rest 之前要加 the。

(五) 受詞 (Object)

受詞的形式：1. 名詞 2. 名詞片語 3. 名詞子句 4. 代名詞

1. 名詞作受詞

例 1

Now even restaurants and grocery stores have prepared such detectors.

中譯 現今甚至餐廳和雜貨店都有準備這樣的偵測器。

文法解析

detectors(偵測器) 作 prepared 這個動詞的受詞。such 是指示形容詞，作「這樣的」解釋。

例 2

The greatest threat to the security lies in the tribal regions of Pakistan, where terrorists train the insurgents to strike into Afghanistan.

中譯 對那項安全最大的威脅來自於巴基斯坦的部落地區，在那裏恐怖份子接受訓練，並且也從那裏出擊阿富汗。

文法解析

本句中的 lie in(在於) 以及 strike into(出擊) 都是動詞片語，都可以接受名詞或代名詞作其受詞，像 the tribal regions of Pakistan 及 Afghanistan。大部分的動詞片語都可接名詞作受詞，只有少數的動詞片語不接受詞，如 drop by(順道拜訪)。

2. 名詞片語作受詞

例 1

The athlete was very confident in winning the contest because she has prepared for the competition for at least one year.

中譯 那位選手對贏得那場比賽非常有信心，因為她已經準備那
場競賽至少一年了。

文法解析

> was confident in(對…有信心) 是形容詞片語，是一種習慣用法，所以
> 其介系詞之後可接動名詞作其受詞，具它類似的還有像：be sure of(確
> 定)，be glad of(高興)，be proud of(以…為傲), be capable of(能夠)，be
> aware of(留意)，be afraid of(害怕)，be considerate of(體貼)。

例 2

The manager verbally agreed to rent his apartment to me.　　(105 年指考)

中譯 那位經理口頭上同意將他的公寓租給我。

文法解析

> 不定詞片語置於及物動詞之後時作名詞片語用，是動詞的受詞。所以
> 本句中的 to rent his apartment to me 是 agreed 的受詞。某些動詞可以接
> 不定詞片語作其受詞，例如：decide, determine，等等。但是有些卻需
> 要先接受詞，再接不定詞，如以下所示：
>
> 主詞 + { allow, ask, decide / refuse, resolve / pretend, agree / intend, manage } + 受詞 + to + 原形 V

例 3

His wife avoided disturbing him when he talked to his boss.

中譯 當他和他的老闆談話時，他太太會避免打擾他。

文法解析

有些動詞後必須接動名詞作受詞，不能用不定詞。本句中的 avoid(避免) 即是此類動詞，其他相同情形的動詞還有：

$$主詞 + \begin{cases} \text{enjoy, mind, delay, quit} \\ \text{finish, deny, imagine} \\ \text{admit, suggest, appreciate} \end{cases} + \text{Ving}$$

3. 名詞子句作受詞

例 1

In Kenya, researchers found that elephants react differently to clothing worn by men of the Maasai and Kamba ethnic groups.　　(100 年學測)

中譯 在肯亞，研究者發現大象對馬賽與肯巴族群的人所穿的衣服有不同的反應。

文法解析

that elephants react... groups 是名詞子句，作 found 的受格，因為 that 子句是置於 found 之後，所以 that 子句是作名詞子句用。其他以 wh- 開頭的子句也可在及物動詞之後作受格；例如：She knows what his son found. Wh- 作名詞子句時，其後是先接主詞，再接受詞。

Dr.Begall and her colleagues wanted to know <u>whether larger mammals also have the ability to perceive magnetic fields.</u>   (98 年學測)

中譯 貝格爾醫生和她的同事想要知道較大的哺乳動物是否也有察覺磁場的能力。

文法解析

whether larger mammals... fields 是名詞子句作 know 的受格。whether 也可換作 if，涵義與用法皆不變，例如：The women wondered if/whether the man truly loved her.

4. 代名詞作受詞

例 1

He that commits a fault thinks everyone speaks of <u>it</u>.

中譯 做賊心虛。

文法解析

it 作介系詞 of 的受詞。本句是一句俗諺。commits a fault 作「犯錯」解釋。speak of：談到；說到。

例 2

Every ass likes to hear <u>himself</u> bray.

中譯 馬不知臉長。

文法解析

himself 是與指 ass，所以本句中的主詞 ass 與 himself 都是同者。反身代名詞可以作受格，如果主詞與受詞為同一者。有些動詞習慣接反身代

名詞作受詞，例如：enjoy, devote, contribute 等動詞。

She enjoyed herself on the party.(她在宴會中玩的很愉快。)

例 3

Grasp all, lose all.

中譯 貪多必失。

文法解析

all是代名詞，作「所有」解釋。本句是一俗諺，grasp作「得到」解釋。句中的兩個 all 都是代名詞，分別作 grasp 與 lose 的受詞。

例 4

She loves to stay in touch with all of her friends wherever she goes.

中譯 她無論去何處，都喜歡與她所有的朋友保持聯絡。

文法解析

all of her friends 是 with 的受詞，所以 all 在本句中是受詞。All of 作「…的所有」解釋。

例 5

The rich man gave the poor man some of his money from his wallet.

中譯 那個有錢人從他的皮夾中拿出一些錢給了那位窮人。

文法解析

some of his money 是作 gave 的受詞。本句是肯定句，所以要用 some of 來表示「…的一些…。」

◎重點整理◎

構成主詞的詞類

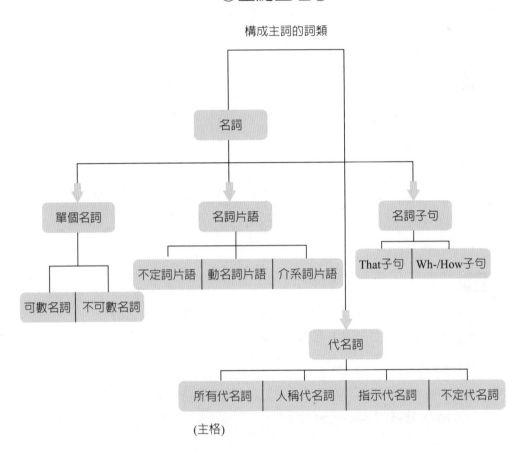

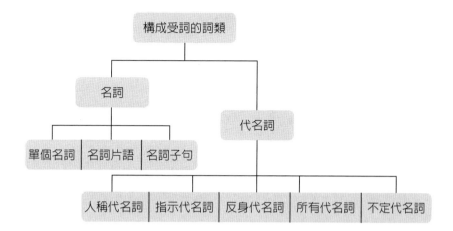

主詞 & 受詞在句中的不同位置

1. 主詞 + 及物動詞 + 受詞

   The bus hit the tree.

2. 主詞 + 不及物動詞 + 介副詞 + 受詞

   He turned down the radio.

3. 主詞 + be／連綴動詞 + 形容詞 + 介系詞 + 受詞

   The old woman was glad of seeing her grandchildren.

4. 主詞 + be + 過去分詞 + 介系詞 + 受詞

   The boy is interested in insects.

5. 介系詞片語：介系詞 + (the) + 受詞

   in the house

Exercise

一、Multiple Choice

1. Most of us _____ comfortable with eye contact lasting a few seconds.

   (A) is　(B) are　(C) have been　(D) was　　　(100 年學測相關試題)

2. The staff in this company _____ a lot of money because their boss raises their salary.

   (A) earns　(B) makes　(C) earn　(D) has made

3. The housewife bought _____ salt in the supermarket.

   (A) two　(B) three packs　(C) four packs of　(D) four pieces of

4. Some of the birds inevitably die during the migration from one place to _____ .

   (A) the other　(B) another　(C) either　(D) any

5. The twins look the same in their appearance; however,their mother can tell one from _____ .

(A) another   (B) others   (C) both   (D) the other

6. The woman tried to avoid _____ the man who bothered her a lot.

    (A) to see   (B) of seeing   (C) seeing   (D) in seeing

7. _____ of the sailors were from the sea after the ship sank. The rescue team sent them to a nearby hospital.

    (A) Both   (B) Neither   (C) Either   (D) Each

8. The _____ of an essay is often a neglected part of the essay.

    (A) conclude   (B) concluding   (C) conclusion   (D) conclusive

                                    (103 年鐵路特考)

9. Now she was given one rule: _____ the cellphone during dinnertime.

    (A) No answer   (B) Not answer

    (C) Not answering   (D) No answering

10. _____ passengers survived from the big fire in the hotel. Most of them died from the burning.

    (A) Little   (B) Many   (C) Few   (D) A lot of

二、Cloze Test

More people than ever thinking about   1   to cut down on greenhouse gas emissions. Some scientists suggest that   2   on our meat diets would help. The raising of livestock like pigs and cows occupies two-thirds of the world's farmland and cause 20 percent of greenhouse gases   3   some estimates. It   4   that the key to save our planet may not be just reducing our intake of meat; instead, switching our diet to insects may be the answer. In fact, the United Nation (UN) wants   5   for alternatives to the meat in our diet.

The UN Food and Agriculture Organization (FAO) are considering a policy paper on   6   . They already held a meeting on the topic in Thailand in 2008, and a world congress meeting is in the plans for 2013.

1. (A) it (B) ways (C) road (D) ridding of

2. (A) taking off (B) cutting back (C) getting down (D) ridding of

3. (A) for (B) to (C) according to (D) with

4. (A) turns up (B) comes about (C) turns out (D) comes with

5. (A) searching (B) to search (C) to be searched (D) being searching

6. (A) the eating of insects (B) the eat of insects (C) eating insect

   (D) to eat insects   (103 年五等特考改編)

三、Translation

Part A: Translate the following sentences into English.

1. 全球暖化會造成氣候的劇變。

   _____.

2. 說是一回事；做又是一回事。

   _____.

3. 那女孩該明白什麼是貧窮孩子的生活。

   _____.

4. 科學家尚未知道如何預測地震的方法。

   _____.

5. 難民中的一些人會被允許移民到西方國家。

   _____.

Part B: Translate the following sentences into Chinese

6. Some teachers devoted themselves to teaching the children in distant places.

   _____.

7. She loves being able to stay in touch with all of her friends wherever she

   goes.

   _____.(103 年鐵路特考)

8. They also said that polar bear hunting was a regulated activity.

_____ .(103 年關稅特考)

9. The staff in the factory complained of their working environments.

_____ .

10. Most of the graduates of this famous university found good jobs.

_____ .

Answers

一、

1. (B) Most of us 是複數的代名詞，所以動詞要用 are。

2. (C) staff(員工) 是集合名詞，表示複數的涵義，所以其後的動詞要用複數動詞。

3. (C) thee packs of：三小包…。

4. (B) 因為鳥類遷移從一地到任何一處其他的地方，所以要用 another 來表示非特定的一處地方。

5. (D) the twin(雙胞胎) 是指兩人，所以用代名詞取代時，要用 one... , the other...。(一者…，剩下一者…。)

6. (C) avoid(避免) 之後要用動名詞作受詞。

7. (A) 因為後一句中的代名詞是 them，而且動詞又是複數動詞 (were saved)，所以只用 Both 符合題意。both=them。

8. (C) The 與介系詞 of 之間一定要用名詞：conclusion

9. (D) No 之後要接名詞，而 the cell phone 之前要用動名詞來當其文法上的主詞，所以只有動名詞 answering 合適。

10. (C)

二、

1. (B) ways：方法

2. (B) cutting back：減少

3. (C) according to：依據

4. (C) turn out：變成

5. (B) want 之後要接不定詞 (to search) 作其受詞。

6. (A) 介系詞 on 之後要接名詞片語作其受詞。

三、

Part A

1. Global warming will result in the drastic change of climate.

2. To say is one thing ; to do is another.

3. That girl realized what life poor children live.

4. Scientists don't know how to predict earthquakes.

5. Some of the refugees were allowed to migrate to western countries.

Part B

6. 有些老師獻身自己於教導偏遠地方的孩子。

7. 無論她去何處，她喜愛能與她所有的朋友保持聯繫。

8. 他們也說北極熊的捕獵是正規的活動。

9. 在工廠的員工抱怨他們工作的環境。

10. 在這所名校中的大多數畢業生找到好的工作。

二、五種基本句型的次要元素

(一) 名詞的修飾語：1. 形容詞 2. 形容詞片語 3. 形容詞子句
    4. 數量形容詞

1. 形容詞：(1) 限定用法 (2) 敘述用法

(1) 限定用法：形容詞 + 名詞

例 1

The maximum capacity of this elevator is 400 kilograms.　　(104 年學測)

中譯　這個電梯的最大容量是四百公斤。

文法解析

大多數的形容詞是置於名詞的前面來修飾名詞。本句中 maximum 正是
此種形容詞,用來形容其後的名詞 capacity。

例 2

Our country is such a litigious society that people now spend a lot of time
suing one another.　　(104 年臺大轉學生)

中譯　我們的國家是一個非常好訴訟的社會,以至於現在的人花
許多時間彼此互告。

文法解析

本句中的形容詞 litigious(好訴訟的) 是用來形容其後的名詞 society。
而字尾 ous 正是典型常見的形容詞字尾。其他的例子還有:dangerous,
enormous, famous, tedious 等等許多這類的形容詞。此外,還有一些特
別的字尾也是形容詞字尾,如 ive, ful, less, able, al, ent, y 等等皆是常見
的形容詞字尾。所以像 impressive(印象深刻的),useful(有用的),
careless(粗心的),edible(可吃的),national(國家的),insistent(堅持
的),healthy(健康的) 都是這類的形容詞。

例 3

The residents alive after the enormous earthquake were saved by the rescue
team.

中譯　在強大地震後,那些存活的居民被救援隊拯救。

有些形容詞只能置於所修飾的名詞後，不能置於名詞之前。像本句中的 alive 就是這類型形容詞，所以放在名詞 residents 之後。這類的形容詞還有 afraid, afire, afloat, adrift, asleep, alike, content, liable 等等。其中有一些是 "a" 字母開頭的形容詞，剛好都是置於名詞之後。

例 4

You are most likely heard the news by now : A <u>car-commuting,
desk-bound, TV-watching</u> lifestyle can be harmful to our health.

(104 年學測)

中譯 到目前為止，你最有可能聽到：一個以車通勤、固定於辦公桌，以及看電視的生活方式可能對我們的健康有害。

文法解析

由連接符號 (-) 連接的兩個 (含兩個) 以上的詞類所形成的形容詞就稱為：複合形容詞。本句中的 car-commuting, desk-bound 以及 TV-watching 都是兩種詞類所構成的複合形容詞，而且都是：名詞 + 現在 / 過去分詞的形式。其中的差異在於現在分詞所構成的複合形容詞是表示主動的涵義，而過去分詞則表示被動的涵義。因此，以車通勤是指行動者 (人) 是主動者，而被辦公桌束縛的是人，所以用被動語態來修飾人。

其他類似形式的例子如下：

(1) 形容詞 + 名詞 a two-hour class(兩小時課程)

(2) 名詞 + 形容詞 wrinkle-resistant pants(抗皺的褲子)

(3) 形容詞 ┌ 現在分詞 a good-looking woman(漂亮的女人)
          └ 過去分詞 a ready-made shirt(做好的襯衫)

(4) 副詞

　　┌ 過去分詞 a far-fetched analogy(牽強的比喻)

　　└ 現在分詞 a fast-developing country(迅速發展的國家)

例5

They can be identified by their thin, light-colored skin.

中譯　它們可以藉著薄又淺的外皮被認出來。

文法解析

本句中的 light-colored 是「形容詞 + 名詞 +ed」而構成的複合形容詞。因為名詞字尾加 ed，所以看起來像過去分詞，但事實上並非真正的分詞，所以又稱作「擬分詞」。這類的特殊形容詞在涵義上沒有被動的涵義。其他的例子還有：blue-eyed(藍眼睛的)，one-legged(獨腳的)，black-haired(黑髮的) 等等相似構成的字。

(2) 敘述用法：be 動詞 or 連綴動詞 + 形容詞 / 名詞 + 形容詞

例1

Hurricanes are not predictable ; therefore, they always cause severe casualties.

(104 年初等考試)

中譯　颶風是無法預測的；因此，它們總是引起嚴重的死傷。

文法解析

形容詞當作 be 動詞或連續動詞 (包含感官動詞) 的補語時，置於這些動詞之後。像本句中的 predictable 即是此種用法。一般而言，大部分的形容詞都可以置於上述動詞之後來作主詞的補語，所以本句中的 predictable 是用來形容主詞 Hurricanes。

例2

Though the policeman inquired the suspect, he remained silent.

> **中譯** 雖然那個警察質詢那位嫌疑犯，但是他仍然沉默。

文法解析

remain 是連綴動詞，所以其後要接形容詞 silent 來修飾主詞 he。其他類似的連綴動詞還有：become, seem, turn, taste, feel, look, smell. 等等，都要接形容詞。

例3

Applying to college means sending in applications, writing study plans, and so on. It's a long process, and it makes students nervous.

> **中譯** 申請入學意味著送申請表，寫研究計畫等等。這是一個漫長的過程，這使學生緊張。

文法解析

在使役動詞 makes 之後要接受詞與受詞補語，本句中的受詞補語是 nervous(緊張的)，用來形容其前的受詞 students。這是一種特殊句型：主詞 + 使役動詞 (make)+ 受詞 + 受詞補語，受詞補語可以是形容詞或名詞。

2. 形容詞片語：(1) 介系詞片語 (2) 不定詞片語 (3) 分詞片語
(1) 介系詞片語：介系詞 +(the)+ 名詞

例1

Mei-ling has a very close relationship with her parents. (103 年學測)

> **中譯** 美玲與她父母有非常親密的關係。

with her parents(與她父母) 是介系詞片語，用來形容其前的名詞 rela-
tionship，所以 with her parents 是作形容詞片語用。亦即在名詞後的介系
詞片語，都作形容詞片語用。

例 2

John's part-time experience at the cafeteria is good preparation for running
his own restaurant.

中譯 約翰在自助餐的兼差經驗對他經營自己的餐廳是一個好的
準備。

文法解析

at the cafeteria(在自助餐廳) 是介系詞片語，用來形容其前的 experience，
因此，at the cafeteria 也是作形容詞片語用。

(2) 不定詞片語：to + 原形動詞

例 1

Since I do not fully understand your proposal, I am not in a position to
make any comment on it.

中譯 因為我不完全瞭解你的計劃，我沒有立場對它作任何的評
論。

文法解析

不定詞片語 to make any comment on it 是用來形容其前的 position，所以
它是作形容詞片語用。不定詞片語在名詞之後大都作形容詞片語用，
形容其前的名詞。不過其前若是有 too 或其他的相關詞類，則另有其

他的功用。例如：He is too young to go to school. to go to school 是表示結果的副詞片語。

例 2

Generally there are two ways to name typhoons : the number-based convention and the list-based convention.　　　　　　　　　　　(101 年學測)

中譯 通常有兩種命名颱風的方式：依據數字的慣例與依據名單的慣例。

文法解析

to name typhoons 是不定詞片語，用來形容其前的名詞 ways。在翻譯上要先翻不定詞片語，再翻譯其所形容的名詞，所以本句中文翻成：命名颱風的方式。

(3) 分詞片語：名詞 + $\begin{cases} 現在分詞片語 \\ \\ 過去分詞片語 \end{cases}$

例 1

The deletion of both names was due to the severe damage caused by the typhoons bearing the names.　　　　　　　　　　　(101 年學測)

中譯 這兩個颱風名稱的刪除是由於具有這些名詞的颱風引起的嚴重損害。

文法解析

分詞片語有兩種：現在分詞片語與過去分詞片語，現在分詞片語置於被修飾的名詞後，與名詞有主動的關係，亦即名詞通常是現在分詞所表達的動作之發起者。過去分詞片語置於被修飾的名詞之後，與名詞

是被動的關係。所以本句中的 caused by...(由…所引起) 來形容其所造成的傷害，是被動的涵義。而 bearing the names 則表示主動的涵義，形容具有這些名字的 typhoons。

例2

Another new technology being tested is Vehicle-to-Infrastructure communication, or V2I. (103 年學測)

中譯 另一種正在測試中的新科技是車載通訊系統或是 V2I。

文法解析

being tested 是表示被動進行的狀態，用來形容其前的名詞 technology，表示此種新科技是在測試中。

3. 形容詞子句：先行詞 (名詞 / 代名詞) + wh- 子句
(1) 形容人的關係代名詞：who, whose, whom

例1

The hunter who found the bear killed it.

中譯 發現那隻熊的獵人殺死牠。

文法解析

who found the bear 是以關係代名詞主格 who 所引導的形容詞子句，用來形容 who 之前的先行詞 hunter。所以解釋上要先翻譯形容詞子句，再翻譯 hunter。事實上 who 就是指 the hunter。who 之後會接動詞或 be 動詞作形容詞子句中的主要動詞。

例2

Presidential candidate Trump whose wife was once a model won the presidential election of 2016.

中譯 他妻子曾是模特兒的總統候選人川普贏得二零一六年的總統大選。

文法解析

whose 是關係代名詞所有格「…的…」解釋，其後須接名詞來形成關係子句中的主詞。所以子句中主要動詞的單複數要依 whose 後所接的名詞而定。本句中 wife 是單數，所以動詞要用 was。

例3

The old man whom he met in the street is his father's friend.

中譯 他在街上遇到的老人是他父親的朋友。

文法解析

whom 在本句中是關係代名詞受格，作 met 的受詞，所以在解釋上先說「他在街上遇到的…」。在現代英文中 whom 也可以用 who 代替，涵義不變。

(2) 形容事物的關係代名詞：which, whose/of which, which

例1

The dinosaurs which were extinct several million years ago become fossils and were discovered in many areas.

中譯 幾百萬年前滅絕的恐龍變成化石並且在許多地區被發現。

which 所引導的形容詞子句是用來修飾表示人以外的名詞，所以本句中的 which 之前是 dinosaurs(恐龍)。which 在子句中是作主格用，所以其後接 were。翻譯上也是先翻 which 子句，再翻 dinosaurs。

例 2

Everyone is a moon, and has a dark side which he never shows to anybody.

(Mark Twain 名言)

中譯　每個人皆是一個月亮，具有他從未向人顯示的黑暗面。

which 是關係代名詞受格，作 shows 的受詞，用來形容 side。關係代名詞受格 which(或 whom) 可以省略，但涵義不變。

例 3

The missing dog whose master was searching it was found in a small town.

中譯　牠主人正在找的那隻失蹤的狗在一個小鎮中被找到。

表示事物的關係代名詞所有格也是用 whose，其後接名詞，表示「…的…。」

例 4

The greatest pleasure I know is to do a good action by stealth, and to have it found out by accident.　　　　　　　　　　(Lamb 的名言)

中譯　我所知道的最大樂趣就是暗中行善，無意中被人發現。

本句中有形容詞子句 which I know 來形容 pleasure，但是 which 被省略了，所以只有 I know 出現在句中，現代英文中關係代名詞受格 which(或 whom) 常被省略，但不影響原文涵義。

(3) 形容人或事物的關係代名詞：that

例 1

The refugees that escape from their own countries eventually settled in Germany.

中譯　從他們自己國家逃難的難民最後在德國定居。

文法解析

that 作關係代名詞時，可取代其前是人或事物的名詞 (又稱做「先行詞」) 本句中的 refugees 是人，所以可用 that 取代他們，引導形容詞子句來形容 refugees。

例 2

Howler monkeys are named for the long loud cries, or howls that they make every day.　　　　　　　　　　　　　　　　(97 年學測)

中譯　吼猴是以其長嘯聲或吼叫聲而命名，牠們每天都會吼叫。

文法解析

that 在此引導形容詞子句來形容其前的 howls(吼叫)。

例 3

The man and his horse that disappeared a few days ago were found in a woods near the small town.

中譯 幾天前消失的那人和他的馬在靠近那個小鎮的一處樹林中被找到。

文法解析

因為 that 可以取代人或事物，所以形容詞子句之前的先行詞是人與物時，一定要用 that 來引導形容詞子句修飾其前的人與事物，所以本句中的 The man and his horse 就要用 that 來取代。

例 4

These were mainly the same areas that became active when participants actually felt pain. (97 年學測)

中譯 當受試者真的覺得痛時，這些主要相同區塊變得活躍。

文法解析

當形容詞子句之前 the same 的形容詞出現時，其後的關係代名詞一定要用 that，無論其為人或事物。其涵義是「…相同的…」此外，其他像 the only, the very(就是) 等也是必須用 that 引導的形容詞子句來修飾其前的先行詞。

(4) 形容詞子句的非限定用法：①在逗點 (,) 之後②在介系詞
   之後

例 1

New Zealanders have given it the nickname weta, which is a native Maori
word meaning "god of bad looks."   (99 年學測)

中譯　　紐西蘭人給它一個綽號「沙蟲」，它是當地毛利人的用
　　　　詞，意思是「長相難看的人」。

文法解析

> 形容詞子句在逗點之後是作補充說明用。在本句中它是用來補充說明
> weta 是什麼涵義。因為是補充說明，所以在解釋上是不用來形容前面
> 的先行詞，而是另成句子解釋。本句中既使沒有 which 子句也不影響
> 句中的主要意思。這就是形容詞子句作非限定用法的差異。

例 2

The crime was seen as a shame to Norway, which regards Munch's paintings
as among its most valued cultural treasures.   (102 年初等考試)

中譯　　這次犯罪事件被視為挪威的恥辱，挪威視孟克的繪畫為它
　　　　最珍貴的文化寶藏。

文法解析

> 本句中的 which 是指其前的 Norway，它也是加以說明為何是挪威之
> 恥。因為偷盜此畫的犯行造成挪威國寶畫作的失去，所以 which 子句
> 也是進一步說明前面句子的涵義，它是用作補充之說明。

4. 數量形容詞：one, the other, another, some, any, neither, few, a few, little, a little, many, much, plenty of, all, both

例1

The two students wear different clothes: One student wears white shirt and a blue jeans; the other student puts on a yellow T-shirt and a dark jeans.

中譯 那個學生穿著不同的衣服：一個學生穿白襯衫和藍色牛仔褲，另一個學生則穿黃色 T 恤及黑色牛仔褲。

文法解析

> one... the other... 表示「一個…另一個…。」是指兩個中的兩者。

例2

Two women got lost in the forest and neither women knew how to find the way out of the forest.

中譯 那兩位婦女在森林中迷路，他們兩人都不知如何找到走出森林的路。

文法解析

> neither 在本句中作形容詞用，修飾其後的 women，指「兩者都不」neither 只能用於兩者的否定，三者以上的否定常用 no，例如 No students in the classroom admitted cheating in the exam.(班上沒有同學承認在考試中作弊。)

例3

Some teenagers play computer games so often that they ignore their studies.

(105 年初等考試)

有些青少年太常玩電玩以致他們忽略了他們的課業。

> some 是不定形容詞，表示有些。它只用於肯定句與少數的疑問句中。
> some= a few，在下列表示希望獲得對方肯定答覆的問句中，要用
> some。
> would you like some coffee? 一般的疑問句要用 any 來表示「有些」的涵義。

例 4

Other parents worry that if they have more than two children, it will increase the world's population.

中譯 其他的父母則擔心他們如果有超過兩個孩子，這將增加世界的人口。

文法解析

> Other(其他的) 是表示非特定的多數，所以 other 之後要用複數名詞
> parents。另一個相關的用法是 the other + 複數名詞，但是 the other 的涵
> 義是「其他剩下的」是有限定的多數。例如，Many people escaped from
> the theater in fire, but the other people died from the fire。

例 5

The lecturer asked the audience if they have any questions about his speech, few people asked him questions.

中譯 那位演講者詢問觀眾他們是否有任何有關他演講的問題，幾乎沒人問他問題。

few(幾乎沒有) 是用於修飾可數複數名詞，但是其涵義卻有部分的意思，因此它所形容的字也有部分否定的涵義。另一個相關的用法是 a few(一些) 則是表示肯定的涵義也是形容可數複數名詞，a few = some。a few 在所有句型中皆可使用。

例 6

A little pollution of water may hurt people's health.

中譯 一點水的污染就可能傷害人們的健康。

文法解析

A little(一點的) 用來形容不可數名詞。所以本句中的 a little 用來形容不可數名詞 pollution。a little 是表示肯定的涵義，但是 little(幾乎沒有) 則用來表示部分的否定。例如，There is little food on the table, so the children almost no food to eat.

例 7

There are many, many words in the English language. But there are still lots of things that we don't have name for! (103 年交通特考)

中譯 在英文中有許多、許多的字。但是仍然有許多我們尚未命名的東西。

文法解析

many 是形容複數名詞，所以後面接 words。lots of(許多) 可以接可數名詞或不可數名詞。例如 lots of money。此外，lots of = a lot of，意思不變，都作「許多」解釋。

There are plenty of food in this restaurant and most people go to the restaurant for its delicious food.

中譯 在這家餐廳有許多食物，大部分的人去這餐廳是爲了它可口的食物。

文法解析

> plenty of(許多) 類似 lots of 的用法，可以接可數或不可數名詞，本句中 plenty of 是不可數名詞 food, plenty of places(許多地方) 是接複數名詞 places。most 在本句作形容詞，其後可接可數或不可數名詞，most people(大部分的人) 是接可數名詞 people。most gold 是接不可數名詞 gold。

All roads lead to Rome.

中譯 條條大道通羅馬。

文法解析

> All(所有的) 是形容三者以上的多數。all 也是形容全體的形容詞。本句是一句俗諺，意思是到達目標有很多途徑。All 之後可以接可數名詞也可接不可數名詞，本句中 All 是接可數名詞 roads。all love 是接不可數名詞 love。

A ship sank at the sea near the north of Taiwan and several crew were missing before the rescue ship came.

中譯 一艘船在靠近北臺灣的海域沉沒了，在救難船來到之前，幾個船員失蹤了。

文法解析

several (幾個) 是用來形容複數名詞，本句中的 crew (船員) 是集合名詞，表示多數 (但是沒有複數形式〔加 s〕)，所以 several 可以接 crew。several = a couple of (幾個)。

例 11

Sealed documents protect <u>both</u> adoptees and their natural parents.

(103 年初等考試)

中譯 封閉的文件保護被收養的人與他們的親生父母。

文法解析

both... and...：…與…都…，both 通常與 and 併用，表示「兩者都… 」both 也可以單獨使用，強調「兩者都… 」。例如，They both like the same girl. 通常 both 是置於代名詞之後使用，但是若置於名詞前來形容名詞，這時就往往會和 and 併用。

(二) 動詞的修飾語：1. 副詞 2. 副詞片語 3. 助動詞

1. 副詞

例 1

An area code is a section of a telephone number which <u>generally</u> represents the geographical area that the phone receiving the call is based on.

中譯 地區代號是一個區域的電話號碼，通常代表接受電話時所根據的地理區域。

副詞 generally 可置於動詞前，形容動詞。一般而言，在句中的副詞通常置於動詞前來修飾動詞。但是在較短的句子中，副詞除了置於動詞前，也可以置於句尾來修飾其前的動詞。例如：The athlete runs <u>fast</u>.(副詞)。

例 2

Using a heating pad or taking warm baths can sometimes help to relieve pain of the lower back. (99 年學測)

中譯 使用加熱墊或洗溫水澡有時可以幫助減輕背部下半身的疼痛。

句中若有助動詞時，副詞一般置於助動詞語主動詞之間。因此，本句中的 sometimes(有時) 置於 can 與 help 之間。此外，其他的動詞時式中若有助動詞，副詞的位置也是如此。例如，He has <u>just</u>(副詞)arrived at home.

2. 副詞片語：(1) 介系詞片語 (2) 不定詞片語 (3) 名詞片語 (作副詞用)
(1) 介系詞片語

例 1

On a sunny afternoon last month, we all took off our shoes and walked on the grass with bare feet.

中譯 上個月的某一個陽光燦爛的下午，我們都脫掉鞋子並且赤腳走在草地上。

文法解析

with bare feet(以赤足) 是一個介系詞片語，在本句中用來形容其前的動詞 walked。介系詞片語用作副詞片語來形容動詞時，通常置於句尾。

例2

For safety reasons, this elevator shouldn't be overloaded. (104 年學測)

中譯 為了安全的理由，這架電梯不應超載。

文法解析

For safety reason(為了安全的理由) 是介系詞片語，置於句首用來修飾後面的句子。換言之，副詞片語也可以修飾整個句子，其修飾全句時，通常置於句首。

(2) 不定詞片語

例1

To promote the new product, the company offered some free samples before they officially launched it. (104 年學測)

中譯 為了促銷新產品，這家公司在他們正式推出它之前提供一些免費的樣本。

文法解析

不定詞片語 (To promote the new product) 在句首時通常當作副詞片語用，用來修飾其後的句子。本句的不定詞片語是表示為了某種目的的副詞片語，所以要解釋為：「為了…。」

Scientists are working hard to find out what leads to this destruction.

(102 年學測)

中譯　科學家正在努力工作，爲了找出是什麼導致了這次的毀滅。

文法解析

> to find out what leads to this destruction 是一個不定詞片語。它是表示目的的不定時片語，用來形容其前的動詞 are working 所以在本句中，它作爲副詞片語用，用來修飾句中的主要動詞。

(3) 名詞片語

例句

Tom and Mary take the school bus to school every morning.

中譯　每天早上湯姆和瑪莉搭都乘校車去學校。

文法解析

> every morning 雖是名詞片語的形式，但在本句中卻用作表示時間的副詞片語，用來修飾全句。這類的名詞片語很多，像 each day, every month, this afternoon 等等皆是。

3. 助動詞：can, could, may, might, shall, should, will, would, need, dare, must

例 1

Using the camera function provided by smartphone, people can take pictures of themselves, their family and friends and even things that interest them.

中譯 人們能使用由智慧型手機所提供的相機功能，自拍、拍攝他們的家人與朋友，甚至引起他們興趣的東西。

文法解析

can 是助動詞，用來加強動詞的語氣，可以視其為一種修飾動詞的詞類。can 的涵義表示能力，作「能夠」解釋。can 也可以表示許可，作「可以」解釋。依據本句前後文的涵義，can 應該視作「能夠」解釋。

例2

Bill: Could you tell me where the taxi stand is?   (102 年地方特考)

中譯 比爾：請您告訴我計程車候車站在哪裏？

文法解析

could 雖然是 can 的過去式，但是在本句中卻不是表示過去的時間。Could 用作問句開頭時，是表示比較客氣的問法。所以 Could you ...? 是表示類似中文「請您…?」的客氣問話，是用於現在的狀況。

例3

You may have the same size as someone else.   (102 年私醫聯招)

中譯 你可能有和別人同樣的尺寸。

文法解析

may 有兩種主要的意思：一、表示許可，二、表示可能性。在本句中的 may 是表示「許可」時，常用在疑問句中。例如，May I come in? May I use your bathroom? 等等。

例 4

The speaker said, "May I have your attention, please?"

中譯 那講者說，「請大家注意」。

文法解析

May 在本句中表示詢問許可，但是卻暗示一種委婉的要求。換言之，此處的 May I 表示一種請求。

例 5

Blessed are those who mourn, for they shall be comforted.　（聖經名言）

中譯 憂傷痛悔的人有福了，因為他們必得安慰。

文法解析

shall 原是表示未來時間的助動詞，一般作「將要…」解釋，而且限定於第一人稱的未來簡單式，例如 We shall meet their representative tomorrow. shall 也有另一種涵義，表示決心和意願，作「必定」解釋。在本句中 shall 就作「必然」解釋。

例 6

He that has no silver in his purse should have silk in his tongue.

（英語格言）

中譯 身上無錢，說話要甜。

文法解析

should 不僅是 shall 的過去式，而且也可以用來表示現在的情況，此時 should 作「應該」解釋，表示一種責任或義務。本句中的主要動詞是 have，所以 should 置於其前用來加強語氣指名他應該做什麼。此外，should = ought to，都是表示「應該」。

例 7

Women would need to meet the same standard as men to get those jobs.

中譯 為了獲得那些工作，女性將需要達到與男性同樣的標準。

文法解析

> 本句中的 would 是 will 的過去式，表示在過去的時間終將發生的事。
> 所以本句中的 would 是女性要達到像男性那樣的標準，這也是一種表
> 示條件的情況。

例 8

Whoever asks him of the matter, he will answer that he doesn't know it.

中譯 無論誰問他此事，他都會回答他不知道。

文法解析

> Whoever 是表示「無論誰」的一種假設的情況，所以這是一種表示尚
> 未發生的事，因此後面主要的子句要用未來簡單式的時式：will + 原
> 形動詞，表示未來可能發生的事。

例 9

All of the staff will attend the meeting at eight o'clock tomorrow morning.

中譯 所有的員工都必須在明早八點參加會議。

文法解析

> 本句中的助動詞 will 是表示未來將進行的事情。通常句中都有表示未
> 來時間的副詞片語，本句中的 tomorrow morning 就是表示未來時間的
> 副詞片語，所以本句是表示未來時間的句型。

例 10

Students needn't follow the instruction that is not available.

中譯 學生不需遵守不可行的指令。

文法解析

need(需要) 是助動詞，其後要接原行動詞：follow。need 像其他的助動詞一樣，可以結合 not 構成否定句。need 也可作一般動詞，但是其後要接不定詞作其受詞。例如，The patient needed to be sent to a big hospital.

例 11

The timid person dare not walk in the dark street.

中譯 那個膽小的人不敢在黑暗的街道走路。

文法解析

dare(敢) 是助動詞，用來加強其後主要動詞的語氣，所以 dare 之後要用原形動詞。在本句中 dare 與 not 構成否定句，其後接原形動詞 walk。

例 12

Mankind must stop global warming; otherwise, the Earth will become unsuitable for human's living.

中譯 人類必須停止地球暖化；否則地球將變得不宜人居。

文法解析

must(必須) 是表示不得不做的語氣。must=have to，因為 must 是助動詞，所以其後要接原形動詞 stop。must 沒有過去式，其相同涵義的過去式用法是 had to。例如，she had to finish the work yesterday.

(三) 副詞 & 形容詞的修飾語

1. 副詞修飾語

例句

Mt. Everest is far higher than Mt. Jade.

中譯 埃佛勒斯峰 (聖母峰) 比玉山高太多了。

文法解析

修飾比較級形容詞的副詞是 far 或 much，其涵義是「…得多」，所以本句中的 far higher 是表示「高得多了」。本句不能用 very 來修飾比較級 higher，因爲 very 只能修飾原級形容詞。例如，very good, very fast 等等。

2. 形容詞的修飾語

例 1

As a matter of fact, it is often <u>very difficult</u> for adoptees to find out about their birth parents because the birth records of most adoptees are <u>usually sealed</u>. (103 年初等考試)

中譯 事實上，對被收養者而言，要找出他們的親生父母是非常困難的，因爲大多數的被收養者的出生記錄通常是封閉的。

文法解析

修飾形容詞的是副詞，所以本句中的 difficult(形容詞) 是用 very(副詞) 來修飾。usually 也是副詞，副詞也可以修飾過去分詞或現在分詞。所以 usually 在句中修飾 sealed。

例 2

Michael Muller's day job is photographing Hollywood stars, like Brad Pitt, but his hobby is <u>much more exciting</u>. （103 年關務特考）

中譯 麥可‧慕勒的日常工作是拍攝好萊塢的明星，像布萊德彼特，但是他的嗜好更刺激多了。

文法解析

more 在本句中是副詞，修飾形容 exciting。爲了加強 more 的語氣，本句中用 much 來修飾副詞 more，表示「更…多了)」。在英文中表示更進一步的副詞也可用 (much 作「之後」解釋時，也可作形容詞用)。此外，much 表示「非常的」涵義時，也用來修飾分詞，包括過去與現在分詞，意思是「十分地」。例如，much surprised, much satisfied 等等，修飾比較級的形容詞，只能用 much，而不用 very。much better (O), very better (X)。

(四) 句子的修飾語

例 1

Traditionally, Tyson has sold its non-food-grade fats to producers of soaps, cosmetics and pet food. （103 年政大轉學考）

中譯 傳統上，泰森銷售它非食品級的脂肪給肥皂化妝品和寵物食品的製造商。

文法解析

副詞置於句首時，也用來修飾全句。本句的 Traditionally(傳統上) 就是副詞修飾其後的句子，通常都有逗點將其與後面句子隔開。

In fact, Jacky Chan's movies are more than simple action movies -- they are action-comedies.　　　　　　　　　　(103 年初等考試)

中譯　事實上，成龍的電影不僅是簡單的動作片 —— 它們還是喜劇動作片。

文法解析

> 由介系詞片語 (In fact) 所構成的副詞片語，置於句首時也是修飾後面的句子。這類的用法不少，例如，In reality(事實上)，In winter(在冬天時)，等等皆是。

◎重點整理◎

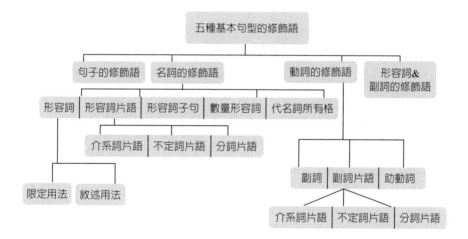

句子修飾語在句中的位置與功用的例句說明

一、名詞的修飾語

The woman met her sister.(her 在本句中是代名詞所有格修飾 sister)

➡ The old woman met her sister with her child.(old 是形容詞修飾 woman, with her child 是介系詞片語修飾 sister)

➡ The old woman alone met her sister with her child living in Taipei. (alone 是敘述用法的形容詞放在 woman 後面，living in Taipei 是現在分詞片語來形容 child)

➡ The old woman alone, who found her missing sister, met her sister with her child living in Taipei.(who 引導的形容詞子句形容 woman, missing 是形容 sister 的現在分詞)

二、動詞的修飾語

A lion can easily catch a zebra.(can 與 easily 都是用來加強或修飾動詞 catch)

➡ To feed its cubs, a lion can easily catch a zebra.(To feed its cubs 是表目的的副詞片語，修飾 catch)

➡ To feed its cubs, a lion can easily catch a zebra in five minutes. (in five minutes 是介系詞片語，作副詞片語用，修飾動詞 catch)

➡ To feed its cubs, a lion can easily catch a zebra in five minutes every time.(every time 是名詞片語，作副詞片語用，修飾動詞 catch)

三、形容詞 & 副詞的修飾語

A leopard is a very quick predator(副詞 very 修飾形容詞 quick)

➡ A leopard is a very quick predator and runs fairly fast while chasing its prey.(副詞 fairly 修飾副詞 fast)

四、句子的修飾語

People need to take a rest after a day's work.

➡ Sometimes, people need to take a rest after a day's work.(副詞 Sometimes 修飾全句)

➡ From time to time, people need to take a rest after a day's work.(副詞片語 From time to time 修飾全句)

Exercise

一、詞類變化題：請選出最適合句中上下文的詞類

1. With the worsening of global economic conditions, it seems wiser and more _____ to keep cash in the bank rather to in the stock market.

    (A) sensibly   (B) sensitive   (C) sensible   (D) sensitively

    (98 年學測延伸題)

2. The man _____ at sea was eventually saved by a ship passing by.

    (A) float   (B) afloat   (C) floated   (D) to floating

3. Jason is very busy. He does not have _____ time reading newspapers or watching TV.   (102 年鐵路特考)

    (A) lots   (B) several   (C) much   (D) some

4. Online classes are _____ taught by professors who have been trained in online teaching.

    (A) usual   (B) seldom   (C) usually   (D) frequent.

5. Students should be especially _____ of programs that offer a degree in return for little or no work.

(A) carefully　(B) care　(C) careless　(D) careful

6. The Sunday peace was broken by the shouting of the two men _____ into the exhibition area.　　　　　　(102 年初等考試)

(A) storms　(B) stormed　(C) storming　(D) storm

7. Some people prefer to adopt infants; _____ people adopt children from foreign countries.　　　　　　(103 年初等考試)

(A) other　(B) the other　(C) another　(D) most

8. Collocations are words in a text _____ are usually next to each other.

(A) who　(B) whose　(C) that　(D) of which　　(103 年臺大轉學考)

9. The couple was looking for their missing child _____ his friend went to a park.

(A) whom　(B) with that　(C) to whom　(D) with whom

10. Most of the articles in this academic journal seem rather _____, with no immediate implication for our daily life.　　(103 政大轉學考)

(A) esoteric　(B) esoterically　(C) esotery　(D) especially

二、配合題：請將下列空格中的字，依其前的字母填入下列文章中。

A. interesting　B. camera's range　C. after all　D. to sit still　E. aferwards
F. above the camera　G. to get appealing portrait
H. by simply snapping a picture　I. possibly　J. some

　　Animals are a favorite subject of many photographs. Cats, dogs, and other pets top the list, followed by zoo animals. However, because it's hard to get them ___11___ and "perform on command," Some professional photographers refuse to photograph pets.

One way ___12___ is to hold a biscuit or treat ___13___. The animal's longing look toward the food will be captured by the camera but the treat won't appear in the picture because it's out of the ___14___. When you show the picture to your friend ___15___, they'll be impressed by your pet's loving expression.

If you are using fast film you can take ___16___ good, quick shots of a pet ___17___ right after calling its name. You'll get a different expression from your pet this technique. Depending on your pet's mood, the picture will capture an interested, curious expression or ___18___ a look of annoyance if you're awakened it from a nap.

Taking pictures of zoo animals require a little more patience ___19___, you can't wake up a lion! You may have to wait for a while until the animal does something ___20___ or moves into a position for you to get a good shot. When photographing zoo animals, don't get too close to the cage, and never tap on the glass or throw things between the bars of a cage. Concentrate on shooting some good pictures, and always respect the animals you are photographing.

(101 年學測)

三、克漏字

My little brother is so ___21___. All day ___22___ he says, "Eddie, I wonder why people can talk but animals can't." or "I wonder why the ocean looks ___23___" of course. I don't know the answers, but I don't let him know that. I just make up ___24___ explanations, and he accepts them as if I were the ___25___ person in the world before I answer one of his questions, I ___26___ tell him that he is pretty stupid and asks ___27___ many questions.

Will, yesterday we both got out report cards. I got B's and C's and he got straight A's. Under the "Comments" section __28__ my report card, it said, "Eddie __29__ get better grades if he asked more question." Of course, on my brother's report card, it said __30__ the opposite.　　　(103 年地方特考)

21. (A) irritated　(B) irritate　(C) irritating

22. (A) alone　(B) long　(C) longing

23. (A) blue　(B) a blue　(C) blues

24. (A) reasonably　(B) reason　(C) reasonable

25. (A) smart　(B) smarter　(C) smartest

26. (A) usual　(B) usually　(C) as usual

27. (A) very　(B) a lot　(C) too

28. (A) of　(B) on　(C) at

29. (A) would　(B) will　(C) is going to

30. (A) only　(B) just　(C) just now

Answers

一、

1. (C) sensible(明智的)，依照本句的上下文意，sensible 合乎上下文意。more 是副詞修飾形容詞 sensible，在連綴動詞 seem 之後要用形容詞，所以只有 (C) 切合上下文法規則。

2. (B) 在名詞之後要用敘述用法的形容詞 afloat(漂浮的)。

3. (C) time 是不可數名詞，所以要用形容不可數名詞的數量形容詞 much。

4. (C) who 所引導的形容詞子句是用來形容 professors。所以 professors 所教導的課程是上網教導的，因此要用 usually 比較適合。

5. (D) be careful of：對…小心。

6. (C) storming into the exhibition area，這個現在分詞片語來形容 men。

7. (A) Some...; other...：有些…；有些…。這是慣用的句詞。

8. (C) that 是引導形容詞子句 (that are usually ... other)，用來形容 text。

9. (D) 從 his friend 後面動詞 went 得知 went 應與 with 合用，而其前是主要子句，所以要用表示受格的 whom 與 with 合用，介系詞之後不能接 that 作為關係代名詞。

10. (A) seem 是連綴動詞，其後要用形容詞 esoteric(奧祕的)。

二、

11. (D) to sit still(安靜地坐著) 是不定詞片語，做形容詞用，用來修飾其前的 them。get+ 受詞 +to+ 原形動詞：使…(做)…。

12. (G) to get an appealing portrait(獲得令人心動的畫面) 是不定詞片與用來形容 one way。

13. (F) above the camera(在鏡頭之上) 是介系詞片語，作副詞片語用，用來形容動詞 hold。

14. (B) out of the camera's range(在鏡頭範圍之外)，它是介系詞片語做形容詞片語用，修飾 it。

15. (E) afterwards(之後) 是副詞，形容動詞 show，意思是「在那之後顯示」。

16. (J) some(一些) 是數量形容詞，形容 shots(拍攝)。

17. (H) by simply snapping a picture ... 是一個介系詞片語，作副詞片語用，修飾 take(拍攝) 這個動詞。

18. (I) possibly(可能地) 是副詞，用來形容 a look of annoyance(受困擾的樣子)。

19. (C) After all(畢竟) 是慣用的介系詞片語，通常置於句首，修飾全句。

20. (A) 形容詞要置於不定代名詞之後，修飾不定代名詞，所以本句

中的 interesting(有趣的) 是置於 something 之後。

三、

21. (A) 主詞是人時，be 動詞之後要用過去分詞 irritated 來作主詞補語，形容主詞 (My little brother)。

22. (B) all day long(整天之久), long 置於 day 之後是敘述用法。

23. (A) 感官動詞 (look) 之後要接形容詞 blue。

24. (C) reasonable 是形容詞，形容其後的名詞 explanations。

25. (C) 本句空格之前有 the，之後有 in the world ，所以應該用最高級來形容 person ，表示「在世上…最…的人」。

26. (B) usually 是頻率副詞，形容其後的動詞 tell。

27. (C) too(太…) 有否定的意味，前面說 he is pretty stupid(太笨了)，所以用 too 來表示否定意涵。

28. (B) on：在…上面。

29. (A) 本句是表示「與現在事實相反的假設句型」：主詞 + would + 原形動詞…，if + 主詞 + 過去式動詞。

30. (B) just：正好，just 是副詞，用來形容 the opposite。

三、句子 & 子句的連接：連接詞的用法
(一) 對等連接詞：and, or, but, for, so, nor (neither)
1. and 的用法

例句

Although Mr.Chen is rich, he is a very stingy person and is never willing to
spend any money helping those who are in need. (101 年學測)

中譯　雖然陳先生富有，但是他是非常吝嗇的人，未曾願意花任何錢去幫助那些有需要的人。

and 是連接兩個涵義相關或動作連貫的句子。在本句中 and 之前是指一個小氣的人，而 and 之後則說明那人如何小氣，因此是兩句涵義相關的句子，要用 and 連接。

2. or 的用法

例句

As soon as the first traveler got a "yes" answer from a driver, he motioned with his hand or fingers for his friend to come -- or he held both thumbs up in an "ok" sign or made a circle with the thumb and the next finger of one hand. (101 年地方特考)

中譯 一旦第一位旅客從第一位駕駛得到「是的」回答，他就用他的手或手指向他的朋友召喚 —— 或是他將兩個大拇指以 ok 的手勢舉起或是用大拇指與手上另一個手指形成圓圈圈。

文法解析

or 是連接兩個涵義相似中相反的句子或字。本句中 or 連接 hand(手) 與 fingers(手指) 是涵義相似的字，所以用 or。同樣的，ok sign 與 made a circle with the thumb... of one hand 也是指 ok 的手勢，所以也用 or 來連接兩個片語。

3. but 的用法

例句

It may not be what we listen to, but how we listen to it that turns music into therapy. (101 年特考)

中譯 它可能不是我們所聽的音樂，但是我們如何聽它的方式會
　　　　將音樂轉變成治療。

文法解析

> but 是連接兩個涵義相反的句子。but 除了置於句子中間，也可以置於
> 句首，表示與前面句子或前文不同的涵義，例如：He said that he had
> lost the money. But it was not true. In fact, he stole the money.

4. for 的用法

例句

It might have rained last night, for the ground is wet.

中譯 昨晚可能有下雨，因為地是濕的。

文法解析

> for(因為) 通常用於表示推論的句子中。本句中的推論是：地現在是
> 濕的，所以推論昨晚可能下雨了。for 做連接詞用時，不可置於句首。
> 只能置於句子連結兩個表示因果關係的句子。

5. so 的用法

例句

I have only gone skiing once before, so I would consider myself a novice.

　　　　　　　　　　　　　　　　　　　　　　　(104 年臺大轉學考)

中譯 之前我只去滑雪過一次，所以我自認是新手。

文法解析

> so 連接表示結果的句子，其前一定是表示原因的句子。所以本句因為
> 只滑雪過一次，所以自認是新手。前一句不可以像中文用 Because(因
> 為)，在英文句子中只能用一個連接詞。

6. nor 的用法

例句

Syria's troops did not stop attacking the rebel army, nor did the rebel army stop counterattacking the government army.

中譯 敘利亞的部隊並未停止攻擊反抗軍，反抗軍也未停止反攻政府軍。

文法解析

nor 表示「…也不…」的否定涵義連接詞，其慣用句型為：nor+ 助動詞 + 主詞 + 原形動詞。其句中的助動詞需與前一句中的動詞時式一致，在本句中都是過去簡單式。

(二) 附屬連接詞

1. 表時間的附屬連接詞：when、while、as、before、after

例 1

When I open a book, I look first at the table of contents to get a general idea of the book and to see which chapter I might be interested in the reading.

(100 年學測)

中譯 當我打開一本書時，首先我會看書目，為了獲得該書的概念，並且會看我可能在閱讀中會產生興趣的那一章。

文法解析

when 是引導表示時間的副詞子句的關係副詞，作「當…之時」解釋。when 所引導的子句之時式可以是現在簡單式，如：本句中的 open，也可以是過去簡單式，例如：When World War II broke out, France declared war on Germany.

While the man was watching TV, the telephone rang.

中譯 當那人正在看電視時，電話鈴響了。

文法解析

> while(當…的時刻)所引導的句子中要用進行式，不論是現在或過去
> 進行式，因為 while 的涵義是強調「正在…如何」。本句中 while 是用
> 過去進行式：was watching，而主要子句是用現在簡單式的動詞時式：
> rang。While 引導的子句，也可用現在進行式。例如：While he is walking
> in the street, he runs into his friend.

例3

Germany openly apologized to Israel for the massacre of Jews during
World War II while Japan denied the slaughter of residents of Nanking City
in China.

中譯 德國就二次大戰期間所屠殺的猶太人向以色列道歉，然而
日本卻否認屠殺中國南京的居民。

文法解析

> while 除了引導時間的副詞子句之外，也可引導表示對比或相反涵義的
> 句子，表示「然而」之意。本句的前後句之涵義成對比，所以 while
> 在本句中作「然而」解釋。

例4

Before the police reached the suspect's house, he had already run away.

中譯 在警方趕到那個嫌疑犯的家中之前，他已經逃走了。

Before(在…之前) 是連接兩個一前一後的連接事件或動作，通常時間在前的句子要用過去完成式，時間在後的句子則用過去簡單式。因此，在本句中 Before 所接的句子，因為時間較晚，所以用過去簡單式 reached，而發生較早的事情則用過去完成式：had already run away。

例5

After terrorists struck New York City on September 11, 2001, airport videotapes from Boston revealed a lost opportunity.　　(103 年地方特考)

中譯　在恐怖份子於 2011 年 9 月 11 日攻擊紐約市後，從波士頓機場的錄影帶顯示出一次錯失的機會。

文法解析

After(在…之後) 與 before 正好相反，它連接發生較早的事情或動作。本句中恐怖攻擊發生較早，所以要用 After 來連接。雖然較早的動作可以用過去完成式，但是用過去簡單式也是可以的。

2.　表示原因的附屬連接詞：because, since, as, seeing that / considering that, now that

例1

The ending of the movie did not come as a surprise to John because he had already read the novel that the movie was based on.

中譯　這部電影的結局對約翰來說並不令其驚訝，因為他已經讀過那部電影所依據的小說。

because(因爲) 是連接表示原因的子句，其前的句子通常是原因，所以本句是一個表示因果關係的句子。Because 的子句中動詞時式較早，因爲他表示一個先前已發生的事由，所以用過去完成式：had already read。而表示較晚發生的事情則用過去簡單式：did not come。

例2

Since I do not fully understand your proposal, I am not in a position to make any comment.

中譯　因爲我不完全瞭解你的計畫，我也沒有立場去評論。

文法解析

since 置於句首時當作「既然；因爲」解釋，與 since 在句中時不同，因爲 since 也可做「自從」解釋。但是依據本句的上下文意，since 應該是連接表示原因的子句，而後半句則是表示結果。

例3

As the old man walked down the street, he ran into an old friend of his.

中譯　當那個老人家往街上走去時，他遇到他的一位老朋友。

文法解析

As 有許多種涵義，依據本句的前後文，As 應作「當…時候」解釋。As 在此句中相當 when 的用法。此外，as 也可作「因爲」、「雖然」等解釋，要依據前後文來判斷 as 在句中的涵義。例如：As young he is, he knows a lot of adult world. 在本句中 As 作「雖然」解釋。

例 4

Seeing that the terrorists attacked the citizens of Paris, the French government reinforced the security of most of the cities in France.

中譯 由於恐怖份子攻擊巴黎的市民，法國政府加強法國大部分城市的維安。

文法解析

> Seeing that 是表示原因的連接詞，後接子句。它表示「因為；由於；」的意思，是一種慣用的表達。與分詞的用法無關。

例 5

Now that they become affluent, they can live a comfortable life.

中譯 因為他們變得富有，他們能過著舒適的生活。

文法解析

> Now that 也是引導表示原因的子句，如同其他原因的附屬連接詞，其引導的句子也要用現在簡單式：become。

3. 表示附屬連接詞：so that, in order that, lest, for fear that, in case that

例 1

She drew on her memories from childhood and expanded upon them using her imagination so that the characters developed a life of their own.

中譯 她藉著童年的回憶，並且運用她的想像力來擴展它們，好使那些角色能發展出自己的生活。

文法解析

so that+ 子句 (為了…) 是表示目的附屬連接詞。在本句中半句是表示某種的作為，後半句則表示達到的目的。so that 不可以拆開，否則意思會不同，so that = in order that，都是表示目的附屬子句。

例 2

The man asked his wife to keep silent in order that he could hear the radio.

中譯　為了能聽到收音機，那人要求他的太太保持安靜。

文法解析

in order that 子句表示「為了… 」後皆表示原因的子句，前後子句的時式一致，所以本句中的主要動詞都是過去式。

例 3

The residents prepared fresh water and food lest they should lack clean water and enough food when typhoon reached.

中譯　那些居民準備了水與食物，以免當颱風來臨時，他們缺少乾淨的水和足夠的食物。

文法解析

lest(以免) 是表示目的附屬連接詞，其後面常出現 should 的助動詞，should 美式英語中常省略，而使用原形動詞：lack。lest 也可以相當於 for fear that ... (should) + 原形動詞 (唯恐)。

例 4

The student took a coat for fear that it should become cold at night.

中譯 那個學生帶一件外套，唯恐晚上天氣會變冷。

文法解析

for fear that 子句是擔心未來發生的事情，後面也要用 should 來接原形動詞。它也可以相當於 in order that... not... 表示否定目的之句型，例如：
The thief ran away in order that he might not be caught.

例 5

In case that you need further information about the trip, please give me a call.

中譯 如果你需要進一步有關這個旅程的資訊，請打電話給我。

文法解析

In case that 原意是「防止…發生」，其後是接現在簡單式動詞。本句 In case that 意思是「如果」，這是表示未來可能發生的情況。

4. 表示結果的附屬連接詞：so ... that 子句，such ... that 子句

例 1

It rained so hard yesterday that the baseball game had to be postponed until next Saturday.

中譯 昨天雨下得太大，以至於棒球比賽被迫延期到下週六。

文法解析

so + 形容詞 / 副詞 + that 子句：太…以至於。這是一個表示結果的片語式連接詞，經常用在英文句子中。so 之後用形容詞，因為 be 動詞

之後接形容詞，若是一般動詞，則 so 之後接副詞，如本句的 rained 和 hard。

例 2

The pianist played Chopin in such an expressive way that he brought the audience to tears. (103 年東吳轉學考)

中譯 那位鋼琴家以非常感性的方式演奏蕭邦，以至於他的聽眾流淚了。

文法解析

such + 單數 / 複數名詞 +that 子句：太…以至於…。such 的句型與 so…that 的句型在涵義上是相似的。但是 such 之後接名詞，因為 such 是形容詞，要注意其複數形式。

5. 表示條件的附屬連接詞：if, supposing, provided, unless

例 1

Keeping pets can be troublesome if vaccination visit is also considered besides regular feeding and bathing. (103 成大轉學考)

中譯 照顧寵物可能是麻煩的，除了例行的餵食與洗澡，去打疫苗也要考慮在內。

文法解析

if 是引導表示條件或假設的子句，所以本句中的 if 是表示某種條件考量，if 的子句中，動詞要用現在簡單式。

例 2

Supposing (that) the World War III breaks out, what would the world become?

中譯 如果第三次世界大戰爆發,世界會變成怎樣?

文法翻譯

Supposing (that) 在本句中是連接詞,引導表示假設的子句。前半句說到假設的原因,後半句說到假設的結果,所以後半句的助動詞要用 would,表示一種未來可能發生的情況之假設。

例 3

The picnic will be cancelled provided (that) it rains.

中譯 如果下雨的話,那個野餐將被取消。

文法翻譯

provided (that) 表示「如果」,是連接詞 (不是分詞) 的特殊用法,在 provided 所引導的句子中要用現在簡單式,主要子句則用未來簡單式,provided (that) = supposing (that) = if。

例 4

The epidemic cannot be prevented unless a new vaccine is discovered.

中譯 除非一種新的疫苗被發現,否則那個傳染病無法被阻止。

文法翻譯

unless(除非) 與表示否定涵義的主要子句合用,表示在某種條件下才不會發生的事或動作。因此,本句的主要子句是否定句:The epidemic cannot be ... ,表示一種假設的條件下才不會發生的事。

6. 表示讓步的附屬連接詞：though/although, even if/ though, as, whereas, while

例 1

Although many people believe that cloudy and stormy weather interfere with the strength of GPS signals, the effect is actually not significant enough to affect the use of consumer GPS devices. (103 年東吳轉學考)

中譯 雖然許多人相信多雲與暴風雨的天氣會干擾衛星定位的訊號之強度，但是那種影響不是真的明顯到足以影響使用者的衛星定位裝置之使用。

文法解析

Although(雖然) 用來引導表示對比的子句，它也可以用 though 來取代。有時也可以置於句尾，例如：The residents luckily survived after the tornado passed, it was huge and powerful though.

例 2

Even though Jackson was smaller than his teammates, his persistent attitude allowed him to accomplish as much as he did. (103 私醫轉學考)

中譯 既使傑克森比他的室友小，他堅持的態度使他能盡最大努力完成。

文法解析

even though(既使；縱然) 是表示讓步的附屬連接詞，通常用過去或現在簡單式作句中的動詞。even though = even if 意思與用法皆不變，例如：Even if he studied English very hard, he still failed to pass the exam.

例 3

Young as he is, he knows a lot about international issues.

中譯 他雖然年輕，但是知道許多國際事件。

文法解析

> as 作「雖然」的解釋與用法時，要用倒裝句的方法：(形容詞/副詞)as + 主詞 +(Be 動詞/一般動詞)：雖然…。再看一例：Hard as she works, she is still as poor as a church mouse.

例 4

Third, independence is important for both groups -- they are conscious of wanting it, whereas young adults and middle -- aged people take it for granted.

(98 年二技入學考)

中譯 第三點，對雙方團體而言，獨立是辛苦的——他們意識到他們需要它，然而年輕人與中年人卻視其爲理所當然。

文法解析

> whereas(然而)連接兩個涵義相反的句子，其前要有逗點隔開，這與一般的附屬連接詞不同，本句中前後句子涵義相反，所以用 whereas 來連接。

例 5

While advertisers see this as a great opportunity to reach their target customers, some people feel that this kind of profiling is an invasion of their privacy.

(103 年私醫轉學考)

中譯 雖然廣告商視這個爲一次打動他們目標中顧客之大機會，

但有些人覺得這種側錄是對他們隱私的侵犯。

文法解析

While 在本句中作「雖然」解釋，引導一個與主要子句形成對比的附屬子句，所以本句中的前後兩子句涵義是成對比的。While 也作「當…之時」解釋，但是依據本句的前後涵義，應當作「雖然」解釋。

7. 表示比較的連接詞：as... as, than

例 1

Usually a horse runs as fast as a zebra.

中譯 通常馬跑得像斑馬一樣快。

文法解析

本句是表示同等級的比較，意思是「像…一樣的…」。它的句型如下：
主詞 +(be 動詞 / 一般動詞)+ as +(形容詞 / 副詞)+ as + 主格 / 名詞。as 之後要用形容詞或是副詞是依其前的動詞決定，若是 be 動詞，則用形容詞，若是一般動詞，則用副詞，因為 as 中的詞類是修飾其前的動詞。

例 2

Pluto is even smaller than seven of the moons circling other planets, including Earth's moon. (103 年臺灣聯大轉學考)

中譯 冥王星甚至比包括地球在內的七個環繞其他行星的衛星還小。

文法解析

本句是表示比較級的比較句型，其句型如下：

主詞 +(be 動詞 / 一般動詞) + $\left\{ \begin{array}{l} 形容詞 +er \\ more/less+ 形容詞 \end{array} \right\}$ + than + 主格 / 名詞：
比…更…。

(三) 片語式連接詞：not only... but also, both... and...,
either... or..., neither... not..., not... but..., as well as, as
soon as rather than, as..., so...

例 1

The book is not only informative but also entertaining, making me laugh
and feel relaxed while I read it.　　　　　　　　　　(102 年學測)

中譯 　這本書不僅是有資訊的，而且也是有趣的。當我閱讀它
　　　　時，它使我發笑，也使我覺得輕鬆。

文法解析

not only ... but also...：不但…而且…。它是連接兩個詞類相同的字，其
中 but 也可省略。本句中 not only 與 but also 都是接形容詞：informative
和 entertaining。後半句中的 making ... relaxed 是分詞構句，表示接續動
作：使得…。

例 2

Although they have different characteristics and meanings, both the lotus
and water lily are highly appreciated in various cultures.

中譯 　雖然他們有不同的特色和涵義，蓮花與水蓮在不同的文化
　　　　中都被欣賞。

文法解析

both... and; …與…都…。這也是片語式的連接詞，連接兩個相同的詞
類。本句中 lotus 與 water lily 都是名詞，所以符合文法規則，both...
and... 也可置於 be 動詞後連接形容詞，例如：The band is both famous
and popular among young people.

例 3

The man had to make a decision, that is, he either stayed in the company or quit his job.

中譯 那個人必須作決定，亦即，他不是待在公司，就是辭去他的工作。

文法解析

either... or...；不是⋯就是⋯。這是表示二選一的連接詞，在兩者之間選擇一者，同樣的，either... or... 也是接兩個相同詞類的字。

例 4

When the tsunami reached the land, neither the residents nor their houses could escape from the destructive power of huge waves.

中譯 當海嘯到達陸地時，那些居民和他們的房子都無法逃脫那些巨浪的摧殘力。

文法解析

neither...nor...：既不⋯也不⋯；兩者都非⋯。這是代表雙重否定的連接詞。the residents 與 houses。neither 與 nor 也可置於主詞之後接動詞或形容詞等詞類，例如：The price of the car is neither expensive nor cheap.

例 5

Colleges in New Zealand do not refer to undergraduate study, but to senior high school.

中譯 在紐西蘭 colleges 不是指大學的求學，而是指高中。

not...but... : 不是…而是…。本句不能依字面的涵義來解釋 (還是…但是…) ，它有特別的涵義：不是…而是…。所以在解釋上要注意，以免誤會句子的涵義。but 之後可接單字或片語，如本句中的 senior high school。

例 6

People can watch videos and movies online as well as play many different online games either with themselves or with others. (102 年鐵路特考)

中譯 人們可以上網看影片或電影，而且也可以與自己或別人玩許多不同的線上遊戲。

文法解析

as well as : 與…；不同…。as well as 有表示「進一步」或「更加」的涵義。其用法也是連結兩個相同的詞類。

例 7

As soon as the thief saw the policeman, he ran away from the house.

中譯 那個小偷一看到那個警察，就從屋中逃走。

文法解析

As soon as : 一…就…。本句型連接兩個一前一後的動作，表示連接發生的事。As soon as 所引導的子句與後面的主要子句中所用的動詞之時式須一致，所以本句中前半句用過去簡單式 saw，後半句也用過去簡單式：ran。

The German soldiers would kill themselves <u>rather than</u> be captured by Russian army.

中譯 那些德國士兵寧願自殺，也不願被蘇聯軍隊抓到。

文法解析

> would...rather than...：寧願…而不願…。不僅 would 之後要用動詞原形，連 rather than 之後也要用動詞原形。所以本句中的 would 之後要用 kill，而 rather than 之後要用 be 動詞原形。

例 9

As you make the bed, so you must lie on it.

中譯 因為你鋪好床，所以你必須躺在其上。(另解：自作自受。)

文法解析

> As..., so...：因為…，所以…。這是一種慣用句型，表示因果關係與涵義。一般說來，英文句子只能有一個連接詞，但是本句是一種特殊句型，所以有兩個連接詞：as/so 而且前者作為「因為」解釋，後者 so 則是表示結果。它常出現在俗諺上，例如：As you sow, so shall you reap. 種什麼就收什麼。有時候後半句的主詞與助動詞可以前後顛倒：shall you。

(四) 連接 (性) 副詞
1. 表示因果關係的連接性副詞：therefore, hence, thus, accordingly

例 1

The house is too far from his office; <u>therefore</u>, he has to rent an apartment near the office.

中譯 那間房子離他的辦公室太遠了；因此，他必須租一間離他的辦公室近的公寓。

文法解析

therefore(因此)是表示結果的連接的性副詞，因為它是用來作為語氣轉換的連接詞，所以稱作連接性副詞，也因為它本身是副詞，所以其前若有句子時，須加上分號 (;) 來連結兩個句子，分號本身有連接詞的作用，相當於 and(並且) 的用法。

例2

A powerful earthquake happened near one of the islands of Indonesia; hence, a tsunami occurred later on and resulted in death of thousands of people.

中譯 一場強大的地震發生在靠近印尼的其中一個島嶼；因此，稍後就發生海嘯並且造成數以千計的人死亡。

文法解析

hence(因此) 也是表示因果關係的連接性副詞。他是與 therefore 相似涵義相似的連接性副詞，所以本句的前半句是原因，後半句則是表示結果。result in 是動詞片語，表示「造成…的結果」。occur 是 happen 的同義字，表示「發生」。

例3

None of the villagers was aware of the coming of the debris flow. Thus, it destroyed the whole village.

中譯 村民中沒有人留意到土石流的到來，正因為如此，它摧毀了整個村莊。

Thus(如此；於是) 表示前面已經有了願意，而在這語氣上說明這種原因導致的結果時，用 thus 來表達，它在語氣上要比 hence 或 therefore 更強。

2. 表示相反或對比的連接性副詞：however, nevertheless, in contrast

例 1

The main language of instruction will be English; <u>however</u>, candidates must also conduct some courses in Chinese. (97 年二技學測)

中譯 教學的主要語言將是美語；然而，候選人也必須用中文教導一些課程。

文法解析

however(然而) 是表示相反涵義的連接性副詞。however 連接兩個意思相反或成對比的句子，其前也需有分號作其連接句子的憑據。本句前半句是指出以英文教學，後半句則是強調中文也用來教授一些課程。因此，用 however 來連接這兩個句子。

例 2

She studied Japanese very hard; <u>nevertheless</u>, she didn't pass the test.

中譯 她非常努力的學習日文；然而，她未能通過測驗。

文法解析

nevertheless(不過) 也是連接兩個涵義相反的句子，nevertheless 與 however 是意思相似的連接性副詞，可以彼此互換使用。

例 3

When the protesters broke into the government building, the police did not stop them. Instead, they withdrew from the building.

中譯 當那些抗議的人闖入那幢政府建築時，警方並未阻止他們，反而他們從那幢政府建築撤退。

文法解析

> Instead(反而；取而代之) 是表示不同於之前的情形，用來表示一種成對比狀況，像本句中的前半句與後半句的情形就是對比的狀況。

例 4

All people in the world live in the same globe. Accordingly, global warming will affect each one of us.

中譯 所有人都住在同一個地球，因此，地球暖化將影響我們每個人。

文法解析

> Accordingly(因此) 是表示結果的連接性副詞，它與 consequently(結果) 是相同涵義的連接性副詞。Accordingly 連接兩個互為因果關係的句子，它經常用於句首。

3. 表示進一步的附屬連接詞：moreover, furthermore, in addition, besides

例 1

Nikola Tesla invented an x-ray machine, a neon light and a remote-controlled boat; moreover, he also invented a type of radar to hunt German submarines.

中譯 尼可拉‧特斯拉發明 X 光機器、霓虹燈以及遙控船。此外，他也發明一種獵捕潛艇的雷達。

文法解析

Moreover(此外) 是表示更進一步的涵義，是延續前一句的涵義或延伸前一句的意思。本句中提到特斯拉發明了一些東西，不僅如此，他還發明了其他的東西，這兩句都是有關發明的東西。

例2

The athletes won the gold medal in the contest. Furthermore, he also won the silver medal in another competition.

中譯 那位運動選手在比賽中贏得金牌，此外，他也贏得另一場比賽中的銀牌。

文法解析

furthermore(此外；再者) 與 moreover 相似的涵義，用來連接兩句相關語義的句子，作進一步的說明或舉例。

例3

Robots can help people do many different and dangerous tasks. In addition, they can be used to do chores in the houses, which will be great help to housewives.

中譯 機器人能協助人做許多困難有危險的工作，此外，它們在屋內能被用作做家事，這對家庭主婦而言，有很大的幫助。

In addition(此外) 通常用於句首，用來連接兩句語意相關的句子，它也是用來表達進一步的涵義的語氣轉換詞。因此，in addition = moreover = furthermore。不過，in addition 可以加 to 連接名詞，表示：除了…此外。例如：In addition to air pollution, water pollution is another serious problem in China.

例 4

Leonardo da Vinci was a distinguished artist whose oil painting, Mona Lisa, is well-known to the world. Besides, he was a scientist as well as an architect.

中譯 達文西是一位知名的藝術家，他的油畫蒙娜麗莎聞名於世。此外，他也是一位科學家和建築師。

文法解析

Besides(此外) 也是表示更進一步的意思，它與 moreover, furthermore，以及 in addition 都有相似的涵義。不過，besides 若不加 s，則作介系詞用，表示「在…旁邊」。

4. 表示順序的副詞性連接詞：first, secondly, next, finally, once, then

例 1

First of all, lotus flowers usually reach up out of the water, while the water lily rests on the floating leaves. Secondly, the pads of ridged leaves of the lotus flowers are completely rounded while those of the water lily have a split in them from the outer edge to the center. Finally, the lotus flowers have the religious significance of purity in Asia, while the water lily is mostly associated with feminine beauty and nymphs (water spirits), as in Greek culture. (102 鐵路特考)

中譯 首先，蓮花通常會冒出水面，然而睡蓮則靠在漂浮的葉子上。其次，蓮花隆起的大片葉完全是圓的，但是睡蓮的葉子從外緣到中心有裂開。末了，蓮花在亞洲有宗教的純潔之意義，然而睡蓮，像在希臘文化中，大都與女性的美麗以及水仙 (水精靈) 有關。

文法解析

本段文章中是依照先後的順序來介紹兩種不同的蓮花。First of all(首先) 是放在頭一句來引導文章的開頭，接下來用 Secondly(其次) 表示第二個項目或要點的陳述。最後用 finally(末了) 來結束文章。這是一篇依照先後順序而寫的敘述文。first of all, secondly 與 finally 都是表示這些順序的連結副詞。

例2

Jack saw his brother attacked by a wild dog, and then he hit the dog on its head so as to save his brother from the dog's attack.

中譯 傑克看到他兄弟被一隻野狗攻擊，然後他就打那隻狗的頭，為了從那隻狗的攻擊中救他的兄弟。

文法解析

英文中的 then(然後) 通常表示接下來的動作或事件。then 是指時間上的順序，通常 then 的前面已有發生的動作或事件。所以 then 之後通常都用過去簡單式來表達。hit 在本句中是過去式動詞，因為 hit 的現在式與過去式都是同樣的拼法。

◎重點整理◎

(一) 對等連接詞

1. 單字 / 片語 / 句子 + $\begin{cases} \text{and(和；並且)} \\ \text{or(或者；否則)} \\ \text{but、and yet(但是)} \end{cases}$ + 單字 / 片語 / 句子

2. 句子 + $\begin{cases} \text{so(所以)} \\ \text{for(因爲)} \end{cases}$ + 句子

3. 句子 + $\begin{cases} \text{and(…也…)} \\ \text{nor、neither(…也不…)} \end{cases}$ + 助動詞 /be+ 主詞

(二) 附屬連接詞

1. 表示時間的附屬連接詞：when, while, as, before, after

2. 表示原因的附屬連接詞：because, since, seeing that/considering that now that

3. 表示目的的附屬連接詞：so that, in order that, lest, for fear that, in case that

4. 表示結果的附屬連接詞：so... that 子句，such...that 子句

5. 表示條件的附屬連接詞：if, supposing, provided, unless

6. 表示讓步的附屬連接詞：though/although, even if/though, as, whereas, while

7. 表示比較的附屬連接詞：as... as, than

(三) 片語式連接詞

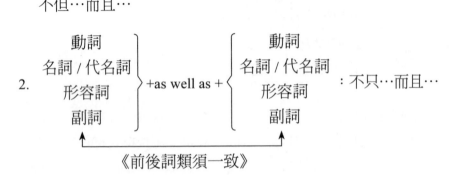

1. not only + 動詞 / 名詞 / 代名詞 / 形容詞 / 副詞 + but (also) + 動詞 / 名詞 / 代名詞 / 形容詞 / 副詞 :

《前後詞類須一致》

不但…而且…

2. 動詞 / 名詞 / 代名詞 / 形容詞 / 副詞 +as well as + 動詞 / 名詞 / 代名詞 / 形容詞 / 副詞 : 不只…而且…

《前後詞類須一致》

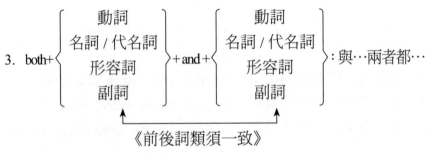

3. both+ 動詞 / 名詞 / 代名詞 / 形容詞 / 副詞 +and+ 動詞 / 名詞 / 代名詞 / 形容詞 / 副詞 :與…兩者都…

《前後詞類須一致》

4. either+ 動詞 / 名詞 / 代名詞 / 形容詞 / 副詞 +or+ 動詞 / 名詞 / 代名詞 / 形容詞 / 副詞 : 不是…就是…

5. neither+ $\left\{\begin{array}{l}\text{動詞}\\\text{名詞 / 代名詞}\\\text{形容詞}\\\text{副詞}\end{array}\right\}$ +nor+ $\left\{\begin{array}{l}\text{動詞}\\\text{名詞 / 代名詞}\\\text{形容詞}\\\text{副詞}\end{array}\right\}$ ：既不是…也不是

6. not+ $\left\{\begin{array}{l}\text{動詞}\\\text{名詞 / 代名詞}\\\text{形容詞}\\\text{副詞}\end{array}\right\}$ +but+ $\left\{\begin{array}{l}\text{動詞}\\\text{名詞 / 代名詞}\\\text{形容詞}\\\text{副詞}\end{array}\right\}$ ：不是…而是…

7. $\left\{\begin{array}{l}\text{動詞}\\\text{名詞 / 代名詞}\\\text{形容詞}\\\text{副詞}\end{array}\right\}$ + as well as + $\left\{\begin{array}{l}\text{動詞}\\\text{名詞 / 代名詞}\\\text{形容詞}\\\text{副詞}\end{array}\right\}$ ：不但…而且…

8. As soon as + 主詞 + 動詞… ，主詞 + 動詞… ：一…就…

《前後時式須一致》

9. 主詞 +not 動詞… rather than ... ：不是…反而是…

10. As + 主詞… ，so… ：因為…所以…

(四) 副詞性連接詞 (又稱作「語氣轉換詞」)

下表為各種語氣的副詞性連接詞

	因果關係	相反 / 對比	此外 / 而且	順序
副詞性連接詞	therefore hence thus accordingly consequently as a result in conclusion in other words in summary otherwise	however nevertheless instead in contrast likewise similarly on the contrary in fact	moreover furthermore besides in addition	first second next finally eventually then

Exercise

一、選擇題：請從下列每題的選項中選出最切題的答案。

1. The contract can't be considered valid, _____ one party did not sign it. (92 年二技學測改寫題)

   (A) when (B) because (C) whereas (D) though

2. You should definitely see the Great Wall _____ you go to China.

   (A) because (B) for (C) but (D) when (98 年二技學測改寫題)

3. _____ John got on the stage to give the speech, he took a deep breath to calm himself down. (103 年大學學測改寫題)

   (A) After (B) When (C) Before (D) Until

4. _____ student enrollment continues to drop, some programs at the university may be eliminated.

(A) Though　(B) If　(C) As　(D) For　　　(103 年學測改寫題)

5. The liquid is as colorless as water, almost tasteless, and _____ quite imperceptible in coffee, cocoa, or any other beverage.

(A) then　(B) so　(C) neither　(D) thus　　(102 臺師大轉學考)

6. The travesty was _____ outrageous that the whole country came together to protest against the injustice.

(A) such　(B) very　(C) so　(D) much　(102 年臺大轉學考改寫題)

7. We must reinforce the river bank. _____, there is bound to be flooding in the winter.

(A) As a result　(B) Otherwise　(C) In fact　(D) However

(102 年淡江轉學考)

8. I think I'd rather have tea _____ coffee.

(A) instead of　(B) in favor of　(C) because of　(D) in case of

9. Most of the herbs now growing in Britain, culinary and domestic, _____ medicinal, resulted from the Roman invasion.

(A) as well as　(B) but　(C) and　(D) since

(103 年成大轉學考改寫題)

10. Our goal to maintain a dynamic and creative College of Liberal Arts, _____ it becomes a valuable asset for the university, the local community, and the world.　(103 成大轉學考改寫題)

(A) thus　(B) and then　(C) so that　(D) lets

二、克漏字

Getting a good camera shot is a difficult challenge for amateur photographers. In order to get a successful picture, there are many things to consider. ___11___, what do you want to appear in the foreground of the photo you are taking and what will be in the background? ___12___, you will have to choose between getting a close-up ___13___ a distant shot. Third, how will you need to adjust the camera ___14___ the film is not under-or over-exposed because of the amount of light? ___15___ you are indoors, the lighting may be close-up and you can use the indoor setting. ___16___, when you are outdoors, you will need to adjust the camera settings so as not to get too much glare from the sun.

___17___ there are so many factors to take into consideration, most people with a lot of practice can succeed in getting excellent photographs.

11. (A) Then　(B) Moreover　(C) First　(D) However

12. (A) Thus　(B) Second　(C) In addition　(D) Therefore

13. (A) and　(B) as well as　(C) or　(D) but

14. (A) so that　(B) for　(C) so　(D) as

15. (A) As　(B) When　(C) Since　(D) If

16. (A) Accordingly　(B) Instead　(C) However　(D) Hence

17. (A) Even though　(B) Though　(C) Now that　(D) As soon as

三、中翻英填空

18. Young _____ he is, he can understand adults' feelings. 他雖然年幼，他瞭解成人的感受。

19. That movie is _____ a _____ _____ that attracts many people to see it. 那部電影非常好，以至於吸引很多人去看它。

20. The student _____ forgot _____ ignored the homework that his teacher asked him to do.
那個學生不是忘記就是忽視他老師所要求他做的回家功課。

21. The ship quickly sailed back to the seaport _____ the typhoon hit it.
那艘船迅速地駛返那個港口，以免颱風打擊它。

22. Those Japanese would die _____ _____ yield.
那些日本兵寧死不屈。

23. They haven't visited Toroko Gorge, _____ _____ their friends.
他們從未去過太魯閣峽谷，他們的朋友也未去過。

24. _____ _____ _____ the parents saw their missing child, they burst in to tear.
那對父母一看到他們失蹤的孩子，就不禁流下眼淚。

25. _____ Tom and his partner took a small boat to the island.
湯姆與他的夥伴兩人都搭小船去到那座島上。

Answers

一、

1. (B) 前半句是結果：那個合約不被認為有效，後半句是表示原因：有一個政黨並未簽它，所以應用表示原因的 because

2. (D)

3. (C) 本句有表示動作的先後順序，所以較早的動作 (約翰上臺要演講) 要用 before 來引導。

4. (B) 表示條件的狀況，所以用 if

5. (D) 因為前半句說出那個液體是無味像水般的液體，所以是無法識別的，因此用 thus(正因為如此)。

6. (C) so...that 子句：太…以至於

7. (B) Otherwise：否則，前、後兩句是一種表示否定條件的情況。

8. (A) instead of：取代…

9. (A) as well as：不但…而且…

10. (C) so that：為了

二、

11. (C) 從後面的句子中的語氣轉換詞 Third：第三點，所以倒推回來，本句的句首應是第一點，所以用表示首先的語氣連接詞：First。

12. (B) Second：第二 (點)

13. (C) 因爲 close-up 和 distant shot 是兩個相反涵義的字，所以用 or 來連接它們。

14. (A) so that：爲了，調整相機 (adjust the camera) 是爲了底片的合適曝光。

15. (D) 後面主要子句中有 may be(可能是)，所以這是一種表示假設的狀況，要用 If。

16. (C) When you are outdoors(當你在戶外時) 是與前一句中的 you are indoors(當你在戶內時) 相反涵義，所以要用 However。

17. (A) Even though：即使

三、

18. as，形容詞 +as+ 主詞 +be 動詞：雖然… (要用倒裝句型表達)

19. such good movie

20. either, or

21. lest：以免

22. rather than

23. nor have

24. As soon as

25. Both

一、否定句型

(一) 主詞 + 助動詞/be 動詞 + $\begin{Bmatrix} \text{never} \\ \text{not} \end{Bmatrix}$ ... without + 名詞/

動名詞：…不…就不…

例句

The divorced couple never met without quarreling.

中譯　那對離婚的夫婦每次碰面就爭吵。

文法解析

"never...without" 是雙重否定，作「不…就不…」也可作「…就必定…」
解釋。本句的涵義就是表示加強語氣的涵義，因此翻作「…就會…」
比較合適。

(二) ... not/never... but(=except that)：…沒有…不…；…必定…

例句

It never rains but pours.

中譯　每逢下雨，必定傾盆大雨。(又譯作：屋漏偏逢連夜雨)

文法解析

never ... but 中的 but，其涵義相當於 except(除了…之外)，所以它是指
例外的狀況 pours(傾盆大雨)。此外，but 也可用作關係代名詞作「…
不是…」，相當於 that ... not，who...not 或 which...not. 例如：President

Trump is not a rude person but makes a foolish decision.(川普總統不是那種作愚蠢決定的鹵莽之人。

(三) ... not ... until + $\left\{ \begin{array}{c} 名詞 / 名詞 / 片語 \\ 子句 \end{array} \right\}$ + ：直到…才…

例句

American government did not declare war on Japan until Japanese fighter planes raided Pearl Harbor.

中譯 美國政府直到日本戰機空襲珍珠港才對日宣戰。

文法解析

"not ... until ..." 不能照字面解釋，作「不…直到… 」。其表達是肯定的涵義，作「直到…才… 」來解釋。因此，本句要先翻譯 until 的子句，再翻前句的主要子句。

(四) anything but + 形容詞：絕非

例句

Though Mr. Smith saves some money, he was anything but rich.

中譯 雖然史密斯先生存了一些錢，但他絕非富有。

文法解析

anything but 是一個慣用片語，表示「絕不」。anything but =never，其後要接形容詞。but 在本句中作「除了…之外」，相當於 except。因此，就 anything but 字面的解釋就是「除了…之外其他都是」，亦即「絕不是」的意思。

二、倒裝句型

(一) 以否定副詞或副詞片語開頭的倒裝句型

Never, Hardly, Scarcely, Rarely, Barely ⎫
Seldom, Little, No longer, No sooner ⎪
Nowhere, By no means, In no way ⎬ + 助動詞 + 主詞 + 原
On no account, Not until, Not only ⎭ 　　形動詞 / 過去分詞

例 1

Never has she seen such a beautiful scenery.

中譯 她從未看過如此美景。

文法解析

> 否定副詞置於句首時，通常都是為了加強語氣用，也因此要用倒裝句
> 型來表達：Never + 助動詞 (has)+ 主詞 + 過去分詞…。若是一般動詞則
> 用：do/does/did 來構成倒裝句型，請看下列說明：Hardly did I recognize
> her.(我幾乎認不出她來。)

例 2

No sooner did the police come, the robbers ran away.

中譯 警方剛到，搶匪就逃走了。

文法解析

> No sooner(一…就…) 可以置於句首，形成倒裝句。其後的主詞與助動
> 詞前後互相顛倒，主要動詞要用原形動詞。因為本句是表示過去發生
> 的事，所以要用助動詞的過去式：did 。

Johnson's behavior seemed weird. Hardly could his friends understand him.

中譯 強生的行為看起來似乎奇怪，他的朋友幾乎不瞭解他。

文法解析

Hardly 作「幾乎不」解釋，有部分否定的涵義。Hardly 置於句首形成加強語氣的句子，助動詞也與主詞前後對調。因為前一句是過去式，所以本句的助動詞也是過去式：could。

Not only can people use them to make and receive phone calls, they can also use them to surf the Internet, send and receive emails, communicate with each other through video calls and make new friends.

中譯 人們不僅使用它們打或接電話，他們也可以使用它們來漫遊網絡，收發電子信函，經由錄影片彼此溝通並且結交新朋友。

文法解析

本句是 not only... (but) also 的連接詞句型，表示「不但…而且…」因為有否定副詞 not，所以也可以置於句首，形成加強語氣的句子，本句中的 but 不可省略，所以只剩下 also，但是後半句並未用倒裝句型，所以仍是主詞在助動詞之前：they can。

(二) 以加強語氣的副詞開頭的倒裝句型

$$\text{Only} + \begin{cases} \text{受詞} \\ \text{副詞子句} \\ \text{副詞} \\ \text{副詞片語} \end{cases} + \text{助動詞} + \text{主詞} + \text{原形動詞}$$

例 1

Only in the past decade have sun-bathers begun to understand the risk of skincancer associated with excessive exposure to the sun's harmful rays.

中譯 只有在已過的十年，日光浴者才開始明白皮膚癌的風險是與過度的曝曬及有害的太陽光有關。

文法解析

Only 置於句首且後面接著其他的副詞、受詞或副詞子句時，only 之後的句型就要用倒裝句：助動詞置於主詞前，主詞之後要用原形動詞，本句因為是現在完成式：have begun，所以 have 就置於 sun-bathers 之前，而 sun-bathers 之後用過去分詞 begun。

例 2

Only when he saw his friend did he realize that his friend lived a poor life.

中譯 只有當他看到他的朋友時，他才明白他的朋友過著貧窮的生活。

文法解析

Only 之後是接副詞子句 when he saw his friend，所以要用倒裝句型：did he realize，這是強調 Only 之後的子句涵義。

(三) 主詞補語 (形容詞 / 介系詞片語)＋ 不及物動詞 (包含 be 動詞在內)＋ 主詞

例 1

Blessed are the poor in spirit, for theirs is the kingdom of Heaven.

（聖經名言）

中譯 靈裡貧窮的有福了，因爲天國是他們的。

文法解析

本句中的 blessed(有福的) 原在 are 之後：The poor in spirit are blessed，但爲了強調，所以將 blessed 移到句首。這就形成以形容詞開頭的倒裝句型。theirs 是所有代名詞取代 their kingdom。

例 2

Between the top and the hillside of the mountain are steep rocks.

中譯 在山頂與山坡之間是陡峭的岩壁。

文法解析

本句原來的句型應是：Steep rocks are between the top and the hillside of the mountain. 主詞是 Steep rocks。但爲了加強位置的語意，所以用倒裝的句型將介系詞片語 between the top and the hillside 置於句首形成倒裝句，來強調 steep rocks 的位置。

(四) 介副詞 / 位置副詞 ＋ { 代名詞作主詞 ＋ 不及物動詞 / 不及物動詞 ＋ 名詞作主詞

例 1

Instead of escaping from the battlefield, on they marched.

中譯 他們未逃離戰場，反而前行。

文法解析

如同上句，本句中的 on 原本在 marched 之後，是一個動詞片語 marched on(往前行)。但是為了加強繼續前進的涵義，所以把介系詞 on(有繼續的涵義) 置於句首。

例 2

The children who had hardly seen snow before shouted loudly, "Down comes the snow!"

中譯 那些之前幾乎從未看過雪的孩子大聲喊叫「下雪了！」

文法解析

本句中的介副詞 Down 原在 comes 之後，作「降下」解釋。為了加強語氣，所以將主詞與動詞顛倒，並且將 down(下來) 置於句首以強調「降下」的涵義。

三、省略句型
附屬子句的省略句型

例 1

When old and poor, he became a tramp.

中譯 當他又老又窮時，他成為遊民。

文法解析

本句的前半句省略了 he was，以附屬連接詞 when 連接形容詞 old and poor. 英文句子中有附屬連接詞 + 主詞 +be 動詞 + 形容詞的子句，常可以省略主詞 be 動詞，形成像本句中的省略句型。

Though exhausted and hungry, the woman still cooked dinner for her children.

中譯 雖然筋疲力盡又飢餓，那婦人仍然為她的孩子煮晚餐。

文法解析

如同上句，本句也是省略主詞與 be 動詞：the woman was，因此，只留下附屬連接詞 though，這是一種類似分詞構句和句型。只是它沒有分詞 being 連接 exhausted and hungry，因為 being 也被省略了。

The passengers handed in their passports as requested.

中譯 照著他們被要求的，旅客們交出他的護照。

文法解析

本句中的省略句型在後半句 as requested 省略了 they were 的主詞與 be 動詞的形式。但省略句型原是被動語態：be + 過去分詞，所以從 requested(過去分詞) 可以看出本句的原來句型與涵義。

If possible, please reserve a table for me.

中譯 若是可能的話，請保留一個桌子給我們。

文法解析

if possible 的原句是 if it is possible，省略 it is。類似的用法還有 if necessary(=if it is necessary) 以及 if convenient 等等。

四、加強語氣句型

例1

It is the scientist that invents the smart cell phone.

中譯 就是那位科學家發明了那種智慧型手機。

文法解析

It is + 被加強的部分 +that 不完全子句 (就是…) 表達一種加強語氣的說法。that 子句中除了動詞以外，其他的部分都可以移至 is 之後作為被加強的部分。所以本句中 the scientist 是被加強的部分，若要強調 the smart cell phone，也可以將其移至 is 之後形成：It is the smart cell phone that the scientist invents.

例2

It is necessary that European countries should help those refugees escaping from their countries because of civil wars or natural disasters.

中譯 歐洲國家應該幫助那些因為內戰或天災而逃離他們國家的難民，這是必要的。

文法解析

本句也是加強語氣的句型：It is + 形容詞 +that + 主詞 +(should)+ 原形動詞…。句中的形容詞大都是表示勸告、建議、說服等涵義的形容詞，其後的 that 子句要用動詞原形，should 也可以省略。再看一例：It is urgent that the doctor examine the injured patient immediately.

例3

Those scientists suggested that all countries in the world should work together to prevent global warming.

中譯　那些科學家建議世界上所有的國家應該共同出力防止地球的暖化。

文法解析

> 當句中的主要動詞是表示「建議、勸告或命令」的語意時，其後面的 that 子句中就要用動詞原形。句中的 should 也可省略，其他類似的動詞還有：advise、insist、command、recommend 等動詞，其句型如：主詞 + {advise/insist/command/recommend...}+that + 主詞 +(should)+ 原形動詞⋯。

五、附加問句句型

例 1

Eric: "Tom works in this company, doesn't he?"

中譯　艾瑞克：「湯姆在這個公司工作，是嗎？」

文法解析

> 在文字末了，加上附加問句，是表示確定前面句子的涵義的正確與否。通常附加問句的時態是與前面句子一致，所以本句中的附加問句是現在簡單式，因為前半句中的動詞是現在簡單式：works。在翻譯上只要翻出「是嗎？」不需把「他」翻出 (這樣更接近中文表達。)

例 2

The policeman asked the suspect, "You don't tell the truth, do you?"

中譯　那位警察詢問那位嫌疑犯，「你沒有說實話，有嗎？」

附加問句的另一個用法就是它是與前半句的句型相反。若是前半句是否定句，則後半句用肯定句，反之亦然。因此，本句中的 don't tell 說出本句是否定句，後面的附加問句要用肯定形式的問句：do you?

例 3

The mother thought that the boy bullied her daughter, didn't he?

中譯 那位母親認為那位男孩霸凌他的女兒，他有嗎？

文法解析

句子中有 that 子句時，附加問句是回應 that 字句的內容，所以在時式、句型與人稱上都要與 that 子句一致。因此，本句中的附加問句是用 he(指 that 子句中的 boy)，而非 she。

六、感嘆句型

例 1

When the westerners saw the Great Wall, they exclaimed, "What a fantastic view!"

中譯 當那些西方遊客看到萬里長城時，他們驚嘆道：「多麼奇妙的景色！」

文法解析

以 what 為開頭且句尾是驚嘆號 (!) 的句子，都是表示驚訝或訝異的感嘆句。驚嘆號的句型是：What +{ 單數名詞 / 複數名詞 }+ 主詞 +be 動詞 / 一般動詞！但是句中若有 be 動詞時，往往可以省略主詞，用 be 動詞，形成本句句型，亦即本句原來句型有 it is，但被省略了。

After a long trip, the passengers went to a local restaurant and had their dinner. As the food was served, they all said, "How delicious these dishes are!"

中譯 在一個長途旅行後，旅客去到一間當地餐廳用晚餐，當食物被推出時，他們全都說：「這些菜多麼可口啊！」

文法解析

以 How 開頭的驚嘆句是另一個用法，但其涵義與 what 引導的驚嘆句相似。How 的驚嘆句型是：How + {形容詞 / 副詞 }+ 主詞 +{be 動詞 / 一般動詞 }！所以本句中的主要動詞是 be 動詞，因為 How 之後是形容詞 delicious，而本句也與 What delicious dishes they are! 同義。

◎重點整理◎

一、否定句型

1. 主詞 +not/never...without...(不…就不…)
2. 主詞 +not/never...but...(沒有…不)
3. 主詞 +not...until+ 名詞 / 名詞片語子句 (直到…才…)
4. 主詞 +anything but + 形容詞 (絕非)

二、倒裝句型

(一) 否定副詞 / 副詞片語

1. Never, Hardly, Not only ...+ 助動詞 + 主詞 + 原形動詞 / 過去分詞
2. Only + 副詞 / 副詞片語 / 副詞子句 / 受詞 + 助動詞 + 主詞 + 原形動詞 / 過去分詞

(二) 主詞補語 (形容詞 / 介系詞片語)+ 不及物動詞 (包括 be 動詞在內)+ 主詞

(三) 介系詞 / 位置副詞 +{ 代名詞作主詞 + 不及物動詞 / 不及物動詞 + 名詞做主詞 }

三、省略句型

附屬子句的省略句型：附屬連接詞 (when, though, if ...)+ 形容詞…，主詞 + 動詞…(大都省略 be 動詞)

四、語氣加強句型

(一)It is + 被強調的部分 +that 不完全子句 (除了動詞之外，子句中其他部分都可被強調。)

(二) 主詞 + 表示命令、勸戒、建議等涵義的動詞 (suggest, recommend, require...)+that + 主詞 +(should)+ 原形動詞…。

五、附加問句句型

三項規則：

(一) 主詞 + <u>動詞 /be 動詞</u>…，<u>助動詞 /be 動詞</u> + 主詞？

〈前後時式須一致〉

(二) <u>主詞</u> + 動詞 /be 動詞…，+ 助動詞 /be 動詞 + <u>主詞 (代名詞)</u>

〈前後人稱須一致〉

(三) 否定句，肯定助動詞 /be 動詞 + 主詞 (前後句子句型相反)
　　 肯定句，否定助動詞 / 否定 be 動詞 + 主詞 (前後句子句型相反)

六、感嘆句

What +(形容詞)+{ 單數名詞 / 複數名詞 }+(主詞 +be 動詞)！：…多麼…。

=How +{ 副詞 / 形容詞 }+{be 動詞 (連同主詞皆可省略)/ 一般動詞 (不可省略)}

Exercise

一、選擇題：請從下列每題的選項中選出最切題的答案。

1. Only after he saw the evidence _____ what the police said.

    (A) he believed   (B) he had believed

    (C) did he believe   (D) had he believed

2. The aircraft carrier did not sail to Taiwan Straight _____ the midnight.

    (A) while   (B) until   (C) as   (D) for

3. It was _____ that the woman saw in the street last night.

    (A) he   (B) she   (C) her   (D) his

4. Not since the Great Depression _____ a more urgent demand for unemployment compensation.

    (A) there has been   (B) has there been

    (C) there have been   (D) have there been

5. I lay as my habit apart from the others _____ without disturbing my companions.

    (A) when necessary   (B) when necessarily

    (C) when is necessary   (D) when to be necessary

6. John: Hello, Mary. How are you?

    Mary: John! _____. The last time I saw you was months ago. How are you?

    John: Fine, thanks.

(A) What a nice surprise!　　　　(B) What a handsome boy!

(C) Nice to meet you.　　　　(D) Christmas is two days away.

7. The policeman has found the criminal last night, _____ he?

(A) did　(B) hasn't　(C) hadn't　(D) didn't

8. When the travelers visited the glaciers of South Island of New Zealand, they all exclaimed, " _____ a marvelous view!"

(A) How　(B) What　(C) That's　(D) This is

9. The accident was _____ a coincidence because the driver had drunk lots of wine.

(A) everything but　(B) anything but　(C) not because　(D) but because

10. The doctor thought that the patient would become better, _____ ?

(A) didn't he　(B) did he　(C) would he　(D) wouldn't he

二、翻譯填空

1. 當觀眾看到那場表演，他們都驚嘆：「好棒的表演！」

When the audience saw the performance, they all exclaimed, " _____ _____ performance!"

2. 若是方便，你能借我車子嗎？

_____ convenient, can you _____ me your car?

3. 當她在衝浪時，她看見一隻鯊魚游向她。

_____ _____ , she saw a shark swimming to her.

4. 那些群眾大喊：「空污滾出我們的都市！」

The crowd shouted, " _____ of the pollution from our city!"

5. 直到他走近那個人，才認出是他兒子。

He _____ recognize the man _____ he walked close to him.

一、

1. (C) 此為倒裝句型,因為 only 子句中是過去簡單式,所以要用 did he believe。

2. (B) not... until...

3. (C) It is 的加強語氣句型

4. (B)

5. (C) when necessary=when it is necessary

6. (A)

7. (B) 前半句的動詞是現在完成式,所以附加問句中的助動詞用 has。

8. (B)

9. (B) anything but:絕非

10. (D) 以 that 子句中的助動詞為對應的助動詞。

二、

1. What a

2. If, lend

3. While/When, surfing

4. Out

5. didn't, until

一、代名詞 & 名詞的慣用句型

(一) It is/was + adj. + to + V (原形動詞)
　　　　(虛主詞)　　　　(真主詞)

It is wrong to cheat people.

中譯 欺騙人是不對的。

文法解析

> 因為 It is + adj. + to + V = To + V + is + adj. 所以本句也可以寫成 It is wrong to cheat people = To cheat people is wrong.

(二) It is + adj. + for + 受詞 + to + V

It is easy for an English teacher to understand an English conversation.

中譯 對英語老師而言，明白英語會話是容易的。

文法解析

> for + 受詞，若是受詞是人的話，是指行為的性質，常是形容客觀的描寫，如 necessary, convenient, impossible, important 等等。

(三) It is + adj. + of + 受詞 (人) + to + V

It is kind of you to help me.

中譯 你人真好願意幫我忙。

文法解析

> of + 人作受詞時，是形容人的行為及對行為者行為的感受，例如 kind, cruel, stupid, foolish。

(四) It is no use + 動名詞 (Ving)：…是無用的

It is no use crying over the spilt milk.

中譯 覆水難收。

文法解析

It is no use + Ving = It is of no use + to + V，兩句涵義是相同的，只是後面主詞的形式不同，不過 Ving 與 to + V 都可作主詞用，所以依文法而言是相同的用法。此外，It is of no use + to + V = It is useless + to + V, of no use 相當於 useless。

(五) It is/was + adj + that，子句：…是…

It is unbelievable that he won the game.

中譯 他贏得比賽是令人難以置信的。

文法解析

that 子句是句中真正的主詞，that 子句在本句中做名詞子句用。

(六) It is/was + 主詞 + who/which + V...：就是…

It was Steve Jobs who invented the first smart phone.

中譯 就是史帝夫・賈伯斯發明第一支智慧型手機。

文法解析

除了 that 之外，關係代名詞 who, whom, which 皆可以形成此類加強語氣句型。

(七) Those + who 引導的子句：凡是…的…

God helps those who help themselves.

中譯 天助自助者。

文法解析

Those 是慣用的指示代名詞，此種慣用句型常用於格言上，表示一種特定的情形。

(八) 主詞 + ⎰ be ＋ 形容詞比較級 ⎱ ··· than ＋ ⎰ that ⎱ ＋ of
　　　　 ⎱ 一般動詞 ＋ 副詞比較級 ⎰　　　　　 ⎱ those ⎰

　　　 ＋ 名詞：···比···更···

同類人、事物

　　The climate of Singapore is hotter than that of Japan.

　　　　　　　　　that 取代 climate

中譯 新加坡的天氣比日本的天氣熱。

　　The ears of rabbits are longer than those of cats.

　　　　　　　　　those 取代 ears

中譯 兔子的耳朵比貓的耳朵長。

文法解析

當比較兩種不同人、事物所屬的東西時，為避免重複，所屬的東西 (如例句中的 climate 與 ears) 可以由 that(取代單數名詞) 或 those(取代複數名詞) 取代句子前面已出現的字詞。

(九) Some..., others... : 有些···，有些···

Many young solders joined in the battle: Some were dead there, others were wounded and were sent back to their countries.

中譯 許多年輕的士兵加入戰場：有些死在那裏，有些受傷並被送返他們的國家。

Some 與 others 在本句中都是代名詞，代替句中的 soldiers，但是 others 並非只剩下其他的人，而是指其中一部分的人，所以只作「有些」解釋。

(十) All + 主詞 + have/has to do is (to)...：只要⋯就⋯

All you have to do is (to) wait for the result.

中譯 你只要做就是等待結果。

文法解析

All you have to do 是特殊的名詞子句，所以被視為一件事情，其後的動詞要用單數。

(十一) 主詞 + 及物動詞 + whether 子句：⋯是否⋯

The police could not confirm whether the prisoner escaped from this area or not.

中譯 警方無法確認那個犯人是否從此區域逃脫。

文法解析

因為 whether 表示「是否⋯」，所以其前的動詞是表示不確定語氣的動詞，像 don't know, wonder, be not sure, doubt 等等動詞，此外，whether 也可用 if 來取代，請看下列說明：

He wondered if she knew his friend, Peter.

他想知道她是否認是他的朋友彼得。

(十二) That ⎤
       What ⎥
       Who ⎥
       Which ⎬ ＋ 主詞 ＋ be 動詞 / 一般動詞
       Why ⎥
       When ⎥
       How ⎦

That the Earth is round is true.

地球是圓的這件事是真的。

What you say is not right.

你所說的是不正確的。

Who she is has nothing to do with you.

她是誰與你無關。

Which decision is correct is still controversial.

那個決定是對的仍然有爭議。

Why he disappeared suddenly is still a mystery.

他為何突然消失仍舊是個謎。

When he discovered the island is left unanswered.

他何時發現那個島仍舊無人知道。

How the killer murdered the queen was not mentioned in the novel.

在小說中並未提到兇手如何謀殺那位皇后。

文法解析

幾乎所有的關係代名詞與關係副詞皆可以形成名詞子句，通常置於句首或及物動詞或 be 動詞之後。換言之，上列句型中的名詞子句也可放於動詞後，作動詞的受格。請看下列說明：

The scientist said that the Earth is round.

The judge pointed out what the lawyer said was wrong.

The host did not know who the woman was.

He could not judge which decision was proper.

The little girl still doesn't understand why her mother left her alone.

(十三) What
　　　　Where
　　　　When ⎰ + to + 原形動詞 + be 動詞 / 一般動詞
　　　　Why
　　　　How

What to do is often difficult for a newcomer in a big company.

對一位在大公司的新進者而言，做些什麼經常是困難的。

Where to find help is usually difficult for a traveler in a foreigner country.

對一個身處異國的遊客而言，去那裏尋找援助通常是困難的。

When to report his boss became a key point in his work.

何時向他的老板回報成爲他工作中的關鍵點。

Why to make such a decision is still a mystery.

爲何作此決定仍舊是個謎。

How to get to the museum is shown on the map.

如何去那個博物館顯示在地圖上。

文法解析

Wh- 或 How 引導的不定詞片詞可以置於句首或及物動詞之後作名詞片語。這樣的名詞片語被視爲一件事，所以後面的動詞要用單數。它也可以置於動詞之後作受格用，請看下列說明：

The woman did not know what to do when the house is afire.

當那房子失火時，那婦人不知如何是好。

The tourist asked the policeman how to get to the train station.

那位旅客詢問警方如何去火車站。

The teacher told her students when to leave school.

那位老師告訴她的學生何時離校。

The artist asked the audience why to appreciate his work.

那位藝術家詢問觀衆爲何欣賞他的作品。

The bus driver told the passenger how to get to the destination.

那位公車司機告訴乘客如何到達目的地。

二、動詞慣用句型

(一) It takes + 時間 / 金錢 + to + V：…花了…(去做)…

It takes the passenger an hour to complete the procedure of checking in.

中譯 完成登機手續花了那位乘客一個小時的時間。

文法解析

take 在此作「花費」解釋，後面通常接時間或金錢，而 to +V 才是全句眞正的主詞。

(二) 主詞 + have + 受詞 + ⎧ 動詞原形 / 現在分詞：使…做… / 過去分詞 ⎫

The teacher had his students write their homework.

那位老師叫他的學生寫他們的家庭作業。

The man had the taxi driver wait for him.

那個人叫那位計程車司機等著他。

The woman had her long hair cut.

那個婦人使她的長髮被剪掉。

have 在本句中是使役動詞，所以作「使得…」解釋。其後的受詞與其後的受詞補語的關係十分密切。若是表示事實或現況，通常用原形動詞。若是表示受詞是處於一種正在進行或發生的狀態，就要用現在分詞來修飾受詞。若是表示受詞是處於被動的狀態，則要用表示被動涵義的過去分詞來修飾受詞。

(三) 主詞 + get + 受詞 + to + V：使 (叫)…做…

The master got his dog to get the ball back.

中譯 那位主人叫他的狗撿回那個球。

文法解析

get 在本句型中也作「使得…」解釋。但是其所接的受詞之後要用不定詞。本句的涵義與用 have 是完全一樣的。所以本句也可改寫為：

The master got his dog to get the ball back.

= The master had his dog get the ball back.

(四) 主詞 + 連綴動詞 + 形容詞

Leaves turn yellow when autumn comes.

當秋天來臨，樹葉就變黃。

The driver seemed tired because he kept yawning.

那位司機似乎累了，因為他不斷打呵欠。

The old man remained weak after he took a two-day rest.

在休息兩天後，那位老人仍然虛弱。

文法解析

英文中的連綴動詞 (linking verbs) 是不完全不及物動詞，也就是動詞後面必須接主詞補語來修飾主詞，否則句子涵義不完全。因此，連綴動

詞之後必須接形容詞或名詞作主詞的補語，再看下列說明：

The weather became worse.
                  （形容詞）

The man became a doctor.
               （名詞）

(五) 主詞 + 感官動詞 + 形容詞

The little girl felt sad when her mother was sick.

當她的母親生病時，那個小女孩覺得難過。

The food tastes delicious.

那個食嚐起來美味。

The tofu smells stinky.

那塊豆腐聞起來很臭。

The music sounds wonderful.

那個音樂聽起來美妙。

The queen looks beautiful.

那位皇后看來很美。

文法解析

感官動詞其實是屬於連綴動詞中的一種與感官有關的動詞，其用法與詞性與連綴動詞一樣。但是要注意的是有些感官動詞與介系詞(或介副詞)合用，就可以接受詞，例如：

Romeo looked at Julia when she appeared in the palace.

當茱麗葉出現在宮庭中，羅密歐就注視她。

(六) 主詞 + 感官動詞 + 受詞 + $\begin{cases} 原形動詞 \\ 現在分詞 \\ 過去分詞 \end{cases}$

The man saw the thief steal money from the woman.

那人看到那個小偷偷那個婦人的錢。

The boy watched his father running away from him.

那個男孩看到他的父親跑離他。

The police heard the animal beaten by some people.

警方聽到有些人打那隻動物。

文法解析

如同使役動詞，感官動詞所接的受詞之後也有三種形式的受詞補語，其用法和涵義也與使役動詞相似。

(七) 主詞 + 特定動詞 + $\begin{cases} Ving \\ to + V \end{cases}$

Children usually love to play toys.(孩子通常喜愛玩玩具。)

= Children usually love playing toys.

People often like to swim in summer.(在夏天人們經常喜愛游泳。)

= People often like swimming in summer.

文法解析

有些動詞可以接不定詞或動名詞，涵義相同。例如：start, begin 等動詞。

(八) 主詞 + 特定動詞 + $\begin{cases} Ving \\ to + V \end{cases}$

The man stopped to smoke his cigarette.

那人停下來開始抽菸。

The man stopped smoking his cigarette.

那人停止抽菸。

【文法解析】

有些動詞接不同的詞類會有不同的涵義。本句中的 stop 接不定詞 (to + V)，意思是「停下來去做其他的事」，所以 to + 動詞原形中的動詞是指要去做的事。若是接動名詞作受詞，則是指停下動名詞表示的動作。意思與不定詞正好相反。類似的動詞還有：forget, regret, remember 等等動詞。

(九) 主詞 + 特定動詞 + 受詞 + to + 原形動詞

Taiwan's government does not allow her people to own guns.

臺灣政府不允許她的百姓擁有槍枝。

The librarian asked the noise-maker to leave the library.

那個圖書館員要求那位製造噪音者離開圖書館。

【文法解析】

有些動詞要先接一般名詞或代名詞作受詞，再接不定詞作受詞補語。這類動詞有：advise, beg, enable, encourage, force, help, order, permit, persuade, remind, request, warn, cause 等等動詞。

(十) 主詞 + 特定動詞 + 受詞 + 原形動詞 (help, find...)

The police helped the worried parents find their missing child.

警方協助那對掛心的父母找到他們失蹤的孩子。

The master found his dog lie on the deck.

那位主人發現他的狗躺在甲板上。

help 與 find 這兩個動詞並非使役或感官動詞，但是它們的用法與使役動詞相似，就是在其後出現的動詞要用原形動詞。help 之後也可加 to 或不加 to 在動詞之前。

三、動狀詞慣用句型 (動名詞、不定詞 & 分詞)

(一) 主詞 + have + $\begin{cases} \text{difficulty} \\ \text{problem} \\ \text{trouble} \end{cases}$ + Ving：有…困難

The poor man had difficulty finding enough food for his family.

那個窮人在為他的家人找到食物上有困難。

The tourists had problem finding their way to the hotel.

那些遊客在尋找飯店的路上有困難。

The child had trouble understanding what his teacher taught.

那個孩子難以明白老師所教導的。

在 have 之後的 difficulty, problem 或 trouble 在解釋上是相同的，都作「在…(方面) 有困難」或「無法… 」解釋。這些用詞之後都要用動名詞。

(二) 主詞 + spend + 時間/金錢 + $\begin{cases} \text{Ving(動名詞)} \\ \text{on + 名詞} \end{cases}$ ：在…花費…

Koalas spend a lot of time sleeping on the trees.

無尾熊花許多時間睡在樹上。

Women usually spend much money on clothes.

女人通常在衣服上花許多的錢。

有 spend(花費) 動詞的句型，其後要用動名詞或名詞，用動名詞時強調動作，用名詞時則說明在那一方面如此花費。

(三) 主詞 + feel like + Ving：想要…

The student who stayed up late last night felt like sleeping.
那個昨晚熬夜的學生覺得想睡。

文法解析

feel like 中的 like 是介系詞，所以其後要接動名詞作受詞，表示某種狀態。其他類似的用法還有：look forward to + Ving(期望)object to + Ving(反對) 等等都接動名詞作受詞，因為 to 是介系詞。

(四) 主詞 + cannot help + Ving：不得不…

The Jews could not help giving up their houses and property when Nazis invaded France.
當納粹入侵法國時，猶太人不得不放棄他們的房子和財產。

文法解析

cannot help + Ving = cannot but + 原形動詞 = cannot choose but + 原形動詞 = have no choice but + to + 原形動詞，意思都作「不得不」解釋。請看下例說明：

The man couldn't help giving his money to the robber.(那人不得不將他的錢給那搶匪。)

= The man couldn't but give his money to the robber.

= The man couldn't choose but give his money to the robber.

= The man had no choice but to give his money to the robber.

(五) 主詞 + be +
- worth + Ving / N
- worthy +
  - of + being + p.p.
  - to + be + p.p.
- worthwhile + to + V

：值得

Freedom is worth fighting for.

自由是值得爭取的。

The game is worthy of being played again.

那個遊戲值得再玩一次。

The lousy movie is not worthwhile to be seen.

那部爛片不值得看。

文法解析

worth 可當作介系詞或名詞用，worthy 是形容詞，其後要接 of 或可直接置於名詞前，作其修飾語，例如：a worthy goal, worthwhile 通常作形容詞用。

(六) 主詞 + be +
- used
- accustomed

+ to + Ving：習慣於…

It is difficult for Westerners to be used to using chopsticks to eat food.

對西方人而言，習慣用筷子吃東西是困難的。

文法解析

be used to + 動名詞表示現在或已存在的習慣，但要注意 be used to 也可接原形動詞，作「被用來…」解釋，此外，used to + 原形動詞是作「以往常常」解釋，表示過去的習慣。

(七) 主詞 + have + { a good time / fun / pleasure } + Ving：在…有樂趣

The couple had a good time visiting the resort.

那對夫婦在遊覽那處名勝上玩得很愉快。

The young people have fun singing English songs at the beach.

那些年青人在海灘唱英文歌唱得很快樂。

They had pleasure playing chess yesterday.

昨天他們下棋下的很愉快。

文法解析

have a good time + 動名詞的用法是與 have difficulty + Ving 相似的句型用法，但是涵義正好相反。

(八) 主詞 + be + { addicted(沉迷於) / dedicated(獻身於) / opposed(反對) / reduced(淪為) / devoted(對…有貢獻) } to + Ving

The man is addicted to surfing the net.

那人沉迷於網路漫遊。

The soldier is dedicated to fighting against the enemies.

那些士兵獻身於對抗敵人。

The students are opposed to accepting the new regulation of their school.

那些學生反對接受他們學校的新規定。

The orphan was reduced to stealing money.

那個孤兒淪為以偷竊為生。

The scientist was devoted to inventing the new machine.

那位科學家對發明那架新機器有貢獻。

文法解析

以上的過去分詞加 to 介系詞的用法都是慣用語，所以需要特別留意其涵義及用法。

(九) 主詞 +had better + 原形動詞：最好⋯

The boy had better follow the rule, or he'll be punished.

那個男孩最好遵守規則，否則他將被處罰。

文法解析

had better 是帶有警告意味的勸告，其語氣要比 should(應該) 強。

(十) 主詞 +ought to + 原形動詞

The young ought to respect the old.

年青人應該尊重老年人。

文法解析

ought to=should，其後都接動詞原形。ought 的疑問句型是 ought+ 主詞 +to+ 原形動詞。

(十一) 主詞 +used to + 原形動詞

Chinese used to live on rice, but now more and more Chinese like to eat Western food.

中國人習慣以米食維生，但是愈來愈多的中國人喜歡吃西方的食物。

used to 與 be used to 的差異不僅是前者皆原形動詞，而後者接動名詞，而且兩者的涵義也不同。used to 指的是過去的習慣，而 be used to 則是指現在的習慣。

(十二) 主詞 + { suggest, recommend, propose, advise
command, order, demand, request
ask, urge, require, desire, insist
persist, maintain, decide, project } +

that+ 主詞 +(should)+ 原形動詞

The doctor suggested that his patient take medicine regularly.
那位醫生建議他的病人規律地服藥。

The expert advises that obese people should have a diet.
那位專家建議肥胖的人應該節食。

上述帶有建議、命令、要求等語氣的動詞在 that 子句後的動詞要用原形動詞或加上 should(應該) 的助名詞，這種前後語氣一致的用法是常考的句型之一。

(十三) 主詞 +be able to+ 原形動詞

Most people are able to finish their studying at senior high schools.
大多數人能夠完成他們的高中學業。

We will be able to see the drastic change of climate in the future.
我們未來將會看到氣候的極端變化。

be able to=can，涵義完全一樣。但是因爲一個句中只能有一個助動詞，所以遇到此種情況，只能以 be able to 來取代 can，正如第二個句子所顯示的情況。

(十四) 主詞 +can't... too+ 形容詞 / 副詞：如何…都不爲過

Parents can't be too careful about taking care of their children.

父母再怎樣照顧他們的孩子都不爲過。

文法解析

本句的涵義不能照字面領會，因爲本句的解釋爲：父母再怎麼小心照顧孩子都不爲過，轉爲正面的解釋。試比較下列的語句涵義之差異：

The box is too heavy to lift.(無法舉起)

The box is very heavy to lift(可以舉起)

(十五) Ving..., S + 現在式動詞 / 未來式動詞…

Hearing the merry rhythm of the music, the girl begins to dance.

聽到那個音樂愉快的旋律，那個女孩開始跳舞。

文法解析

以現在分詞開頭的句子，通常表示兩種時間的狀態。一種是現在正在發生的事情，另一種則是未來可能發生的事情。

(十六) Ving..., S + 過去式動詞…

Seeing the lion run to him, the hunter ran away quickly.

看到獅子奔向他，那個獵人很快地跑走。

文法解析

從後半句中的動詞可以看出本句是表示過去時間的句子。所以原句應為：When the hunter saw the lion run..., the hunter...。因為前、後子句皆是以 the hunter 為主詞，所以可以省略附屬連接詞 When 與 the hunter，將 saw 改成 Seeing 而形成分詞構句。

(十七) Having + p.p...., S + 過去式動詞

Having wrapped the presents, Alice went to bed.

愛麗絲包好禮物後，就去睡覺。

文法解析

本句以完成式的分詞構句開頭，表示前後不同時間的連貫，所以 Having wrapped 表示已完成的動作，要比其後半句中的 went 發生的早，所以它應是過去完成式。

(十八) Being + Ving..., S + 現在式動詞…

Being chasing the cat, the dog hits a tree.

被那隻貓追趕時，那隻狗撞到一棵樹。

文法解析

Being + Ving 在本句中視表示現在進行的狀態，所以是用現在進行式的分詞構句型式。

(十九) S + 動詞…, Ving...

He found the treasure, hiding it in his car.

他發現那個寶藏並且把它藏在他的車中。

分詞構句若出現在後半句，通常表示在時間的順序上是較晚或較後發生的動作或事情。事實上，hiding it... 可以改成 and hid it...。

(二十) p.p...., S + 動詞…

Reared up on a farm, Angela loves rural life.

安琪拉是在農場養大的，她喜愛鄉村生活。

以過去分詞開頭的分詞構句通常是被動句型，它是省略了 Being + 過去分詞中的 Being，而以過去分詞呈現。

(二十一) 連接詞 + 分詞構句…，S + 動詞…

Though failing in the entrance examination of college, Peter still studied hard to prepare other tests.

雖然彼得大學入學考試失敗，但是他仍然努力讀書來準備其他的考試。

有些分詞構句因為缺了附屬連接詞就會變得語意不清，所以仍然得保留附屬連接詞 (Though)，而形成連接詞 +Ving 的形式。

四、形容詞 & 副詞慣用句型

(一) 不定代名詞 $\begin{cases} \text{something, somebody, someone} \\ \text{nothing, nobody, anything, anyone, anybody} \end{cases}$

+ 形容詞

The police didn't find anything dangerous in the park.

警方在公園未找到任何危險物品。

There is nothing usual in the area.
在此地區沒有不尋常的事情。

文法解析

形容詞在不定代名詞的後面來修飾不定代名詞，這與一般的形容詞用法不同(一般皆置於被修飾的詞類前)。

(二)主詞 + { be 動詞 / 一般動詞 } + so + { 形容詞 / 副詞 } + that 子句：

太…以至於…

The car runs so fast that it hits the tree by the road.
那輛車行駛太快以致撞上路邊的樹。

The girl is so charming that she attracts many people.
那女孩非常迷人，以致她吸引許多的人。

文法解析

so ... that ... 表示一種情形造成的結果，so 之後用形容詞或副詞是由其前的動詞型式而決定，若用 be 動詞，則 so 之後要用形容詞。若用一般動詞，so 之後則用副詞。

(三)主詞 +be+such+ { a/an+ 單數名詞 / 複數名詞 } + that 子句：

十分…以至於…

The scientist is such a wise person that he invented the invisible plane.
那位科學家是非常聰明的人以致他能發明隱形飛機。

文法解析

本句型與前項(二)的句型涵義相似。只是本句型中的 such 之後要接名詞而非形容詞，其後 that 子句的用法一致。

(四)A ＋ be ＋ as ＋ adj ＋ as ＋ B：A 像 B 一樣的…

The giant serpent is as long as a car.

那巨大的蛇像車子一樣長。

文法解析

> as ... as 中第一個 as 之涵義是「這般的…」做副詞用，而第二個 as 作
> 「像…一樣」是介系詞，as 相當於 like 的涵義與用法，所以整個句型
> 的涵義爲：像…一樣的…。

$$(五)A ＋ be ＋ \begin{cases} 原級形容詞 ＋ er \\ \begin{Bmatrix} more \\ less \end{Bmatrix} ＋ 原級形容詞 \end{cases} ＋ than ＋ B：$$

　A 比 B 更…

Usually foxes are smarter than wolves.

通常狐狸比狼聰明。

Children are more innocent than adults.

孩子比大人更單純。

文法解析

> 當形容詞爲單音節的字 (如：wise, cruel 等等) 都在字尾加 er 形成比較
> 級形容詞。三個音節以上的形容詞則在其前加上副詞 more 或 less 來形
> 成比較級形容詞。

(六) A + be + the +
$\left\{\begin{array}{l}\text{原級形容詞 + est} \\ \left.\begin{array}{l}\text{most} \\ \text{least}\end{array}\right\} + \text{原級形容詞}\end{array}\right.$
$\left\{\begin{array}{l}\text{of + 三者 (含三者)} \\ \text{以上的團體} \\ \text{in+ 位置 / 地點} \\ \text{(在…那裏)} \\ \text{among+ 三者 (含} \\ \text{三者) 以上的群體} \\ \text{(在…之中)}\end{array}\right.$

Taipei 101 is the tallest building in Taiwan.
在臺灣 101 大樓是最高的建築。

Sam is the most intelligent student of all the students.
山姆是班上最聰明的學生。

Swimming is the most competitive game among the contests.
在這些競賽中游泳是最競爭的比賽。

文法解析

最高級比較級都是三者 (含三者) 以上的比較，而其後的介系詞都是接全體或整體的人或事物，只是涵義有所不同。of+ 三者以上的團體，有「屬於」的涵義。in則皆是位置或地點，among則強調「在…之中」。

(七) A+be
$\left\{\begin{array}{l}\text{形容詞 + er} \\ \text{more/less+ 形容詞}\end{array}\right\}$ + than+
$\left\{\begin{array}{l}\text{any other+ 單數名詞} \\ \text{all the other+ 複者名詞}\end{array}\right\}$: …是最…

Mt Everest is taller than any other mountains in the world.
埃佛勒斯山比世界任何其他的山更高。

Apes are more intelligent than all the other animals in the world.
人猿比世界上所有其他的動物更聰明。

Helen Keller is more persistent than anyone else.

海倫・凱勒比任何其他的人更有恆心。

文法解析

本句型雖然是以比較級的形式表達，但是卻是表達最高級的涵義。注意 than 之後的涵義是表示排除其他的人事物的情況。

(八) A+be+ $\left\{ \begin{array}{l} \text{倍數} + as + \text{原級形容詞} + as \\ \text{倍數} + the + \text{名詞} + of \end{array} \right\}$ +B：

…是…的…倍…

New Zealand is seven times as big as Taiwan.

紐西蘭是臺灣的七倍大。

Ostrichs' eggs are five times the size of chickens'.

駝鳥的蛋是雞蛋的五倍大。

文法解析

time 在本句型中作「倍數」解釋。其他的用法如同形容詞原級比較的用法。

(九) The+ 比較級 +S.+be/V…, the + 比較級 +S+be/V…：

愈…就愈…

The better her mother's health becomes, the happier she feels.

她母親的健康愈好，她就愈覺得高興。

文法解析

這是表示相對比較的情況，可以是正比也可以是反比。若動詞為 be 動詞，則比較級是形容詞。反之，若動詞是一般動詞則比較級是副詞，用來修飾動詞。

$$(\text{十}) \ S+be \begin{cases} \text{senior} \\ \text{junior} \\ \text{superior} \\ \text{inferior} \\ \text{prior} \end{cases} to + \text{受格} : \begin{cases} \text{比…更年長} \\ \text{比…更年輕} \\ \text{比…更優越} \\ \text{比…更差} \\ \text{比…更前面} \end{cases}$$

The residents here are usually senior to those in other places.
在此地的居民通常是比其他地方的居民年長。

Anyone who is junior to Tom should help clean the classroom.
任何比湯姆年幼的人皆能幫忙清理教室。

Some white people think that they are superior to colored people.
有些白人認為他們比有色人種優越。

文法解析

這些表示比較涵義的特殊用字，他們的字型皆有 or 作字尾並且用 to 作其介系詞來接另一者比較。

(十一) S + be not + so much A as B：…與其說是 A，不如說是 B

They are not so much co-workers as competitors.
與其說他們是同事，不如說他們是競爭對手。

文法解析

這是一種很特別的句型，所強調的對象是 B，而非 A，所以本句是強調後面的 competitors(競爭者)。

(十二) S + be + too + 形容詞 + to + 原形動詞…：太…以至於不…

China was too weak to fight against Western countries at the turn of twentieth century.
在二十世紀初中國太弱以致無法對抗西方國家。

too(太…) 本身是隱含否定涵義的副詞，所以其後的動詞受其影響而轉變爲否定的意思。

(十三) S + be + $\left\{\begin{array}{l}\text{always, regularly, usually, frequently} \\ \text{often, sometimes, occasionally, rarely} \\ \text{seldom, scarcely, ever, never}\end{array}\right\}$ +

形容詞

He is usually late for his class in the morning.

他通常早上上課會遲到。

Wind is often wild in winter.

在冬天風經常是狂暴的。

Mr. Brown is a nice person who is seldom angry.

伯朗先生是一個很少生氣的好人。

文法解析

上述框內的副詞都稱爲頻率副詞，表示某個行動或某件事發生的頻率或次數，從 always(總是，一直都是) 到 never(從未) 的表達各種情況的頻率副詞都有。他們都放在 be 動詞之後修飾其後的形容詞。

五、連接詞慣用句型

(一) S ... not ... until/till ...：直到…才…

He did not see his uncle until he arrived in Taipei.

直到他到臺北，他才看到他叔叔。

文法解析

本句型不能從字義去解釋 not ... until ...，因爲本句的涵義是肯定的意思並未將 not 的否定涵義表達出來。

(二) not because ... but because ...：不是因為…而是因為

The young girl married the rich old man <u>not because</u> she loved him <u>but because</u> she wanted to inherit his wealth.

那個年輕女孩嫁給那個富有的老人，不是因為她愛他，而是因為她想繼承他的財富。

文法解析

本句型其實是將 not ... but ... 的涵義再加上 because 而形成。所以在解釋上，仍不可以將 but 作「但是」解釋。

(三) in that 子句：在於…

Man is different from animals in that man is rational.

人之異於禽獸在於人是理性的。

文法解析

in that 中的 that 不是關係代名詞，是連接詞，這是一種特殊句型，in that 不可拆開使用。

(四) S...
$$\begin{cases} \text{so that 子句…} \\ \text{in order that 子句} \\ \text{to the end that 子句} \end{cases} ：…為了…$$

The man worked very hard <u>so that</u> he could earn more money.

那個人非常努力工作，為了他能賺更多的錢。

= The man worked very hard <u>in order that</u> he could earn more money.

= The man worked very hard <u>to the end that</u> he could earn more money.

文法解析

so that 在一起時作「為了」解釋，是表示目的之連接詞。其前後句子的動詞時式須一致。

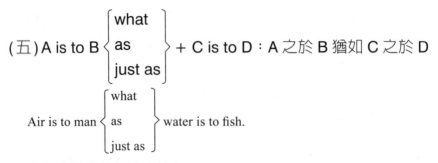

(五) A is to B ⎧ what / as / just as ⎫ + C is to D：A 之於 B 猶如 C 之於 D

Air is to man ⎧ what / as / just as ⎫ water is to fish.

空氣之於人猶如水之於魚。

⟨ 文法解析 ⟩

這是一種相對比喻的用法，雖然不常見到，但是它是一種相對比較的用法。

Exercise

一、選擇題：請從選項中選出最適合句子的答案選項

1. It is (A. she   B. hers   C. her) that James saw in the street.

2. The earthquake occurred suddenly. Some people rushed to the street, (A. the other   B. the others   C. others   D. another) hid under the desks or tables.

3. The climate of Taipei is much hotter than (A. those   B. this   C. that D. it) of Tokyo.

4. It is cruel (A. for   B. to   C. of   D. from) the murderer who killed the six-year-old little girl.

5. (A. Most   B. Each   C. Either   D. Little) of the scientists agree that dinosaurs died out because of the tremendous explosion caused by the collision between the Earth and a huge asteroid.

6. The nose of an elephant is much longer than (A. it   B. this   C. that D. those) of a monkey.

7. Many rich people think they are (A. inferior　B. senior　C. junior
D. superior) to poor people.

8. The more money you save now, the (A. easy　B. easier　C. easiest
D. easily) life you will have in the future.

9. The policeman asked the man (A. that　B. how　C. whether　D. which)
he drank or not.

10. The mother (A. had　B. got　C. forced　D. asked) her child buy a
bottle of milk for her.

11. It is no use (A. to regretting　B. regretting　C. of regretting　D. for
regretting) what already happened.

12. The tourist who got lost in the city had difficulty (A. to find　B. finding
C. of finding　D. to finding) his way to the station.

13. The kind person helped the young boy (A. return　B. returning　C. to
returning D. of returning) his home.

14. Many westerners are not (A. used to　B. accustomed to　C. use to
D. A&B are correct) eating Chinese food.

15. The considerate clerk gave her customer a bag to put in his glass lest it
(A. fell　B. to fall　C. fall　D. falling) to the ground.

16. Only when the election came to an end (A. the citizens could enjoy
B. the citizens can enjoy　C. do the citizens enjoy　D. could the citizens
enjoy) the quiet life.

17. The witness told the police that the truck ran (A. so quick　B. so fastly
C. so quickly　D. such a fast) that it hit a tree by the road.

18. The child cried very loudly (A. so that　B. for which　C. so to　D. so as
to) he could attracted his mother's attention.

19. New Zealand is not only famous for her beautiful views, but also (A. distinguish
B. distinguished　C. to distinguish　D. fame) for her multiple cultures.

20. (A. Whatever   B. Whenever   C. But for   D. As soon as) the thief saw the policeman, he ran away at once.

21. The rich woman spent a lot of money (A. buy   B. to buy   C. buying D. for buying) expensive clothes and jewelry.

二、克漏字

Smart phones are a revolutionary invention that become a communication means to contact people. It was not popular ___1___ iPhones were created by the Apple company. Nowadays smart phones are ___2___ prevalent that almost everyone owns one. The phones also bring some problems because many people are ___3___ to them. Some people are ___4___ involved into using smart phones to notice the danger around them. For example, they cross roads without watching cars toward them and ___5___ causes traffic accidents. It ___6___ that more and more traffic accidents happened because of using smart phones.

___7___ who use smart phones also surf the Internet quite often. It ___8___ them plenty of time to watch the screen of phone and waste their time and energy. Experts suggest that this kind of people ___9___ quit this bad habit. They remind them that it is not ___10___ spending so much time ___11___ smart phones. Using smart phones is not ___12___ studying or working in our daily life. We ___13___ save our time to do ___14___ in our life. ___15___ your smart phone on the table, walk out of your room to see things around you instead of those on the screen of your smart phone.

1. (A) when   (B) until   (C) that   (D) because
2. (A) so   (B) very   (C) such   (D) too
3. (A) like   (B) love   (C) addicted   (D) amazed
4. (A) so   (B) very   (C) too   (D) much

5. (A) this　(B) that　(C) they　(D) so

6. (A) reports　(B) is reported　(C) was reported　(D) says

7. (A) These　(B) Them　(C) Those　(D) That

8. (A) costs　(B) takes　(C) spends　(D) makes

9. (A) would　(B) might　(C) could　(D) should

10. (A) worth　(B) worth of　(C) worthy　(D) worthless

11. (A) in　(B) at　(C) on　(D) for

12. (A) as important as　(B) less important

　　(C) more important　(D) as soon as

13. (A) could　(B) would　(C) had best　(D) ought to

14. (A) meaningful something　(B) something meaningful

　　(C) something mean　(D) meaning something

15. (A) You leave　(B) Leaving　(C) To leave　(D) Having left

三、翻譯填空：依據中文句子的涵義填入適當的英文字詞

1. 最近天氣不好。不是下雨就是陰天。

　 The weather is bad. It is ＿＿＿＿＿ rainy ＿＿＿＿＿ cloudy.

2. 澳洲幾乎和美國一樣大。

　 Australia is almost ＿＿＿＿＿ America.

3. 那個旅客對那隻大白鯊感到驚嚇。

　 That tourist was ＿＿＿＿＿ the big white shark.

4. 他運氣不好。每次去日本必定遇到颱風。

　 He had a bad luck. He never went to Japan ＿＿＿＿＿ encountered typhoons.

5. 就是這場暴風雨使得我的旅程耽延。

　 It was the storm ＿＿＿＿＿ made my trip ＿＿＿＿＿.

一、

1. C 2. C 3. C 4. C 5. A 6. C 7. D 8. B 9. C 10. A
11. B 12. B 13. A 14. D 15. C 16. D 17. C 18. A 19. B 20. D
21. C

二、

1. B 2. A 3. C 4. C 5. A 6. C 7. C 8. B 9. D 10. A
11. C 12. A 13. D 14. B 15. B

三、

1. either, or 2. as big as 3. shocked at 4. but 5. that, delayed

03

克服閱讀障礙的第三關
── 找出文章主題與大意

- 第一節
  主題句 & 主旨句的定義與位置

- 第二節
  段落文脈的結構與發展

- 第三節
  文章的文體 & 語氣

閱讀導引

一、主題句的定義 & 主旨句的定義：文字解說→實例說明 (包
含文章內容 & 問題)

二、主題句的位置 & 主旨句的位置：圖示說明→實例講解 (包
含文章內容 & 問題)→重點整理

三、文章發展結構的形成：文章結構說明→七種文章結構解說
→範例說明→重點整理

四、用字遣詞對文章風格的影響：文章中修飾語的運用→圖示
說明→實例說明→重點整理

英文文章的
閱讀障礙

- 無法明白段落的主題
- 無法掌握全文的主旨
- 無法領悟文章的結構
- 無法瞭解文章的風格

破解方法

- 找出或推論出段落的主題
- 找出或歸納出全文的主旨
- 分析文章發展的依據
- 研究文章中的用字遣字

英文閱讀能
力的增進

- 迅速掌握全段/全文的主題
- 應付英文閱讀測驗相關的問題
- 明白文章作者的目的和語氣

一、主題句的定義

　　現今閱讀測驗中最常見的問題之一就是下列有關詢問全段或全文主題的問題：

1.　What is the main $\begin{cases} \text{subject} \\ \text{idea} \\ \text{point} \\ \text{purpose} \\ \text{theme} \end{cases}$ of the $\begin{cases} \text{passage} \\ \\ \text{reading} \end{cases}$?

2.　What is the best topic for this $\begin{cases} \text{passage} \\ \\ \text{reading} \end{cases}$?

3.　The article/passage/essay/reading is mainly about _____.

4.　From the passage, we learn that _____.

5.　The $\begin{cases} \text{passage} \\ \\ \text{reading} \end{cases}$ is mainly to describe _____.

6.　The first (second, third ...) paragraph is mainly about _____.

　　以上的問句都詢問文章或段落的主旨或主題。這不僅是現今閱讀測驗考題的趨勢，也是閱讀英文文章的主要目的之一，因為讀完一篇文章，卻不知其所言重點或主題為何，這樣的閱讀是無效的。因此，找出一篇文章中的主旨或一段文章中的主題，是很重要的閱讀技巧 (reading skills)。在英文文章

的段落中常有表達主題 (main idea/topic) 的句子，它被稱作「主題句 (topic sentence)」，一段只有一個主題句。同樣地，在整篇文章中也有表達全文主題的句子，其被稱為「主旨句 (thesis sentence)」，全文也只有一個主旨句。接下來的章節就是教導讀者如何找出主題句或主旨句。

※ 以下是「主題句」的範例說明：

The ideal season to visit the city of Mumbai is the months in the middle of September and April. Around this time the rains and typhoons have stopped unleashing their power and the humidity levels are at their most minimal. Actually guests can visit at whatever time of the year. However, summer months have a tendency to be too humid and hot, making a tour not extremely charming. But if you are arranging a business trip and will stay indoors and in a cooled solace, then the climate doesn't make a difference. (105 年公務人員特考)

中譯

　　到訪孟買的理想季節是九月和四月中旬的月份。大約這個時期雨和颱風已經停止發威並且濕度是最小。

　　事實上，訪客可以在一年的任何時段到訪。然而，夏天的月份趨於太潮濕又太熱，這使得旅遊不是非常吸引人的。但是如果你正在安排出差並且待在一個令人涼爽舒適的室內，那麼天氣就無所謂了。

內容解析

　　本段的主題句是本段的首句：The ideal season to visit the city of Mumbai is the months in the middle of September and April. 因為接下來的句子 (Around this time ...) 都在說明第一句中的那個適宜拜訪 Mumbai 的季

節之原因，而且用對比的方式來呈現其他季節不適合的原因：However, summer months have a tendency to be too humid and hot, making a tour not extremely charming.(太潮濕且炎熱…不是非常吸引人)。因此，本段第一句就是主題句，因為它涵蓋了後面句子內容的大意。

※ 現在以下列一篇文章為例，說明何謂「主旨句」：

The World Heritage Centre develops relationships with universities that are committed to research and education for the protection, conservation, and management of cultural and natural heritage through the international network entitled Forum UNESCO-University and Heritage (FUUH).

There are two ways to become affiliated to this network: individually or institutionally. Individual affiliation to this network is free and simple. Academic staff, researchers, heritage professionals, and students (above Masters level) may join the network on an individual basis. Individual members receive the FUUH monthly electronic newsletter informing them about worldwide news on natural and/or cultural activities. As an interactive communication tool, FUUH invites individual members to send news about their respective activities, provided that they relate to heritage. These items of news are reflected in the next FUUH newsletter, thus providing members instant worldwide dissemination and visibility. Institutional affiliation is made through the signature of a Memorandum of Understanding (MOU) in which the World Heritage Centre of UNESCO and a University agree to work together in a spirit of cooperation to reinforce links between their institutions, and contribute to World Heritage research and knowledge.

Universities interested in working with the World Heritage Centre of UNESCO through signing a Memorandum of Understanding can contact the World Heritage Centre.

中譯

　　世界遺產中心與經由聯合國教科文組織與大學暨遺產論壇的國際網絡與大學發展關係，這些大學承擔對文化與自然遺產的保護、保存以及管理。

　　有兩種加入這個網絡的方式：個人或組織。個人加入此網絡是免費且簡單的。學術成員、研究者、遺產專業人士以及學生(碩士學位者以上)可以以個別處理的方式加入此一網絡。個人會員每月會收到此論壇的電子報通知他們有關世界各地在自然和/或文化活動的消息。作為一種互動的溝通工具，如果與世界遺產有關，該論壇會邀請個人會員送出個別的活動消息。

　　這些消息的事項會在下一期的論壇報中發布，如此就提供會員立即的全球性之傳播與可見度。機構的加入是經由備忘錄(MOU) 的簽定所完成，其中聯合國教科文組織的世界遺產中心與某所大學同意以合作的精神共同工作來加強它們之間的聯繫並且對世界遺產研究和知識有貢獻。

　　對於聯合國教科文組織的世界遺產中心有興趣的大學經由簽署備忘錄就能接觸世界遺產中心。

內容解析

　　在本文的第一段中就指出世界遺產中心與聯合國教科文組織以及大學暨遺產論壇經由國際網絡 (the international network) 建立合作關係來使大學承擔對文化與自然遺產的保護、保存以及管理。接下來的第二段就介紹加入上述網絡 (FUUH) 的方式，接下來的第三段也是說明此網絡的功用。因此，本文的手段就是表達本文的主旨，因為只有一句，所以也是本文的主旨句。主旨句常出現的位置除了第一段之外，還有文章的最後一段。這兩個段落是最常出現主旨句的地方。知道主

旨句就可回答下列相關的問題：

What is the main idea of this article?

(A)To introduce a global network, FUUH.

(B)To promote UNESCO World Heritage sites.

(C)To persuade people to interact with their cultures.

(D)To inform universities of the importance of signing an MOU.

Answers

(A)

二、主題句的位置

(一) 在段首的主題句——開門見山：

　　前一例的兩段文章中，主旨句通常可在第一段的句首找到。然而閱讀文章中只有一段時，段落的主題句即是全文的主旨句，正如下例所示：

例題

　　The individual human brain and mind is the most complicated and highly organized piece of machinery that has ever existed on this Earth. So-called electronic brains can perform extraordinary tasks with superhuman rapidity; but they have to be given their instructions by men. The human organism can give instructions to itself, and it can perform tasks outside the range of any inanimate machine. Though at the beginning it is a feeble instrument equipped with conflicting tendencies, it can in the course of its development achieve a high degree of integration and performance. It is up to us to make the best use of this marvelous piece of living machinery.

Instead of taking it for granted, or ignorantly abusing it, we must cherish it, try to understand its development and explore its capacities.

中譯

　　個人的頭腦與心智是這世上現有最複雜，且非常有組織的一件機器。所謂的電腦能以超人般地速率執行特別的工作；它們仍需由人來下令執行。人腦卻能給他自己指令，並且它能執行超出沒有生氣機器所能做的範圍外之工作。雖然，在開始時人腦是個具有不同傾向的脆弱設備，但是在它發展的過程中它能達到高度的整合及表現。好好利用這種令人驚嘆的活機器是由我們來決定。我們不要視其為理所當然或無知地濫用它，而必須珍惜它，試著去瞭解它的發展及開發它的能力。

內容解析

　　本文的第一句即是本文的主題句，這種開宗明義的方式這是主題句在段落中最常見的位置，而就文章發展的型式而言，本文是以開頭的主題句來標明本文的題旨：人腦比電腦複雜且優秀，而後接著以解釋此主旨的演繹式文體展開，最後以一種結論式的語氣 (我們必須珍惜…。) 來結束本文。所以找出本文的主題句及其所含的主旨可以幫助我們回答下列有關這種詢問主題的問句：

This passage mainly discussed _____ .

(A) electronic computers　　　　(B) the human brain

(C) how to calculate　　　　　　(D) how we should live

Answers

(B)

(二) 主題句位於段首的第二句——好戲在後：

　　這種情況發生於段首的起始句，通常是引入 (引介) 句 (introductory sentence) 來引出下一句 (亦即主題句) 中的主題或提出問題，而引出主題句作答，所以在這種情形下，段首句通常是作過渡或介紹的功用，來切入或引出主題，請看下列說明：

　　The locations of stars in the sky relative to one another do not appear to the naked eye to change, and as a result stars are often considered to be fixed in position. In reality, though, stars are always moving, but because of the tremendous distances between stars themselves and from stars to Earth, the changes are barely perceptible here. It takes approximately 200 years for a fast-moving star like Bernard's star to move a distance in the skies equal to the diameter of the Earth's moon. When the apparently negligible movement of the stars is contrasted with the movements of the planets, the stars are seemingly unmoving.

(問題)

Which of the following is the best title for this passage?

(A) The Evermoving Star

(B) Planetary Movement

(C) Bernard's Star

(D) What the Eye Can See in the Sky

Answers

(A)

(中譯)

　　天空中星星之間相對的位置對肉眼而言並未顯出改變，結果星星經常被認為是固定在其位置上。事實上，雖然星星一直在移動，但是由於它們之間的巨大距離以及它們與地球之間的距

離，這些改變幾乎是無法辨識的。像伯納德的這類快速移動的星星要花費將近二百年的時間在天空中來移動一個相當於月球直徑的距離。當星星顯而易見的動作與行星的動作對照時，星星似乎是沒有在動。

內容解析

> 本文第一句是引介句 (introductory sentence) 引出本文所說的對象：星星。它也是作為與本文主題成對比的句子，因為第二句 (也是本文的主題句) 與第一句是涵義相反的句子。換言之，作者藉著 In reality(事實上) 這個語氣轉接詞來說出本文真正的主題。接下來的句子都是在解釋說明第二句中的主題：星星一直在移動 (stars are always moving)。因此全文的脈絡分析如下：
>
> 第一句：引出本文探討的對象 (星星) 以及一般對星星位置的觀念
>
> 第二句：道出不同於傳統對星星認知的觀念，與首句成對比而凸顯主題。
>
> 第三句以後的句子：印證第二句中的主題所以本文的標題 (the best title) 是與主題有關，因此答案是 (A)：一直移動的星星。

(三) 在段末的主題句──追根究底：

　　置於段末的主題句通常是將段落發展的細節歸納的結果，也就是說段末的主題句是具有結論的功能。將段落發展中的說明、舉例、比較、定義等闡述性的文意歸納在一起，而形成暫時的結論 (或一段的結論)，所以主題句在段末的段落又稱為歸納型段落，請看下例說明：

The rules of etiquette in American restaurants depend upon a number of factors: the physical location of the restaurant, e.g., rural or urban; the type of restaurant, e.g., informal or formal; and certain standards that are more universal. In other words, some standards of etiquette vary significantly while other standards apply almost anywhere. Learning the proper etiquette in a particular type of restaurant in a particular area may sometimes require instruction, but more commonly it simply requires sensitivity and experience. For example, while it is acceptable to read a magazine in a coffee shop, it is inappropriate to do the same in a more luxurious setting. And, if you are eating in a very rustic setting, it may be fine to tuck your napkin into your shirt, but if you are in a sophisticated urban restaurant this behavior would demonstrate a lack of manners. It is safe to say, however, that in virtually every restaurant it is unacceptable to indiscriminately throw your food on the floor. The conclusion we can most likely draw from the above is that while the types and locations of restaurants determine etiquette appropriate to them, some rules apply to all restaurants.

問題

With what topic is this passage primarily concerned?

(A) rules of etiquette in different restaurants

(B) instruction in proper etiquette

(C) the importance of good manners

(D) variable and universal standards of etiquette

Answers

(D)

中譯

　　美國餐廳的禮節規則是因幾個因素而定：餐廳外在的位置，例如鄉村或城市；餐廳的形式，例如非正式的或正式的；以及更普通的某些標準。換言之，某些禮節的標準化很顯著而其他的標

準則幾乎可在各處運用。在特定區域的特別型式的餐廳學習適當的禮節有時可能需要教導，但是更普遍地是這樣的學習只需要敏銳及經驗。例如，雖然在咖啡店裡看雜誌是可被接受的，但是在一種更華麗的布置下做同樣的事卻不合適。如果你在一家非常樸素布置的餐廳用餐，將餐巾塞入你的襯衫裡也許可以，但是如果你在一家精緻的都會餐廳用餐此種行為會證明缺少體貌。然而，可以確切的說實際上每家餐廳對你雜亂地將食物丟到地板上這件事是無法接受的。我們幾乎可以從以上的陳述獲得這樣的結論，雖然餐廳的形式與位置決定了對它們合適的禮節，但是某些規則仍可運用到所有的餐廳。

內容解析

　　本文一開始就說出與主題相關的要點：美國餐廳的禮節規則是因幾個因素而定。接下來對這幾個因素作了進一步的舉例與說明。然而對這幾個 (事實上是三種) 因素的個別舉例與說明並未作進一步的分析。直到最後一句，作者清楚地用 The conclusion(結論) 來總結全文的涵義，並歸納出全文的主題 (也是結論)：餐廳的形式與位置決定了對它們合適的禮節，但是某些規則仍可運用到所用的餐廳。所以本文的文脈發展可以分析如下：

引介句 (引介與主題相關的論點)：The rules of etiquette in American restaurants depend on a number of factors: *1*. the physical location of restaurant *2*.The type of restaurant *3*. certain standards that are more universal.

⇩

對提出的論點舉例說明：Learning the proper… and experience. For example, …

⇩

結論句 (總結以上的三種因素並作簡單的分析) 也是本文的主題句

就以上分析可以得知詢問本文主題的問題之答案應是 (D)：變動與普遍的禮節標準。

(四) 在段落中的主題句——若隱若現：

與段首、段尾中的主題句比較，在段落中的主題句是比較少見，其在段落發展的程序上是依照「次要的引題→重要的主題思想→次要的闡述」的原則，請看下例說明：

When children begin school in the United States, at the age of five or so, they are usually clearly either right-handed or left-handed. In schools in the United States, left-handed children are usually allowed to learn to write, cut with scissors, and work with art supplies with their preferred hand. But in the past, it was often the custom to force a left-handed child to learn to write and do other work with the right hand. In some countries, this is done today. Researchers do not agree on the effects of such a change. Some say that forcing a left-handed child to be right-handed can cause emotional and physical problems and even learning difficulties. They say such a child may start to confuse the directions left and right and reverse letters and numbers accidentally, such as writing 36 instead of 63. Other specialists laugh at such findings and say that changing a child's handedness will have no such effects. Perhaps part of the disagreement is due to the fact that children differ in how strong their hand preference is. Some left-handers are so strongly left-handed that they fight any change, and if they are forced, they may indeed develop problems. Others are not so strongly left-handed and can make the change without any great difficulty.

問題

How do the authors of this passage feel about teaching left-handers to use their right hands?

(A) They think it should not be done to children who strongly prefer the left hand.

(B) They think it prevents many serious problems.

(C) We do not know what their opinion is.

(D) They think it should never be done to any left-handers.

Answers

(A)

中譯

　　當五或六歲左右的孩子在美國開始上學時，他們通常很清楚是用右手或用左手。在美國的學校，用左手的孩子通常被允許用他們所喜好的手來學習寫字，用剪刀剪以及用美術用品工作。但是在過去強迫使用左手的孩子以右手來學寫字及做其他的工作經常是一種慣例。在某些國家今天依舊如此做。研究人員不同意這樣的一種改變的效果。有些研究人員說強迫用左手的孩子使用右手會引起情緒與生理上的問題以及甚至學習的困難。他們說這樣的孩子可能開始弄混左右的方向並且偶爾會顛倒字母與數字，就像把 36 寫成 63。其他的專家對這樣的發現置之一笑並且說改變孩子的用手方式不會有這樣的結果。也許部分的不同意是因為基於孩子在他們用手偏好的程度上有差異的這個事實。某些使用左手的人是非常傾向使用左手，他們抗拒任何的改變。如果他們被迫改變，他們實際上有可能會有問題產生。其他的人不是強烈的左手使用者，他們可以不會很困難的有所改變。

內容解析

　　本文開頭就介紹本文探討的對象：使用左手的孩童。接下來以美國使用左手的孩童的例子舉例說明。一直到文章的中間才點出與本文主題相關的句子：Researchers do not agree on the effects of such a change.

接下來就將兩種不同研究者對使用左手的孩童的不同看法進一步解釋說明。末了作者對上述不同的論點提出其看法 (也是本文的主題)：

Perhaps part of the disagreement is due to the fact that children differ in how strong their hand preference is.

本文的脈絡可分析如下：

(1) 引介本文討論的對象：When children begin school ... or left-handed.

(2) 舉例說明：在美國的例子 (In schools in the United States ... with the right hand)，古今的例子 (But in the past ... this is done today)

(3) 指出與主題相關的陳述 (不同研究者的看法)：Researchers do not agree on the effects of such a change.

(4) 進一步舉例說明上述看法：Some say ... Other specialists laugh at.(不同的研究觀點)

(5) 對上述不同看法的結論 (亦是本文主題)：Perhaps part of disagreement is due to…

(6) 對結論進一步說明：Some left-handers are ... Others are not so strong ...

瞭解本文的主題 (作者的看法) 就可以順利回答上述問題。

(五) 在段落中無主題句：

有些段落並無明確的主題句。段落的中心思想，是藉由對細節敘述或暗示而來。所以要從段落的細節中，找出文中主要論述的對象，進而找出與此對象相關的論點。這個論點可能只是一個字詞或片語也就是關鍵字詞，不過這個關鍵字詞還是與全段的細節相當有關係，請看下例說明：

Once upon a time there was a king who had three daughters. He wanted to choose one of them to be the queen. He called the daughters to him and said, "My dear children, the one who brings me a birthday present which is most necessary to human life shall be queen. Go and make your plans."

The king's birthday arrived. The two oldest daughters brought him presents that were very necessary, but were also very expensive. However, the youngest daughter only brought him a small pile of salt. When the king saw her present, he became very angry. He told the daughter to leave his castle and never come back.

The daughter left her father's castle. She had nowhere to go. As she wandered in the forest, cold and hungry, a prince saw her and fell in love with her at once. She agreed to marry him and a great party was held at the prince's castle. The king was invited, but he did not know that the bride was his daughter.

The girl told the cook to make all the dishes for the party with no salt. At the wedding, everyone started eating and they found that the food had no taste. Then the king sighed, "I now know how necessary salt is. But, because I didn't know that before, I sent my own daughter away and I will never see her again." Hearing this, the daughter went to the king and made herself known. They all lived happily ever after.

中譯

　　很久很久以前有一位有三個女兒的國王。他要選擇他們其中之一成為女王。他叫女兒們到他那裡去並且說：「我親愛的孩子，那位帶給我對人類生活最需要的生日禮物者將成為女王。去進行你們的計畫。」

　　國王的生日到了。兩個大女兒帶給他十分需要但也是十分昂貴的禮物。然而，最小的女兒只帶給他一堆鹽。當國王看到她的禮物就很生氣，他告訴那個女兒離開他的城堡，永遠別回來。

那個女兒離開她父親的城堡。她無處可去。當她在森林中徘徊時，又冷又餓，有位王子看到她並且立刻愛上她。她同意嫁給他而且一場盛大的宴會在王子的城堡中舉行。那位國王被邀請，但是他並不知道新娘是他的女兒。

　　那個女子告訴廚師在宴會中所有的菜中都不用鹽。在那場婚禮中，大家開始進餐，他們發現食物沒有味道。然後那位國王就嘆氣：「我現在知道鹽是多麼需要。但是先前我並不知道，我將我的親生女兒送走，而我也再見不到她了。」聽到這些話，那個女兒走到國王那裡，讓國王知道她。從那以後他們都過著快樂的生活。

內容解析

　　本文是一個敘述含有人生哲理的故事，有點類似寓言的故事。從故事的描述中歸結出富有人生哲理的觀點。在首段中故事的主題就被間接的點出：the one who brings me a birthday present which is most necessary to human life shall be queen.(那位帶給我對人類生活最需要的生日禮物者將成為女王。) 接下來的故事發展都圍繞在此一主題中。其發展的脈絡如下：

第二段重點：他最年幼的女兒帶給國王一小堆的鹽，作為她所認為生活最需要的東西。

第三段重點：國王如何來到她女兒的婚宴，作為下一段故事發展的背景。

第四段重點：指出國王如何發現鹽是生活最主要之物。

※　從以上 2〜4 段的分析可以看出這些故事的發展與細節皆是圍繞在鹽是生活中最需要之物。由此可以歸納出本文的主題，也可回答本文的相關問題：

The best title for this story could be _____ .

(A) "A Wise King"

三、主題句的位置與文章發展的關聯

(一)演繹式段落發展 (Deductive development of paragraph)：主題句在段首類似自然科學中的假設，亦即先提出主題或論點，而後來印證此一主題或論點是正確的。因此，主題或主題句嘗試出現在段落的首句，而後延伸出其他支持主題句中主題的細節，像解釋、說明或舉例等等。現以下列例子說明演繹式的文脈發展：

例題

"Stay inside" is no longer a safe way to escape from unhealthful air. Recent studies have shown that indoor air pollution is almost always two to five times worse than outside pollution. Buildings create their own pollution, and the air inside many homes, office buildings, and schools is full of pollutants including chemicals, bacteria, and smoke. These pollutants are causing a group of unpleasant and dangerous symptoms such as eye or throat discomfort, headaches, dizziness, and tiredness, which experts call "sick building syndrome."

中譯

「待在室內」不再是一種逃離不健康空氣的安全方式。近來的研究已顯示室內空氣的污染幾乎都是比室外污染還糟二到五倍。建築製造它們本身的污染，在許多家中、辦公室中以及學校中的空氣充滿包括化學物、細菌與煙霧的污染物。這些污染物不

斷引起一類像眼睛或喉嚨不適、頭痛、頭暈以及疲倦這種不舒服或危險的症狀。專家稱之為「致病建築症候群」。

內容解析

　　本段的首句是主題句，開宗明義的將主題呈現："Stay inside" is no longer a safe way to escape from unhealthful air.(「待在室內」不再是一種逃離不健康空氣的安全方式。) 接下來的句子就是針對此主題句中的主題加以解釋與說明。並且舉例說明「待在室內」不再是一種逃離不健康空氣的安全方式。因此，本段的文脈發展就是一種演繹式的發展，先提出主題，再加以說明或舉例。所以演繹式的發展之段落通常主題或主題句會出現在段落的首句。其段落的發展如下圖所示：

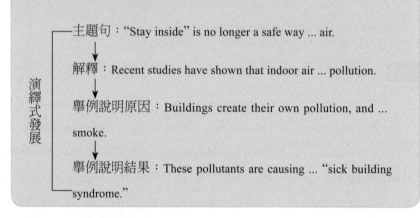

演繹式發展

主題句："Stay inside" is no longer a safe way ... air.

解釋：Recent studies have shown that indoor air ... pollution.

舉例說明原因：Buildings create their own pollution, and ... smoke.

舉例說明結果：These pollutants are causing ... "sick building syndrome."

(二) 歸納式段落發展 (Inductive development of paragraph)：主題句在段尾

　　文章中歸納式的發展就是先敘述現象、問題、解釋或舉例，而後將所陳述的這些細節歸納出一個結果或結論，也就是此一段落的主題或主題句。因此，歸納式發展的段落之主題句通常出現在段落的最後一句，也就是結語。現以下列說明歸納式的文脈發展：

In our busy modern world, doctors do not always take the time to explain illness and possible remedies to their patients. Doctors may even not give any scientific details in words that are easy to understand either. For this reason, many hopeful people take advantage of Internet resources to find the facts they need for good medical decisions. On the subject of physical and medical research, there are thousands of amazing websites where people can get information. Some people believe that the great amount of medical information available on the Internet can improve their health, while others claim that these facts and opinions may be inaccurate and therefore dangerous. Indeed, to find out the best ways to solve difficult health problems, we may still need to seek advice from doctors.

中譯

　　在我們現代繁忙的世界中，醫生不一定花時間向他們的病人解釋他們的疾病和可能的醫療方式。醫生甚至可能也不會告知任何精確易懂的細節。因此許多帶著期盼的人會利用網路資源來找到他們需要的有關好的醫療選擇的真相。在生理與醫藥的研究主題上，有數以千計令人訝異的網站，人們從這些網站可以獲得資訊。有些人相信大量可獲得的網路資訊能有助於他們的健康，然而有些人宣稱這些事實與意見可能是不準確的，因而具有危險性。事實上，要找出最佳解決困難的健康問題之途徑，我們也許仍然需要尋求醫生的忠告。

內容解析

　　本文開頭是描述一種醫療問診的現象：醫生不詳述病人的病因，所以病人自己利用網路資源來做更好的醫療決定。接下來的句子進一步說明對這些資訊的正反兩面的反應。最後一句則是作者表達自己的看法：我們仍然需要尋求醫生的忠告，這也是本段的結語，亦即本段

的主題句。英文中的 indeed(事實上) 是表示轉換語氣的轉折詞，凸顯之前所談論並非事實，indeed 之後的所說的事實才是正確的。其段落的發展如下：

演繹式發展

現象的描述：In our busy modern world, doctors do not ... Doctors may even not ... understand.

↓

對此現象的反應：For this reason, many ... decisions. On the subject of physical ... information.

↓

對網路資訊正反兩面的反應：Some people believe ... , while others ... dangerous.

↓

作者的看法 (結語)：Indeed, to find ... seek advice from doctors.

◎重點整理◎

一、定義：
1. 主旨句：全文的主旨所在 (不論段落多寡)。
2. 主題句：整段的主題所在 (一個段落只有一個主題句)。
3. 結論句：歸納整篇或整段文章的細節闡述，為加強或引申主題的句子，有時與段首的主題句前後呼應。

二、主旨句、主題句及結論句的位置及相關作用：
1. 主旨句的常見位置：第一段的段首和末段的段尾。
   主旨句的少見位置：中間段落。
2. 主題句的四種位置：
   (1) 段首：表明段落主題，以演繹方式闡述支持主題的細節。

(2) 段首第二句：由引介句來引出主題，再以答題或闡述的方式切入主題句。

(3) 段尾：在段末歸納前面句子所闡述的細節，以歸納的方式，提出結論，其功能與結論句類似，但卻無前後呼應。

(4) 段中：隱藏在段落中，由一連串的闡述句來引入主題，再由主題進而引申或列出相關的細節闡述。

※ 以下表列主旨句在全文中兩種常見的位置：

(1) 位於全文的首段

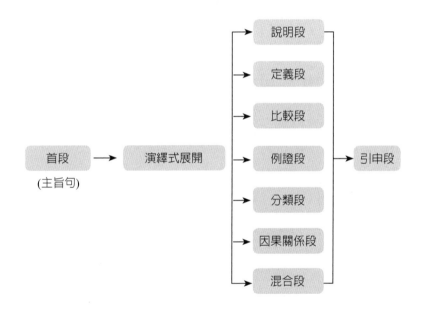

附註：上述的各種段落形式請參考本書第二節段落文脈的結構與發展的說明。

(2) 位於全文的末段

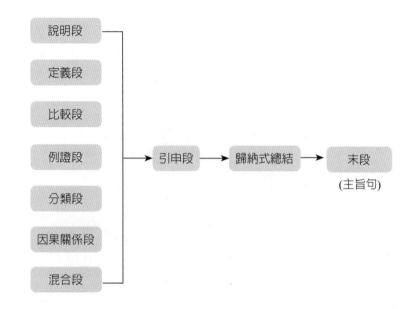

※ 以下表列主題句在段落中的四種位置：

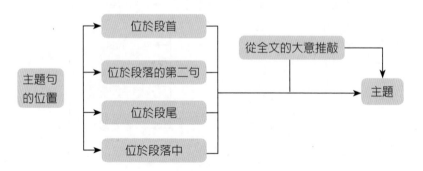

3. 無主題句的段落其實是將主題句化整為零，分散到某些句中的關鍵字了。而這些<u>關鍵字</u>往往就是段落中一直出現或圍繞的主要字眼或對象。

三、主旨句的位置與文章發展的關聯

1. 演繹式段落的發展

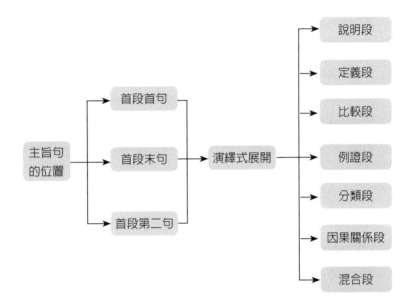

2. 歸納式段落的發展

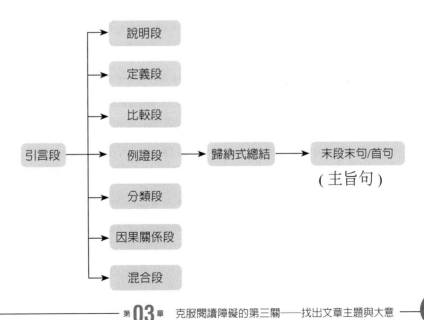

Exercise

找出下列文章中的主旨或主題句：

1. When a couple marries, the groom gives his bride a wedding ring. Many marriages are double-ceremonies-that is, both the bride and groom exchange rings. The wedding ring is customarily a simple, plain gold band.

   The roundness of the ring symbolizes eternity and announces that the couple is united for life. The wedding ring is wore on the third finger of the left hand. People used to believe that a vein from that finger ran directly to the heart.

   主旨／主題句：_____

2. The British Government has made some laws to reduce noise. Moreover, it has spent a lot of money for the same purpose. As a result of these laws, a worker can make a claim for money if he becomes deaf after working in a noisy environment for a long time. America and Norway have similar laws. In Taiwan, there are only few laws to keep city noise from increasing. But there is no law to make an employer pay compensation to a worker who becomes deaf. Recently, it was discovered that many teenagers in America could hear no better than 65-year-old people. Furthermore, in addition to making people deaf, noise makes people less efficient. Workers in noisy offices are not as efficient as workers in quiet offices. On the other hand, however, workers in the factories doing dull jobs work better when lively music is played to them. Do you think there is too much noise near your school or your home? Since we cannot measure the increase or decrease of noise, we never know in what dangerous situation we are put. Therefore, we hope our government can enforce more strictly their anti-noise laws.

主旨 / 主題句：_____

3. Few institutions are more important to an urban community than its police, yet there are few subjects historians know so little about. Most of the early academic interests developed among political scientists and sociologists, who usually examined their own contemporary problems with only a nod towards the past. Even the public seemed concerned only during crime waves, periods of blatant corruption, or after a particularly grisly episode. Party regulars and reformers generally viewed the institution from a political perspective; newspapers and magazines–the nineteenth century's media-emphasized the vivid and spectacular.

Yet urban society has always vested a wide, indeed awesome, responsibility in its police. Not only were they to maintain order, prevent crime, and protect life and property, but historically they were also to fight fires, suppress vice, assist in health services, supervise elections, direct traffic, inspect buildings, and locate truants and runaways. In addition, it was assumed that the police were the special guardian of the citizens' liberties and the community's tranquility. Of course, the performance never matched expectations. The record contains some success, but mostly failure; some effective leadership, but largely official incompetence and betrayal. The notion of a professional police force in America is a creation of the twentieth century; not until our own time have cities begun to take the steps necessary to produce modern departments.

主旨 / 主題句：_____

4. An old saying tells us that if you want something done well, you should do it yourself. Today many people seem to take this saying to heart. They do not buy furniture and other things already made. Instead, they prefer to make things themselves. They have become do-it-yourself fans. In the

United States many store sell parts for making desks, chairs, tables, bookcases, and other things. All you have to do is put parts together, add some paint or varnish, and you will have made a fine piece of furniture. You will find a lot of satisfaction in doing it yourself. Besides being economical, it's fun, too.

主旨 / 主題句：_____

5. Giving gifts can be great fun. It can be even more exciting than receiving presents. If you think it too unimaginative to give toys to children, or roses and chocolates to lovers, you can take gift-giving as a challenge to your creativity. Some people do have fresh ideas about what to give. At a baby shower, the young mother was over-joyed to receive a gift of 24 hours' free babysitting. The offer of service was not only welcomed by the receiver but taken as an expression of the giver's talent. Give more thought to what you are going to give, and you can make your gift original and unique.

主旨 / 主題句：_____

6. An election year is one in which all four numbers are evenly divisible by four (1944, 1948, etc.). Since 1840, American presidents elected in years ending in zero have been destined to die in office. William H. Harrison, the man who served the shortest term, died of pneumonia several weeks after his inauguration. Abraham Lincoln was one of four presidents who were assassinated. He was elected in 1860, and his untimely death came just five years later. James A. Garfield, a former Union army general from Ohio, was shot during his first year in office (1881) by a man to whom he wouldn't give a job. While in his second term of office (1901) , William Mckinley, another Ohioan, attended the Pan-American Exposition at Buffalo in New York. During the reception, he was assassinated while

shaking hands with some of the quests. Three years after his election in 1920, Warren G. Harding died in office. Although it was never proved, many believed he was poisoned.

主旨 / 主題句：_____

_____

Answers

1.　沒有明確的主題或主旨句，the wedding ring(結婚戒指) 爲本文的關鍵字。

2.　Therefore, we hope our government can enforce more strictly their antinoise laws.

3.　The notion of a professional police force in America is not a creation of the twentieth century; not until our own time have cities begun to take the steps necessary to produce modern departments.

4.　Today many people seem to take this saying to heart.

5.　Giving gifts can be great fun.

6.　Since 1840, American presidents elected in years ending in zero have been destined to die in office.

在前一單元中已就文章的大意主題提供相關的找尋方法。本單元將分析段落中及段落間的發展型式，以便瞭解及掌握段落中的具體訊息，進而加深對段落內容的明瞭以及回答詢問段落內容的問題，而按段落內容發展的型式可分為以下七種：

一、時間排列型段落 (Chronological paragraph)

時間型段落是以時間的順序或事情發展的先後次序來呈現的段落，大都用來記敘事物、記載歷史或事件發展的過程。請看下例說明：

例題

According to the best historical and archaeological evidence, it is estimated that it took about 8 million years for the Earth's population to reach the 250 million total which existed at the end of the first century after Christ. For some time after that, disease, famine, and war kept the population increase down to a fraction of 0.1% a year so that more than 15 centuries passed before the population reached 500 million. But in the next 250 years, up to 1850, the population of the world shot up to the 1 billion mark, and today it has reached 3 billion. It is predicted by United Nations investigators that in the next 36 years the population of the world will double, reaching almost 7 billion by 2000.

中譯

根據最佳的歷史及考古證據，據估計地球上的人口花了八百

萬年才在西元第一世紀末達到總數二千五百萬人。在那之後的某段時間，疾病、飢荒及戰爭使得人口成長降低到一年只有百分之零點一，所以過了十五個世紀多人口才達到五千萬人。但在接下來的二百五十年中，直到一八五〇年，世界人口突增至十億人的數字，而今天它已達三十億。根據聯合國的調查預估在下一個三十六年中世界人口將會於西元二〇〇〇年之前倍增至將近七十億。

內容解析

　　本文是以時間為主軸，將事件倒敘回來。從最早的時間(八十萬年前)到西元第一世紀末，再到十五紀中，而後再說到一八五〇年代。最後結束於公元二〇〇〇年之前。不過本文是以數字混合時間來呈現時間的先後。所以其數字及時間就變成本文的兩個重心。其發展的脈絡如下：

時　　間	對應的數目
Stage1 { from 8 million years B.C. to / to 100 years A.D.	250 million
Stage2 { from the end of the first century / to about 16th century	500 million
Stage3 { from 16th century / to 1850	1 billion
Stage4 { from 1850 / to about 2000	7 billion

從以上的圖表中可對時間及數字的發展經過一目瞭然，並可輕而易舉回答下列的問題：

1. It is estimated that in the year A.D. 100 the population of the Earth was about

   (A) 800 thousand   (B) 1 million

   (C) 250 million   (D) 500 million

2. The population of the world doubled between the year

   (A) 1850 and today   (B) 100 and the year 1600

   (C) 100 and the year 1400   (D) 1 and the year 100

3. By the year 2000, the Earth's population will probably exceed its present population by

   (A) 1 billion   (B) 3 billion   (C) 4 billion   (D) 7 billion

---

Answers

1. (C)   2. (A)   3. (C)

二、空間排列型段落 (Spatial paragraph)

　　描繪人與事、物、地點或場所之間的位置關係的文章大都用空間位置排列的相關順序來寫。而描寫的過程一般是按順序來描寫的，通常由一特定的地點或位置為對象，而後按空間的順序由上到下或由下到上或自左而右或自右而左，以及自中心向四周或四周向中心，由近到遠或由遠到近等等的順序來描述。

例題

　　Manhattan, an island about thirteen miles long and two miles wide, forms the principal of New York City, from whose mainland it is separated by the Harlem River. It was discovered by Verrazano in 1524 visited by Hudson in 1609, and first occupied as part of New Netherland by the

Dutch. They applied the name Manhattan to the local Indians, and in 1626 the accomplished fact of its settlement was given some semblance of legality by its purchase from the Indians for sixty guilders($24). One of the five boroughs of New York City, the island houses the principal business districts and includes Wall Street, Greenwich Village Broadway, the Bowery, the East Side, Harlem, and the Batter.

中譯

　　形成紐約市主體的曼哈頓島是一座大約十三英哩長兩英哩寬的島嶼，其本土是哈林河所分割。它於一五二四年為 Verrazano 所發現，而於一六〇九年由哈德生首次探訪。也首度由荷蘭人占據而為其國土的一部分。他們使用當地印第安大對該島的稱呼一曼哈頓，並且在一六二六年藉著六十元的荷幣從印第安人那購得此地，而使荷人對其地已完成開墾的事實賦予某種合法的外貌。作為紐約市的五大區之一曼哈頓島容納了主要的商業區以及包括華爾街、格林威治村、百老匯、包爾瑞大道、東區、哈林區，以及百特區。

內容解析

　　本文介紹地理景觀的短文。是以空間的排列位置為主軸，從曼哈頓島的大小外觀開始，介紹與其相關的歷史 (按時間先後陳現)，最後終結於其所包含的精華區。所以針對其地形的問題也就躍然紙上：

(1)　In shape, Manhattan Island is apparently

　　(A) long and narrow.　　　(B) short and wide.

　　(C) almost square.　　　　(D) similar to a boat.

由 13 英哩長與 2 英哩寬的描寫中可以看出曼哈頓島是一狹長的島嶼。所以答案為 (A)，針對此類敘述空間位置的文章，要對數目及表位置的形容詞 (如 long, wide, high 等等) 及介系詞 (in, on, between, over 等等)

敏銳。

而本文的主題也是與地理的重要性有關，所以有針對此主題而提出的
問題：

(2) The main purpose of this passage is to

    (A) give details about the location and early history of New York City.

    (B) give readers some interesting and important facts about Manhattan
        Island.

    (C) convince readers that the Indians were cheated out of an important piece
        of land.

    (D) explain how New York City came to be called Manhattan.

(3) The island of Manhattan is separated from the rest of New York City by

    (A) one of the City's boroughs.   (B) the Verrazano Bridge.

    (C) the Hudson River.   (D) the Harlem River.

題 (2) 的答案應為 (B) 是曼哈頓，不是紐約市 (考對地名的清楚與否)。
題 (3) 的答案也是考對文中地理位置的瞭解與否，答案應為 (D)。在原
考題中問地理位置的問題就占了 3 題，可見本文是測驗考生對空間位
置這類文章的熟悉度。

三、例證型段落 (Paragraphs developed by examples)

例證型段落是透過舉例的方式來印證文章的主題或中心思
想。而舉例的方式及位置視文章展開的模式及規模而定，也就
是說文章展開的方式若為演繹式，則舉例在主題之後。反之，
若舉例在前，主題在後 (作結論式的主題) 則其展開的方式為
歸納式。也就如下表所示：

$$\text{演繹式文體：主題 (句)} \begin{cases} \text{長文→舉例 (1) →舉例 (2) →} \\ \text{舉例 (3)…→結論句} \\ \\ \text{短文→一個長例或一連串的} \\ \text{短例 (單字或片語的形式) →} \\ \text{有時會有與主題呼應的結論} \\ \text{句} \end{cases}$$

$$\text{歸納式文體：} \left. \begin{array}{l} \text{長文→舉例 (1) →舉例 (2) →} \\ \text{舉例 (3)…} \\ \\ \text{短文→一個長例或一連串的} \\ \text{短例 (單字或片語的形式)} \end{array} \right\} \begin{array}{l} \text{主題 (句)} \\ \text{(亦為結論句)} \end{array}$$

例 1

Ice ages, those periods when ice covered extensive areas of the Earth, are known to have occurred at least six times. Past ice ages can be recognized from rock strata that show evidence of foreign materials deposited by moving walls of ice or melting glaciers. Ice ages can also be recognized from land formations that have been produced from moving walls of ice, such as U-shaped valleys, sculptured landscapes, and polished rock faces.

(88 國小特教甄試)

According to the passage, what happens during an ice age?

(A) Ice melts six times.

(B) Evidence of foreign materials is found.

(C) Ice covers a large portion of Earth's surface.

(D) Rock strata are recognized by geologists.

Answers

(C)

中譯

　　冰河時期 (當冰雪覆蓋地球的區域之時期) 已知發生過至少六次。過去的冰河時期可以由岩石層被確認，這些岩石層顯示為移動的冰層或融化的冰河所堆積的外在物質之證據。冰河時期也可以從由冰層所造成的地形而認出，就像 U 形峽谷，刻劃過的地形以及光滑的岩石表層。

內容解析

　　本位的主題句位於段首，所以本文為先說出主題的演繹式文體。接下來以兩個短例來證明段首的主題句：冰河時期已知發生過六次。因此文章的脈絡可以如下：主題(Ice age ... six times)→例1(Past ice ages ... glaciers) →例2(Ice age can also be…polished rock faces)。其中第二例更進一步以 such as 的方式來列舉說明。所以本文是一典型的例證型段落。對於上述的問題，它是與主題句中的解釋有關的 (those periods covered extensive areas of the earth)，所以答案應是 (C)。

例2

　　Folk music in the early 1960s was a medium for social criticism. It reflected young peoples ideals, hopes, fears, and their anger, confusion, and rebellion. Folk singers sang about the importance of brotherhood, the horror of war, and the dignity of the individual human being.

　　What confuses and angers idealist young people? One thing is the difference between many adults, words and their actions. Many parents say, "God wants us to love each other and be honest." However, these same parents are often dishonest in business. How can people love each other and be dishonest, too? Such behavior troubles idealistic young people. Their high moral values were expressed in the folk music of the 60s.

What do young people fear? Their greatest fear is destruction of their future by war. Science can improve life, but it can destroy life, too. Scientists can make artificial kidney machines, and they can transplant human hearts. Many scientists, however, work on nuclear bombs, chemical and biological weapons, and other instruments of war. Young people fear the unwise use of this scientific power for destruction.

Why do young people rebel? They rebel because they hate conformity. They don't want to live in the same kind of houses, wear the same kind of clothes, study the same subjects, or work at the same kind of jobs as their fathers. They want to be individualistic. They want the right to choose their way of life. They want equal opportunity for all men. Their songs said it all for them.

(90 國小教師學分班)

中譯

　　民謠在一九六〇年代早期是作社會批評的一種媒介。它反應年青人的想法希望、恐懼以及他們的憤怒混亂和叛逆。民歌手歌唱有關同胞情誼的重要性，對戰爭的恐懼以及人類的個人尊嚴。

　　是什麼混亂激怒了理想的年青人？一是許多成人在言行之間的差異。許多父母說，「神要我們彼此相愛與誠實相待。」然而，這些同樣的父母在事情上經常不誠實。人們如何能彼此相愛而又不誠實相待？這樣的行爲困擾理想主義的青年。他們高度的道德評價在六〇年代的民謠中被表達出來。

年青人恐懼怎麼？他們最大的恐懼是他們的未來會爲戰爭所毀滅。科學能改善生活，但它也可以摧毀生活。科學家能製造人工腎臟機器，他們能移植人體心臟。但是許多科學家研究核彈、生化武器以及其他的戰爭武器。年青人害怕這樣的科學毀滅力量的不智使用。

　　年青人爲何叛逆？他們叛逆是因爲他們痛恨墨守成規。他們不要住同樣的房子，穿同樣的衣服‧讀相同的科目，或者像他們的父親做同樣的工作。他們要個人主義。他們要選擇他們生活方式的權利，他們要所有人同等的機會，他們的歌爲他們說出這一切。

內容解析

　　本文也是一種例證性的文章。在第一段中主題就已陳現：It reflected young peoples ideals, hopes, fears; and their anger, confusion, and rebellion. 接下來的三段文章就是就主題中所提到的三種青年人的反應來一一舉例說明。作者是以問句的方式來說明這三種的年青人反應之原因。因此本文的脈絡可分析如下：

首段：主題呈現 (It reflected young peoples…rebellion.)
　　↓
第二段：說明年青人的混亂與憤怒的原因 (主題句中提及的反應)
　　↓
第三段：　明年青人的恐懼 (主題句中提及的反應)
　　↓
第四段：解釋年青人叛逆的原因 (主題句中提及的反應)

瞭解上述文章的脈絡，對相關問題就能一一回答

1.　Young people are confused because

(A) many adults differ from each other in their opinions.

(B) many adults have no sense of social and personal responsibility.

(C) many parents do not follow what they themselves teach.

(D) many parents say that people don't love each other.

2. Young people fear

(A) that scientists can make artificial kidney machines and transplant human heart.

(B) that science doesn't help human beings.

(C) that they will be as poor and miserable as ever.

(D) that their future will be destroyed by the use of modern weapons in war.

3. Young people rebel because

(A) they hate their parents and society.

(B) they want to live their own way.

(C) they want to be like other young people.

(D) they want to make the older generation accept their political views.

第一題的答案要在第二段中找，答案為 (C)，第二題很自然就在第三段中來找，答案為 (D)，最後一題則是在最後一段中來找解答，答案是 (B)。其實這三個問題都是包括在全文的主題範圍內。

四、定義型段落 (Paragraphs developed by definition)

許多解釋事物、術語、現象的文章常用定義式的段落來表達。文章中也常直接以下列的字詞提到被定義人事物的涵義、屬性、範圍等等：

$$\text{被定義的} \atop \text{人、事、物} + \left\{ \begin{array}{l} \text{be 動詞} \\ \text{be equal to(等於)} \\ \text{mean(s)} \\ \text{denote(s)} \\ \text{be known as} \\ \text{be called (as)} \\ \text{be defined as} \\ \text{be described as} \\ \text{refer(s) to} \end{array} \right\} + \text{下定義的詞、片語或句子：}$$

就是；等於；稱為；指～

　　下定義的字組或句子可分為兩類：
(一) 單句定義：以一個句子來說明解釋。
(二) 延伸定義：以二個 (含二個) 以上的句子來說明 (有時可擴展為整段)。

例 1

　　Carbohydrates, which are sugars, are an essential part of a healthy diet. They provide the main source of energy for the body, and they also function to flavor and sweeten foods. Carbohydrates range from simple sugars like glucose to complex sugars such as amylose and amylopectin. Nutritionists estimate that carbohydrates should make up about one-fourth to one-fifth of a person's diet. This translates to about 75-100 grams of carbohydrates per day. A diet that is deficient in carbohydrates can have an adverse effect on a person's health. When the body lacks a sufficient amount of carbohydrates, it must then use its protein supplies for energy, a process called gluconeogenesis. This, however, results in a lack of necessary protein, and further health difficulties may occur. A lack of carbohydrates can also lead to ketosis, a build-up of ketones in the body that causes fatigue, lethargy, and bad breath.

中譯

　　碳水化合物，也是醣類，是健康飲食的必需成分。它們是提供身體活力的主要來源，並且它們也具有添加香味與使食物變甜的功能。碳水化合物分布的範圍從像葡萄糖這種單純的醣類到像澱粉顆粒質與澱粉酵素這類複雜的醣類。營養師估計碳水化合物應該構成一個人飲食中的四分之一到五分之一。這說明一天大約有 75～100 克的碳水化合物。碳水化合物不足的飲食可能會對個人健康有負面的效果。當人體缺少足夠份量的碳水化合物時，它就必須使用它的蛋白質供應來提供活力，一種稱為糖質合成的過程。然而這將造成所需蛋白質的缺乏。其他的健康難題可能發生。缺少碳水化合物也可能導致酮症。身體中內酮體增強所引起的疲倦，昏睡以及呼吸不順。

內容解析

　　本文是一篇對碳水化合物 (Carbohydrates) 的定義與解釋，並且舉例說明它對人體的功用。若就內容而言，它的用字算是艱深，其中相關的專業用詞不少，不過由於文章本身是重在定義與解釋，所以其中的舉例皆與此有關。而舉例也是說明碳水化合物的功用。因此，本篇文章是屬於一種定義與相關舉例的文章。知道文章的結構，就可以回答以下的問題：

Which of the following best describes the organization of this passage?

(A) definition and example　　(B) comparison and contrast

(C) specific to general　　　　(D)cause and result

Answers

(A) 定義與舉例。

He was what we would call a Bohemian: that is, he was a careless dresser, scorned regular employment, had no permanent address and was vague about money.

But Franz Schubert possessed two attributes that set him apart from other Bohemians: he was a genius and he had work to do. There was music to be written and if he had to starve in the process of writing it, he did not mind it.

Thanks to the good offices of a group of actual starvation; but his existence was a precarious one. He "boarded around," so to speak, staying with any friend who could give him a place to sleep. Legend has it that when he was put up for the night he frequently went to bed wearing his spectacles so that he could set to work immediately should an idea for a melody awaken him. That melody, when it arrived, was more than likely to be the setting for a song poem.   (82 雄師學分班)

中譯

他就是我們所謂的豪放不羈之人；也就是說，他是個穿著隨便的人，對固定的工作嗤之以鼻，居無定所而且用錢隨便的人。然而 Franz Schubert 有兩項使他與其他這類人不同的屬性：他是位天才而且有工作要做。若有想寫的樂譜，既使在寫的過程中必須挨餓，他也毫不介意。由於一群真正飢餓之人的好心協助；但是他的生活仍是不安定的。他「到處投宿」，也就是，與任何能供他睡覺之處的朋友待在一起。而傳奇的事就是當他晚上投宿時他經常戴著他的眼鏡去睡覺，為的是他能立刻起來工作，萬一某個旋律的靈感使他醒過來時。當那個旋律來臨時，其極可能成為一首韻詩的曲調。

　　本文的第一段的首句就是將主題點出的主題句：Bohemian，而本文也就是繞著這個表達主題的關鍵字在發展全文。也由這句中的 what we would call... 可知其為定義型的段落。然而從第二段開始，對文中主要人物 Franz Schubert 的 Bohemian 式的格性作了更仔細的定義：其兩種不同於其他 Bohemian 的特性。之後就以實例來具體說明這兩種特性。所以本文的發展脈絡可分析如下：

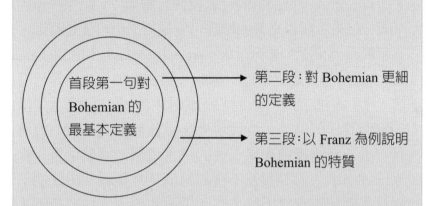

所以由上表看來，本文是一典型由中心至圓周的延伸性定義型段落，由兩句以上的多重定義來呈現主題，並且逐漸擴充為整段。以下這題乃是針對 Bohemian 定義的問題：

What are Bohemians like as a rule?

(A) They wear fashionable clothes.

(B) They are good office workers.

(C) They like to live in the same house for a long time.

(D) They are happy-go-lucky with their money.

Answers

(D)

五、因果型段落 (Paragraphs developed by cause & effect)

因果型段落主要是在解釋或說明某件事物或事件發生的原因及導致的結果，譬如說許多松樹突然之間枯死了，這是結果。而找出其枯死的原因，這是原因。而反過來說，植物學家發現某種導致針葉科樹木枯死的病菌，進而推測或發現某區域松樹的枯萎與此有關。這是先發現原因後找出結果的因果關係，所以表示因果型段落的發展模式有兩類：1. 結果─原因或 2. 原因─結果，所以文章的結論可能是結果也可能是原因。

而就原因來說，亦分近因 (immediate cause) 和遠因 (remote cause)，近因通常是立即而明顯的。譬如突然發生中等程度的地震，所以橋被震垮了。這顯示原因和結果在時間上是接近的。然而若仔細調查可能發現老早以前橋就有龜裂的痕跡，而且在近一年來遭遇颱風引發的洪水侵襲，因此地震一來就使原已逐漸擴大的裂痕及不穩的結構突然傾塌。由此例子可知文章有兩種表達原因的方法：近因和遠因。由於近因本身的性質 (立即而明顯的關聯性)，所以表達近因通常是以引導原因子句的連接詞或片語來表達，例如：because, since, as(因為), as a result of(由於), because of, owing to, due to(用在 be 動詞之後), thanks to(由於), on account of(因為), so, therefore, thus(正因如此), accordingly(因此), consequently(因此、結果) 等等。而表示遠因的方式通常是間接且綿長的說明段落。有時並沒有上述的連接詞或片語，而是由上、下文的涵義來表達。偶爾會以連接性副詞來轉接語氣，例如：therefore(因此), hence(因此), thus, so, accordingly, consequently 或片語：To sum up(總歸), On the whole(總而言之) 等等。

Elections are at the heart of the American political system, but in 1976 only 54 percent of voting age population went to the polls. Does it make a difference that so many Americans fail to vote?

Wolfinger and Rosenstone, two professors of political science, used the surveys conducted in 1972 and 1974 by the Bureau of Census, which interviewed over 88,000 people, about 50 times the number usually questioned by pollsters. For the first time, statistically precise descriptions of the voting rates of specific social and economic groups became available.

Furthermore, the size of the samples permitted them to isolate the turnout of particular groups-women, the poor, Chicanos, the elderly, and the young.

The core finding was the overwhelming importance of education. Age is second, with voting rates rising well into the seventies. Other variables have little effect on voting. From these and other findings, it is clear that some groups are underrepresented among voters, while others are overrepresented variables. But Wolfinger and Rosenstone showed that the political preferences of the groups that vote are not substantially different from the views of the entire adult populations, so the difference to the American political system is remarkably small.　　(85 師大教分班)

中譯

　　選舉是美國政體的核心。但在一九七六年在達到投票年齡的人口中只有百分之五十四前去投票。這許多的美國人不去投票會造成影響嗎？

　　Wolfinger 及 Rosenstone 這兩位政治學教授運用國家統計局在一九七二年及一九七四年所做的 8,000 人次的面訪調查，這份調查大約是一般民意調查員所做的問卷數量的五十倍。也是頭一次

在統計上對某些特定社經團體的投票率之準確敘述成為可行的。

　　此外，調查樣本的規模也容許他們區隔特定團體的投票率——婦女、低收入、墨裔美國人、老年人以及年青人。

　　這項調查的重要發現是教育程度是具有壓倒性的重要性。年齡則次之，投票率在七十歲的年齡層升高不少。其他的變數對投票率影響甚小。從這些和其他的發現，很清楚可知有些團體在選民中代表性不足，而有些團體則是代表性過高的變數。但是 Wolfinger 與 Rosenstone 指明某些投票團體的政治偏好與整體美國成人的觀點並無實質上的差異，所以這樣的投票率之差異對美國政體的影響是相當小的。

內容解析

　　本文是一典型的因果型文章，首段的第一句為介紹背景的引句，接著提出針對本文主題的問句：Does it...to vote? 而藉著這問句就將本文的原因提出。接下來的三段皆是就此問題而有的答案探尋。以 Wolfinger 及 Rosenstonef 所使用的民意調查結果來作本的結論，並且將這結論於末段的最後一句中提出。所以本文是遵循「原因—結果」的發展模式而展開的文脈。以一九七六年美國大選的這項近因來探尋投票率低落所可能造成的影響。本文的展開脈絡可分析如下：

Paraghph1
┌ Line 1 引言句 (introductory sentence)：
│ Elections are…to the polls.
│ 　　↓
│ Line 2 主題詢問句 (rhetoric question)：
└ Does it make… to vote?
　　↓

Paraghph
2～3　　例證段落：提出 Wolfinger 與 Rosenstone 兩人所採用的民意調查資料及其背景

↓

Paraghph4
{
引申段落：將第 2 及第 3 段落的例證加以歸納

結論句：But Wolfinger and Rosenstone showed that ...
is remarkably small.
}

所以要找本文的主題句可直接找與主題有關的問句，再就問句的主題
在後面段落尋找答案 (通常在最末段或段尾)，也就是找出表結果的
結論句。以下兩句是針對題旨及原因所作的問句：

1. A most appropriate topic of this passage should be

    (A) The Low Voting Rates in the United States.

    (B) New Techniques in Measuring Voting Rates.

    (C) The Overwhelming Importance of Education.

    (D) Variations in Turnout Among Voter Groups.

2. The 1972 and 1974 surveys are significant because

    (A) they give precise figures of voting rates of different groups.

    (B) they are the first large-scale surveys conducted by the government.

    (C) they represent a cooperation of the government and the colleges.

    (D) they are conducted on individuals in isolated groups.

Answers

1.(D)　2.(A)

六、比較與對比型段落 (Paragraphs developed by comparison & contrast)

比較或對比型的段落是常見的段落，透過比較或對比可呈現事物的相同或相異性，進而瞭解文章的主題或重點所在。這類文章通常是透過比較或對比來加深讀者對正、反、好、壞、優、劣兩面事物的印象，進而影響讀者的價值判斷。其展開的方式主要有三類：

(一) 個別比較法

亦即先集中說明某一特定對象的特徵或特性，然後再接著說明另一特定對象相似或不同的特徵或特性來作前、後的兩區段式比較。

對象 A：特徵 1+ 特徵 2+ 特徵 3…自成一區段
對象 B：特徵 1+ 特徵 2+ 特徵 3…自成一區段

對象 A 和 B 之特徵 1 的相同或差異 + 特徵 2 的相同與差異 +…

結論

(二) 逐項比較法

把兩個對象的相同或不同特徵作立即的比較，而且逐項進行，不區分兩區段。

對象 A 的特徵 1 與對象 B 的特徵 1 作比較
↓
對象 A 的特徵 2 與對象 B 的特徵 2 作比較
↓
對象 A 的特徵 3 與對象 B 的特徵 3 作比較

(三) 綜合比較法

把上述兩種比較法綜合運用，穿插進行比較。也是比較複雜的比較法。

例 1

In some cultures, the act of touching another person is considered very intimate and is therefore reserved for people who know each other very well. In the United States, for example, young children are taught that it is rude to stand too close to people. By the time they are adults, Americans have learned to feel most comfortable when standing at about arm's length away from people to whom they are talking. And many Americans do not touch each other with great frequency while talking (this is particularly true of men). In contrast, other cultures have more relaxed rules regarding touching. For example, it is usual for friends-both men and women—to embrace each other when they meet. When they talk they generally stand closer than Americans do, and they touch each other more often. They are as much at ease doing this as Americans are with more space between them.

中譯

在某些文化裡，與別人觸碰的舉動被視為很親密的，因此，也只有彼此很熟悉對方的人，才會有這種舉動。例如在美國，大人會告訴小孩，站得離別人太近是不禮貌的。到了長大成人，美國人已經學會了當他站在離談話對象前一臂之遙處，他會覺得最自在。很多美國人在談話時都不會常常去碰觸對方 (男士尤其如此)。相反地，其他的文化在身體接觸方面規範比較鬆。例如，不論是男是女，朋友見面時相互擁抱是很常的事。他們談話時通常站得比美國人近，也比較常碰觸對方。他們這麼做很自在，就像美國人保持距離一樣。

　　本文的前五句在描述及說明美式交化的人際接觸，其中提到身體的碰觸 (特徵 1) 兩個美式文化特徵及說話時的距離 (特徵 2)。而從下半段的第六句開始，由 In contrast(相反地) 這個片語式連接副詞清楚地表明與其前相反的比較，而且也就是就身體的碰觸 (特徵 1) 和談話的距離 (特徵 2) 按相同順序 (先身體後談話) 與對象 1(美式文化) 作相反的比較，因此本文是一篇典型的個別比較法 (亦即作兩區段分隔開的比較)，其細節如下：

(1) 對象 1(美式文化)：

　　① 特徵 1：the act of touching another is ... intimate.

　　② 特徵 2：many Americans, ... while talking.

(2) 對象 2 (其他文化)：

　　① 特徵 1：other cultures have more ... touching.

　　② 特徵 2：when they talk, ... than Americans do.

在瞭解上比較發展的相異點後就可毫無困難地回答下列問題了：

(1) According to this passage, different cultural backgrounds _____ .

　　(A) have little to do with human behaviors.

　　(B) influence human interaction.

　　(C) show that one people is superior to another.

　　(D) have produced the same human behavior.

(2) The polite space between two persons talking to each other _____ .

　　(A) is not very important in American culture.

　　(B) is very important in American culture if they are intimate.

　　(C) is about arm's length in all cultures.

　　(D) varies from culture to culture.

例2

Mrs. Allen and Mrs. Baker differ from each other in many ways except age. Ruch Allen is taller and slimmer than Emily Baker. She walks faster and she gets things done more quickly than Mrs. Baker does. Mrs. Bakers, on the other hand, is less busy than Mrs. Allen because she only keeps house, she doesn't teach. She is much more interested in politics than Ruch Allen is. She's a member of women's club.

中譯

Mrs. Allen 和 Mrs. Baker 除了年齡之外，有許多地方是不一樣的。Ruch Allen 比 Emily Baker 高且瘦。她走得較快，而且做事的速度也比 Mrs. Baker 快。另一方面，Mrs. Baker 並不像 Mrs. Allen 那樣忙碌，因爲 Emily Baker 只是個家庭主婦；她沒有教書這門職業，她比 Ruch Allen 對政治來得有興趣多了。她是位女性俱樂部的會員。

內容解析

本文是典型的逐項比較法，其展開結構如下：
主題句 (建立命題及比較的主要項目或限定比較的範圍)：Mrs. Allen and Mrs. Baker differ from each other in many ways except age.
(1) 特徵 1：身高與身材
　　① 對象 A：Ruch Allen — taller and slimmer
　　② 對象 B：Emily Baker
(2) 特徵 2：走路及做事
　　① 對象 A：Ruch Allen — walk faster and things done more quickly

② 對象 B：Emily baker

(3) 特徵 3：忙碌的程度

① 對象 A：Ruch Allen

② 對象 B：Emily Baker — less busy and not teach

(4) 特徵 4：政治興趣

① 對象 A：Ruch Allen

② 對象 B：Emily Baker — much more interested in politics; a member of women's club

所以本文是除了年紀之外，其他皆不同的比較文章。

(1) Mrs. Allen and Mrs. Baker are the same in their _____.

(A) age　(B) taste　(C) character　(D) interest

(2) This paragraph is about _____.

(A) language　(B) politics　(C) comparison　(D) relationship

(3) Mrs. Allen is a _____.

(A) housewife　(B) politician　(C) teacher　(D) saleswoman

問題 (1) 是就兩人的相同點而問，答案在主題句中 (except age)：(A)。問題 (2) 是就本章的型式而言，答案為 (C)。問題 (3) 是由特徵 3 的比較中推論出來，所以 Allen 太太是位老師：(C)。

例3

In seeking to solve their problems, social scientists encounter greater resistance than physical scientists. By that I do not mean to belittle the great accomplishments of physical scientists, who have been able, for example, to determine the structure of the atom without seeing it. That is a tremendous achievement; yet in many ways it is not so difficult as what social scientists are expected to do. The conditions under which social scientists must work would drive a physical scientist frantic. Here are five of those conditions. He can make few experiments; he can not measure the results accurately; he can not control the conditions surrounding the experiments; he is often expected to get quick results with slow acting economic forces; and he must work with people, not with inanimate objects.

中譯

　　在找尋如何解決他們的問題上，社會學家要比自然科學家遭遇更大的抵抗。我那樣說不是有意要輕視自然科學家的偉大成就，他們也曾經能夠在沒有看到的情況下判定原子的結構。那是項偉大的成就；然而在許多方面其不像社會學家所預期完成的事物那樣的困難。社會學家工作時必須所處的情況將會使自然科學家抓狂。以下是五種這樣的情況。他幾乎無法作試驗；他不能精確地衡量結果；他不能控制試驗四週的情況；他經常被期待在緩慢進行的經濟力量下得到迅速的結果；並且他必須與人在一起工作，而非與沒有氣息的物品在一起工作。

內容解析

He can make few experiments.	He can make more experiments.
社會學家 (被直接指明)	自然科學家 (被間接影射)
He cannot measure the results accurately.	He can measure the results accurately.
He cannot control the conditions surrounding the experiments.	He can control the conditions surrounding the experiments.
He is often expected to get quick results with slow acting economic forces.	He is not often expected to do such a thing.
He must work with people, not with inanimate objects.	He only work with inanimate objects.

本文是綜合個別比較及逐項比較的綜合比較法。第一段的首句正是本文的主題句：In seeking to solve ... physical scientists. 而這主題句是以比較的語氣來呈現，也就是一開始就點出本文爲比較型的段落。接下來略略地提出本文中兩個對象的相互比較 (接近逐項比較法)。不過話鋒一轉就再切入本文主題的重心：社會科學家所遭遇的更大困難。並且細分五項，逐項說明。雖然這五項並未直接提到自然科學家，不過其的確間接地與自然科學家的研究情況作比較試看下列說明，所以本文是混合了「明顯的個別比較法」及「隱含的逐項比較法」的「綜合比較法」。根據此瞭解也就可輕而易舉地回答下列問題：

According to this author, social scientists

(A) make more contributions to society than physical scientists.

(B) have solved more problems than physical scientists.

(C) are no more important than physical scientists.

(D) face more obstacles than physical scientists in their research.

Answers

(D)

七、分類型段落 (Paragraphs developed by logical division)

爲了便於書寫及明瞭文章內容，對作者及讀者來說，分類型段落都是便於表達思路的方式。而分類型段落主要有三種展開結構：

1. 由總類到分類：
   由一般性原則到特定的細則。

2. 由分類到總類：
   由特定的細則歸納爲一般性 (或結論性) 的原則，與此分法有關的分類指示字、詞包括：types, kinds, classes, sorts,

sources, varieties items, categories 等等，常見的動詞則是：classify, divide, break into 等等。

3. 順序性分類。

然而有些文章並未清楚標明上述的字詞或寫明出來。而是以類似順序般的字詞來逐項列出，例如：first, secondly, first of all(首要的是)，third, ...；或更間接口氣的語氣連接詞：then, next, now, furthermore, moreover(此外) 等等，這類不明顯分類的用詞也表明另一種含蓄式的分類，或說按照主題作前後輕重的闡述。

例 1

The human brain, with an average weight of fourteen kilograms is the control center of the body. It receives information from the senses, processes the information, and rapidly sends out responses; it also stores the information that is the source of human thoughts and feelings. Each of the three main parts of the brain-the cerebrum, the cerebellum, and the brain stem-has its own role in carrying out these function.

The cerebrum is by far the largest of the three parts, taking up 85 percent of the brain by weight. The outside layer of the cerebrum, the cerebral cortex, is a grooved and bumpy surface covering the nerve cell beneath. The various sections of the cerebrum are the sensory cortex, which is responsible for receiving and decoding sensory messages from throughout body; the motor cortex, which sends action instructions to the skeletal muscles, and the association cortex, which receives, monitors and processes information. It is in the association cortex that the processes that allow humans to think take place.

The brain stem, which connects the cerebrum and the spinal cord, controls various body processes such as breathing and heartbeat. It is the major motor and sensory pathway connecting the body and the cerebrum.

What is the author's main purpose?

(A) To describe the functions of the parts of the brain.

(B) To explain how the brain processes information.

(C) To demonstrate the physical composition of the brain.

(D) To give examples of human body functions.

Answers

(A)

中譯

　　有著平均重十四公斤的人腦是人體的控制中心，它接受從感官來的訊息，處理這些訊息並且迅速地發送反應；它也儲存人類思想與感受的來源之訊息。腦部三個主要部分的每一部分一大腦、小腦以及腦幹在實行這些功能上有它自己的角色。大腦到目前為止是三部分中最大的，占了腦部重量的百分之八十五。大腦的外層，大腦皮質，是一層覆蓋神經細胞於其下的凹凸不平的表層。大腦不同的區域是感官中樞皮層，負責接受及解讀全身而來的感官訊息；運動神經皮層對整個骨架肌肉送出行動指示，以及聯繫中樞皮層，接受、偵測以及處理資訊。就是在聯繫中樞皮層，使得人類思考的過程才會發生。

　　位於頭蓋骨後方大腦之下的小腦是由一團隆起的神經細胞所構成。小腦就是控制人的平衡、協調以及姿勢。

　　連接小腦與脊髓的腦幹控制身體不同的步驟，就像呼吸與心跳。它是連接身體與大腦的主要運動和感官的途徑。

> 　　本文是一篇典型的分類式段落。在第一段中本文的主題句就指出三種的腦部區域：Each of the three main parts of the brain-the cerebrum, the cerebellum and the brain stem-has its own role in carrying out these functions. 接下來的三段分別說明每一種腦部功用，並且依主題句中所提及的腦部區域之順序來依序說明，從大腦 (cerebrum) 到小腦 (cerebellum) 再到最後一段的腦幹 (brain stem) 說明。瞭解文章此種的結構，有助於回答上述的問題：作者主要的目的是 (A) 描寫腦部的功能。

例2

　　Besides providing an ideal environment for sea plants and animals to live in, seawater has other valuable properties, one of which is that it constantly moves and its movements produce energy.

　　The most obvious movements are the waves and the tides. Winds cause the waves, and the gravitational pull of the moon and the sun causes the tides. In places like the Bay of Fundy in Canada, the difference between the high and low tide level can be as much as 40 feet.

　　France and Britain are now trying to use energy in the tides to produce electricity. Waves can produce electricity and some small-scale experiments are taking place to learn more about this. One of the most encouraging areas of research uses the difference between the temperature of seawater at the surface and deep down to produce electricity.

中譯

　　海水除了提供海裏動植物理想的生活環境之外，還有其他珍貴的特質。其中之一便是海水會不斷地流動，產生能量。

　　最明顯的運動便是波浪與潮汐。風造成波浪，而日月的引

力則造成潮汐。有些地方像加拿大的芬地灣，漲潮與退潮的差距可高達四十呎。

　　法國和英國目前正嘗試利用潮汐的能量來發電。波浪能產生電子，而一些小規模的實驗正在進行，以對這方面有更深入的暸解。最有希望的研究範疇之一，是利用海面以及海底深處的差異來產生電力。

內容解析

　　本文並無任何明顯表示分類的指示詞式句子。而是以上、下文意及代名詞來串連及說明海水的流動。由句首的主題句提出本文的主題：海水不停的流動 (it constantly moves)，接下來以代名詞 its 來連接文意。到了第二段的開頭又將此一流動分為兩種：海浪 (the waves) 和潮汐 (the tides) 接著是一連串的說明及舉例 (like the Bay of Fundy in Canada) 來先解釋海浪的形成及功用。

　　到了第三段則以例證來證實第二種海水流動的功用——潮汐的功用 (發電)。所以，本文雖未明顯分類，然其也是按照由一般性概念到特定的細節來說明或舉例。這是比較活的表達手法。暸解此發展脈絡就能很快找出問題的重點及解答：

(1) One of the valuable properties of seawater is that _____.

　　(A) it has no plants in it

　　(B) it pulls the sun and the moon

　　(C) it flows all the time

　　(D) it feeds all kinds of animals

(2) Waves and tides are caused by _____.

　　(A) the same forces　　　　(B) different forces

　　(C) their own movements　　(D) plants and animals

　　另外，許多文章的段落進展通常是混合以上若干種的段落型式而成，很少有單型式的段落，也就是說例證型常以時間型的順序在文中展開。而定義型的也可能與例證型文體相輔相成。這種混合沒有一定原則，視實際的文章主題及內容而定，稱爲「混合型段落 (Paragraphs developed by mixed types)」。

例 1

　　The marathon is a race with a long history. It was first run over two thousand years ago in Greece by just one runner. The race became a part of the ancient Olympics. The first marathon in the United States took place almost one hundred years ago. It was held in New York City. The year was 1896. Another marathon was run in that same year in Boston. But these races did not get a lot of attention at that time. There were not many runners then and only a few were willing-or able-to run a race of more than 26 miles.

　　But in recent years jogging has become a very popular sport. People who at one time could barely run a few yards to catch their morning buses are now jogging. Many people run one or two miles a day. And marathon running appeals to many of them. The number of marathons has grown to keep pace with the new public interest. Now, a marathon is run somewhere in the United States every week of the year.

中譯

　　馬拉松是一項歷史悠久的賽跑。最早起源於兩千多年以前的希臘，跑者只有一個。這種賽跑後來成爲古代奧林匹克運動會的一部分。美國最早的馬拉松，大約是在一百年前舉行的。地點

在紐約市。

時間是一八九六年。同年在波士頓也有另一項馬拉松開跑。但是這些比賽在當時並未受到太多的注意。跑者並不多。而且只有少數人願意──或是能夠──跑二十六哩以上。

但是近幾年來，慢跑成為很受歡迎的運動。以前想趕上早班公車，跑個幾碼幾乎都不行的人，現在也在慢跑。很多人一天跑個一兩哩。而且其中很多人對馬拉松跑步很有興趣。馬拉松比賽的數目隨著大眾對它的注意而增加。如今，馬拉松在美國每個星期都舉行。

內容解析

　　本文是混合型段落混合定義型段落及時間型段落。句 (1) 為單句定義句，而由句 (2) 開始是一連串按時間排列的歷史敘述。而其中的年代 (1896) 及表順序副詞 (first, another, now 等) 皆為敘述時間或順序的詞。

Which of the following sentences best states the main idea of the above passage?

(A) The marathon is a Greek sport.

(B) The marathon was already quite popular in the United States about one hundred years ago.

(C) Jogging is a popular sport.

(D) The marathon is more popular in the United States now than it was in the in the nineteenth century.

Answers

(D)

An Augustinian monk named Gregor Mendel was the first person to make precise observations about the biological mechanism of inheritance. This happened a little over a hundred years ago in an Austrian monastery, where Mendel spent his leisure hours performing experiments with pea plants of different types. He crossed them carefully and took notes about the appearance of various traits, or characteristics in succeeding generations. From his observations, Mendel formed a set of rules, now know as the "Mendelian Laws of Inheritance," which were found to apply not only to plants but to animals and human beings as well. This was the beginning of the modern science of genetics.

中譯

　　一位名叫孟德爾的奧斯定會的僧侶是對有關生物遺傳機能做了準確觀察的第一個人。這件事發生在一百多年前的一處奧地利的修道院，在那裏孟德爾花費他閒暇時間以不同種類的豌豆科植物做實驗。他使異種互相交配並且對其下一代不同的特徵外形或特性予以記錄。從他的觀察中，孟德爾形成了一套規則，也就是現在所知的「孟德爾遺傳定律」，其不僅可應用於植物上，也可應用於動物以及人類上。這也是現代基因學的開始。

內容解析

　　本文是綜合定義型及例證性的兩種混合型文體。不過是以解釋「孟德爾定義」的由來為主體。所以可以說是對這個定義的由來背景作說明，而輔以由豌豆這事例加以解釋。段首的句子為本文的主題句，說出孟德爾在生物遺傳的重要性，而段尾的末句的涵義則指出其該學科的創始者，可以說這末了的一句是類似本段的結論句，這可由其 beginning 的涵義與第一句中的 first 之涵義前後呼應而看出。因著本

文為綜合性的文體，其問句涵蓋甚廣；請看以下題目：

一、對主題的另一種問法：

The importance of Gregor Mendel is that he was the first person to

(A) imagine that there existed a precise mechanism of inheritance

(B) approach the problem of inheritance scientifically

(C) think about why animals and plants inherit certain characteristics

二、詢問時間

When did Mendel perform his experiments?

(A) in ancient times   (B) in the 1680s

(C) in the 1860s   (D) at the beginning of this century

三、詢問原因

Why did Mendel do this work?

(A) Because it was part of his duties.

(B) Because he enjoyed it.

(C) Because he lived in Austria

(D) Because he was paid for it

四、詢問定義的內容

The Mendelian Laws of Inheritance describe the transmission of biological traits in

(A) plants   (B)animals   (C) human beings   (D) all of the above

Answers

一、(B)   二、(C)   三、(B)   四、(D)

◎重點整理◎

段落結構 & 型式	段落發展型式的特性
時間排列型段落	依據時間的順序或事情發展的先後次序來呈現的段落，大都是記敘文。
空間排列型段落	以空間位置排列的相關順序來描寫人、事、時、地、物之間的關聯。
例證型段落	透過舉例的方式來印證文章的主題或中心思想。
定義型段落	針對特定的事物、人物、術語、用詞以及現象等等加以定義或解釋，常出現在說明文中。
因果型段落	依據因果關係來呈現文章的內容，常出現在論說文中。
比較 & 對比型段落	採取個別 / 逐項 / 混合比較法。
分類型段落	以演繹式或歸納式逐項分類，配上序數或表示順序的文字來分項說明。

※ 明白上述文章內容的架構與發展有助於對文章內容與主題的掌握。

Exercise

確認下列各篇文章的結構：

1.　本文是：_____型段落

History has long made a point of the fact that the magnificent flowering of ancient civilization rested upon the institution of slavery, which released opportunity at the top for the art and literature, which became the glory of antiquity. In a way, the mechanization of the present-day world produces the condition of the ancient in that the enormous development of labor-saving devices and of contrivances which amplify the capacities of mankind affords the base for the leisure necessary to widespread cultural pursuits. Mechanization is the present-day slave power, with the difference that in the mechanized society there is no group of the community which does not share in the benefits of its inventions.

(A) 例證　(B) 時間　(C) 定義　(D) 比較

2. 本文是：_____型段落

What can one boy or girl do to preserve the world's rain forests? Ask Jiro Nakayama. He's the twelve-year-old leader of a band of school-children in Nagano, Japan, who have already saved 40 acres of forest land in Costa Rica. On their way to and from school, they collect old newspapers and empty aluminum cans for sale to a recycling plant at 63 cents per kilogram. The money they have made, together with donations from parents and neighbors, is sent to the International Children's Rainforest Program, which buys and preserves virgin rain forests at the rate of $50 an acre. So far, Jiro and his friends have raised more than $5,000.

(A) 定義　(B) 時間　(C) 因果　(D) 混合

3. 本文是：_____型段落

When you buy a share of stock, you buy a little part of an incorporated business. The corporation uses your money to help run or expand its business. If the corporation makes a profit, it sends you a check for or your share of the profit-say $1.00 for each share of the stock. The money is called a dividend. If the corporation makes a very big profit, it may decide to make the dividend bigger, say $2.00 for each share of the stock, and you get more money back even though the amount you invested is the same. But if the corporation doesn't make a profit, your share earns you nothing. If your stock keeps paying good dividends, people will want that stock so much that you can sell it for more than you paid for it. But if that stock never pays a dividend, few people will want to buy it. If you can sell it at all, you will get much less money than you paid for it.

(A) 定義　(B) 分類　(C) 例證　(D) 混合

4. 本文是：＿＿＿＿型段落

Ten years ago, there were more than 1.3 million elephants in Africa. Over the past ten years, that number has been cut down to around 600,000. African elephants are hunted for their valuable ivory tusks. Most have been killed by poachers. Poachers are hunters who kill animals illegally. An adult elephant eats as much as 300 pounds a day. In their search for food, elephants often move great distances. When they cannot find the grasses they prefer, they may strip the land of trees.

Today, the area in which elephant herds live is much smaller than it used to be. Many areas in their path have been turned into farms. And some elephants have been killed by farmers for trampling their crops.

What can we do here in our country about a threatened animal that lives so far away? Our government has passed a law to protect it. People cannot import or bring in items made from ivory or any part of the elephant's body.

Most countries throughout the world have also stopped ivory imports. It is hoped that the ban on the sale of ivory will help save the African elephant. But the world's largest land animal needs other help. The countries where these animals live are often poor and unable to manage the herds. If the elephant is to survive, this animal is going to need our support for many years to come.

(A) 分類　(B) 因果　(C) 比較　(D) 時間

5. 本文是：＿＿＿＿型段落

Friendship is both a source of pleasure and a component of good health. People who have close friends naturally enjoy their company. Of equal importance are the concrete emotional benefits they derive. When something sensational happens to us, sharing the happiness of the occasion with friends intensifies our joy. Conversely, in times of trouble and tension, when our spirits are low, unburdening our worries and fears to compassionate friends alleviate the stress. Moreover, we may even get some practical suggestions for solving a particular problem.

From time to time, we are insensitive and behave in a way that hurts someone's feelings. Afterward, when we feel guilty and down in the dumps, friends can reassure us. This positive interaction is therapeutic, and much less expensive than visits to a psychologist.

Adolescence and old age are the two stages in our lives when the need for friendship is crucial. In the former stage, teens are plagued by uncertainty and mixed feelings. In the latter stage, older people are upset by feelings of uselessness and insignificance. In both instances, friends can make a dramatic difference. With close friends in their lives, people develop courage and positive attitudes. Teenagers have the moral support to assert their individuality; the elderly approach their advanced years with optimism and an interest in life. These positive outlooks are vital to cope successfully with the crises inherent in these two stages of life.

(A) 時間　(B) 空間　(C) 比較　(D) 例證

Answers

1. (D)　2. (C)　3. (D)　4. (B)　5. (D)

一、文章的文體

(一) 記敘文 (Narrative essay)

　　針對人、事物所做的描述，常出現在對過去人物或事件的描述，例如：歷史、軼聞或故事等類的敘述。記敘文有下列幾種特點：

　　1. 常依據時間的順序 (time order) 來呈現事情的經過。

　　2. 常以動詞過去簡單式作為敘述中的主要動詞時式。

　　3. 人、事、時、地、物是文章主要描述的對象。

　　4. 常用舉例來說明人或事物。

　　現以下列範例說明敘述文的文體特點：

　　Samuel Morse accomplished something that is rarely accomplished he achieved fame and success in two widely differing areas. Throughout his youth he studied art, and after graduation from Yale University he went on to London in 1811, where his early artistic endeavors met with acclaim. In London, he was awarded the gold medal of the Adelphi Art Society for a clay figure of Hercules, and his paintings *The Dying Hercules* and *The Judgement of Jupiter* were selected for exhibition by the Royal Academy. Later in life, after returning to America, Morse became known for his portraits. His portraits of the Marquis de Lafayette are on exhibit in the New York City Hall and the New York Public Library.

　　In addition to his artistic accomplishments, Morse is also known for his work developing the telegraph and what is known as Morse Code. He first had the idea of trying to develop the telegraph in 1832, on board a ship returning to America from Europe. It took eleven long years of ridicule by his associates, disinterest by the public, and a shortage of funds before Congress finally allocated S30,000 to Morse for his project. With these funds, Morse hung a telegraph line from Washington, D.C., to Baltimore, and on May 24, 1844, a message in the dots and dashes of Morse Code was successfully transmitted.

中譯

　　撒姆耳・摩斯完成了一些很少完成的事：他在兩種極大不同的領域中功成名就。他整個年輕時期研習藝術，而且自耶魯大學畢業後他於一八一一年去到倫敦，在那裏他早期藝術方面的努力得到喝采。在倫敦他以海克力斯的陶製肖像獲頒艾得費藝術協會的金牌獎，而他的畫作「垂死的海克力斯」以及「丘比特的審判」為英國皇家學院獲選為其展示品。在他人生的後來時期，返美後摩斯以他的肖像畫而聞名。他的拉法葉的瑪吉斯肖像畫在紐約市政廳和紐約公立圖書館展示。

　　除了他藝術上的成就之外，摩斯也以他發展出的電報與為人所知的摩斯密碼的成果聞名。他早於一八三二年 (在一艘自歐返美的船上) 有嘗試發展電報的想法。在美國國會終於撥款三萬美元給摩斯的計畫之前的十一年期間，他被他的同事嘲笑，被大眾冷漠以對以及缺乏資金。有了這些基金，摩斯牽了一條從華盛頓特區到巴爾的摩的電報線路，並且在一八四四年五月二十四日一條以摩斯密碼的長短音訊息成功地被傳送。

內容解析

　　本文是一篇典型的敘述文，描述摩斯密碼發明者摩斯的成就。文章內容是依據時間的順序而發展：從 1811 年他去倫敦在藝文界出名到

1832 年他想出電報的想法以及他在 1844 年成功了發明摩斯密碼的電報。因為是描述過去的歷史，所以文中大部分動詞都用過去簡單式動詞，只有說到不變的事實時 (像 Morse is also known for his work developing the telegraph and what is known as Morse Code.) 才用現在簡單式動詞 is。此外，文章中也舉出一些實例說明摩斯在藝術與科技兩方面的成就。因此，在依據時間發展的順序、動詞時式以及舉例上，本文是一種敘述文的呈現方式。

　　本文的第一句即是本文的主旨句，將全文的主題呈現出來。這種開宗明義的方式正說出了主旨句的型式及位置。就型式而言，本文是先標明主旨 (he achieved fame and success in two widely differing areas) 的演繹式段落，也就是主旨句出現在全文的起首，而後有一連串的闡述細節之句子來舉例說明主旨句的主題，換言之，第一段是舉例說明摩斯的第一種成就 (在藝術方面)，第二段則描他的第二種成就。根據這個主旨下列問題有關，全文的標題 (由主旨簡化而來) 就是選項 (D) 摩斯不同的成功。

Which of the following is the best topic of this passage?

(A) Samuel Morse's artistic talents

(B) The use of Morse Code in art

(C) The invention of the telegraph

(D) Samuel Morse's varied successes

(93 臺南市國小教甄)

(二) 抒情文 (Descriptive essay)

　　抒情文是抒發作者主觀的感受與感情或想法的文體，經常會以第一人稱來表達。文章中會用許多的形容詞或副詞來描寫其中的情境。這種文體常表達一種作者的經驗或激勵，使讀者

身有同感。

現在以下列範例說明抒情文的特點：

I attended my 43 year-old uncle's wedding last Sunday afternoon. It was not a traditional wedding held in a church with a simple cake-and-tea or coffee reception afterwards. Instead, my uncle and his fiancée exchanged their vows of marriage in a beautiful garden at a five-star hotel. Since both my uncle and his fiancee were already working at good-paying jobs in two of the most successful computer companies in the city, they didn't need to depend upon their parents to help pay for their wedding. The couple invited many co-workers and friends besides their relatives. The wedding guests drank pink champagne and ate a variety of special delicacies prepared by the hotel's gourmet cooks. Attending this splendid wedding made me think that waiting to tie the wedding knot until one is older and financially independent is a good idea.

中譯

上週六下午參加我四十三歲的叔叔的婚禮。它並非是一場在教堂舉行並且婚禮後有著簡單下午茶或咖啡招待的傳統婚禮。反而，我的叔叔與他的未婚妻在一家五星級飯店的美麗花園中交換他們婚姻的誓約。因為我叔叔與他的未婚妻都已經在城中最成功的兩家待遇不錯的電腦公司工作，他們不需要依賴他們的父母來幫助他們付婚禮的費用。除了他們的親戚外，這對夫婦還邀請許多的同事參加。婚禮的客人喝玫瑰香檳酒以及吃由飯店的美食廚師所預備的特別佳餚。參加這場輝煌的婚禮使我認為等到較大年紀結婚以及經濟上的獨立是個不錯的想法。

> 　　本文以第一人稱「我」來描寫作者叔叔的婚禮。其中用了不少的形容詞，像 simple(簡單的)，beautiful(美麗的)，successful(成功的)，good-paying(待遇很好的) 來形容婚禮的情景。最後一句則表達出作者對這場婚禮的感想：參加這場輝煌的婚禮使我認為等到較大年紀結婚以及經濟上的獨立是個不錯的想法。抒情文的主題並不明顯，有時只是一些感想或想法的表達而已。

(三) 說明文 (Expository essay)

　　說明文是以客觀的解釋或說明人、事物或事理。作者儘量不做任何個人的評論或主張，也不表達個人的想法。文章中常以客觀的事實表達事物或事情，其目的是希望讀者能清楚明白文章中所介紹對象或主題的內容。因此，說明文的目的是提供讀者有關文章主題的資訊。例如，大到像自然界的各種現象，科學的原理。各種理論的解說等等，小至像如何使用某種工具或機械等等。

　　現以下文為範例說明：

　　When thousands of homosexual men began dying in the early 1980s of Acquired Immune Deficiency Syndrome, some public health experts predicted an "AIDS apocalypse. " An official predicted AIDS would make the Black Death the bubonic plague that wiped out one-third of the population of Europe in the Middle Ages-look weak by comparison. Such warnings were based on fear. Panic caused police officers to demand rubber gloves to use when they arrested people with AIDS. Some school principals refused to admit children with AIDS to schools. The panic has largely passed.

There's no vaccine to prevent people from catching AIDS. The main weapon against the disease has been educated. In the last three years, bars and other businesses that cater to gays have distributed literature promoting "safe sex. " Safe sex, such as the use of condoms, has helped stop the spread of the disease. The results have been dramatic. The rate of new infections of gay men has dropped sharply. About 5,000 gay men in San Francisco tested positive for AIDS in 1981; in 1988, there were only 100. The epidemic is all but over among gay men.

But intravenous drug users are still catching the disease from other drug users when they share hypodermic needles. New York City has an estimated 200,000 intravenous drug users, 40 percent of them infected with AIDS. Those who have AIDS may not show signs of the disease for up to 10 years. Also at risk of AIDS are kids whose mothers are intravenous drug users or prostitutes. Most new victims of AIDS are poor blacks and Hispanics.

(81 國中教分班)

中譯

　　當數以千計的男同性戀，在一九八〇年代的初期開始死於後天免疫不全症，某些公共醫療專家預期一種「AIDS 大災難」。一位官員預料 AIDS 將使黑死病——曾在中世紀時橫掃歐洲三分之一人口的黑死病瘟疫——相形見絀。這種警告是基於恐慌。恐慌促使警方在逮捕患有愛滋病 (AIDS) 的人時，要求警員戴上橡膠手套。某些學校校長拒絕愛滋病學童入學。這種的恐慌正擴大蔓延中。

　　沒有疫苗能阻止人們染上愛滋病。對抗這類疾病的最主要之武器乃是教育。在已過三年，那些吸引男同性戀的酒吧和其他類似場所已經散布提倡「安全的性」這種文宣。像使用保險套這類安全的性關係已經幫助阻止此病的傳播。其結果是戲劇化的。

男同性戀的新患者之比率急速下降。一九八一年在舊金山約五千個男同性戀患者被測試有愛滋病，而在一九八八年只有一百位而已。這類的傳染病幾乎皆在男同性戀之中。

　　但是違禁藥品注射者仍然繼續從其他的使用者那染上此病，當他們共享針筒的針頭時。在紐約市據估計就有二十萬的禁藥使用者，而其中百分之四十已染上愛滋病。患有愛滋病的人會有長達十年之久的無癥兆期間 (空窗期)。而且愛滋病的高危險群是那些母親是吸毒者，或妓女的子女。愛滋病的大部分患者皆是貧窮的黑人及南美洲人。

內容解析

　　本文是一篇說明愛滋病 (AIDS) 蔓延的現象。文章是以第三人稱 (The third person) 的敘述方式來說明愛滋病擴散的嚴重性。文章中用第三者的語氣客觀地陳述人們對愛滋病的恐慌 (第一段)，預防愛滋病傳染所採取的步驟 (第二段) 以及使用毒品者染上愛滋病的情況 (第三段)。在這三段中都有清楚或確定的時間或數字。如一九八〇年的愛滋初期發展到一九八一年舊金山大量男同性戀者的患病，又如 20 萬紐約禁藥使用者中百分之四時感染愛滋病的數據等等。這些都顯示時間或數據是常出現在說明文中。因此，說明文有兩種常有的特點：一、常以旁觀者 (第三者) 的角度說明所解釋的對象或事理。二、文章中常出現數據或時間來表達客觀的事實。

(四) 論說文 (Argumentative Essay)

　　論說文是一種針對一個爭議性的主題進行探討，提出正、反兩方或其他不同的觀點或看法，進行理性的討論，並且表達作者對此議題的立場，再引用例證或理由支持此一立場或論點。因此，論說文的目的嘗試說服讀者認同作者的觀點或立

場，是一種勸說式的文章。所以明白作者在議題 (argument) 上的立場是很重要的，因爲這是作者纂寫此文的主要目的。

請看下列範文說明：

"Who is qualified to teach ESP (English for Specific Purposes)?" This is the most frequently asked question and the core of many debates in the field of language education. Because ESP courses incorporate specific content administrators, teachers, and even students, some may believe that content teachers should teach ESP. The rationale for such an argument is it would be difficult to ask traditional English teachers, most of whom are trained in the humanities, to teach from materials related to business, sciences, medicine, engineering, or other content areas. In higher education, content professors are experts in the specialized disciplines, and many possess good English skills from their academic training. Therefore, many administrators and other stakeholders often consider content teachers to be the most effective ESP teachers. However, most content professors put priority on their own research and content teaching and thus are less interested in taking on the responsibilities of teaching English. In those cases where content professors are asked to teach ESP, the classes are likely to lose their original language focus because content teachers tend to spend more time teaching research and content knowledge. In addition, content teachers usually lack appropriate training in teaching methods and in classroom management. Many tend to apply outdated approaches, such as translation or audio-lingual methods, because that was how they learned English.

　　「誰有資格教 ESP(專業英文)？」這是最常被問到的問題，也是許多語言教育領域中爭辯的核心。因為 ESP 課程包括特定的內容，管理者、老師甚至是學生，有些人可能相信專業老師應該教授 ESP。這種論點的原理是要求傳統的英文老師，他們大部分都是接受人文的訓練，來教授從有關商業、科學、醫藥，專科教授在專業學門中是專家，許多人擁有從他們學術訓練所獲得好的英文技能。因此，許多管理者和其他的利益相關者經常認為專業老師是最有效率的 ESP 老師。然而，大部分的專科教師是以他們自己的研究和專科教學為優先，正因為如此他們對承擔教授英語的責任較少感到興趣。在那些被要求教授 ESP 的專業老師的案例中，因為專業老師傾向花更多的時間在教導研究和專業知識，這些課程可能失去它們原初的語言焦點。此外，專業老師通常缺少在教學方法與課室管理合適的訓練。許多人傾向運用過時的方法，就像翻譯或聽與說教學法，因為那就是他們如何學習英文的。

內容解析

　　本文一開頭就提出一個問題「誰有資格教專業英文？」接下來就針對此問題進行說明與討論，文中討論專業領域和一般語文教師有否資格擔任專業英文老師。文章分兩種不同的看法來陳述上述兩種老師的教育背景是否適合擔任專業英文老師。這兩種不同的看法或觀點就形成本文的議題。文中也闡述兩種不同背景的教師擔任專業英文教師的優缺點，這是一篇針對一個論點提出不同正反兩面的看法之文章，也是一篇典型的論說文所常見的表達方式，現以下列圖示說明：

提出論點 / 議題→對論點 / 議題進行討論 ⟨ 正面的說明 / 反面的說明 ⟩ →

→ 對此論點的結論 ⟨ 贊成或反對 / 綜合性的觀點

明白上述文脈的發展就可以找出全文的主題，請看下題示範：

What is the main purpose of this paragraph?

(A) To explain the rationale of how to teach English to students with specific needs.

(B) To summarize the development of ESP teacher training and curriculum design.

(C) To emphasize the importance of providing adequate teacher training to content professors.

因為本文末了的說明是指出專業教師在教學方法與課室管理上的不足，所以間接表達對專業教師在教學上的訓練之需要。上述選項中只有 (C) 為了強調提供專業教師足夠教師訓練的重要性才切合題意。

二、文章的語氣

(一) 文章語氣與修飾語

　　文章中的用字遣詞表達出作者的語氣。若是一篇文章有許多的形容詞或副詞來形容文中的人、事、物，就要分析其中的修飾語是接近文章中所描述對象的實際情形，抑或是作者主觀的看法或想法。例如，作者描述某地發生一場 enormous(龐大的)earthquake(地震)，文章中有否提供這個地震的相關資料，

像地震的強度、深度及受災的情況等等，來證實此一地震確實是 enormous。因此，文章中的用字遣詞會影響到文章的語氣，也就是作者的語氣。由此，亦可看出作者對其描述或討論對象的態度或立場。以下列文章說明文章的語氣：

範文 1

Far too long Europe has closed its eyes to Syria's foul and bloody civil war and tried to keep the suffering multitudes out. Suddenly the continents gates have been pushed open by two political forces. One is moral conscience belatedly wakened by the image of a drowned Syrian child on a Turkish beach. The other is the political courage of Angela Merkel, the German chancellor, who told her people to set aside their fear of immigrants and show compassion to the needy.

Tens of thousands of asylum-seekers flowed towards Germany by rail, bus and on foot, chanting "Germany! Germany!", to be welcomed by cheering crowds Germany is showing that old Europe, too, can take in the tired, the poor and the huddled masses yearning to breathe free. It says it can absorb not thousands, but hundreds of thousands of refugees. Such numbers will inevitably raise many worries: that cultures will be swamped by aliens, economies will be overburdened, social benefits will have to be curbed and even that terrorists will creep in. Anti-immigrant parties have been on the rise across Europe. In America, too, some politicians want to build walls to keep foreigners out.

Yet the impulse to see immigrants as chiefly a burden is profoundly mistaken. The answer to these familiar fears is not to put up more barriers, but to manage the pressures and the risks to ensure that migration improves the lives of both immigrants and their hosts. The starting point is a sense of perspective. (excerpted from *The Economist*)

中譯

　　有很長的一段時間，歐洲對敘利亞的污穢又血腥的內戰視而不見並且試著把大量受苦的人們阻隔在外。突然間藉著兩股政治勢力歐洲的大門被推開了。一個是道德良知，它被在土耳其海灘上溺斃的敘利亞孩童的影像所喚醒。另一個是德國總理安格拉·梅克爾的政治勇氣，她告訴她的百姓把對移民的恐懼擱置一旁，對需要幫助的人表示同情。

　　數以千計的尋求庇護者搭火車、巴士及徒步湧向德國，他們高唱「德國！德國！」被歡呼的人群所歡迎。德國正表明古老的歐洲也能接受那些疲倦的，貧窮且擁擠，渴望呼吸自由的群眾。據說它能吸收不只數千的，而是數十萬的難民。

　　這樣的數目將無可避免地引起許多擔憂：就是文化會被外國人所淹沒，經濟會超出負荷，社會福利將被迫抑制，而且甚至恐怖份子會悄悄混入。反移民的政黨已經在整個歐洲崛起。在美國也是一樣，有些政客要築牆阻隔外國人於牆外。

　　然而視移民為主要負擔的這種推動是很大的錯誤。對這些熟知的恐懼不是去設立更多的障礙物，而是去處理壓力與危機以確保移居能改善移民與他們的東道主之生活。此一出發點是有遠景的觀點。

內容解析

　　在本篇文章描述敘利亞難民的困境中，作者是用不少負面的形容詞，例如，far to long(太長的…)，Syria's foul and bloody(敘利亞骯髒又血腥的)，suffering(痛苦的)，這些文章開頭的用詞都顯示作者對敘利亞難民的同情。而其中的動詞 wakened(被喚醒)，set aside their fear(把

恐懼擱置一旁) 則是加強作者對幫助敘利亞難民者的肯定語氣。

在第二段中作者的用詞仍然是支持敘利亞難民，但是是從敘利亞難民本身的反應來描寫。像 tired(疲倦的)，poor(貧窮的)，yearning to breathe free(可望呼吸自由的) 這些描述這些難民困苦處境的用詞。雖然在第三段中敘利亞難民所帶來的負面影響也被提及，但是在末了的一段作者在結語中指明第三段中的情形是不對的，並且提出更善意的建議來處理難民的事，認爲這是一個「有遠景的觀點」。

在全文中有不少用詞都是同情與支持敘利亞難民的處境。因此，從這些用詞中就可看出作者對敘利亞難民所持的態度，這對瞭解全文的重點有不小的助力。

再看一篇不同語氣的範文：

範文2

Traditionally, mental tests have been divided into two types. Achievement tests are designed to measure acquired skills and knowledge, particularly those that have been explicitly taught. The proficiency exams required by some states for high school graduation are achievement tests. Aptitude tests are designed to measure a person's ability to acquire new skills or knowledge. For example, vocational aptitude tests can help you decide whether you would do better as a mechanic or musician. However, all mental tests are in a sense achievement tests because they assume some sort of past learning or experience with certain objects, words, or situations. The difference between achievement and aptitude tests is one of degree and intended use.

(103 學年私醫插大試題)

中譯

傳統上，心理測驗被分爲兩種。成就測驗是設計來測量所

獲得的技能與知識，尤其是那些被清楚教授的東西。由某些州對高中畢業所要求的能力測驗是成就測驗。性向測驗是設計來衡量個人獲得新技能或知識的測驗。例如，職業性向測驗能幫助你決定你做為技師或音樂家，何者做得更好。然而，所有的心理測驗在某種意義上而言都是成就測驗，因為它們假定某種過去的學習或經驗是某些事物、文字或情況。成就測驗與性向測驗的差異是程度與預期的用途。

內容解析

　　本文是一篇說明文，是在說明心理測驗的分類。文章中所用的字詞皆是清楚明白的專業術語，像 achievement tests(成就測驗)，proficiency exams(能力測驗)，aptitude tests(性向測驗) 都是心理測驗中所用的專業術語，除了說明這些測驗的功能外，作者並未加上任何形容詞來描述這些測驗，因此，它是一篇以客觀的口氣說明一種專業知識的情形。這種不加上描繪用詞的文章並且大都以事物作為句中主詞的陳述方法是一種常用來描述客觀事實的表達方式，避免用個人的感受或想法來表達所描述的事物。所以下列針對作者對文章主題之問題就可以知道如何作答：

The author's attitude toward the subject of mental tests is _____.

(A) indifferent　(B)critical　(C)objective　(D) emotional

Answers

(C)objective(客觀的)

(二) 文章語氣與主題或對象的關係

　　文章的主題會影響到文章的語氣。文章的主題若是有關戰爭的方面或災難方面，文章中的用詞就比較是嚴肅且正式的用

詞，因為輕鬆或幽默的口吻可能不太適宜用於這類的主題或對象。以下是一篇有關二次世界大戰中一位被日軍俘虜的英國護士的回憶：

範文1

"We were five weeks in those houses," the woman recalled, "On Christmas Eve, the Japanese soldiers suddenly ordered us out and moved us to the jail, then into a street of three-roomed bungalows about two miles away, where thirty women were put into each bungalow. There was no furniture in the house, so we had to sleep on the cold tiled floors. We were lack of food and firewood for cooking what little food we had. Sanitary condition there was awful, and there was sickness. We organized ourselves into a so-called "district nursing" and tried to visit and help the sick. There were no medical supplies."

中譯

那位婦女回憶到：「我們在那些房子中待了五週。在聖誕夜前夕，日軍突然命令我們出來並且搬到監牢中，然後我們搬到兩英哩外的一條街上的三房的平房，在那裏有三十位婦女被安置在每一幢平房中。屋中沒有傢俱，所以我們必須睡在冰冷的地磚地板上。我們缺少食物和烹飪我們僅有食物的柴火。那裏的衛生狀況很差，有人生病。我們自行組成所謂的『地方上的護理』來嘗試探視且幫助病人。沒有醫療供給。」

內容解析

本文描述一位英國護理人員在日軍戰俘營中所遭遇的悲慘環境。文字簡潔，文中所描述的情景令人同情，並且是使讀者面對一種嚴肅的情景，因為所描述的對象與場景使人感受當時情境的惡劣。在這樣的文章中相關的用字本身已足以令人感受其嚴肅的一面，例如

像 ordered(命令)，jail(監牢)，sleep on the cold tiled floor(睡在冰冷的地磚地板上)，Sanitary condition...awful(衛生情況很糟糕)，no medical supplies(無醫療供給) 等等用詞皆呈現這段敘述內容的嚴肅性。

現在看另一篇語氣不同的範文：

範文 2

Worshipping Whales and Eating Them Too

As the harpoon pieces its thick skin, the giant whale leaps from the sea and then plunges back into the deep. The fishing boat tosses precariously on the huge waves created by its wake.

Clinging to lifelines, the fishermen chant: "namuamidabusta, namuamidabusta." They are offering Buddhist prayers for the whale that is about to die.

Before they set each year to pursue their quarry, Japanese whalers make a pilgrimage to temples and Buddhist memorials scattered along the seacoast. At the shrines, they pray for the blessing of the whale -- a symbol of growth and development in Japan.

中譯

　　當魚叉刺入牠的厚皮，那隻巨大的鯨魚從海中跳出，然後跳回深海中。捕漁船在由牠尾流所產生的巨浪上不穩地上下搖擺。

　　漁夫緊抓住救生索，他們反覆唸誦：「拿米阿米杜波斯卡（梵語），拿米阿米杜波斯卡。」他們正在為那隻臨死的鯨魚獻上佛教的祈禱。

　　每年在他們啟航去追尋他們的獵物時，日本的捕鯨者都會去散布於海岸邊的寺廟與佛塔。在那些神社中，他們為了鯨魚的福祉而祈禱——一種日本成長與發展的象徵。

本篇文章的標題就顯得矛盾與諷刺：Worshipping Whales and Eating Them Too(敬奉鯨魚同時把牠們吃掉)。文章一開頭就描述日本捕鯨船捕獵鯨魚的情景，但是在第二及第三段中卻說明捕鯨者對鯨魚的膜拜。這是兩種形成強烈對比的描述，充滿矛盾與諷刺。依據 Edgar. V.Roberts 在他 Writing Themes About Literature 中所定義的「諷刺」寫法，本文是呈現「情境式的反諷」，兩種截然不同的情境 (殺死鯨魚 & 敬奉鯨魚) 呈現出強烈的矛盾現象，而形成一種非常諷刺的對比。本文作者運用日本捕鯨者的捕鯨行為以及接下來對鯨魚的祈禱來凸顯本文諷刺的語氣。

範文 3

There men appear be no better than carnivorous animals of a superior rank, living on the fresh of wild animals when they can catch them, and when they are not able, they subsist on grain.

(引用 Michel-Guillaume Jean de Crèvecœur 的文章)

中譯

人不過顯得是一種比較優越層級的食肉動物，當他們能捕獲野生動物時，他們是以野生動物的鮮肉維生。當他們無法捕獲牠們時，他們則以穀物維生。

內容解析

作者將人描寫成一種食肉的動物，並且以捕食野生動物的鮮肉維生。其言下之意即是人也是像動物般的一種動物而已。不過在貶低人類為食肉動物的同時，作者也加上「比較優越層級」的動物來形容人類，語氣中也透露其幽默的口吻。

◎重點整理◎

一、文章的文體

名稱	文體的特性
記敘文	1. 針對特定的人、事、物 2. 常以時間先後的順序來陳述事情的經過 3. 常用動詞過去式的時式作為文中主要的動詞
抒情文	1. 抒發作者主觀的感受或感情 2. 常以第一人稱 ”I”(我) 來敘述事情 3. 有較多的形容詞與副詞用來形容或描述主觀的感受 4. 經常是一種經歷或經驗的表達
說明文	1. 以客觀的解釋或說明人、事物或事理 2. 文中少用表達個人的評論或觀感之詞句 3. 常以傳輸特定的資訊為目的
論說文	1. 針對有爭議的主題進行討論或探討 2. 常提出正、反兩面或其他不同的觀點或看法 3. 常引用例證或理由支持某一論點 4. 文章的目的常是說服或勸說讀者接受文中的觀點

二、文章語氣的解析

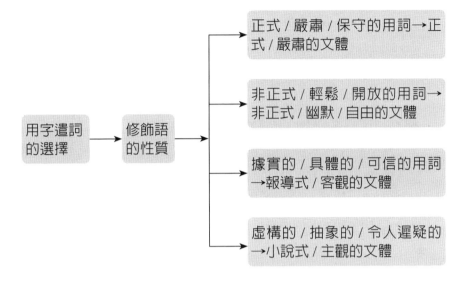

用字遣詞的選擇 → 修飾語的性質 →

- 正式 / 嚴肅 / 保守的用詞→正式 / 嚴肅的文體
- 非正式 / 輕鬆 / 開放的用詞→非正式 / 幽默 / 自由的文體
- 據實的 / 具體的 / 可信的用詞→報導式 / 客觀的文體
- 虛構的 / 抽象的 / 令人遲疑的→小說式 / 主觀的文體

Exercise

確認下列文章的文體與語氣：

1.

A famous painter was worried about his dog, which happened to have a sore throat. He knew that a doctor would not examine a dog, so he decided to pretend that he himself was the one who was sick. In spite of the fact that it was midnight, he made a phone call to a famous throat specialist and asked the doctor to rush to his home right away.

The doctor was very angry, but he tried hard to control himself and said, "I only see patients during the day and by appointment." On hearing this, the painter replied, "But⋯but, Doctor, I'm the famous portrait painter,

Raphael Depicter, and this is an emergency." As the painter was indeed a well known artist, the doctor finally agreed to visit the patient.

When the doctor arrived at the artists home and saw that his patient was a dog, he was raged, but immediately he thought of a plan to get even. Hiding his anger, he said calmly, "I'm afraid this is a very difficult case. I'll have to go back to study the case more carefully. I'll call you when I find out exactly what's wrong with your dog." Then he left.

About the same time the following night, Mr. Depicter was awakened by a phone call. It was the throat specialist and he asked Mr. Depicter to go immediately to his house. Mr. Depicter said, "But, Doctor, it's past twelve. I have an appointment to paint the portrait of a very important person. Can't you wait until tomorrow afternoon?" But the doctor insisted, saying: "That would be too late. Please hurry." Thinking it was about his dog's illness, the painter jumped out of bed, got dressed, and ran to the doctor's house. After opening the door, the doctor said to the artist, "Please tell me, how much would you charge to paint my house?"

(1) 本文的文體是 _____ .

(2) 本文作者的語氣是　(A) 嚴肅的　(B) 諷刺的　(C) 幽默的
(D) 客觀的

2.

　　I live on the 13th floor. You can see the mountains from the top of the building I live in. I must have been to the same place in the mountains thirty times, but every time I go there it feels like the first time. It is a beautiful place; it is quiet and green; it is a place where I feel relaxed and happy. It doesn't take a long time to get there from my building, maybe only thirty minutes by motorcycle, but when I get there it feels like a different world. I don't know the name of the place I go to because I don't need to know. The name is not important. I remember how to get there, and I know that I will feel very different when I get there. The world will look very different, and it will be like I've never been there before.

(1) 本文的文體是 _____ .

(2) 本文作者的語氣是 (A) 批評的　(B) 嚴肅的　(C) 幽默的
(D) 主觀的

3.

It's very difficult for people who sleep silently to put up with the sound of snoring. Some people are asleep the moment they lie down, others stay up half the night waiting for the miracle of sleep to come about. Even insomniacs snore. Insomniacs are those people who need to lie in in the morning to catch up on lost sleep. Snorers will never admit to snoring. They know the rest of the world looks down on them and they just can't face up to reality. My friend, Henry, a champion snorer, has just found a cure and he lets me in on his little secret. He has just spent good money for a band with a stud on it. He wears the band around his head at night and if he tries to sleep on his back. The stud gives him a jab. I'm sure this news will cheer up all snorers, who now have a new experience to look forward to. With one of these on their heads, all they have to lose is their sleep.

(1) 本文的文體是 _____ .

(2) 本文作者的語氣是 (A) 主觀的　(B) 輕鬆的　(C) 保守的
(D) 置疑的

4.

The Marketing Information Center of the Information Industry Institute (I I I) recently announced that sales of PCS in the domestic and overseas markets combined during the first quarter of 1992 jumped 15 percent, compared with the same period of last year. At the same time, the total sales value went up by 23.5 percent.

From January until the end of March, the total amount of locally-made PCS sold both here and abroad was in excess of 619,000 units for a value of US$490 million.

According to statistics compiled by the I I I, of the 619, 000 units sold, portables accounted for 22.3 percent, and tabletop models 77.7 percent of the total.

Many local PC producers agree that, although orders for the first quarter continued to expand, problems created by intense international competition and the sliding of prices for related computer parts have brought great pressure on the ROC computer business. A recession may come in the near future.

North America absorbed the largest portion of ROC personal computer exports during the first quarter, taking 42 percent of the total value, while western Europe took 37 percent.

(1) 本文的文體是_____.

(2) 本文作者的語氣是 (A) 嚴肅的　(B) 客觀的　(C) 輕鬆的 (D) 幽默的

5.

Euthanasia(安樂死)is the practice of ending the life of a person who is hopelessly ill. It is commonly called mercy killing or painless death. It is an issue causing heated debate.

Many people are opposed to euthanasia for four reasons. First, they argue that no matter how you look at it, euthanasia is killing or suicide and thus is wrong and immoral. The second reason is that there is always the possibility of a wrong diagnosis. Doctors are not flawless, and even the best of them makes mistakes. In addition, there is always the chance that some new pain-killing medicine or even a cure is just around the corner. The most important reason to oppose euthanasia, for many, is the risk of abuse. They are afraid that criminals or bad people may use euthanasia to serve their evil purposes.

However, there is the other side of the issue. A large number of people support euthanasia. One common argument for euthanasia is that patients with incurable diseases should not be forced to continue living if they are in great pain and cannot bear this constantly. The second reason is that staying in a hospital for a long time often causes a financial and emotional burden on the family. Incurably ill patients often worry about the hardship and misery that will fall on their families. Moreover, incurable patients often find their lives meaningless. Even if they are alive, they can only lie in bed. For many, this is living death, and they would rather choose to die with dignity. Finally, proponents believe that keeping dying patients alive on life-support systems is cruel and senseless, for it causes great suffering to both the patients and their families, and places great burdens on the community. Therefore, supporters believe, doctors should have the right to end the life of a terminally ill patient with the permission of the patient or the family.

(1) 本文的文體是＿＿＿＿＿＿＿.

(2) 本文作者的語氣是 (A) 嚴肅的　(B) 主觀的　(C) 諷刺的 (D) 開放的

6.

In the early part of the twentieth century, racism was widespread in the United States. Many African Americans were not given equal opportunities in education or employment. Marian Anderson (1897-1993) was an African American woman who gained fame as a concert singer in this climate of racism. She was born in Philadelphia and sang in church choirs during her childhood. When she applied for admission to a local music school in 1917. She was turned down because she was black. Unable to attend music school, she began her career as a singer for church gatherings. In 1929, she went to Europe to study voice and spent several years performing there. Her voice was widely praised throughout Europe. Then she returned to the U.S. in 1935 and became a top concert singer after performing at Hall in New York City.

Racism again affected Anderson in 1939. When it was arranged for her to sing at Constitution Hall in Washington, D.C., the Daughters of the American Revolution opposed it because of her color. She sang instead at the Lincoln Memorial for over 75,000 people. In 1955, Anderson became the first black soloist to sing with the Metropolitan Opera of New York City. The famous conductor Toscanini praised her voice as "heard only once in a hundred years." She was a U.S. delegate to the United Nations in 1958 and won the UN peace prize in 1977. Anderson eventually triumphed over racism.

(1) 本文的文體是_____.

(2) 本文作者的語氣是 (A) 支持的　(B) 反對的　(C) 客觀的
(D) 悲傷的

7.

It has been estimated that up to 100 million sharks may be killed each year as a result of commercial fishing operations. Ninety percent of these are a by-catch, which means they are not targeted by fishermen and have little or no commercial values.

There is serious concern that such dramatic impact on shark numbers will eventually affect the whole marine ecosystem. This is because sharks are highly predators, one of the last links in the ocean food chain, helping to maintain the quantity of other fish populations by preying on them.

If marine ecosystems begin collapsing because of the removal of sharks in great amount, the ultimate commercial ramifications are obvious. As top-end members of the food chain, sharks tend to be particularly vulnerable to the massacre of humans. Compared with millions of eggs laid by other fish in a lifetime, most sharks produce only one or two pups every year. This makes them less capable of sustaining their populations as a result of commercial fishing pressures, especially those from Asian countries. For example, many sharks are taken in the driftnets of Chinese fishermen who supply shark fins to lucrative Asian markets, where they are sold at high prices and are used as a main course of a banquet or a medicine for preventing tumors. The decrease of sharks may result in an unbalanced marine ecosystem that may be harmful to human benefits.

Despite serious concerns expressed by marine biologists about the decline of sharks, the public pay little attention to such an issue. There appears to be some reasons for this situation: the negative and completely false image of all sharks being ferocious man-eaters that leads to people's disgust at sharks: a lack of firm statistics indicating that their populations really are endangered, and their existence as far-away issue out of people's sight and mind. These factors may explain people's indifference to the decline of sharks and thus ignore the related problem caused by such a decline.

(1) 本文的文體是_____.

(2) 本文作者的語氣是 (A) 輕鬆的　(B) 諷刺的　(C) 客觀的
　　(D) 同情的

8.

I am from Nantou. I used to have a happy family. My grandfather spent his whole life in Nantou. So did my father. My grandfather never had any formal education. He was very poor-he had no land, but he had many mouths to feed. His dream was to have his own farm, so he worked very hard and finally saved enough money to buy the land that he rented from his landlord. His dream came true because of his hard work.

My father was lucky in the sense that he could inherit my grandfather's land as he was the only son. But he was not rich-he had a farm, but his income was low. He received little education-he was just a primary school graduate. However, he had a dream, too, just like my grandfather. His dream was for me to go to college in order to become an educated person. He often told me, "Being a farmer does not make a decent living. I want you to live a better life than I. Education is the key to a better life and a great future." My mother, a traditional woman who was the best helper to my father on the farm, shared my father's dream as well. Besides taking good care of me, she always encouraged me to study hard.

Unfortunately, the 921 earthquake, which took away many lives and left many people homeless, also deprived me of my happy family. I was the only survivor in my family on that terrifying night. I am now entirely on my own, but I will never feel discouraged or frustrated. I will bravely face whatever difficulties that may lie ahead. I will definitely work my way through college because I am always reminded by my father's conviction that knowledge builds wealth.

(1) 本文的文體是 _____.

(2) 本文作者的語氣是 (A) 懷念的　(B) 痛苦的　(C) 客觀的
　　(D) 嚴肅的

1. (1) 記敘文　(2) C
2. (1) 抒情文　(2) D
3. (1) 記敘文　(2) B
4. (1) 說明文　(2) B

5. (1) 論說文　(2) A
6. (1) 記敘文　(2) A
7. (1) 說明文　(2) D
8. (1) 抒情文　(2) A

04 綜合閱讀分析

閱讀導引

一、運用字彙推敲的技巧來找出字義：將文章中畫底線的字彙
　　逐字分析其可能的字義。

二、解釋文章中句子的文法或句型：依據行數來說明各句的文
　　法或句型。

三、找出文章的主題 & 大意：依據主題句常出現的位置以及
　　文脈的發展，尋找段落與全文的主題。

四、達成點 (單字)、線 (句子)、面 (段落) 三方面的立體全
　　文解析：澈底瞭解全文。

全方位的閱讀分析

字彙涵義的推敲　　文法&句型的分析　　文章主題&大意的解析

全方位文章解析步驟

個別範文分析

中文譯文

字義解析

句法分析

文章主題&大意解析

全方位英文閱讀應該包括下列三要素：

(1) 字彙 (2) 文法 & 句型 (簡稱為句法)(3) 文章主題 & 大意，三者的關係，可用點、線、面的關係來說明，圖示如下：

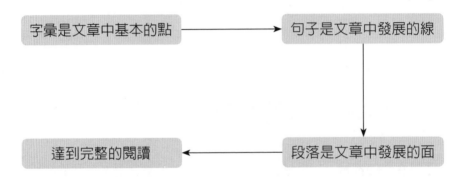

因此，字義的瞭解是最根本的基礎。接下來對句子涵義的明白就需要掌握文法與句型，而找出段落的主題或大意則是閱讀最終的步驟。字義、文法、主題三者缺一不可，因為要有完整的閱讀必須完成這三方面的步驟，否則在文章理解上就有不足之處。並容易產生下列三種情形：

一、對字義的牽強附會：不明白句子文法，就可能誤解上下文意，造成對句中單字的誤解。

二、對文法與句型的誤解：造成以句子字面的涵義解釋，忽略或錯誤解釋句子的涵義。

三、對文章段落的的一知半解：因為無法明白段落的主題，所以即使單字涵義與句子文法都明白，仍然不清楚段落的主

要思想或重點。

※ 文章針對上述的閱讀缺失，運用前三章中所教的有關字彙推敲的技巧，文法與句型的解析以及文章與大意的掌握方法，以範例解說使得前三者所學的得以實際運用在文章的閱讀中。接下來的第二節中有八篇範文分別解說其中單字字義的推敲、句子文法的結構以及文章主題與大意的確認。

範文 1

Line 1　　　　The difference between Presley and Crosby reflected generational differences which spoke of changing values in American life. Crosby's music was <u>soothing</u>; Presley's was disturbing. It is

¹
too easy to be glib about this, to say that Crosby was singing to,
Line 5　　first, Depression America and, then, to wartime America, and that his audience had all the disturbance they could handle in their daily lives without buying more at the record shop and movie theater. Crosby's fans talk about how "relaxed" he was, how natural", how "<u>casual</u> and easy going." By the time Presley began

²
Line 10　causing <u>sensations</u>, the entire country had become relaxed, casual and easy going, and its younger people seemed to be tired of it, for Elvis's act was anything but soothing and scarcely what a parent of that placid age would have called "natural." for a young man. Elvis was unseemly, loud, <u>gaudy</u>, sexual--that

³
Line 15　gyrating <u>pelvis</u>!--in short, disturbing. He not only disturbed

⁴
parents who thought music by Crosby was soothing but also reminded their young that they were full of the <u>turmoil</u> of

⁵
youth and an appetite for excitement. At a time when the country had a population coming of age with no memory of troubled times,
Line 20　Presley spoke to a <u>yearning</u> for disturbance.

6

(84 臺大研究所)

譯文

　　柏理斯與柯茲比的差別反映了時代的差異，而這種差異道出了美式生活中正在改變的價值觀。柯茲比的音樂是舒緩的；柏理斯的音樂卻是擾人的。這樣的說法顯得太輕率以至於不能隨便地如此說，不能說柯茲比所歌頌第一是景氣大衰退的美國，然後是戰時的美國；並且不能說他的觀眾要處理他們日常生活中所有的煩惱而不再到唱片店或電影院去消費。

　　柯茲比的歌迷談論他是多麼地「輕鬆」、多麼地「自然」以及多麼地「隨意及閒混」。到柏理斯開始引起大家的注意之前，全國都變成輕鬆、悠閒以及閒混。然而這國家的年輕人似乎已厭倦這樣的生活，因為艾維絲的行為絕非舒緩的並且也幾乎不是在太平時代的父母所對年輕人稱之為「自然的」。

　　艾維絲是不端莊的、不客氣的，俗麗且性感的──他那晃動的臀部！──簡言之，令人不安的。他不但擾亂了那些認為柯茲比的音樂是舒緩的父母，也提醒他們的年輕子女他們是充滿了年輕人的騷動及渴望刺激。當全國有一種來自於沒有憂患時期回憶的人們，柏理斯道出了騷動的渴望。

(一) 字義解析

1. "soothing" 的字義可從其前句的涵義："The difference between Presley and Crosby ... American life" 及 soothing 後面的句意得知：Presley's was disturbing. 因為第一句告訴我們 Presley 是不同於 Crosby，所以下一句中的 soothing 也是不同於 disturbing。disturbing 是動詞 disturb (騷動) 轉變來的現在分詞作形容詞，所以 soothing 就作 disturbing(騷動的) 相反解釋，表示不騷動的、平靜的。而 soothing 的原意正是接近此意。

2. causal 的字義可由與它並列的 easy going(悠哉的) 及其前的 how 子句推敲出。and 通常用來連接兩個字義接近的單字或片語，所以 causal 的涵義應該與 easy going 類似。而與 how causal…並列的其他 how 子句，在平行語法中 (連接同類詞性的單字、片語或子句)，其涵義也是類似或加強語氣的。所以 how causal 的字義也可從 how relaxed 來進一步證實。由以上兩種方式可推敲出 causal ≒ easy going ≒ relaxed。

3. 類似第二點的方法，gaudy 的字義也可由其先前的字、詞推敲出。在 be 動詞後的形容詞是作主詞補語，所以這些補語應是同樣類似的形容詞，由 loud, sexual 及最後結論的字 disturbing 可推知 gaudy 騷動人的一種情況，而「絢麗」正是使人騷動的一種情況。

4. 破折號 (--) 所連接的前後字、詞在意思上是接近，甚至相等的。所以 pelvis 的字義可由 sexual 來推敲出，sexual 是形容詞 (al 的字尾大部分皆爲形容詞)，表「性感的」，而 pelvis 爲現在分詞 (gyrating) 所修飾，所以是名詞。因此可推知 pelvis 是指男人身上的性感器官 (Elvis 是男性)，這時 pelvis 的大意就出來了。通常閱讀測驗不會考非關鍵性的單字，所以知道 pelvis 是指性感的器官，也就可以了。

5. not only ... but also 是瞭解 turmoil 的關鍵連接詞，因其所連接的字、詞爲同性質涵義的字詞，所以 turmoil 的字義可由 disturbed(擾亂) 的字義推敲出。此外，由 and 所連接的片語：an appetite for excitement(對刺激的渴望) 也可加強「擾亂」的這種解釋。

6. 由 when 子句所顯示的意思：a population ... with a memory of troubled times.(有一個來自於毫無憂患時期回憶的人們)，說明 Presley(由上文知道他是非常渴望騷動)，說明

Presley(由上文知道他是非常渴望騷動) 道出了 "yearning for disturbance"，for 可作「求取…意向或對象」解釋，所以 yearning 的意思也應該與上文所述的一致，而 yearning for 正是 appetite for 的另一種方式的表達。注意同義字的出現對單字涵義的瞭解有很大的幫助。

(二) 句法分析

　　每篇文章皆有作者獨特的用字遣詞以及慣用的句型，本篇亦不例外，本文作者運用文法中的平行語法 (parallelism) 來表達或加強其文意。這種語法在每一段中出現，而形成本文的主要語法。此外，還有一些慣用語及慣用句型，這些對瞭解本文也有舉足輕重的重要性。

1.　主要語法：

　(1) Lines 3～8：不定詞片語的平行語法。

　　　It is <u>too</u> easy <u>to be glib about this</u>, <u>to say</u> that Crosby was singing to... America, and <u>(to say)</u> that his audience had all and movie theater.

　　　【解析】too ... to ... 的慣用語在此句中一直延伸到最一個不定詞片語 (to say) that his audience ...。所以需留心這裏的解釋，有三個否定的解釋：<u>too</u> easy <u>to</u> be .... <u>to</u> say that Crosby and <u>(to say)</u> that his audience ...。

　(2) Lines 8～9：以 how 開頭的名詞子句平行語法。

　　　Crosby's fans talk <u>about</u> how "relaxed" he was, <u>how</u> "natural", <u>(he was)</u> <u>how</u> "causal and easy-going." (he was).

　　　【解析】省略句型再度又出現在這些子句中，因爲同樣主詞 (he) 及動詞 (was) 不必重複出現在同形式的句子中，其都作介詞 about 的受格。

(3) Lines 10～15：以一連串類似涵義的形容詞之平行語法。

... the entire country had become relaxed, causal, and easy going

.... Elvis was unseemly, loud, gaudy, sexual ... disturbing.

【解析】這是一種修辭的句法，將一連串相近涵義的字並連一起，而後由弱至強或從不重要到重要的語氣加強法，此類的字、詞在字義上多有雷同，對其中難字的瞭解頗有助益。

2. 慣用語句：

(1) Lines 9～10：

By the time　Presley began ... the entire country had become...

【解析】By the time 表示「到…為止」，可考慮用在過去完成式或未來完成式。此句是接在過去簡單式 began 的句子，故用過去完成式作主要句子的時式。

(2) Lines 12～14：anything but(絕非)+adj./adv./v ... for Elvis's act was anything but soothing and scarcely what ... for a young man.

【解析】anything but 在此為副詞修飾 soothing，其可以等於 never, by no means 等完全否定副詞。

(3) Lines 15 ～ 18: not only ... but also ...(不但…而且)

He not only disturbed parents ... but also remined ...

(前後所接的動詞時態需一致)

【解析】在語氣上，此句型是強調後者 (but also) 所接的字詞或片語，其也可等於 as well as，不過 as well as 則是強調前者，此點需注意，而動詞的單複

數則與被強調的字一致。試比較下列兩句之差異：

He as well as I is wrong on this matter.

= Not noly but also he is wrong on this matter.

(三) 文章主題與大意

　　三段 (含三段) 以上的文章通常都有表達全文主題的主旨句。本文亦不例外，而主旨句最常出現的位置在第一段中的第一句。本文亦是如此。而針對主題的問題亦常出現在閱讀測驗中，本閱讀測驗中的第一題即是如此。現就本文的主旨句及各段的主題句來探討之。

1. 本文的主旨句為第一段的第一句：The difference between Presley and Crosby reflected generational differences which spoke of changing values in American life.(柏理斯與柯茲比的差別反映了時代的差異，而這種差異則道出了美式生活中正在改變的價值觀。)

   針對此主題所有的問題為：

   ◎ According to the author, Crosby and Presley stand for all but:

   (A) two types of popular music.

   (B) two styles of performance.

   (C) two generations of cultural turmoil.

   (D) two periods in American history.

2. 第二段的主題句為第二段的第一句：Crosby's fans talk about how ... and easy going. 此段的前半段都在描寫 Crosby 的歌迷之生活態度。他們喜歡 relaxed, natural 及 causal 的生活，因為他們經歷了許多憂患的時期，這樣由第一段末了的原因

演變到第二段開頭的結果正是第二個問題所要問的因果關係：

◎ Crosby was a popular singer of his time because:

   (A) troubled time needed a relieving voice

   (B) he stopped disturbance.

   (C) he and his admirers lived in a placid age.

   (D) he fed the appetite for excitement.

就因果關係的推論得知答案 (A) 較為合適。

3. 第三段的主題句，也是本段的結論句——在末了的一句：

At a time when ..., Presley spoke to a yearning for disturbance. 本段第一句描寫 Elvis 的行為：disturbing 與最後一句 a yearning for disturbance 前後呼應，清楚表達出 Presley 與 Crosby 兩代之間在態度上的差異。最後一題的問題與此結論句也有關聯：

◎ Which of the following statements about Presley is incorrect?

   (A) He roused a yearning for turmoil.

   (B) His audience were mainly young people who found peaceful life dull.

   (C) He grew up during the Great Depression.

   (D) His music was loud and his manner improper.

   (A)、(B)、(D) 的描述都可在第三段中找到，惟有 (C) 是例外，為確定此例外，可再回溯前兩段來確定 Presley 不是生長於經濟大衰退時期。

以上三個測驗問題的答案都可從文章的主旨句或段落的主題句中找出，可見主旨句與段落主題句的重要性。

Line 1   Ever since humans have inhabited the earth, they have made use of various forms of communication. Generally, this expression of thoughts and feelings has been in the form of oral speech. When there is a language <u>barrier</u>, communication
1

Line 5   is accomplished through sign language in which motions stand for letters, words, and ideas. Tourists, the deaf, and the mute have had to resort to this form of expression. Many of these symbols of whole words are very <u>picturesque</u> and exact
2
and can be used internationally; spelling, however, cannot.

Line 10   Body language transmits ideas or thoughts by certain actions, either internationally or uninternationally. A wink can be a way of flirting of indicating that the party is only joking. A nod signifies <u>approval</u>, while shaking the head indicates a
3
negative reaction.

Line 15   Other forms of <u>nonlinguistic</u> language can be found in
4
<u>Braille</u> (a system of raised dots with the fingertips), signal flags,
5
Morse code, and smoke signals. Road maps and picture signs also guide, warn, and instruct people. While <u>verbalization</u> is the most
6
common form of language, other systems and techniques also

Line 20   express human thoughts and feelings.   (85 淡江研究所)

譯文

自有人類以來，他們就已使用各式各樣的溝通方式。一般說來，思想與感情這類的表達一直是以口語的形式。當有語言的障礙時，溝通是經由手語來達成，這其中的動作代表了字母、單字與想法。觀光客、聾子與啞吧必須憑藉這種的表達型式。許多

整個字的表徵是非常生動且準確的，且通用於國際上。然而，拼字卻無法如此。

　　肢體語言能藉著某些動作在國際上或國內來傳達觀念或想法。眨眼可能是挑逗的方式或表示當事人只是在開玩笑。點頭表示同意，然而搖頭則表示負面的回應。

　　其他非語音形式的語言可在盲人點字法 (用指頭碰觸的突起之點狀系統)、旗號、摩斯密碼與煙霧訊號被發現。公路地圖與標識也可引導、警示及指示人們。

　　雖然口語是最普遍的語言形式，然而其他的系統與技巧也能表達人的想法與感受。

(一) 字義解析

1. "barrier" 的字義可由其前一句的涵義與其後主要子句而推敲出。因為其前一句的涵義是：「一般而言，思想與感情這類的表達一直是以口語的形式出現。而 "barrier" 之後的主要子句卻出現與它前一句成對比的涵義：「溝通是經由手語來達成，這其中動作代表了字母、單字與想法。」由這前後句子成對比的涵義可推知 "barrier" 應是表達與語言相關的負面涵義。換言之，當語言出現 barrier 之時，則要用手語取代口語。至此 barrier 的涵義已呼之欲出，「障礙、困難」等等的解釋皆已是原意或接近原意。

2. "picturesque" 的字義可由它本身的結構與它前一句的涵義而推敲出。先就 picturesque 本身的結構而言，它的前半部 picture 使人易於聯想與「圖畫有關的涵義。但「非常圖畫的」這種解釋顯然不夠通順。所以需要再從前一句的涵義來推敲：「觀光客、聾子與啞吧，必須憑藉「手語」這種的表達形式。」而「手語」上比「拼字」在整個字的表徵

上能表達的更 "picturesque"。由這種前後的相反描述可推知「拼字」(spelling) 是不能表達 "picturesque"，所以 picturesque 的涵義應是與「圖畫」所引申出的相關涵義——生動的；活潑的。與此相關的問題如下：

◎ Sign language is said to be very picturesque and exact and can be used internationally except for ...

   (A) spelling

   (B) ideas

   (C) whole words

   (D) expressions.

由推敲 "picturesque" 的字義過程中，我們得知 sign language = this form of expression = these symbols of whole words，而 " spelling" 是不包含在這種 picturesque 的 sign language 中，所以答案應為 (A)。

3. "approval" 的字義可從表示相反對照的連接詞 "while" 推敲出。while 在本句中是表示「然而」之意，所以它所連接的前、後子句在涵義上是相反或成對比的。前半句為：「點頭表示…。」，後半句則表示「搖頭表示負面的回應。」可見前句的涵義應是表示「正面的回應」，而依常理判斷，點頭的動作一般是反應出「同意、認同或贊成」的意思，而 approval 正 (接近) 是此意。

4 & 5. nonlinguistic 與 Braille 的字義是相關的，因為 nonlinguistic 的涵義顯然要從 Braille 以及其後的解釋來認定：Other forms of nonlinguistic language can be found in Braille (a system of raised dots with the fingertips), signal flags, Morse code, and smoke signals. 此句中的 Other forms 相當於 Braille, signal flags.... smoke signals. 而 nonlinguistic language 是來形容這些是何種形式的語言。

因此，找出「Braille、旗號、摩斯密碼與煙霧訊號」的共同特徵，就能推敲出接近 nonlinguistic 的語意。此外，因為單字後的括號常是解釋或說明單字的涵義，所以 Braille 的涵義也可從其後括號內的解釋來獲知：「用手指頭碰觸的突起之點狀系統」，按常識來判斷，這應是指盲人所使用的點字法。所以，這些其他形式的方法都有一共同的特徵，就是沒有用口語來表達，也因此 nonlinguistic 可能是指「非口語的」這即已接近它的原意了——非語音的。明白本句中的這兩字之大意也就能回答下列的問題：

◎ Which form other than oral speech would be most commonly used among blind people ?

(A) picture signs

(B) Braille

(C) body language

(D) signal flags.

other than 作「除了…之外」解釋，所以題目所問的除了口語之外，什麼是最常使用的 (非語音) 形式之語言？答案顯然是 (B)。

6. verbalization 的字義可由 while 的功用與前面三段的大意來獲知。如前所述 while 可連接兩個涵義或對比的子句，所以前一句作「雖然 verbalization 是最普遍的語言型式，但是其他系統與技巧也可表達人的想法與感受。」這樣解釋。可見 verbalization 與其他表達人的想法與感受之系統與技巧是不同的。而由前面三段的大意可知這些系統與技巧是指手語、肢體語言或非語音的表達 (如第三段所述)，所以 verbalization 應是指語音的表達，再加上第一段第二句的涵義——一般說來，思想與感情這類的表達一直是以口語的

型式 (the form of oral speech)——所顯示的相關性，因為從這句之後就描述許多不同於口語的表達方法，因此可推知 verbalization 就可能是指先前所提過的 the form of oral speech，只是作者用同義字來表達同樣的涵義。由這些前後字義的呼應 (此外，the most common form 也與 Generally 在涵義上互相呼應) 以及 while 所表達的對比之涵義可知 verbalization 應是指「口語的型式」明白此字的涵義有助於回答下列的問題：

◎ Which of the following statements is not true ?

　　(A) There are many forms of communication in existence today.

　　(B) Verbalization is the most common form of communication.

　　(C) The deaf and mute use an oral form of communication.

　　(D) Ides and thoughts can be transmitted by body language.

Verbalization (the form of oral speech) 是一種的 communication. 所以 B 是正確的。再看 (A)、(D) 也符合原文涵義，只有 (C) 不符合，所以答案 (C)。

(二) 句法分析

　　本文是說到有關不同型式的人際溝通，而以比較的型式來表達，所以每段中都有一些表示對比涵義的句型，它們的型式如下列所分析：

1. 用表示語意成對比或相反的連接詞或語氣轉換詞來引導不同涵義的句子或子句。

　　(1) Lines 7～9: Many of these symbols ... spelling, however, cannot.

　　　　【解析】本句是以 however(然而) 這個表示相反涵義的連接副詞來連接前、後兩句語意表示相反的句子。

　　(2) Lines 13～14: A nod signifies approval, while shaking ... negative

reaction.

Lines 18～20: While verbalization is the most common..., other systems ... thoughts and feelings.

【解析】本文作者對 "while"(然而，雖然) 這個連接詞似乎情有獨鍾。在第二、三段中各用它們來取代 but, though/although 這類的連接詞。

2. 用以表示不同類的形容詞：

Line 15: Other forms of nonlinguistic language can ... in Braille ....

Line 18: While verbalization..., other systems...

【解析】other(其他的) 形容不同類的事物，是另一種表示相異的敘述方法。

(三) 文章主題與大意

　　本文是一篇說明文。全文的脈絡是按照演繹式的方法展開的。所以文章一開始就將全文的主旨點出：Ever since humans have inhabited the earth, they have made use of various forms of communication. 所以第一段的首句就是全文的主旨句。接下來就是說明主旨句中所指的「不同型式的溝通」，它發展的細節如下：

1. 第一段：不同型式的溝通 (主旨) 是分為口語的手語的型式，不過文中側重對手語的說明與舉例 (Lines 3～5)，這也是後續段落的發展重點。

2. 第二段：主題句出現在第一句：Body language transmits ideas ... or internationally. 它接續第一段中的重點，並且更詳細地用例子來說明這類的非口語表達 (Lines 11～14)。

3. 第三段：本段的主題句仍出現於首句，表達另一些較少見之非口語溝通的型式。與第一、二段中所提常見的非口語

型式 (手語與身體語言) 相比較之下，本段中的非口語型式之溝通是比較特定的溝通方法，換言之，全文是依循從一般性 (或普遍性) 到特定性之說明方法 (事實上，這就是演繹法的發展軌跡：由廣泛到細節的描述)。

4. 第四段：本段 (句) 是表達全文的結論：While verbalization is the most common ..., other systems ... and feeling. 換言之，它就是本文的結論句、它與首段中的主旨前後呼應，因爲它同時提到 verbalization 與 other systems and techniques，包含了各種的溝通形式，這與主旨句中的 "use of various forms of communication" 在涵義上是相通的。而它的後半句：other systems and techniques also express human, thoughts and feelings 則表達出全文發展的重點，因爲在 while 所引導的句型中，重點是在後半句中被強調、因此，雖然只是短短的一句話，卻表達出全文的主旨 (前半句) 與文脈發展的重點 (後半句)。由以上的段落分析可知全文發展的脈絡如下：

段落	主旨 (題) 句	展開的軌跡
第一段 引介本文主題	第一句 use of various forms of communication ↓	演繹式：由一般的介紹轉移到一般性的細節說明或舉例。 (oral speech → body language)
第二段 接續主題並加強全文的重點	第一句 Body language...by certain action ↓	演繹式：接續前一段的一般性細節說明做更詳盡的敘述。 (sign language→body language)

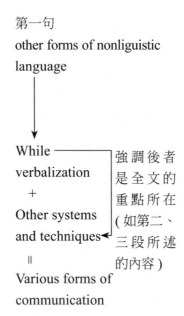

第三段
接續全文的重點說明，並且縮小至更特定的範圍。

末段
結論全文的主旨與發展的重點

第一句
other forms of nonliguistic language

While
verbalization
+
Other systems and techniques
‖
Various forms of communication

強調後者是全文的重點所在（如第二、三段所述的內容）

演繹式：由一般性的說明轉移到特定性的說明。
(body language → other forms of nonlinguistic language)
結論句：呼應首段的主旨並文中段落的重點，是演繹式發展的方式之一。

範文 3

Line 1   If you ever get a blow-out while you are driving, you

1
should know what to do. A blow-out is a sudden flat tire. It
can be a very frightening experience, especially if you are
traveling at high speed. If your car gets a blow-out, the first
Line 5   thing to do is to hold very tightly to the steering wheel. You

2
can easily lose control of the car if you do not have a good
hold on the steering wheel. The next step is to get off the
road. You must not try to stop or turn too quickly, however.
After you check the traffic, you should move over to the side
Line 10   of the road and slow down gradually. Then you should turn
on your flashing lights so other cars will see you. This way

3

you may learn it is a good idea to check the amount of air in your
tires every week.

譯文

　　如果你開車時，曾有過爆胎，你應該知道如何處理。爆胎
就是突然沒了氣的輪胎。這會是個很可怕的經驗，特別是在高速
行駛時。若你的車爆胎了，頭一件要做的事就是緊緊地握住方向
盤。若你不能握好方向盤。你可能輕易地使你的車失控。接著就
是駛離路面。然而，你不能嘗試太快地停車或轉向。在你檢查過
交通狀況後，你應該將車開到路邊，並且緩慢減速。然後你打開
車子的警示燈以讓其他的車輛看到你。從上所述你可以知道每週
檢查你的胎壓是個好主意。

(一) 字義解析

1. blow-out：由第二句中對 blowout 的定義可以得知此字涵義：
   a sudden flat tire(突然洩了氣的輪胎)。而接下的一句涵義，
   則更加強 blow-out 這方面的解釋：It can be a very frightening
   experience, especially if you are traveling at high speed.(這可能是
   很嚇人的經驗，特別是你在高速行駛時。) 綜合此字的定義
   與描述它的狀況，可以得知 blow-out 應是與「爆胎」有關。

2. steering：此字的字義可從其前後句子的描述而看出。因為
   其前的句子是描繪車子發生爆胎的情況，首先要做的事就
   是抓緊 steering wheel。雖然 wheel 是作「輪子」解釋，但是
   依常理分析，這不可能是指「車輪」，而下一句中的 "easily
   lose control of the car"(輕易使車子失去控制) 則意味著 steering
   wheel 應是與控制車子行進有關的車中設備，再加上車中類
   似「輪子」、「車輪」形狀的設備只有方向盤，所以由此
   種種上下文意，可以推敲 steering wheel 應是與控制車子方

向的方向盤有關。

3. flashing：flashing 的字義可從其後的解釋看出：so other cars will see you.(以讓別的車看到你)。因為若是打開燈就可以使別的車見到你，那麼句中就不需要 flashing 這個字來修飾 lights。所以 flashing 應是指警告方面相關的涵義。而字尾有 "ing" 的型式，則進一步意味著此字應是強調正在進行的狀態。依常理判斷，具有進行警示功用的車燈，應該就是會不停閃爍的「閃光」燈。而 flashing 正是此意。

(二) 句法分析

　　本文是屬於說明性的短文。此類試題也是近年來各校的英文閱讀測驗的熱門題型之一。因此種性質，本文綜合了不少表示條件與建議的句型，來表達本文教導性質的內容。

1. Lines 1～7: If you ever get a blow-out while.. especially. If you are ... speed. If your car gets a blow-out, ... You can ... If you do not have ... wheel.

　　【解析】條件涵義的 If 子句在短短的全文中就占了四句的篇幅。由此可見它所表達某種的假設情況，為了是說明與提示讀者有關車況的處理情形。而它所用的句型是一般的條件子句的句型：If 十主詞十現在簡單式…。

2. Lines 2、8、10: If you ever ..., you should know ... You must not try... you should move over ... Then you should turn on ...

　　【解析】因本文具有說明與教導某種車況的處理情形，所以全文有不少表示建議與提示語氣的助動詞，像 should, must。而這些助動詞有些出現在主要子句中，與有 If 的條件子句形成一完整表示建議語氣

的句子，例如：If you ever get a blow-out while you are driving, you should know what to do.

(三) 文章主題與大意

　　因本文是講解發生爆胎狀況時的處理步驟，所以全文是依照處理此一突發狀況的先後順序來展開文脈。也因此有一些表示前後順序的語氣轉換詞出現在全文中，其出現的情況如下：

1. Lines 4～5: If your car gets a blow-out, the first thing to do is to the steering wheel.
   【解析】 "the first thing" 表達出首先要處理的事，它也是表示動作先後順序的語氣轉接詞。

2. Lines 7～8: The next step is to get off the road.
   【解析】 "The next step" 也表達出其次要做的事，同上句中的 the first thing 一樣，它也是語氣轉接詞。不過它們與一般常見表示順次的語氣轉接詞 (first, second, next 等)不太一樣，因為前者是名詞，而後者則是副詞。

3. Lines 9～11: After you check the traffic, you should ... gradually. Then you should turn on ... see you, This way you ... every week.
   【解析】 在 "The next step" 之後，用比較間接的語氣轉接詞 "after" 與 "Then" 來繼續依序地表達處理爆胎的狀況。而最後一句的 This way(從上述的事) 則是作為本文的結論：提醒事先防範的重要。

※ 本段的主題句 (也是本文的主旨句) 是第一句：If you ever get a blow-out while you are driving, you should know what to do. 接下來的句子就是描述這個主題：如何去處理爆胎的狀況。換言之，本文是以演繹的方式展開全文的文脈，而以

逐項的說明——敘述。其發展可歸納如下：

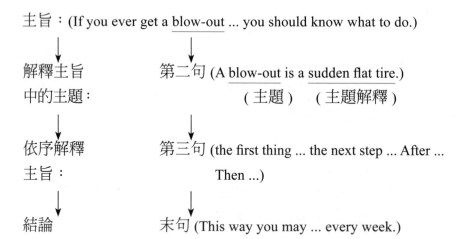

主旨：(If you ever get a blow-out ... you should know what to do.)

解釋主旨　　　第二句 (A blow-out is a sudden flat tire.)
中的主題：　　　　　　(主題)　　(主題解釋)

依序解釋　　　第三句 (the first thing ... the next step ... After ...
主旨：　　　　　　　　Then ...)

結論　　　　　末句 (This way you may ... every week.)
(對主旨的引申)

瞭解本文的主旨與過程就可分別回答下列兩個問題：

1. The topic of the above paragraph is:

    (A) How you feel if you get a blow-out?

    (B) What to do if you are traveling at high speed?

    (C) What to do if you get a blow-out?

    (D) What to do when you check your tires?

2. Which sentence in the above paragraph should be crossed out?

    (A) It can be a very frightening experience, especially if you are traveling at high speed.

    (B) You can easily lose control of the car if you do not have a good hold on the steering wheel.

    (C) After you check the traffic, you should move over to the side of the road and slow down gradually.

    (D) This way you may learn it is a good idea to check the amount of air in your tires every week.

【解析】本問題可謂別出心裁的問法：在以上段落中的那一句應該被刪去？若不瞭解全文的脈絡發展，則很難回答此問題，因為似乎看來都差不多。但是在 (B) 句中的涵義，事實上是介於 The first thing 與 The next step 之間，在語意上有多餘之嫌，並且使語氣未能連貫，所以應選 (B) 為答案。

範文 4

Line 1　　　　As far back as 700 B.C., man has talked about children being cared for by wolves. Romulus and Remus, the legendary twin founders of Rome, were <u>purported</u> to have been cared for by
　　　　　　　　　　　　　　　　　　1
　　　　wolves. It is believed that when a she-wolf loses her <u>litter</u>, she
　　　　　　　　　　　　　　　　　　　　　　　　　　　　　　2
Line 5　　　seeks a human child to take its place.

　　　　　　This seemingly <u>preposterous</u> idea did not become credible
　　　　　　　　　　　　　　　　3
　　　　until the late nineteenth century when a French doctor actually found a naked ten-year-old boy wandering in the woods. He did not walk erect, could not speak <u>intelligibly</u>. nor could
　　　　　　　　　　　　　　　　　　　　　　　　　　　　4
Line 10　　he relate to people.

　　　　　　He only growled and stared at them. Finally the doctor won the boy's confidence and began to work with him. After many long years of devoted and patient instruction, the doctor was able to get the boy to clothe and feed himself, recognize and <u>utter</u> a number
　　　　　　　　　　　　　　　　　　　　　　　　　　　　　　　5
Line 15　　of words, as well as write letters and form words.

(86 師大研究所)

遠溯至西元前七百年前，人們談到被狼照顧的小孩。傳奇中創立羅馬的雙生子羅穆魯斯與瑞莫斯據稱曾被狼撫養過。據信當母狼失去她的幼雛時，她會尋找人類的小孩來取代。

直到十九世紀當一位法國醫生真的找到一個在森林中流浪的十歲男孩時，這種似乎荒謬的想法才變為可信。他不能直立地行走，不能說人懂的話，也不能表明他與別人的關係。他只是對他們咆哮與凝視。最終那位醫生贏得那男孩對他的信任而與他開始一同工作。在多年長期的熱心與耐心的教導後，那位醫生使那男孩能自己穿衣與進食，認識與唸出一些字以及寫字母與拼字。

(一) 字義解析

1. purported 的字義可從 legendary 與前一句的涵義而推敲出，legendary 是 legend(傳奇) 的形容詞 (因其字尾為 ary)，所以 legendary 作「傳奇的」解釋。而 legendary 是用來形容 twin founders，而 twin founders 就是指 Romulus and Remus(因前者為後者的同位語)。而 Romulus and Remus 這兩位「傳奇的」人物是被 "purported to" 由狼所曾撫養。所以「傳奇的」與 "purport" 在涵義上有相當關聯。因此，purported 在涵義上應是指「並非真有的」或「並非存在的」。再加上前一句中說到這種孩子被狼養大的事是「古早」以前的傳聞，這更加強 "purport" 這字作「傳奇中的」或「據說」的解釋。至此，"purport" 的字義已是呼之欲出。

2. litter 的字義是由它之後的 "child to take its place" 涵義而推敲出。此片語中的代名詞所有格 its 是指同句中的 her litter，而 child 來取代 her litter 的地位，可見 child 是與 litter 類似的事物。而 she-wolf(母狼) 的這種身分更加強 litter 這樣的解

釋，所以 litter 應是指「動物的孩子」，這正是本書字彙篇所教的方法：由代名詞來推敲同義字的涵義。知道 litter 的字義後就可回答下列的問題：

◎ In this passage, the word "litter" most nearly means:

  (A) garbage   (B) mate   (C) offspring   (D) temper.

  【解析】乍看之下，本題並無立即明顯的對應答案，而有些字又非熟悉的單字。在此情況下，最好採取刪除不合適答案的剔除法。(A)、(D) 的涵義顯然不符。而 (B) 則需聯想它的類似字彙，如 offspring 就是 litter 的同義字，沒錯，就是它：offspring(後裔)。

3. preposterous 的字義可由前一段中的大意與同句中 "not become credible" 來推敲。preposterous 是形容 idea，而由前一的涵義中可以得知這個 idea 是指由母狼來撫育人的小孩。而在前一段的大意中已指出這種想法是傳奇似的，而非真實的。所以 preposterous 應是較接近這種涵義。而其後的 not credible 更加強這樣的解釋。所以 preposterous 的大意應類似「無法令人相信的；難以置信的」，瞭解這個大意也就可回答下列的問題：

◎ In this passage, the word "preposterous" most nearly means:

  (A) dedicated   (B) scientific   (C) wonderful   (D) absurd.

  【解析】依照找出的解釋，答案 D 最合適。wonderful(奇妙的) 通常是形容肯定 (可信) 的事物，在此並不合適。

4. intelligibly 的字義可從其前後句子的上下文而推敲出。由前一句的 "actually found.. wandering in the woods. " 中的 actually(真地) 與 in the woods(在樹林中) 意味著這個真實

的發現是印證傳說中的假設。所以眞有由狼養育的孩子這件事，接下來的句子都是對這男孩非人性一面的描述 (第八～十行)。他無法直立地行走，不能…，也不能表明他與別人的關係。"intelligibly" 的字尾局 ly，所以應該是副詞，用來修飾 speak，因前文已顯示他是由狼帶大，所以推想他可能不能說人語，因此 "intelligibly" 的涵義應與此種聯想有關。再加上後一句中的進一步說明：他只是對他們咆哮與凝視，更加強 "intelligibly" 作「人明白的話」的解釋。而 intelligibly 正接近此意。下列是與 intelligibly 有關的題目：

The French doctor found the boy:

(A) walking aimlessly in the woods.

(B) growling at him.

(C) quite credible.

(D) speaking intelligibly.

【解析】(D) 顯然不對，(C) 的情況文中並未提到，(B) 的答案很詭異，因爲原文中咆哮的對象是「他們」(them)，而非「他」。稍不留神，就會答錯。只有 A 符合原文，因爲 walk aimlessly = wander. 這也算是測驗考生同義字的概念。

5. utter 的字義可由同一句中的上下文以及前面句子的描述可推敲出。本句前文提到那位法國醫生教導那個男孩自己穿衣與進食，認字與寫字 (to get the boy to clothe and feed himself, recognize.. a number of words, as well as write letters and form words)，換言之，他在教那男孩一些人類生活的基本技能。而穿衣與進食之後的描述都與人所使用的溝通技能有關，文中提到認字與寫字，而缺另兩項溝通的基本技能：說與聽。又 "and" 通常連接兩個動作或涵義相關的單字或片

語，所以recognize(認出)應與「說」方面的動作更有關聯。此外，前文中也提到那男孩不能說人懂的話，只會咆哮，所以由這上文的暗示可以推想 utter 應是針對他不能說人話的需要而作說明。因此，utter 的涵義應是與「說出；讀出」有關。瞭解此意就可作答下列問題：

Which of the following statements is NOT true ?

(A) The young boy never was able to speak perfectly.

(B) The French doctor succeeded in domesticating the boy somewhat.

(C) She-wolves have been said to substitute human children for their lost litters.

(D) Examples of wolves caring for human children can be found only in the nineteenth century.

【解析】由最後一句的描述中得知 A 的答案是正確的：那男孩只會說一些字 (事實上 utter ≒ speak)，而絕不能說地很好。(B) domesticating：教化，somewhat：一些；(C) 已在前分析過，是正確無誤。只有 (D) 與原文不符，因為第一段中提到西元前就有這種的傳說。

(二) 句法分析

　　本文是記敘文，所以全文的時式大都是過去式，第一段因為是引言，所以還有使用現在式來表示普遍性說法。第二段則是對過去特定事件的記載，全部以過去式敘述，現將重要或複雜的句子分析如下：

1. Lines 4～5: It is believed that when she-wolf loses her litter. she seeks a human child to take its place.

【解析】當表示一般或大家都這樣想 / 相信 / 期待…的事物

或觀念時，在英文中要用下列的特殊句型來表達：
It is thought/believed expected ... that 子句，因本句是
表示一種普遍認爲的傳說，所以要用現在簡單式。

2. Lines 6～8: This seemingly preposterous idea did not become
credible until the late nineteenth century ...

【解析】本句不行依字面來解釋，因它爲特殊句型 not ...
until ...：直到…才…。所以要先從後面解釋起，並
且沒有否定的涵義：直到十九世紀…才變的可信。

3. Lines 8～10: He did not walk erect, could not speak intelligibly, nor
could he relate to people.

【解析】爲了避免句型的重複與單調，所以最後一句的否定
句通常可用以下的句型：nor (neither) + 助動詞 /be
動詞 + 主詞，但需留意的是助動詞的時式須與前面
否定句的時式一致。

... could not speak ..., nor could he ...

(三) 文章主題與大意
　　本文是依照時間先後順序敘述的記敘文。全文是以演繹的
方式展開，因此主旨句很自然地就出現於首段，而整個文章的
脈絡發展如下：

1. 第一段：包含全文的主旨與引言。第一句就是主旨句：As
far back as 700 B.C. man has talked about children being cared for
by wolves. 接下來的兩句是舉例說明與背景解釋，所提到的
時間也是本文中最早時間。

2. 第二段：本段是引用一個真實事例來印證前一段中 (未確
定) 的傳說。此段明確地表明這印證的企圖，本段的首句

即開門見山的強調以前的傳聞是真的，所以第一句也就是本段的主題句，接下來的敘述 (Lines 8～14) 是以細節說明這個舉證的事例是真實可信的 (否則，三言兩語何以令人置信！)。所以本段是以全部的內容來印證第一段中的主旨。

由以上的段落分析可知全文的脈絡如下：

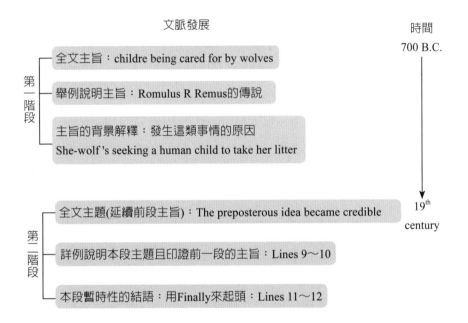

範文 5

Line 1   A satellite is usually launched by a rocket. Once the satellite is in orbit, the plane of the orbit is relatively fixed in space. However, as the satellite goes around the earth, the earth spins on its axis beneath it. Thus on each circuit the
Line 5   satellite passes over a different part of the earth's surface.

The orbit of a satellite is usually not a circle. During launching, variations from the calculations of elevation, altitude and speed are impossible to eliminate. The orbit is
<u>3</u>
then elliptical. Scientists deliberately plan for a satellite

Line 10　　to enter an elliptical orbit so that it will probe a range of altitudes. An <u>elliptical</u> path can bring a satellite into the upper
<u>4</u>
atmosphere. The <u>friction</u> of the atmosphere on the satellite
<u>5</u>
causes its speed to decrease.It is then drawn closer to the earth, and may be heated ultimately to <u>incandescence</u> and be
<u>6,</u>

Line 15　　vaporized as it enters the lower portion of the earth's atmosphere.

A satellite which has been given an initial horizontal speed of 30,000 km/hr orbits about the earth in a circular path at an altitude of about 500 km. If this horizontal speed is raised to 40,000 km/hr, the space vehicle leaves the earth's

Line 20　　orbit and goes into orbit around the sun. The <u>velocity</u> at
<u>7</u>
which this happens is called escape velocity.　　(84 政大研究所)

譯文

　　人造衛星通常是由火箭來發射的。一旦衛星進入軌道,軌道的平面就在太空中相當地固定。然而,當人造衛星環繞地球時,在它之下,地球依著地軸旋轉。正因為如此,每循環一週,人造衛星就經過地球表面不同的區域。

　　人造衛星的軌道通常不是圓形。在發射之際,其仰角、高度及速度的計算之差異是無法去除的:因此其軌道為橢圓形的。科學家故意設計進入橢圓形軌道的人造衛星為了它能偵測高度的範圍。橢圓形的軌道能將人造衛星帶入較高的大氣層。大氣層與人造衛星的摩擦導致它的速度減緩。也因為如此它被更拉近地

球；當它進入地球大氣層較低部分之際，它可能最後被加熱至白熱化而被蒸發掉。

　　一個被施以水平起速達時速三萬公里的人造衛星，以圓形的路線進入在大約五百公里高度的地球軌道。倘若這種水平速度被提高到時速四千公里，那麼這個太空交通工具就會離開地球軌道而進入太陽的軌道。當這種速率發生時，它就被稱之為脫離速率。

(一) 字義解析

1. satellite 是全文的主要關鍵字，因為全文都在解釋 satellite 的運作情形。所以瞭解它，就能對全文的瞭解有莫大的幫助。第一句就說明 satellite 是由火箭所發射的。可見 satellite 為一飛行物體。由此推測其可能為太空梭或人造衛星，但從第二段中的最後一句說到 satellite 最終會被蒸發 (vaporized) 掉，可見其並非太空梭 (因為太空梭還要回到地面來)，而為人造衛星。知道 satellite 為人造衛星的涵義後，就要運用或聯想有關人造衛星方面的常識，例如，人造衛星是固定在地球的某一軌道上之類的常識，這對文中其他字彙的明白有莫大的幫助。

2. circuit 的字義可由其前一句的涵義推敲出：as the satellite goes around the earth, the earth spins on its axis beneath it.(當人造衛星環繞地球時，在它之下，地球依著地軸旋轉。) 而 thus(正因為如此) 這語氣連接詞，說出這前、後兩句緊密的因果關係──在如何的情形之下，人造衛星會經過地表的不同區域。由此可推知 circuit 是意指「一圈或一周」。此外，字首 circ(圓) 的涵義可加強這種涵義的解釋。

3. altitude 的字義可由以下兩點來推敲：

(1) 由字首 at(高的) 及字尾 tude(情況) 來推敲 alti+ tude=altitude；又 tude 通常為名詞字尾，所以 altitude 解釋為高度或高。

(2) 由同句中的上、下文來推測：During launching, variations from the calculations of elevation, altitude, and speed are impossible to eliminate ...(在發射期間，從角度、altitude 及速度的計算上之差異是無法去除的)。and 連接同範圍內的事物，而計算之差異更使我們聯想到可能是高度，因為速度及角度都提及了。

綜合以上兩點推敲 altitude 字義的方法，接下來我們就能回答如下的問題：

◎ According to the passage, satellite orbits are usually not circular because _____.

(A) there is friction in the atmosphere

(B) the earth spins on its axis

(C) variations from precise calculations are difficult to eliminate

(D) too great a speed is needed for circular orbits

(E) present-day satellites weigh too much

答案為 (C)，因為第二段的首句就說出人造衛星的軌道並非圓圈，而第二句很顯然地即在說明其原因，所以找出第二句即可知答案。

4. elliptical 的字義可由以下兩方面來推敲：

(1) 第二段的首句已說出「衛星的軌道非圓形」，第二句為說明其非圓形的原因。第三句則說出其非圓形的結果，而其中的 then(正因為如此) 更加強這種作為結果的解釋。照常理判斷，因為無法避免計算的差異，而依照地

球的軌道來看，應該出現的結果是橢圓形，答案正是如此。換言之，由 not a circle 來推測 elliptical 的涵義。

(2)在 Line 11 中，說到 elliptical 的軌道能將人造衛星帶入較高的大氣層。若讀者對太空常識豐富，則可判斷 elliptical 應為「橢圓形的」，而且字尾 al 為慣用的形容詞字尾。

5. friction 的字義需從其所在的那句及下一句中的文意推敲出：

(1)大氣層怎麼會導致人造衛星的速度的減緩？而介系詞 on(在…之上) 則透露出大氣層的 friction 作用在人造衛星上，所以這可能是一種物理現象。

(2)接下去的句子中，又出現表結果的 "then" 說出人造衛星因為 friction 的作用而被拉近地表，最後在進入地球較低區域時被蒸發掉。

綜合 (1)、(2) 兩點，可知會使人造衛星速度減緩並且最後被蒸發掉的物理現象應該是指「摩擦」，知道 friction 的字義就可回答下面的問題：

◎ According to the passage, an elliptical orbit may cause the satellite to vaporize due to _____.

(A) the vibration of the engines

(B) friction with the atmosphere

(C) the heat of the sun

(D) the earth spinning on its axis

(E) space dust.

答案很明顯地為 (B)：與大氣層的摩擦。

6. incandescence 的字義可由 may be heated ultimately to incandescence and be vaporized as it enters the lower portion of the earth's atmosphere 這句中推敲出。加熱至何種情況之下東西會被蒸發掉？按常理推斷，應該是「白熱」或「高溫」。而表示情形的 as

子句更加強這種推斷，因為人造衛星降落地球時，會因高溫而被燒毀。此句的 heated ultimately to(最終加熱到…) 為解釋 incandescence 的關鍵片語。

7. velocity 的字義可由其前一句的文章及 at which this happens 此子句推敲出：

(1) 最後一段不長，其重點在談人造衛星的速率。所以 velocity 的前一句也在說到某種假設的速率情況，說到在水平速度升至時速 40,000 公里時，此太空工具會離開地球軌道而進入太陽軌道。這種情形就是下一句所要定義的。

(2) at which this happens 中的 this 就是指前一句所發生的情況，而 at 的受詞為 velocity，而 at 在此段中作在 / 以…的 (速度) 解釋 (例如：Lines 17&18 中的 an ... speed of 30,000 km/hr, at an altitude of about 500km)，所以 velocity 也可能作速度解釋，更何況其前一句中就說到速率的情況。此外，escape velocity 中的 escape 已有「脫離」的涵義，故 velocity 不可能解釋為脫離。

所以綜合 (1)、(2) 兩點，知道 velocity 在此作某種速率的定義。事實上它是科技術語中的「速率」來取代一般所用的 speed。與此句有連帶關聯的問題為：

◎ According to the passage, which speed will produce an elliptical orbit of a satellite around the earth?

　(A) 5,000 km/hr.

　(B) 15,000 km/hr.

　(C) 30,000 km/hr.

　(D) 35,000 km/hr.

　(E) 45,000 km/hr.

在知道 velocity 之意後，答案也就明顯得知 (C)。

(二) 句法分析

　　本文內容爲科技性的文章，重在解釋及說明，所以時態多爲現在簡單式或完成式，因爲所說明的皆是事實。也因屬於說明性文章，所以其敘述方式均按部就班，用了不少表時間或因果的語氣連接副詞和子句。此外，有些文中的代名詞也要分清其所代替的字，這樣才不會造成對文章內容的誤解。

1. 表時間或因果的語氣連接副詞和子句：once, however, thus, during, then, ultimately, as, if。

　　第一段：Once(一旦)the satellite ... However(然而)as the satellite ... Thus(正因爲如此)…

　　【解析】表條件關係用 once，而表語氣的轉變用 however，再表因果關係用 thus。

　　第二段：During(在…期間)launching, variations from ... to eliminate. The orbit is then(因此)

　　elliptical ... Line 13：It is then(正因爲如此)drawn…and may be heated ultimately(最終地)..

　　【解析】表時間的 during，及因果關係的 then 將第二段的句子之因果關係表明得很清楚。

　　第三段：Line 18：If this horizontal ...

2. 辨別文中的代名詞：因文中所描寫的皆爲非人稱的事物，故都用 it，所以易產生混淆。例如 Lines 3～4 中的 the earth spins on its axis beneath it. 這一前一後的 it 各有所指，前者指地球，後者指人造衛星，所以務必要辨明其區別，以免誤解文意。第二段中的 it 則皆指人造衛星，第三段的最後一句中的 this 是代替前一句整句的涵義。知此，即對文意的瞭解很有助益。

(三) 文章主題與大意

　　前面四篇文章是提及有關人文、社會、哲學及政治方面的內容，而本篇則說到不同領域的科學——科技。這類文章文體多為說明性的文體，段落分明，所以主題不難掌握，試就以下各段來分別說明：

1. 第一段的主題：第一句為引入句，將題目點出：satellite，接著的第二句就是主題句 (Once the satellite ... in space) 說出 satellite 如何在地球表面運行，這種主題句在第二句的位置較少見，需注意。

2. 第二段的主題：第一句就明白的道出本段的主題—— The orbit of a satellite is usually not a circle. 接下來的句子大都為說明句，說明何以不是圓形而為橢圓形的情況。所以整段大抵以主題句的重點為範圍。

3. 第三段的主題：主題句並不明顯，但可將最後一句視為歸納式的主題句 (也就是結論句)，由兩種速率的說明，來解釋何謂「脫離速率」(escape velocity)。藉由正常速率與超越速率的比較來定義 escape velocity. 這三段都重在解釋定義，所以針對此文體 (說明文) 的題目也就可知其答案了。

　　◎ The author's style can best be described as：

　　　(A) argumentative.

　　　(B) explanatory.

　　　(C) humorous.

　　　(D) rhetorical.

　　　(E) scholarly.

　　　答案為 (B)：解釋的。

Line 1　　　　Watching a baby between six and nine months old will help you observe the basic concepts of geometry being learned. Once the baby has mastered the idea that space is three dimensional, it reaches out and begins grasping various kinds of

Line 5　　objects. It is then, from perhaps nine to fifteen months, that the concepts of sets and numbers are formed. So far, so good. But now an ominous development takes place. The nerve fibers in the Brain insulate themselves in such a way that the baby begins to hear sounds very precisely. Soon it picks up language, and it is then

Line 10　　brought into direct communication with adults. From this point on, it is usually downhill all the way for mathematics, because the child now becomes exposed to all the nonsense words and beliefs of the community into which it has been so unfortunate as to have been born. Nature, having done very well by the child

Line 15　　to this point, having permitted it the luxury of thinking for itself for eighteen months, now abandons it to the arbitrary conventions and beliefs of society. But at least the child knows something of geometry and numbers, and it will always retain some memory or the early halcyon days, no

Line 20　　matter what vicissitudes it may suffer later on. The main reservoir of mathematical talent in any society is thus possessed by children who are about two years old, children who have just learned to speak fluently.　　　　(84 中興研究所)

譯文

　　仔細地觀察六至九個月大的嬰兒，你就會發現他已經學會

了幾何學的基本概念了。只要嬰兒有了三度空間的觀念，他就會開始伸手去抓握各式各樣的東西。大約九至十五個月大的時候，那時就形成了集合數字的概念。至此，一切都很順利。不過，此後不祥的發展就開始了。腦部的神經纖維開始獨立自主，因此嬰兒開始能確切的聽到各種聲音。不久，他就學起語言來，那時也就與成人發生了直接的溝通。從這一刻起，數學的學習一落千丈。因為此時起孩子就完全暴露在這個他不幸得生於其中的社會裡各種無意義的辭藻及信仰裏。大自然，至此點前都對這孩子恩惠有加，讓他享受了十八個月獨立思考的時光，現在拋棄了他，讓他去接觸社會中各種變化無定的習俗規定與信仰。不過，至少這孩子多少也知道了一些有關幾何學及數字方面的事情，而他不論後來經過何等的滄桑，也將永遠保留住這一些早期太平日子裏所得的記憶。所以，任何一個社會中數學天賦的主要儲存庫就是由兩歲大左右的孩子們所把持著，也就是那些剛學會流利講話的孩子們。

(一) 字義解析

1. geometry：通常只有一段的文章，其主題句大都在首句。本文亦不例外。而 geometry 又為此句中的關鍵字，所以欲知其意，可從文中其他的句子找出類似或相關的字，在 Line 6 中 the concepts of sets and numbers are formed (from perhaps nine to fifteen months) 與首句中的 a baby bet ween six and nine months old... the basic concepts of geometry being learned. 在意義上互相呼應。所以可以推斷 geometry 可能與 sets and numbers(集合數字) 有關。這就很接近 geometry(幾何學) 的原意了。此外文中多次提到小孩的 mathematics 或 mathematical talent，所以也可據以加強 geometry 作此解釋的依據。根據對 sets and

numbers 及 geometry 的相關瞭解，就可作答下題：

◎ According to the author, at what age does a child probably begin to learn about sets and numbers?

(A) Six months.

(B) Nine months.

(C) Fifteen months.

(D) Eighteen months.

答案爲 (B)，因爲是從九個月到十五個月知道 sets and numbers。

2. ominous：其字義可由以下兩方面來推敲：

(1) 從其前一句中的 so far, so good(目前爲止，一切都好)，這裏的好是指嬰孩對數字的形成發展良好。而後接著的 But now 改變了句子的涵義及語氣，說到一種 ominous 的發展發生了，這種的發展依前後的語氣來看，顯然是指負面的，不好的發展，因此 ominous 有作此解釋的趨勢。

(2) 而作者說到孩童轉向聲音及語言的注意時，作者用 because the child now exposed to all the nonsense words and beliefs of the community into which it has been so unfortunate as to have been born. "nonsense" 和 "unfortunate" 強烈暗示作者對孩童由對數字轉向對語言的注意所感到的不滿，因此下文也提供了 ominous 作負面解釋的依據。知及於此，也就可回答下面的問題：

◎ The use of the word "ominous" shows that the author believes the child's

(A) linguistic future is threatened.

(B) nerves will deteriorate.

(C) hearing will suffer.

(D) mathematical ability will decline.

答案為 (D)，因為 (A)～(C) 皆為肯定聲音對孩子的影響。

3. downhill：其字義可由其本身的組成及上、下文中推敲出

(1) downhill 是由 down(下)+hill(山坡) 所組成的組合字，所以作「下坡」解釋。

(2) 從 Lines 6～7 的 "But now an ominous development takes place." 開始，作者認為嬰孩開始學習語言是件不好的事，所以強調從這點開始 ("this" 是指嬰兒開始和大人溝通)，它 (這裡指嬰孩) 開始在數學方面一路 downhill。由此推敲 downhill 為負面的字眼。而同一句中解釋 downhill all the way for mathematics 也加強這種負面的解釋：because the child now becomes exposed to all the <u>nonsense</u> words and beliefs of the community... so <u>unfortunate</u> as to have been born.

4. arbitrary 的字義可由上文中看出，Line 15：Nature,... having permitted the luxury of thinking for itself for eighteen months, now abandons it to the arbitrary conventions and beliefs of society. 從上文中我們得知嬰孩有十八個月的獨立思考的時光，不過拋棄它而去接受非自然的社會習俗和信仰。換言之，人類社會的習俗與大自然無拘束的賜予對嬰兒來說是兩種相對的經歷。所以 arbitrary 的字義應是指非自然的、非獨立的，也就是人事的、人意的，瞭解於此，也就能回答相關問題了。

5. reservoir：其字義可由前一句中的同義字 retain 來推敲，因為在這句中孩子對幾何的概念仍有所保留 (retain)，所以接下來的這句為接續前一句的說明，並加以解釋，由 thus(正因如此) 在此句的轉接更可確定 reservoir 是作「保存或保留」來解釋：The main reservoir of mathematical talent ... is thus

possessed by children ....

(二) 句法分析

1. 分詞構句：

Lines 14～17: Nature, having done very well by the child to this point, having permitted it the luxury of ... months, now abandons it to the arbitrary conventions and beliefs of society.

【解析】此句的分詞構句為複合分詞構句，換言之，在主詞 Nature 之後有兩個分詞構句的插句來修飾全句，而這兩個分詞構句意義上的主詞皆為 Nature，其時態為完成式，所以所表達的時間也要比主要子句中的動詞時式早 (abandons)，所以在解釋上應先翻「在此點上對嬰孩恩惠有加之後以及讓它享受十八個月大的…. 之後，大自然才放棄了它。瞭解分詞構句與主要子句時式的先後，能有助於我們對文章的瞭解。此外，找出分詞構句的意義上的主詞也很重要，這兩點是遇到分詞構句時需注意的。

2. 表結果的副詞片語或子句：

(1) Lines 7～9: The nerve fibers in the brain themselves in such a way that the baby begins to ... precisely.

【解析】such+ 單 / 複數名詞 that 子句：如此的…以至於…
= so + adj/adv + that 子句

(2) Lines 9～11: ... into which it has been so unfortunate as to have been born.

【解析】so + adj/adv + as to + 原形動詞：太…以至於…

3. 加強語氣的 it 句型：

Lines 5～6: It is then, ... that the concepts of sets and numbers are formed.

【解析】It is was+ 被強調的人、事物 +that+ 不完全子句：就
　　　　是…

4. 在英文中，baby 為無性別的名詞，故用 it 來取代，所以文
中許多的 it 皆指嬰孩。

(三) 文章主題與大意

　　本文是一篇描述人類心理成長的文章，這類文章也算常
出現的閱讀測驗。不過在這篇說明文中，作者的語氣並非客
觀而中性的。從其用了不少帶價值判斷的修飾語 (如 downhill,
nonsense, unfortunate 等等) 以及相反口吻的連接詞 (But) 來看，
其對孩童學習發展有批判及不滿的價值判斷。本文的發展可以
正→反→正來表示。

1. 主題句仍出現在第一句：Watching a baby between ... geometry
being learned. 接下來的幾句 (Line 4) 皆是說明及延伸這樣的
主題。不過從 Lines 6～11(以第一個 But 來轉變內容)，這
些皆在說明阻礙 geometry 發展的原因。

2. 直到 Line 17 之後 (以另一個 But 來轉變語氣及內容)，又回
到相關本文第一句中的主題，不過是延伸第一句主題的內
容，發展為本段的結論句：The main reservoir ... who have just
learned to speak fluently. 事實上，結論句常是主題句延伸的結
論，這是重要的法則，宜留心！

針對全文正、反兩面的說明，可以判斷作者的語氣為「不
以為然」；所以下列問題的答案也就可得知：

◎ The author's attitude toward early childhood education can best
be described as somewhat?

(A) indifferent

(B) compromising

(C) indulgent

(D) cynical.

答案應 (D)：諷刺的。

同樣地，文中的兩個 But 也表明嬰兒早期學習數學的能力受其學習語言的打擾，也因此可回答下列問到本文結論的問句：

◎ The passage will reach which of the following conclusions?

(A) The language concepts used in early education interfere with mathematical reasoning.

(B) It is hopeless to try to teach children mathematics after the age of two.

(C) Language teaching should incorporate some mathematical formulas.

(D) Preschool education should stress society's beliefs and conventions.

答案為 (A)，這是在讀到段末結論時，所歸納出的答案，下面又是一題相關主題的問題：

◎ What does the passage mainly focus on ?

(A) The impact of language on mathematics.

(B) Children's ability to learn languages.

(C) How basic concepts of physics are learned.

(D) Math-learning strategies for babies.

答案為 (A)。

Line 1　　　There were about 300,000 blind termites or white ants
　　　　in a termite nest. About 100,000 of them grew wings, left
　　　　the darkness they loved, sought the light, and flew away in
　　　　many directions. A male and a female came to earth together.
Line 5　　They lost their wings, found a crack in a rotten log or plank,
　　　　and mated. The male soon died, but the female lived on for
　　　　ten, twenty, thirty, or more years. The female began a new
　　　　colony, laying eggs that hatched out sexless worker and
　　　　warrior ants. This queen laid many thousand eggs a day, perhaps
Line 10　100,000,000 eggs during her lifetime.

　　　　　There millions of termites, eating damp wood, cause
　　　　damage to houses and other buildings amounting to millions
　　　　of dollars every year. There are certain simple rules to be
　　　　followed in guarding against destruction caused by termites.
Line 15　No wooden part of building should touch the ground. The
　　　　supports for a building should be of stone, concrete, or similar
　　　　material. Painting wood nearest the ground with creosote is
　　　　an added caution. Do not build you home so that it may become a
　　　　home for termites!　　　　　　　　　　　　(87 中原研究所)

譯文

　　在一個白蟻窩中大約有三十萬隻的盲眼白蟻。其中約有十
萬隻會長出翅膀,飛離他們所愛的黑暗之地,尋求光源,並且往
各方飛散。雄蟻與雌蟻會一起來到地上。他們失去翅膀,找到朽
壞的樹木或木板的裂縫,然後交配。雄蟻很快地死去,但是雌蟻
卻繼續存活十、二十、三十年甚至更久。

雌蟻便開始了新的群體，產卵並將出無性工蟻與兵蟻。這隻蟻后每天會生下數以千計的卵，終其一生中可以產下一億顆的卵。

數百萬隻的白蟻侵蝕潮濕的木頭，造成數百萬元的房子與其他建築物的損壞。只要遵行幾則簡單可行的方法便能防止白蟻的破壞。建築物木質的部分不應接觸到地面。建築物的支撐物應是石頭、水泥或類似的質料。以防腐劑塗在最接近地面的木頭上則是更謹慎的作法。切勿將你自己的家變成白蟻的窩。

(一) 字義解析

1. termites：要推敲 termites 的字義，關鍵在於其後的 white ants。因為 or 通常連接兩個字義相近的字，or 作「或者」解釋。所以 termites 的涵義可由 white ants 來推敲出：termites white ants(白蟻)。因為本文的描述對象就是 termites，所以瞭解它的涵義有助於對全文文意的掌握。

2. mated：mated 的字義可從它所在句子的前後句來推敲。前一句中的 male 與 female came... together(雄、雌白蟻 .. 來在一起) 強烈暗示有關交配的事，因為在昆蟲的世界中，雄、雌昆蟲會聚在一起，大都是繁殖下一代。此外，mated 之前的主詞是 they，所以這說明 mated 是雄雌白蟻一起做的事，這更暗示 mated 有「交配」的涵義。後一句說明雄蟻做完此事就死去。按常識說，這在昆蟲世界是常有的事，雄性昆蟲盡完傳宗接代的責任，生命就結束而雌性昆蟲則繼續其孵卵的責任。所以綜合前、後句的涵義可以推敲出 mated 的字義。並且也有助於回答下列問題：

◎ After mating, the female died:

   (A) at once.

(B) soon.

(C) in two years.

(D) after many years.

【解析】本題除了測驗 mate 的字義外，也考驗考生是否細心，因為此題是問 "female" 的死去，而非 male。然而，原文只說到 female 最少可活到三十年以上，所以言外之意就是在幾十年後才會死去。因此，答案應為 (D) after many years. 此題需要考生的腦筋稍微急轉彎。

3. hatched：它的字義可由與它在文法結構上相關的字來推敲出。因 hatched 所在之處是一句修飾 eggs 的形容詞子句，所以 hatched 的字義與 eggs 關聯密切。而 laying eggs 作「產卵」解釋，所以 hatched 的字義也與此有關，而 hatched 之後的 out sexless workers and warrior ants 則更加強此種字義的解釋，因為雌蟻會生出無性工蟻(sexless workers)這是普通的常識。由此 hatched 的字義也就躍然紙上。

4. creosote：不同於 1～3 項單字的推敲方式，creosote 的字義需從它所在段落的頭一兩句來推敲。第三段的第一句就說出白蟻對房屋的危害。接下來的一句則提到防治之法。一項接著一項的提到。所以 creosote 所在的那句也是與防治白蟻危害有關：Painting wood... with creosote(用 creosote 漆在…的木頭上)，可見 creosote 是某種防止白蟻之害的藥劑(因為它可作附著於木頭的液體)。而 an added caution(更為謹慎)是用來描述 "Painting wood... with creosote" 的防治方法之情形。綜合上述種種前文之推敲可以得知 creosote 應是防止蟻害的物質。瞭解於此也就足以回答下列問題：

◎ The function of creosoting is to：

(A) minimize destruction

(B) facilitate mating

(C) reducing egg-laying

(D) multiply males.

【解析】本問句的意思是問「"creosoting"的功用為…」，只有 A 減少毀損切合題意。(B) 助長繁殖、(C) 減少孵卵 (D) 繁增雄蟻皆是答非所問。

(二) 句法分析

　　本文是說明文，是以過去式的時式來描寫白蟻的生態。全文大都是以簡單句的句型所構成，因此，其中的文意就比較簡單易懂。不過，還有下列幾個句子的結構需要加以解釋：

1. Lines 2～4: About 100,000 of them grew wings, left the darkness they loved, sought the light, and flew away in many directions.

　　【解析】本句是以介系詞片語 "About 100,000 of them" 作主格，並且它也是 grew, left, sought 與 flew 這些動詞的主格，所以本句的結構是單個主詞加上一連串表示連續動作的動詞，而本句中的介系詞片語因為作主格用，所以其性質為名詞片語。與此句相關的問題如下：

◎ How many of termites in the nest grew wings?

　　(A) one-quarter

　　(B) one-third

　　(C) one-half

　　(D) all

　　【解析】(B) one-third：三分之一，是與第一句中的數字 (300, 000) 作比較。

2. Lines 15～17: The supports for a building should be of stone, concrete, or similar material.

【解析】of+ 名詞―形容詞，而它的用法與位置通常有兩種：

(1) 在名詞後修飾名詞，例如：

the door of car

(2) 在 be 動詞之後，作主詞補語用。就像本句中的 of stone(像石頭般的)，of concrete 像水泥般的。爲避免重複 concrete 與 material 之前的 of 都被省略。

3. Lines 18～19: Do not build your home so that it may become a home for termites!

【解析】not ... so that+ 主詞 + may/can+ 原形動詞：以免：免得，它是 "so that+ 子句" 的否定句型，而 so that+ 子句作「爲了…」解釋。

所以，本句中要注意以否定祈使句開頭的涵義：
Do not ... 注意 so that 與 so ... that 的不同型式與涵義：

表結果：He ran so fast that he caught the bus. 他跑得快以致能趕上公車。

表目的：He ran fast so that he might catch the bus. 他跑得快爲了要趕上公車。

(三) 文章主題與大意

　　本文是描述自然現象的說明文。全文主要分成兩大部分：第一部分涵蓋第一、二段，是描寫會發生的自然現象 (白蟻的生態)，是以過去簡單式來依序描述，第三段則是描寫一再發生的事實 (白蟻對住家的破壞)，是以現在簡單式來依序描述這種重複發生的事實。本文兩種不同的時式意味著不同的語

氣，尤其當後者是帶有建議語氣時，一般都用現在簡單式，本文並無明顯的表達全文主旨的主旨句。不過，在全文的末了一句，是類似結論語意的結論句：Do not build... for a termites! 它以命令句來表達，並且在最後一句，這意味著它是本文的重點所在。

1. 第一～第二段：這兩段說到白蟻的生活，尋偶以及繁殖的過程，文脈的發展是依循時間先後的順序。第一段的首句將本文所要描並的主要對象 termites 就已點明，但它並非本文的主題句。只是介紹本文的引介句 (introductoy sentence)：第二段則全都在描述白蟻孵育的情形。雖然這兩段都無表達全文主題的主題句，然而作者已在字裏行間透露出白蟻的驚人數量與繁增，這對引入下一段的文意是很自然的強調。

2. 第三段：本段的主題句是第二句：There are certain simple. caused by termites. 因為從第三句開始就是詳細列舉這些簡單的可行方法」，末句則是強調防治白蟻的重要性：Do not... for termites!。而第一句則是本段主題的引介句，所以它在本段中有連接語意的功用。

所以全文的脈絡發展如下：

第一段：引入全文所要討論的對象：白蟻

第二段：依時間先後順序，介紹白蟻一生最後的重任：養育下一代

突現白蟻驚人的數量

第三段：引介句 (白蟻的危害) → 本段主題句 (防治之道) → 詳述其細節 → 結論句 (以命令來實現其重要性)

Line 1   Fish are easy to recognize. They do not have arms or legs, like animals, but fins and a strong tail. Animals use their legs to move, but fish use their tail and fins. Most fish are covered with scales, and they feel slimy. They have eyes

Line 5   and what appears to be a nose; they can hear, and they have a skeleton. The slime on fish helps them to swim more quickly in water. More importantly, it helps to keep the water out of their bodies. Without slime, water gets into the fishes, muscles. The scales also help to keep the water out. If you take fish out of the

Line 10   water, be careful with the scales and the slime. (86 北師研究所)

譯文

　　魚是易於辨認的。牠們沒有像動物那樣有手臂或腿,但卻有鰭與有力的尾巴。動物使用他們的腿來走動,而魚卻使用尾巴與鰭來游動。大部分的魚都覆有魚鱗,而這些魚鱗讓人感覺滑溜溜的。他們有眼睛與好像鼻子的東西:他們能聽,而且他們有骨架。在魚身上的黏液會幫助他們在水中游地更快。更重要的是,它有助於隔絕水於體外。若無這種黏液,則水會進入魚的肌肉中。魚鱗也有助於隔絕水於體外。你若將魚拿出水外,要小心牠的魚鱗與黏液。

(一) 字義解析

1. fin 的字義可從其前的 "arms or legs" 與其後的 "a strong tail" 推敲出。這裡的 "arms or legs" 是指陸上動物的四肢,由 but 是連接對比或相反涵義的用法來看:"fins and a strong tail" 也應是指陸上的肢體或對比的肢體,而魚的肢體就是鰭與尾巴。所以 fins 應是指鰭(若 tail 作「尾巴」的涵義是已知的),

此外，後一句成對比的描述也有助於這樣的解釋：動物使用腿來行動、而魚卻使用 tail 與 fins 來行動。所以由上下文意的解釋可知 "fin" 的涵義。

2. scale 的字義可由其前的動詞片語 "are covered with" 與本文倒數第二句中的解釋而找出。"are covered with" 作「覆蓋著」。依常理推斷，魚的身上所覆蓋的應是魚鱗，但並非所有的魚都有鱗 (如鰻魚即無)，所似句中的 Most fish 來說明此種情形。再加上倒數第二句中所提這種 scales 也有助於水隔絕於體外，這種說明更加強 scale 作「魚鱗」的這種解釋。

3&4. slimy 與 slime 的字義是類似的，只是前者是形容詞 (從字尾 y 可識出)，而後者卻是名詞，它們的字義可由兩字前後文的涵義推敲出。關於 slimy 的涵義，要先弄清楚 "they" 所指為何，因為這裡極易誤認 "they" 是指 "Most fish"，事實上，they 是指 scales。所以是魚鱗使人覺得 "slimy"。按常理判斷，摸魚鱗的感覺是黏黏的或滑溜溜的。因此，they feel 這兩個字就提供對 slimy 涵義很好的聯想。而在魚身上的 slime 有助於他們在水中游的更快，並且也有助於隔絕水於體外。我們知道魚鱗可隔絕水於體外，但 slime 卻非魚鱗，不過它卻是與魚鱗有密切關聯的東西，因為它使得魚鱗摸起來 slimy(滑溜溜或黏黏的)。這種滑溜溜的東西又可使魚游的更快，且有防水性，但卻不明顯 (因為魚鱗是魚可見的最外層表面)，綜合上述對 slime 的特性描述可知，它應是與「黏液」有關的涵義。

明白上述 1～4 的字義解析後，以下列出與其相關的問題：

◎ According to the passage, the following are true EXCEPT

(A) Fins and tail help fish to swim in water.

(B) Skeleton helps fish to hear in water.

(C) Slime helps fish move faster in water.

(D) Most fish have scales on their bodies.

◎ Which of the following helps fish to keep the water out of their bodies?

(A) Slime

(B) Fins and tail

(C) Slime and scales

(D) All of the above.

【解析】

1. 1.(A)、(B) 與 (C) 顯然都與原文文意符合，只有 (D) 不對。雖然你可能對 skeleton 的涵義不清楚，但用剔除與問題不合的選項，就可以找出答案──這是當你無法立即辨識出答案的間接答題方式。

2. 在解 slime 與 scale 的字義後，可以確定答案為 (C)。當然！本題也可直接從上下文中判斷 slime 與 scales 的防水功能。不過此處是訓練考生對單字字義解析的能力，況且考題也是千變萬化，難以預料。增加此種推敲字義的能力，是有備無患。

(二) 句法分析

　　本文屬於說明性的短文，句型簡單，大都為簡單句或複句。用字常前後重復。這樣的句子與用詞是常出現在介紹自然科學的短文中。然而，仍有些句子的文法易引起混淆，現分析如下：

1. Lines 1～3、6 中的 "fish" 是魚類的總稱，泛指所有的魚。因為 fish 是單、複同字型的字彙，所以其後要用複數動詞，例如：Fish are easy to recognize. fish 作複數的型式也可由其後的代名詞可看出：They do not have arms or legs. 然而，fish 若未涵蓋所有的魚類或意指某些的魚類，則要用複數的型式

來表達：Without slime, water gets into the fishes' muscles.(Line 8)
這裡的魚類是前面所指那些大部分有鱗的魚類。所以說到
不同種類的魚類時，需用複數來表達。再看一例：There are
many kinds of fishes in this lake.

2. Line 8: Without slime, water gets into the fishes' muscles.

【解析】Without + 名詞 / 名詞片語：若非

$$= \text{But fot} + 名詞 / 名詞片語$$

$$= \text{If it} \begin{cases} \text{had not been} \\ \text{were not} \end{cases} \text{for} + 名詞 / 名詞片語$$

(三) 文意主題與大意

　　本文是以演繹的方式展開全文。第一句即是全段的主題
句：Fish are easy to recognize，接下來則是以比較與說明來解釋
全文的主題：easy to recognize(易於辨識)。而說明的重點則集
中於魚在水中的特性：不怕水。也因此 slime 與 scale 就占了全
文大部分的篇幅。甚至結語 (If you take ... with the scales and the
slime) 仍與此相關。現以簡略圖示呈現本文的發展如下：

Line 1 主題句：Fish are easy to recogniza.

↓

Lines 1～3 比較句：They do not ... like ... animals ... tall. Animals use
　　　　　　　　　　... and fins.

↓

Lines 3～6 說明句：Most fish are covered with ... to keep the water out
　　　　　　　　　　... (自此說明的重心轉到對 slime 與 scales
　　　　　　　　　　解釋)

↓

Lines 9～10 結語句：If you take ... the slime.(與主題句中的主題
　　　　　　　　　　稍有不同，另一個由主題衍生的推理)

Exercise

一、閱讀測驗：請依下列文章的內容作答

1.

      Is there too much violence on TV? Every day and every night there is a murder on the tube. Some viewers become violent after certain programs. Other viewers see so much violence that they don't care when they see bad things happen in real life. Frequent violence on TV often causes people to stop caring. On the other hand, violence is part of life. TV must show murders and fights because these help to tell complete stories. Our knowledge of art, science, and history is not complete without knowledge of violence. Perhaps the negative influence of TV violence is powerful on some people. But shouldn't we ask, "Is there a balance between evil and good on TV?"   (83 金融特考)

請回答下列問題：

(1) _____ The main idea of the reading is that _____

  (A) there is too much violence on TV

  (B) violence makes people stop caring

  (C) some viewers become violent after certain programs

  (D) TV should be banned altogether

  (E) seeing too much violence can be bad, but some violence must part of life

(2) _____ What dose violence refer to in this passage?

  (A) TV show

  (B) murders and fights

  (C) art and science

  (D) positive influence

2.

I am more of a host than a guest. I like people to stay with me but do not much care about staying with them, and usually say I am too busy. The only people we ask to stay with us are people we like--I do not believe in business hospitality, which has the seed of corruption in it--and all Fridays I work in a pleasant glow just because I know some nice people are coming down by the last train. I am genuinely glad to see them. But I suspect that I am still more delighted when they go, and the house is ours again.

(84 世華銀行)

請回答下列問題：

(1) _____ What is the main idea of the passage ?

(A) The writer lives to be a host.

(B) The author dislikes guests.

(C) The author thinks guests are more important.

(D) The writer is too busy to greet guests.

(2) _____ What is the meaning closest to the word "glow"?

(A) bloom

(B) radiance

(C) manner

(D) fire

3.

One of the nice things about the city of Washington, D.C, the capital of the United States, is that it has a number of large museums. People who live there can visit one of the fine national museums many times during the year. Although some exhibits are permanent, there are also many special travelling exhibits which are only shown for a short period of time. The entrance fees are not expensive, and they have special rates for groups. So if you like art, natural sciences, technology, American Indian history, or just want to take a walk inside a nice clean air-conditioned museum at a reasonable price, museum visiting is one of the best pastimes.

請回答下列問題：

(1) _____ The writer of excerpt likes Washington D.C. mainly because _____.

(A) it is a very large city.

(B) is has some good museums

(C) it is the capital city of the United States

(D) it is her hometown

(2) _____ According to the passage, the price of visiting museums in Washington D.C.is _____.

(A) too high.

(B) not high enough

(C) just about right

(D) too cheap

(3) _____ According to the passage, a "special exhibit" in a museum is one which is _____.

(A) only temporary

(B) very expensive

(C) always on display

(D) not open to the public

4.

Ellen Glanz lied to her teacher about why she hadn't done her homework; but, of course, many students have lied to their teachers. The difference is that Ellen Glanz was a twenty-eight-year-old high school social studies teacher who was a student for six months to improve her teaching by gaining a fresh prospect of her school.

She found many classes boring, students doing as little as necessary to pass tests and get good grades, students using tricks to avoid assignment, and students skillfully persuading teachers to do the work for them. She concluded that many students are turned off because they have little power and responsibility for their own education.

Ellen Glanz found herself doing the same things as the students. There was the day when Glanz wanted to join her husband in helping friends celebrate the purchase of a house, but she had homework for a math class. For the first time, she knew how teenagers feel when they think something is more important than homework.

請回答下列問題：

(1) _____ According to the article, it can be inferred that Ellen Glanz felt that

    (A) she shouldn't have lied because she herself is also a teacher

    (B) students have the right to lie to the teachers

    (C) teachers should be partly responsible for students lying to them

    (D) students should never lie to their teachers

(2) _____ Ellen Glanz became a student again because she

    (A) wanted to know whether the teacher would recognize her as an older student

    (B) wanted to learn new teaching skills

    (C) wanted to find out why her students lied to her

    (D) had felt tired of always being a teacher

(3) _____ According to the article, the phrase "turn off" is closest in meaning to _____

    (A) lose interest in something

(B) refuse the request

(C) dislike certain people

(D) change attitude completely

(4) _____ What is the main den of the article?

(A) In order to fully understand students, teachers should sit in another teacher's class every once in a while,

(B) Students feel he classes boring because they are cheating and irresponsible.

(C) In order to encourage students, teachers should tolerate students lying

(D) Teachers should allow students to have more control over their learning.

(5) _____ What is Ellen Glanz s attitude toward students' lying?

(A) understanding

(B) negative

(C) positive

(D) cheerful

5.

Salt and sugar act differently in our bodies, but when it comes to causing thirst, their effects are pretty much the same. Here's why particles of salt on sugar enter the bloodstream soon after we eat them. As they move through the body, they pull water out of our body cells. The cells notice the change right away, and they do not like it. So they try to hold in water and send chemical messages to the brain.

The brain also has its own sense organs that detect when the blood contains too much sugar or salt. After the brain gets the message that the body needs water to reduce the amount of the sugar or salt, you start to feel thirsty. That is why cookies, candy or even very sugary soda or juice, can make you just as thirsty as salty foods.

請回答下列問題：

(1) ＿＿＿＿＿ According to the article, why does sugar make us thirsty?

(A) Because particles of sugar cannot enter the bloodstream.

(B) Because particles of sugar keep water in our body cells.

(C) Because particles of sugar increase water in our body cells.

(D) Because particles of sugar reduce water in our body cells.

(2) ＿＿＿＿＿ Which of the following statements is true?

(A) Salt cannot move through the body.

(B) The function of our body cell is to keep water out of them.

(C) Like candy, salty foods can make us thirsty.

(D) Particles of sugar can send chemical messages to the brain.

(3) ＿＿＿＿＿ Which of the following words is closest in meaning to the word "notice" in line 5?

(A) Raise.

(B) Prove.

(C) Sense.

(D) Waste.

(4) ＿＿＿＿＿ Which of the following is NOT mentioned as a cause of thirst in the passage?

(A) Soda.

(B) Heat.

(C) Juice.

(D) Candy.

(5) ＿＿＿＿＿ What is the best title of this article?

(A) Why do we feel thirsty after taking sugary soda or salty foods?

(B) Why do salt and sugar send chemical messages our body cells?

(C) Why do salt and sugar act differently in our bodies?

(D) Why do particles of salt or sugar enter the bloodstream?

6.

    Catherine sell houses for a company. A man has agreed to buy a house for $450,000, but then he changes his mind. Her boss calls her into office. He is so anger that he speaks rudely to her. She knows it is not her fault, and she bursts into tears.

    Having just finished dinner, Jim is talking in the backyard with his wife and children. The phone rings. It is Jim's mother calling from another city. Jim's father has just had a heart attack and died. Jim starts crying as he tells his mother he will come as soon as possible.

    How do people feel about crying? Catherine was embarrassed and very angry with herself. Jim felt better after he let out his feelings.

    Chemists have been studying why people cry. They say the body produces two kinds of tears. One kind cleans out the eye if it gets dirt in. But when people cry because of their feelings, these tears have poison chemicals in them. The body is getting rid of chemicals produced by strong feelings.

請回答下列問題：

(1)   Witch of the following is the best title for the passage?

(A) Business.

(B) Feeling.

(C) Anger.

(D) Crying

(2)   Catherine's boss speaks rudely to her because

(A) he thinks that she didn't do her job well

(B) she sold the house at a lower price

(C) she was late for the appointment with the buyer

(D) she refused to listen to his advice

(3) _____ Which of the following statements is true about Jim?

(A) He cried because he had a heart problem.

(B) He did not cry because he hated his father.

(C) He felt better after he cried.

(D) He felt relieved on hearing the news of his father's death.

(4) _____ According to the passage, Jim and his mother are living

(A) together

(B) in different cities

(C) in the same neighborhood

(D) with Jim's grandparents

(5) _____ Which of the following statements is true about the passage?

(A) Catherine sells cars.

(B) Jim learned from his mother's letter that his father died.

(C) Crying is a way of removing chemicals from the body.

(D) People cry only when they feel very sad.

7.

Making a good speech in public is a big challenge for most people, but there are some basic rules you can follow. First of all, you need to know what kind of audience you have. Maybe they are friendly audience who knows you already, or maybe they are strangers you need to get acquainted with. Next, the topic of your speech needs to be something you know a lot about. If you are a fashion designer, for example, you should not give medical advice. You had better talk about what styles are best for what kinds of body shapes. Also, you will want to give your audience strong images that will linger in their minds after the speech is over. Finally, don't make your speech too long. Nobody wants to go hungry or go to bed late because of a long speech.

請回答下列問題：

(1) _____ The writer of this passage is _____

(A) teaching people how to be good fashion designers

(B) telling how to speak to a friendly audience

(C) giving advice to people who may want to give a speech

(D) telling people how to make long speeches

(2) _____ When giving a speech, one had better _____

(A) talk about something that is new and exciting

(B) talk about the subject as long as you can

(C) talk about all the friends you have

(D) talk about a topic you are very familiar with

(3) _____ For a fashion designer, body shapes are important because

(A) people should lose weight to look like fashion models

(B) people should always look for the newest fashions

(C) people should wear clothes which fit their own figures

(D) people basically all have the same shape

(4) _____ The writer of the passage is most probably _____

(A) a medical doctor

(B) an experienced public speaker

(C) a fashion designer

(D) a successful politician

(5) _____ How many rules does the writer give for making a good speech?

(A) Two.

(B) Three.

(C) Four.

(D) Five.

8.

On the afternoon of May 12, 2008, an earthquake measuring 7.9 on the Richter scale hit Sichuan Province, a mountainous region in western China. By the next day, the death toll stood at 12,000, with another 18,000 still missing. Over 15 million people live in the affected area, including almost 4 million in the city of Chengdu. Nearly 2,000 of the dead were students and teachers caught in schools that collapsed.

Since the Tangshan earthquake in 1976, which killed over 240,000 people. The people from morning and do not seem able to get going very well until afternoon; during the evening, they are wide-awake and hate to go to bed. People can usually adjust to a different schedule if necessary, but it seems to be more difficult for some people than for others.

China has required that new structures withstand major quakes. But the collapse of schools, hospitals and factories in several different areas around Sichuan may raise questions about how rigorously such codes have been enforced during China's recent, epic building boom.

Many parents have said their children were crushed in shoddy school buildings that toppled while nearby apartments and government offices stayed.

請回答下列問題：

(1) ＿＿＿＿＿ What does "affected" in the sentence "over 15 million people live in the affected area"-- mean ?

(A) Influenced

(B) Infected

(C) Validated

(D) Affective

(2) _____ According to the article _____

    (A) China had enforced rigorous building codes

    (B) Buildings collapsed because of lack of rigorous building codes

    (C) Rigorous codes had helped China's recent building boom

    (D) China's recent building boom had been praised

(3) _____ According to the article, which one of the following statements is Not true?

    (A) The Tangshan earthquake killed over 240,000 people.

    (B) Many people died because of the collapse of schools, hospitals, and factories

    (C) About 30,000 people were dead or missing when the news came out

    (D) China has required that new structures withstand major quakes only after the Sichuan earthquake

(4) _____ According to this article, how many people were killed by the Sichuan earthquake?

    (A) 12,000

    (B) 18,000

    (C) 2,000

    (D) 240,000

(5) _____ According to the article, "epic building boom" refers to

_____

    (A) the bombing of buildings

    (B) the collapse of buildings

    (C) the fast construction of buildings

(D) the booming sound of buildings

9.

American Indians played a central role in the war known as the American Revolution. To them, however, the dispute between the colonists and England was peripheral. For American Indians, the conflict was a war for American Indian independence, and whichever they chose they lost it. Mary Brant was a powerful influence among the Iroquois. She was a Mohawk, the leader of the society of all Iroquois matrons, and the widow of Sir William Johnson, Superintendent of Indian Affairs. Her brother, Joseph Brant, is the best-known American Indian warrior of the Revolution, yet she may have exerted even more influence in the Confederacy than he did. She used her influence to keep the western tribes of Iroquois loyal to the English King, George II. When the colonists won the war, she and her tribe had to abandon their lands and retreat to Canada. On the other side, Nanny Ward held positions of authority in the Cherokee nation. She had fought as a warrior in the war against the Creeks and as a reward for her heroism was made "Beloved Woman" of the tribe. This office made her chief of the women's council and a member of the council of chiefs. She was friendly with the white settlers and supported the patriots during the Revolution. Yet the Cherokees too lost their land.

請回答下列問題：

(1) _____ What is the main point the author makes in the passage?

(A) Regardless of whom they supported in the Revolution, American Indians lost their land.

(B) The outcome of the Revolution was largely determined by American Indian women.

(C) At the time of the Revolution, the Superintendent of Indian Affairs had little power.

(D) Siding with the English in the Revolution helped American Indians regain their land.

(2) _____ According to the passage, Mary Brant's husband had been a

(A) revolutionary hero

(B) government official

(C) Mohawk chief

(D) Cherokee council member.

(3) _____ To which tribe did Nancy Ward belong?

(A) Mohawk

(B) Creek

(C) Cherokee

(D) Iroquois

(4) _____ How did Nancy Ward gain her position of authority?

(A) By bravery in battle

(B) By joining the Confederacy

(C) By marriage of a chief

(D) By being born into a powerful family.

(5) _____ According to the passage, what did Mary Brant and Nancy Ward have in common?

(A) Each went to England after the American Revolution.

(B) Each influenced her tribe's role in the American Revolution.

(C) Each was called "Beloved Woman" by her tribe.

(D) Each lost a brother in the American Revolution.

10.

Pragmatically, while absolute translatability is impossible in the same way that a perfect act of reading is unthinkable, some degree of translatability, whatever the languages and problems, is always possible. And in practice, what appears to be on the surface untranslatable offers the translator the best. possibilities of an interesting success. Although it is impossible to reproduce the same sounds and meanings in intra and interlingual translation, I think that what is most interesting to translate and most susceptible of success is the impossible or, even better, the untranslatable. And there are some truly untranslatable words and phrases by any standards. These "untranslatables," like the unwilling but much desired Colombian drug "extraditables," are the richest linguistic sources to transfer to the target language, are a challenge to art and ingenuity, and stimulate the imagination of the artist-translator, who in confronting the untranslatable cannot be lazily seduced by the surface obvious into producing an unimaginative, mechanical version.

(Taken from *The Poetics of Translation,* by Willis Barnstone)

請回答下列問題：

(1) _____ In the passage, the author thinks that _____

(A) absolute translatability, like a perfect act of reading, is impossible.

(B) a perfect act of reading is possible, but absolute translatability is unthinkable.

(C) both absolute translation and perfect reading are possible.

(D) both absolute translatability and a perfect act of reading depend on one's skill.

(2) _____ According to the author, the untranslatable feature of language _____

(A) makes the translator annoyed and depressed.

(B) forces the translator to give up.

(C) demands the translator to be Columbus.

(D) provides the translator with a chance to succeed.

(3) _____ The author thinks the "untranslatables" of words _____

(A) can stimulate the translator's imagination.

(B) can make the source language easy and clear.

(C) can add the surface value of target language.

(D) can encourage the translator to be a drug addict.

(4) _____ From the passage, the word "extraditables" is related to

_____

(A) medicine and wine

(B) crime and fugitives

(C) war and weapon

(D) art and ingenuity

Answers

1. (1)E (2)A   6. (1)A (2)C (3)B (4)C (5)D

2. (1)A (2)B   7. (1)C (2)D (3)C (4)B (5)C

3. (1)B (2)D (3)A   8. (1)C (2)D (3)C (4)B (5)C

4. (1)C (2)B (3)A (4)D (5)A 9. (1)A (2)B (3)C (4)A (5)B

5. (1)D (2)C (3)C (4)A   10. (1)A (2)D (3)A (4)B

NOTE
筆　記

國家圖書館出版品預行編目資料

全方位英文閱讀／劉遠城著. —— 初版.
—— 臺北市：五南, 2019.11
　面；　公分
ISBN 978-957-763-707-9（平裝）

1.英語　2.讀本

805.18　　　　　　　　　　108016596

1X5J

全方位英文閱讀

作　　　者 — 劉遠城（360）

發 行 人 — 楊榮川

總 經 理 — 楊士清

總 編 輯 — 楊秀麗

副總編輯 — 黃文瓊

責任編輯 — 吳雨潔

封面設計 — 姚孝慈

美術設計 — 吳佳臻

出 版 者 — 五南圖書出版股份有限公司

地　　　址：106台北市大安區和平東路二段339號4樓

電　　　話：(02)2705-5066　　傳　　真：(02)2706-6100

網　　　址：http://www.wunan.com.tw

電子郵件：wunan@wunan.com.tw

劃撥帳號：01068953

戶　　名：五南圖書出版股份有限公司

法律顧問　林勝安律師事務所　林勝安律師

出版日期　2019年11月初版一刷

定　　價　新臺幣590元